LED ASTRAY

the best of

KELLEY ARMSTRONG

20th
ANNIVERSARY

Tachyon | San Francisco

Cover art copyright © 2015 by Liliana Sanches
Cover and interior design by Elizabeth Story
Author photo © 2015 by Kathryn Hollinrake

Tachyon Publications
1459 18th Street #139
San Francisco, CA 94107
415.285.5615
www.tachyonpublications.com
tachyon@tachyonpublications.com

Series Editor: Jacob Weisman
Project Editor: Jill Roberts

ISBN 13: 978-1-61696-202-9

Printed in the United States by Worzalla

9 7 8 6 5 4 3 2 1

"Rakshasi" copyright © 2011 by Kelley Armstrong. First appeared in *The Monster's Corner: Stories by Inhuman Eyes*, edited by Christopher Golden (St. Martin's Griffin: New York).

"Kat" copyright © 2009 by Kelley Armstrong. First appeared in *The Eternal Kiss: 13 Vampire Tales of Blood and Desire*, edited by Trisha Telep (Running Press: Philadelphia, PA).

Praise for Kelley Armstrong

On *Bitten*

"Frisky. . . . Tells a rather sweet love story, and suggests that being a wolf may be more comfortable for a strong, smart woman than being human."
—*New York Times Book Review*

"Filled with romance and supernatural intrigue, this book will surely remind readers of Anne Rice's sophisticated refurbishings of the vampire story."
—*Publishers Weekly*

On *The Gathering*

"She has a great, image-evoking writing style that's fun to read. . . ."
—*Dark Faerie Tales*

On *Omens*

"Author Kelley Armstrong has done it again. . . . In *Omens*, she has moved to another fascinating tale of paranormal circumstance, and riddled it with feeling and eerie happenstance."
—*Blogcritic*

On *Visions*

"I was so interested in the characters I could barely put *Visions* down. Frankly, I enjoyed the hell out of it. . . . I cannot wait for the next installment."
—*Tor.com*

On *The Awakening*

"*The Awakening* is one heckuva ride—from beginning to end, there is not a dull moment or even an opportunity to catch a breath and relax."
—*The Book Smugglers*

"Will exhilarate even readers new to the series. . . . Dark alleys, undead bodies and bountiful blood will cause shivers. . . ."
—*Kirkus*, starred review

On *Sea of Shadows*

"*Sea of Shadows* is a great fit for both the male and female reader who are looking for something more in their historical fantasy, especially if it's tinged with enough horror-filled moments to bring shivers to your late night reading."
—*Lost in a Great Book*

On *The Summoning*

"Teen readers might scream loud enough to raise the dead."
—*Kirkus*, starred review

OTHER TITLES BY KELLEY ARMSTRONG

DARKEST POWERS

The Summoning (2008)
The Awakening (2009)
The Reckoning (2010)

DARKNESS RISING

The Gathering (2011)
The Calling (2012)
The Rising (2013)

CAINSVILLE

Omens (2013)
Visions (2014)
Deceptions (2015)

AGE OF LEGENDS

Sea of Shadows (2014)
Empire of Night (2015)

STANDALONE

The Masked Truth (2015)

AS K. L. ARMSTRONG (WITH MELISSA MARR)

THE BLACKWELL PAGES

Loki's Wolves (2013)
Odin's Ravens (2014)
Thor's Serpents (2015)

Contents

Rakshasi

For two hundred years, I have done penance for my crimes as a human. After twenty years, I had saved more lives than I took. After fifty, I had helped more people than I had wronged. I understand that my punishment should not end with an even accounting. The balance between good and evil is not that simple. I expected my good deeds must exceed my evil ones before I am set free.

Yet now, after two hundred years, that balance has long passed equilibrium. And I have come to realize that this life is no different than my old one. If I wish something for myself, I cannot rely on others to provide it.

Reliance on Fate is the refuge of the weak. The strong know that free will is all. What I want, I must take.

I waited in the car while Jonathan checked the house. Jonathan. There is something ridiculous about calling your master by his given name. It's an affectation of the modern age. In the early years, I was to refer to them as *Master* or *Isha*. When the family moved west, it became *Sir*, then Mr. Roy.

My newest master, Jonathan, does not particularly care for this familiarity. He pretends otherwise, but the fact that I must call him by his full name, where his wife and others use the simplified "Jon" says much about my master. I have attempted to revert to Mr. Roy, for his comfort, but he won't allow it. The formal appellation smacks too loudly of slavery, and he prefers the illusion that I am merely an employee.

He called my cell phone. Yes, I use cell phones. They are a convenient method of communication and I am very capable of learning and adapting.

"Amrita?" he said, as if someone else might be answering my phone. My name is not Amrita. My name is not important. Or, perhaps, too important. I have never given it to my masters. They call me Amrita, the eternal one.

"The coast is clear," he said. He paused. "I mean—"

"I understand American idiom quite well," I said. "I have been living here since before you were born."

He mumbled something unimportant, then gave me my instructions, as if I hadn't been doing this, too, since before he was born.

I got out of the car and headed for the house.

As Jonathan said, there was an open window on the second floor. I found a quiet place away from the road, not yet on the property of the man I'd come to visit. Then I shifted to my secondary form: a raven. Fly to the bedroom window. Squeeze through. Shift back to woman.

There wasn't even an alarm on the window to alert the occupant to my intrusion. Quite disappointing. These jobs always are. I long for the old days, when I would do bloody battle against power-mad English sahibs and crazed Kshatriyas. Then came the murderers and whore-masters, then the Mob, then the drug dealers. It was, with the drug dealers, that the Roys began to rethink their strategy. Getting one alone was not easy. On the streets, they came with well-armed friends. I may be immortal, but I can be injured, and while my personal comfort is not a concern, my income-earning potential is. They tried targeting drug dealers at home, but there they were often surrounded by relative innocents. So, in this last decade, they have concentrated on a new source of evil. A dull, weak, mewling source, one that bores me to tears. But my opinion, like my comfort, is of little consequence.

I took a moment to primp in the mirror. I am eternally young. Beautiful, too. More beautiful than when I was alive, which was not to say that I was

ugly then, but when I look in the mirror now, I imagine what my husband—
Daman—would say if he saw me. Imagine his smile. His laugh. His kiss. I
have not seen him in two hundred years, but when I primp for my target, it
is still him I imagine I am readying myself for.

I found the target—Morrison—in the study, talking on his speaker phone
while punching keys on his laptop. I moved into the doorway. Leaned against
it. Smiled.

He stopped talking. Stopped typing. Stared.

Then, "Bill? I'll call you back."

He jabbed the phone off and shut his laptop. "How'd you get in here?"

"My name is Amrita. I am a surprise. From a very pleased client."

I slid forward, gaze fixed on his. For another moment he stared, before
remembering himself.

"But how did you get—"

I smiled. "I would not be much of a surprise if I rang your front bell,
would I?" I glanced back at the door. "I trust we are alone?" Jonathan said
Morrison was the only one in the house, but I always checked.

"W-we are."

"Good."

I sidled over and pushed his chair back, away from the desk and any
alarms under it or guns in the drawers. That was all the security men like
this had.

I straddled Morrison's lap. I could see indecision wavering in his eyes. He
was a smart man. He knew this was suspicious. And yet, as I said, I am a
beautiful woman.

I put my arms around him, hands sliding down his arms, fingers entwining
with his. I leaned over, lifting our hands . . . then wrenched his arms back
so hard he screamed. I leapt from his lap, over the back of the chair, then
bound them with the cord I'd used as a belt on my sheer dress.

I have subdued lapdogs that gave me more trouble than Morrison. By
the time he recovered from the shock and pain of that first strike, he was
secured. He fought, but my bonds have bound warriors. He was no warrior.

Next, I tortured him for information. It was a bloodless torture. Necessity,
not preference. There are ways to inflict pain without leaving marks. Mental

pain is the most effective of all, and with the power of illusion, it is easy for me to torture a mind. I can make a man believe he is being rent limb from limb, and scream with imagined agony.

As for the information I needed, it was a simple accounting of his misdeeds. Details on the financial scam that paid for this mansion. I had him write out those details, in a confession. Then I tortured him for the location and combination to his home safe.

With my help, the Roys kill—sorry, *eliminate*—the basest dregs of the criminal bucket. This is their divine mission, handed down to them millennia ago, when they were granted the ability to harness the powers of my kind. They seek out evil. I eliminate it. A very noble profession but one that, as you would say, does not pay the bills. Finding targets, researching them and preparing for my attack is a full time job. So the Roys, like other *isha* families, also have divine permission to take what they require from their victims.

I did so. Then I forced Morrison to take out his gun and shoot himself, leaving the confession of his crimes on the table, and compensation for his victims still in his safe.

Before he pulled the trigger, he looked at me. They always do. Seeking mercy, I suppose. But I know, better than anyone, that such sins cannot be pardoned in this life. If they are, it will be seen as a sign of weakness, the perpetrator reverting to his or her old ways as soon as the initial scare passes.

They always look at me, though, and they always ask me the same thing.

"What are you?" he said.

"Rakshasi," I replied, and pushed his finger on the trigger.

Rakshasi. Morrison didn't know what that meant. They never do. Even those of my own heritage rarely have more than a vague inkling of my kind, perhaps a story told by a grandmother to frighten them into obedience.

Rakshasa. Rakshasi for women, though there are far fewer of us. The word means protector, which has always made me laugh. We are demon warriors, cursed after a life of evil to walk the earth as monsters, wreaking havoc wherever we go. Disturbers. Defilers. Devourers.

Though the word is used for all my kind, it is only after we accept the bargain of the isha that we become protectors. When we rise from our death-bed, we are met by a member of an isha family. He tells us our fate. Misery and guilt and pain. We shall forever feel everything that we did, in life, visited upon others. Yet we can redeem ourselves. Submit to their bargain, work for them until we have repaid our debt, and then we will be free.

I did not take the offer. I doubt any rakshasa does, at that death-bed visit. We are men and women of iron will. We do not snivel and cower at the first threat of adversity. I truly do not believe the isha expect agreement. Not then. They simply offer the deal, and when it is rejected they leave. Then, on every succeeding anniversary, they find us, and they offer again.

In the end, it was not the misery or guilt or pain that wore me down. It was the loneliness. We are doomed to be alone as we walk the earth, and after almost eighty years, I could take it no longer. I would have held out, though, if the isha did not bring me a letter one year. A letter from Daman. He too had been doomed to this existence. Our crimes were shared, as was every part of our lives from the time we were children.

Daman had accepted his isha's bargain, and he pleaded with me to do the same. Take the deal and we would be together again. So he had been promised. So I was promised. And I accepted.

We returned to the house. It is the same house I have lived in for sixty years, though Jonathan and Catherine only came a few years ago, when he took over from his uncle as my isha. I came with the house. Or, I should say, it came with me.

It was no modest family home. For size and grandeur, it was on scale with Morrison's mansion. There were no vows of poverty in this family of crusaders. Like the Templar Knights, they lined their pockets extravagantly with the proceeds of their good deeds, which may explain part of the logic behind the switch from petty drug dealers to corporate sharks. We are in a recession. To some, that means tightening the purse-strings. To others, it means seeking richer sources of income. I cannot argue with that. I felt the same way when I walked the earth as a human. But it does beg the question, how prosperous were the Roys before I agreed to their bargain? The answer is that they'd been barely able to feed their families. If they free me, they will lose the prosperity I bring them. Which gives them little incentive for agreeing I have repaid my debt to humankind.

Jonathan took me to my apartment. As cages go, it is a gilded one. Sleeping quarters, living area, kitchen, and bath, all well furnished. The shelves are lined with books. There is a computer for my amusement. Anything I wish will be brought to me. Anything except freedom. The walls are endued with magic that prevents me from leaving without my isha so long as I am bound to him.

Beyond a recitation of events, Jonathan and I had not spoken on the four-hour drive from Morrison's house. Every isha is different. With some, I have found something akin to friendship. Most prefer a more businesslike relationship. Jonathan takes that to the extreme, talking to me only when necessary. He is not rude or unkind. He simply pays me no heed. It is easier for him to treat me as an object. To engage me in conversation might lead to asking my thoughts or feelings, which would imply I possess such things. That I am not a robot warrior, but a sentient being. Best not to think on that.

In my apartment I prepared dinner. A glass of human blood. A plate of human flesh. It is what I need to survive and my ishas provide it. At one time, they used their victims. Now, that is inconvenient. One of the isha families without a rakshasa saw a market of their own and filled it. Jonathan orders my meals. They come in a refrigerated case, the blood in wine bottles and flesh neatly packaged and labeled as pork. He can bring me the case and leave, never even needing to look at the contents.

I fixed a plate of curry with the flesh. I may be a cannibal, but I have retained some sense of taste. When I'd finished, I waited for Catherine. She gives me time after a job to eat, preferring not to visit while the scent of cooked flesh still lingers in the air. As a courtesy, I opened the windows. Yes, I did have windows, though I couldn't reach out them—the magical shield that kept me here blocked these exits as well.

Catherine extended me a return courtesy by knocking before she entered.

Most of my ishas do not—either they forget I may have a human's need for privacy or they wish to remind me of my place. Jonathan regularly "forgets" to knock, which is his way of asserting his position without challenging me. I would hold him in higher regard if he simply barged in.

"Did it go well today?" Catherine asked as she entered. One might presume she'd already spoken to her husband and was simply asking to be polite, but with this couple, such a level of communication was not a given.

I told her it had, as I accompanied her to the living area, walking slowly to keep pace with her crutches. Catherine suffers from a crippling disease that today has a name—multiple sclerosis. In general, I'm not interested in the advances of science, but I have researched this particular ailment to help me better understand the first wife of an isha who has chosen to seek my companionship.

For most wives, it is not an option because to them, I do not exist. They have no knowledge of their husband's otherworldly abilities, and thus no knowledge of me. For decades, I have been shunted in and out a side door while the wives are out, and otherwise kept in my soundproof apartment, which they are told contains whatever brand of toxicity is currently popular. With the last isha, it was asbestos.

Occasionally, though, the Roys take a wife from within the isha community. That is where Jonathan found Catherine. And if such a choice—not only an isha's daughter but a poor cripple—helped him win his position over his brothers. . . ? It is not my concern. I say nothing to Catherine and she pretends, if poorly, not to believe it herself.

We chatted for a while. As to what we could possibly have in common, the answer is "little," which gave us much to discuss. Catherine was endlessly fascinated with my life. To her, I was the star in some terrible yet endlessly thrilling adventure. I reciprocated by asking about her life, but she rarely said much, preferring instead to talk about me.

"Have you been doing better?" she asked as I fixed tea.

"I am surviving. We both know that I would prefer it wasn't so but . . ." I smiled her way. "You have heard quite enough on that matter."

"I wish you could be happier, Amrita."

"I've been alive too long to be happy. I would prefer to be gone. At peace." I handed her a cup. "But, again, we've talked about this enough. It's a depressing way to spend your visits. I would prefer to talk about you and *your* happiness. Did you ask Jonathan about the trip?"

Her gaze dropped to her teacup. "He said it wasn't possible. He'd love to, but he can't take you and he can't leave his duties here."

"Oh. I had thought perhaps he would be able to take me. That the council would consider it acceptable for me to revisit my roots. I am sorry I mentioned it then."

"Don't be. You know I want to see India. You make it sound so wonderful. I just hope . . ." She sipped her tea. "I hope by the time he's free of his obligation, I'm still in good enough health . . ."

She trailed off. I didn't need to remind her that was a fool's dream. By the time the next generation was ready to take over as my isha, she would not have the strength to travel.

"He would like to take you," I said.

"I know."

"He would like to go himself."

"I know. But his obligation . . ."

Could be over any time he chooses. Those were the words left unspoken. Also the words: but he does not have the strength of will to do it, to defy his family by making that decision on his own, despite the fact it is his to make, and the council will support it. They have no choice. I have clearly earned my freedom.

"I would miss you," she blurted. "I'd miss our talks."

I smiled. "As would I. If you were free to travel, though, you would see these places for yourself, do these things for yourself, make new friends. Here, you are as much a prisoner as I am. Jonathan must worry about you—about retaliation from those we attack—so he must insist you stay here, in this house, for your own safety."

Did she believe that? No. She suspected, I'm sure, that he kept her here because it was convenient. She was as much his property as I was. Birds in our gilded cages. I simply gave him the excuse to keep her here. Without that, I knew she was thinking, she'd have more freedom, whether he liked it or not.

She shook her head. "Jonathan knows best. He will free you. I know he will. It just isn't time."

It never would be. These nudges weren't enough. Time for a push.

There were many things Daman and I agreed on, as partners in life, in love, in ambition. One was that, despite the teachings of the Brahmins, all men are essentially created equal. Each bears within him the capacity to achieve his heart's desire. He needs only the strength of will to see those ambitions through.

Daman's story was an old one. A boy from a family rich in respect and land and lineage, poor in wealth and power and character. His family wanted him to marry a merchant's daughter with a rich dowry. Instead he chose me, his childhood playmate, a scholar's daughter. I brought no money, but I brought something more valuable—intelligence, ambition and a shared vision for what could be.

A hundred years ago, when my ishas lived in England, one saw the play *Macbeth*, and forever after that, when he was in an ill-temper, he would call me Lady Macbeth. I read the script, to see what he meant, and found the allusion insulting. Macbeth was a coward; his wife a harpy. Daman did not need me to push him. Every step we took, we took as one.

In our twenty years together, we recouped everything his family had lost over the centuries. And more. Our supporters would say that we brought peace and stability and prosperity to the region, far outlasting our deaths. Our detractors would point out the trail of bodies in our wake, and the growing piles in our coffers. Neither is incorrect. We did good and we did evil. We left the lands better than we found them, but at a price that was, perhaps, too steep.

I do regret the path we took. Yet if given a second chance, I would not sit in a corner, content with my lot. My ambition would merely be checked by an appreciation for the value of human life. That appreciation has stayed my hand in this matter. And it has gotten me nowhere. So it will be stayed no more.

———

My next assignment came nearly four months later. That is typical. While one might look at the world and see plenty of wrongdoers, it is a rare one that ought to be culled from our society altogether. Jonathan must search for a target. Then he must compile a dossier on the client and submit it to the council, who will return "elimination approval" or request more information. Then comes the weeks of surveillance, at which point my participation is required, my talents for illusion and shape-shifting being useful.

How much of the surveillance work is left to me depends on the isha. Jonathan lets me do almost all of it, claiming he's conducting his own elsewhere, though when I've followed, I've found him relaxing in coffee shops, flirting with serving girls or working on his novel.

There is a reason he is supposed to supervise me. Because I could shirk my duties, perhaps find a coffee shop of my own. I've considered doing so. I even have an idea for a novel. While it amuses me to think of this, I could not do it. I enjoy these unsupervised times too much to risk them, and I do not have the personality for lounging and storytelling.

However, this time, when I did my surveillance, I was . . . less than forthright about my findings.

The target was yet another financier. Unlike Morrison—and the others— this one had more than a security alarm and a handgun to keep him safe. Having been the subject of death threats, he had employed a bodyguard, in the form of a young man he passed off as his personal assistant.

I learned about the death threats only by eavesdropping. I left them out of the report. I discovered the "assistant's" true nature only by surveillance. I left that out of the report as well. My official conclusion was that this man—Garvey—was no more security conscious than the others, but that his assistant was rarely away from his side, which could pose a problem if we proceeded as usual. I suggested I lure the assistant away and let Jonathan subdue him while I dealt with Garvey.

It went as one might expect. My plan for separating the two went perfectly. Such things are minor obstacles for one who has spent hundreds of years practicing the art of illusion.

I got the bodyguard upstairs, where Jonathan was waiting. Then I hurried back to Garvey before the confrontation could begin.

Jonathan's cries for help came before I even reached the bottom of the stairs. They alerted Garvey, as I knew they would. My job, then, was to subdue the financier before he could retrieve his gun. Then it would be safe for me to go to my isha's aid.

It took some time for me to subdue Garvey. He was unexpectedly strong. Or so I would claim.

By the time I returned upstairs, the bodyguard had beaten Jonathan unconscious and was preparing the killing blow. I shot him with Garvey's gun. Then I returned to Garvey and carried on. This was my mission and my mission superseded all else, even the life of my isha.

When I was finished with Garvey—after he confessed to killing his guard and then taking his own life—I took Jonathan to the hospital. Then I called Catherine.

"I take responsibility for this," I said to Catherine as we stood beside Jonathan's hospital bed. "My job was to protect him and I failed."

"You didn't know."

"I should have known. That too is my job. We are both to conduct a proper survey—"

"If Jon didn't find out about the guard, you couldn't have. There was no way to know he'd have need of one. He wasn't being investigated yet."

I fell silent. Stared down at Jonathan, still unconscious after surgery to staunch the internal bleeding. As I feigned guilt and concern, I sneaked looks at Catherine, searching for some sign that she would secretly have been relieved by his death. I'd seen none so far and caught none now, even as she thought I wasn't watching.

She claimed to love him. She did love him. Either way, I could work with this. I had simply needed to know which it was. Now I did.

"It's becoming so much more dangerous," I murmured. "There were always problems, but it is so much harder to keep an isha safe these days."

"Problems?" she said. "This—this hasn't happened before, has it?"

I kept my gaze on Jonathan.

"Amrita."

I looked up slowly, hesitating before saying, "The council has assured me that my rate of accidental injury is far below that of most rakshasas."

"Rate of accidental injury?" Her voice squeaked a little. "You mean the little mishaps, right? A bruise? A cut? I've never heard of an isha getting more than a few broken bones. That's what you mean, isn't it?"

I said nothing.

"Amrita!"

Again, I looked up. Again I hesitated before speaking. "There have been . . . incidents. Jonathan's great-uncle's car accident. It was . . . not an accident. That was the story the council told the family. And there have been . . . others." I hurried on. "But they say that the risk with me is negligible, compared to that of others."

Which didn't reassure her in the least.

I said nothing after that. I had planted the seed. It would take time to sprout.

A week later, Jonathan was still in the hospital, recovering from his injuries. I had not yet returned to my apartment—once I entered, I wouldn't be able to leave. Catherine had to get my food from the refrigerator. She didn't like that, but the alterative was to sentence her only help-mate to prison until Jonathan recovered.

The day before he was due to come home, Catherine visited me in the guest room.

She entered without a word. She sat without word. She stayed there for nearly thirty minutes without a word. Then she looked up at me and said,

"Tell me how to release you."

We had to hurry. The only way to free me without Jonathan's consent was while he was unable to give that consent.

We withheld his fever medication until his temperature rose and he became confused. With the aid of a few illusory tricks, he parted with the combination to his safe.

While Catherine treated his fever, I retrieved what we needed from the safe. I fingered the stacks of hundred dollar bills taken from our victims, but I took none. I had no need of it.

"Are you sure this is what you want?" she asked as I prepared for the ritual. "They say that when a rakshasa passes to the other side, there is no afterlife. You're living your afterlife. There'll be nothing."

"Peace," I said. "There will be peace. It is for the best. The council will not judge you harshly if I am gone. Nor will Jonathan."

She nodded. She knew this, which was why she'd agreed to it. The only reason she'd agreed to it.

I drew the ritual circle in sand around Jonathan's bed. I lit tiny fires in the appropriate locations. I placed a necklace bearing one half of the amulet around my neck, the other around his. I recited the incantations. Endless details, each of which had to be done in exactly the right order. Endless details that were etched into my brain, the memories of my kind, as accessible as any other aspect of my magic, but requiring Jonathan's assistance. Or the assistance of his bodily form—hair to be burned, fingernails to be ground into powder, saliva and blood to be mixed with the powder.

Finally, as Catherine waited anxiously, I injected myself with the mixture. The ritual calls for it to be rubbed into an open wound. I'd made this one modernized alteration, and Catherine had readily agreed it seemed far less barbaric than the original.

Next I injected Jonathan. Then I began the incantations.

Jonathan shuddered in his sleep. His mouth opened and closed, as if gasping for air. Catherine grabbed his hand and wheeled on me.

"What's happening?" she said.

"The bond is breaking."

I shuddered myself, feeling that hated tie tighten, as if in reflexive protest. Then slowly, blessedly, it began to loosen.

Catherine began to gibber that something was wrong. Jonathan wasn't breathing. Why wasn't he breathing? His heartbeat was slowing. It wasn't supposed to be slowing, was it?

I kept my eyes closed, ignoring her cries, ignoring her tugs on my arm, until at last, the bond slid away. One last deep shudder and I opened my eyes to see the world as I hadn't seen it in two hundred years. Bright and glimmering with promise.

Catherine was shrieking now.

I turned toward the door. She lunged at me, her crutches falling as she grabbed my shirt with both hands.

"He's dead!" she cried. "You're still here and he's dead! Something went wrong."

"No," I said. "Nothing went wrong."

She screamed then, an endless wail of rage and grief. I picked her up, ignoring her feeble blows and kicks, and set her gently in a chair, then leaned her crutches within reach.

She snatched them and pushed to her feet. When I tried to walk out, she managed to get in front of me.

"What have you done?" she said.

"Freed us. Both of us."

"You lied!"

"I told you what you needed to hear." I carefully moved her aside. "I do not want annihilation. I want what I was promised—a free life. For that, I need his consent and the council's approval. There is, however, a loophole. A final act of mercy from an isha to his rakshasi. On his deathbed, he may free me with his amulet and the ritual. You will tell the council that is what happened here. The poison I injected with the ritual potion will be undetectable. We have used it many times without incident. They will believe he has unexpectedly succumbed to his injuries."

"I will not tell them—"

"Yes, you will. Otherwise, you will be complicit in his death. And even if you manage to convince them otherwise, you will forfeit this house and all that goes with it. It is yours only if he dies and I am freed. They may contest that, but even if they do, you'll have already removed the contents of his safe. I left everything for you."

That was less generous than it seemed. For years, I'd been taking extra from our targets and hidden it away in my room as I'd used my computer to research life on the outside. I would not leave unprepared. I was never unprepared.

Now that the bond was broken, there was nothing to stop me from entering and exiting my apartment, and taking all I had collected as I began my search for Daman. I passed Catherine and headed for the door.

She was silent until I reached it.

"What will I do now?" she said.

"Live," I said. "I intend to."

KAT

A Darkest Powers / Darkness Rising Universe Story

THE VAMPIRE HUNTERS came just before dawn. I was sound asleep—a total knock-out sleep, deep and dreamless, after a night spent sparring with Marguerite. I woke to her cool fingers gripping my bare shoulder.

"Kat?" she whispered. "Katiana?"

I pushed her away, muttering that I'd skip the bus and jog to school, but her fingers bit into my shoulder as she shook me.

"It's not school, *mon chaton*," she said in her soft French accent. "It's the hunters. They've found me."

My eyes snapped open. Marguerite was leaning over me, blue eyes wide, her heart-shaped face ringed with blond curls. When I was little, I used to think she was an angel. I knew better now, but it didn't change anything. She was still *my* guardian angel.

I rolled out of bed and peered around the dark room. If I blinked hard enough, I could see. Cat's-eye vision, Marguerite called it. I was a supernatural, too, though not a vampire. We had no idea *what* I was. At sixteen, I still didn't have any powers other than this bit of night vision.

Marguerite pushed clothing into my hand. For two years, we'd slept with an outfit and packed backpack under our beds, ready to grab if the hunters came. Two years of running. Two years of staying one step ahead of them. Until now.

"Where are they?" I whispered as I tugged on my jeans.

"Outside. Watching the house."

"Waiting for daylight, I bet." I snorted. "Idiots. Probably think once the sun comes up, you'll be trapped in here."

"If so, they will be in for a surprise. But I would like to be gone by then, to be sure they are not waiting for reinforcements."

"Going up, then?" I asked.

She nodded and we set out.

We snuck through the top-floor apartment we rented in the old house. In the living room, I hopped onto the couch, and Marguerite handed me a screwdriver. I popped off the ventilation shaft cover, passed it down to her, grabbed the edge and swung up and through.

Ever seen a TV show where the hero sneaks into the villain's lair through a ventilation shaft? Ever thought it looked easy? It's not. First, your average ventilation shaft is not hero-sized. Second, they're lined with metal, meaning it's like crawling through a tin can, every thump of your knee echoing.

Fortunately, neither Marguerite nor I are action hero-sized either. And we know how to move without making a sound. For Marguerite, it comes naturally. Vampires are predators, and she's never sugar-coated that for me. My skill comes from training. I'm a competition-level gymnast, a brown belt in karate and a second-degree black belt in aikido.

I'd been taking lessons since I came to live with Marguerite eleven years ago. All supernaturals need to be able to defend themselves, she says. I might eventually get powers that help me, but if I turn out to be something like a necromancer, I'm shit outta luck. Not that she'd use those exact words. Marguerite doesn't swear, and doesn't like me to either. She has no problem with me kicking someone's ass—she just doesn't want me saying the word.

When my elbow bumped the metal side, I managed to swallow my curse, turning it into a soft growl.

"You're doing fine," her whisper floated to me. "Keep going."

We finally reached the attic, where we'd removed the screws from the vent right after moving in. As I pushed it up and out of the way, I mentally cursed again, this time cussing out the landlady for nailing shut the attic hatch, which would have made for a much easier escape route. That was why we'd rented the place—Marguerite had seen the hatch in our apartment and slapped down the cash . . . only to realize it was nailed closed, the wood too rotted to pry open.

Once in the attic, Marguerite took over. She can see better in the dark than I can. In the vent, she'd let me go first to cover my back, but here she led to make sure I didn't trip or step on anything nasty. That's the way it's always been. She trains me to defend myself, but when she's there, she's always the one taking the risks. When I was five, it made me feel safe and loved. Now . . . well, there's part of me that wants to say it pisses me off, but the truth is, I still like it.

Marguerite walked to the dormer window. Oak branches scraped against it like fingernails on a chalkboard, setting my already stretched nerves twanging. She wrenched off the rotted window frame. Those branches, creepy as they were, made excellent cover, hiding us as we swung up and onto the roof. Following her lead, I slid across the old shingles, feeling them scrape a layer or two off my palms. We crept along to the shadow of the chimney, then huddled against it and peered out into the night.

Marguerite started to close her eyes, then opened them wide, her nostrils flaring.

"Yes, I'm bleeding," I whispered. "Scraped palms. I'll live."

She handed me a tissue anyway. Then she closed her eyes, trying to pinpoint the vampire hunters with her special senses. A vampire can sense living beings. Marguerite doesn't know how it works, but years ago I saw this TV show on sharks and how they have this sixth sense that detects electrical impulses, making them perfectly-evolved predators. So I've decided that's what vampires have—a shark's electro-sensory system. Perfect predators.

Tonight her shark-sense wasn't up to snuff, and Marguerite kept shaking her head sharply, like she was trying to tune it in. She looked tired, too, her eyes dim, face drawn. I remembered how cool her skin had been when she woke me up.

"When's the last time you ate?" I whispered.

"I had a storage pouch—"

"Not that stale blood crap. A real meal, I mean."

Her silence answered. While she can get by on packaged stuff, it's like humans eating at McDonald's every day. She needs real food, hot and fresh. Though she doesn't have to kill people to feed—she just drinks some blood, like a mosquito—it's always dangerous, and since we've been on the run she doesn't do it nearly enough.

"You can't do that. You need to feed more to keep up your energy."

"*Oui, maman.*"

I made a face at her and hunkered down, letting her concentrate. After a moment, she pointed to the east.

"Two of them, over there. Watching and waiting. We must go."

I nodded, and followed her back to the rear of the house and down the tree, hidden by its branches. We hop-scotched through yards as the darkness lifted, giving way to predawn gray, pink touching the sky to the east. The rising sun wasn't a problem. Bram Stoker got one thing right with Dracula—vampires *can* walk around in daylight.

We headed for the bus station three blocks away. These days, when we looked for a place to live, Marguerite didn't ask how many bedrooms and baths it had or even how much it cost. She picked apartments based on how easily we could escape them—and the city—fast.

"I'm sorry, *mon chaton*," she said for the umpteenth time as we ran. "I know you liked it here, and I know you were looking forward to your date Saturday."

"I'll live."

"You liked him."

I shrugged. "Just a guy. Probably turn out to be another jock-jerk anyway."

Being on the run meant home schooling. Home schooling meant limited opportunities to meet guys. So I did most of my socializing at the gym, which had lots of really hot guys. Unfortunately, most of them knew how hot they were. Luke had seemed different, but I told myself it was just a front. That always made leaving easier.

We dashed behind a convenience store. I leapt onto the wooden fence and ran along the top of it.

"Slow down, Kat," Marguerite called behind me. "You will fall."

I shot a grin back. "Never. I'm a werecat, remember?"

She rolled her eyes. "There is no such thing."

"Because I'm the first."

It was an old routine, and we knew our lines by heart. I've loved cats for as long as I can remember, and I'm convinced it has something to do with my supernatural type. Marguerite says no—there are no werecats. She says the reason I like felines so much is just because, when I was little, people always told me I looked like one, with my golden brown hair and tilted green eyes. Even from the day we met, Marguerite had called me *chaton*—kitten.

Back when I lived with my parents and was named Kathy, I'd always wanted to be called Kat, but my mother said that was silly and Kathy was a perfectly good name. When I went away with Marguerite, I had to change my name, and I'd done so happily, wanting something fancier, more exotic, like her name. So I became Katiana, but everyone called me Kat.

I darted along the top of the wooden fence, then hopped down behind the bus station. When I headed for it, Marguerite caught my arm.

"You will stay close to me when we are inside," she said. "No running off."

"I'm not five, Mags," I said.

I could also point out that she was the one the hunters were after, but she'd only say that still put me in danger. Given a chance, they'd grab me as bait for her. I'd say if they did grab me expecting a hysterical sixteen-year-old girl, they'd be in for a shock, but I wasn't dumb enough to put myself in harm's way. Rule one of martial arts: never underestimate your opponent, and I didn't know a thing about these opponents. Marguerite said they'd be supernaturals—all vampire hunters are, because humans don't know about our world—so we could be facing anything from spellcasters to half-demons to werewolves.

As we entered the trash-strewn alley, I noticed a foot poking out from a cardboard box.

"Dinner," I said, pointing.

"We do not have time—"

"We'll make time," I said, lowering my voice as I strode to the box. "You need your energy."

I bent and peered into the box. The guy inside was sound asleep. I motioned Marguerite over. She took a look and hesitated, glancing over at me. She'd rather not do this with me watching, but I was right—she needed the energy boost. So, she daintily wedged her shoulders into the box, moving soundlessly. Another pause. I couldn't see her face, but I knew what she was doing—extending her fangs.

When she struck, it was with the speed and precision of a hawk. Her fangs sank in. The homeless guy jerked awake, but before he could make a sound, he slumped back into the box, out cold again. A vampire's saliva contains a sedative to knock their prey out while they feed. Like I said, perfectly-evolved predators.

I didn't look away as Marguerite fed. Why would I? She didn't turn her head when I downed a burger. Humans kill animals for food. Vampires knock out humans and borrow some blood. People would donate that pint at a clinic to keep a human alive, so what's wrong with taking it fresh from the source to keep a vampire alive? Marguerite says I'm oversimplifying things. I say she overcomplicates them.

When Marguerite finished feeding, she took a moment to seal the wound and make sure the man was comfortable. Then she tucked a few twenty-dollar bills into his pocket, and motioned for me to fall in behind her as she continued to the end of the alley.

Of the five people inside the bus depot, two were sprawled out asleep on the seats. They clutched tickets in their hands, as if to prove they had a reason to be there, but I bet if I checked the tickets they'd be months old. Homeless, like the guy in the alley.

Marguerite caught my elbow and whispered, "We will go home, Katiana. I promise."

"I wasn't thinking about that."

But, of course, I was. I missed home. Not the house or even the neighborhood, just the feeling of having a house and a neighborhood. Even as I walked past the posted bus schedule, I couldn't help looking down the list of names, finding my city. Montreal. Not the city where I was born, but my real home with Marguerite, the one we'd been forced to leave when the hunters tracked us down two years ago.

We walked to the counter.

"Kathy," a woman called.

I didn't turn. Marguerite had drilled that instinct out of me years ago. But I still tensed and looked up. Reflected in the glass of the ticket booth, I saw a woman approaching me, smiling.

"Kathy."

Marguerite caught my hand, squeezing tight. I glanced over, slowly, saw the woman and my gut went cold—a sudden, mindless reaction, something deep in me that said I knew her, and I should run, run as fast as I could.

Still gripping my hand, Marguerite started for the door. The woman only watched us as we hurried outside.

"She knew my name," I said.

"Yes, they know about you. That is why—"

"She knew my *real* name."

Marguerite looked away. I stopped walking. When she tugged my hand, I locked my knees.

"What's going—?"

"Not now. We must leave."

I didn't move.

She met my gaze. "Do you trust me, Kat?"

I answered by letting her lead me to the sidewalk.

"We will call a taxi," she said, fumbling with her cell phone.

Two figures stepped from behind the bus depot and started bearing down on us.

"Marguerite?"

She looked up. *"Merde!"* She grabbed my hand again. "Run, Kat."

"But we're in a public place. Shouldn't we just go back inside—?"

"They will not care. Run!"

I raced back down the alley, past the homeless guy in his cardboard box, and vaulted the fence, Marguerite at my heels. As I tore down the next alley, two more figures stepped across the end of it. I wheeled. The other two men were coming over the fence.

Trapped.

The men in front of us didn't say a word, just started walking slowly our way. I squared my shoulders and flexed my hands, then broke into a sprint, running straight for them, hoping that would catch them off-guard. If not, I'd rather start the fight before the other two joined in.

One of the men reached into his pocket. He pulled out something. It was still barely dawn, the alley dark with shadows, and I saw only a silver object. A cell phone maybe. Or a radio. Or—

He lifted a gun. Pointed at me.

"Kat!" Marguerite shrieked.

She grabbed my shirt and wrenched me back. I flew off my feet. She dashed in front of me. The gun fired—a quiet *pfft*. The bullet hit her in the chest. She toppled beside me, hands clutching her heart, gasping. Her face, though, was perfectly calm. No blood flowed between her fingers.

"On my count," she whispered. "Three, two, one . . ."

We leapt up. Marguerite went for the guy with the gun. He fell back in surprise. She grabbed the gun as I caught the second guy by the wrist and threw him down. Behind us, the other two were running, feet pounding the pavement, getting louder by the second.

Marguerite kicked her opponent to the ground, and we ran. As we did, I glanced over. The hole in her chest was closing fast, leaving only a rip in her shirt.

"—vampire?" one of the men behind us was saying. "Why the hell didn't someone know she was a vampire?"

I looked at Marguerite. She met my gaze, then tore hers away, and we kept going.

On the next street, we saw a city bus and flagged it down. The driver was nice enough to stop. We climbed on. I looked out the window as we pulled away from the curb, but there was no sign of our pursuers.

"They aren't vampire hunters, are they?" I murmured.

"No."

I looked over at her. "Were there ever vampire hunters?"

She shook her head, gaze down. "No. Only them."

"Coming for me, not you. They're from that place, aren't they? Part of that group that experimented on me."

"The Edison Group. Yes. At first, I thought they might be vampire hunters. There is such a thing, though rare, so I should have known . . ." She shook her head. "I wanted them to be vampire hunters. When I realized otherwise . . . I should have told you."

"Yeah." I met her gaze. "You should have."

"I'm sorry."

I nodded. She put her arm around my shoulders and I rested my head on hers and closed my eyes.

I don't remember much about my mother and father. They'd always seemed more like paid guardians than parents. They'd treated me well and given me everything I needed. *Almost* everything. There was no cuddling at my house. No curling up on Daddy's lap with a book. No bedtime tuck-in with hugs, kisses and tickles from Mommy. I hadn't known I was missing anything, only that I wasn't a happy child.

The hospital visits didn't help. Once a month, late at night, my father would wake me up and we'd drive to this place that he said was a hospital, but looking back, I know was a laboratory. We always had to go in through the back door, where we'd be met by a tall man named Dr. Davidoff. He'd whisk us into a room and run all kinds of tests on me. Painful tests that left me weak and sore for days. My parents said I was sick and needed these visits. I'd say I felt fine, and they'd say, "Yes, that's why you need to keep going."

When I was in kindergarten, a new library assistant came to our school. Her name was Marguerite and she was the prettiest lady I'd ever seen. The nicest, too. All the kids wanted to help her put away books and listen to her talk with that exotic French accent. But I was her special pet. Her kitten. Whenever I was alone at recess, she'd come over and talk to me. And she'd keep me company after school, while I waited for my father to pick me up.

One day, Marguerite said she had to leave, and asked me to come with her. I said yes. Simple as that. I was five and I loved Marguerite, and I didn't particularly love my parents, so it seemed like a good trade-up. I went to live with her in Montreal, where I was Katiana and she was my Aunt Marguerite, and the story of how I came to live with her was a delicious secret between us.

When I'd been with her for a few years, Marguerite told me the truth. I was a supernatural, and a subject in a genetic modification experiment, supposedly to reduce the negative side-effects of supernatural powers. Marguerite had been part of a network of supernaturals concerned about the experiments. She'd been assigned to monitor me, so she'd taken the job at my school.

When she saw how miserable I was, she told the group, but they wouldn't let her do anything—her job was to watch and report only. Marguerite couldn't do that. So she'd asked me to come away with her, and no matter what has happened since, I've never regretted saying yes.

The bus went downtown, so that's where we got off.

"There is a car rental place on the other side of the river," Marguerite said. "We will go there."

I nodded and said nothing. It was barely seven a.m., and the downtown streets were almost empty. A vehicle rolled by now and then, most of them cube vans making early deliveries. A few police cars crawled along the streets, looking for trouble left over from the night before.

Sleepy-eyed businessmen dragged themselves into office buildings, coffee clutched in their hands, the smell making my stomach perk up. If we'd been back at the apartment, I'd be just rolling out of bed, a steaming mug of hazelnut coffee on my nightstand, Marguerite knowing that woke me better than any alarm clock.

As we reached the end of the block, the smell of coffee was overwhelmed by a far less enticing odor: the river. I could hear it, too, the crash of the dam not yet swallowed by the roar of downtown traffic. As we turned the corner, a blast of wind hit and I swore I could feel the spray of water.

I shivered. Marguerite reached for my backpack. "Let me get your sweater."

"I'm okay."

"A coffee then." She gave a wan smile. "I know you like your morning coffee. It will not be your fancy flavored sort, but—"

"I'm okay."

She turned another corner, getting us out of the wind. "You're not okay, Kat. I know that. I . . ."

"You thought it was for the best. I get that." I cleared my throat, anxious to change the subject. "I recognized the woman in the bus station. I think she was one of the nurses from the lab. I guess they finally tracked me down, and now they want to kill me."

"No. They would not do that. You are too valuable."

I snorted. "Yeah, as a trophy. If you didn't think he meant to shoot me, you wouldn't have jumped in the way."

She walked a few more steps before answering. "I am certain they would not kill you. But certain enough to risk your life on it? No." She looked over at me. "You *are* valuable, Kat. Even in their experiment, you were special. That is why you had to go to the laboratory at night, away from the other children, hidden from most of those who worked there."

"So I was a top-secret part of a top-secret experiment?"

A tiny smile. "Something like that."

"A werecat. Gotta be."

I expected her to roll her eyes, shoot back her usual line, but she only hunched her shoulders against the cold morning air, and stared off down the empty street.

"The bullet," I said. "Is it still . . . in you?"

She nodded. When I tried to press her on that, worried that it might be dangerous, she brushed my concern off with uncharacteristic impatience, her gaze fixed on the next corner. Then she caught my arm.

"Someone is there. He stopped at the corner."

I could come up with a dozen logical explanations for someone to pause at a corner, but Marguerite held me still as she strained to look, listen and sense.

"Someone else is approaching," she whispered. "He stops beside the first . . ."

It was so quiet that even I could pick up the murmur of conversation. Marguerite pushed me into an alcove as footsteps sounded. Then a man cursed. Marguerite pushed me farther into the alcove and we huddled there, listening.

"Are you sure your spell picked them up?" the man asked.

"It detected the girl," a woman said. "It only works on the living. And only intermittently with her."

The man said something I didn't catch.

"I suppose so," his companion replied. "Let me cast again."

She murmured words in a foreign language. A spell. I shivered. Marguerite rubbed my arm, but it wasn't the cold that made me tremble now. I might be a supernatural, and I might live with one, but their world was still foreign to me, mysterious. I don't like mysteries. I like what I can see, feel, touch and understand. I like what I can fight. Spells? I had no idea how to defend myself against those.

We pressed deeper into the shadows as the voices approached.

"Nothing," the woman said.

"We—"

"Shhh," she said. "I heard something."

We'd barely breathed, so it wasn't us. A door creaked open. Footsteps again, but it was another pair, coming from the opposite direction, like someone had stepped out of a shop down the road. The footsteps headed our way.

Marguerite's slender hands flew in familiar code, outlining a plan. I barely needed to watch—I knew what she'd be thinking. With a bystander approaching, our pursuers would be focused on getting past him, their weapons hidden. So when they reached the alcove—

Marguerite sprang first, grabbing the man as he stepped into view, then yanking him into the darkened alcove. I leapt out behind her. The woman backpedaled, hands sailing up, lips parting. An invisible blow hit me in the chest. I tottered backward. That was it—just thrown off balance. I smiled. Now *that* I could handle.

I charged. Her hands flew up again. I chopped them down, disrupting her spell. She started to cast again, this time not using her hands. A witch spell. A roundhouse kick knocked her off her feet and cut that one short.

Marguerite leapt between us. She grabbed the woman and dragged her into the alcove. Inside, the man lay on his back, out cold from her bite.

As Marguerite took the woman into the shadows for the same treatment, I looked down the street. A chubby guy in a business suit stood twenty feet away. Just stood there, travel mug raised halfway to his lips, like he'd been frozen there the whole time, watching the fight.

"Morning," I said.

He skittered across the road and took off the other way.

"Looks like he didn't want to play Good Samaritan today," I said as Marguerite joined me on the sidewalk. "But he probably has a cell, so he might call . . ." I stopped, seeing her holding what looked like a phone. "Did *they* manage to call someone?"

"A radio with a GPS." She lifted the box. "They sent our coordinates."

She dropped it over the side of a trash bin and we took off. As we turned the corner, we saw the woman from the bus station rounding the next one down the block. I wheeled. Two unfamiliar men were approaching from the rear. I hesitated, telling myself they were just humans, bystanders, heading off to work. Then one reached into his coat and pulled out a gun.

Marguerite grabbed my shoulder, steering me to the nearest exit: a service lane just ahead. At the mouth, she caught my arm and peered down the lane, making sure it wasn't a dead end. There was a wall thirty feet down, but the lane continued, turning left.

We raced to the end, veered around the corner . . . and found a single parking space, enclosed on all other sides by soaring walls.

"No, no, no," Marguerite whispered.

I pointed. "A door."

As we ran to it, Marguerite pulled out her lock picks. I tried the handle, just in case, but of course it was locked. She pushed a pick into the keyhole.

Footfalls pounded down the service lane. She stopped and turned.

"Just open—" I began.

"No time."

She looked around, then her chin shot up. I followed her gaze to a fire escape. I ran for it. She boosted me and I grabbed the bottom rung. I scrambled up, hand over hand, as fast as I could. At a shout, I looked down to see the woman skidding to a halt at the end of the alley . . . and Marguerite, still on the ground.

"Marguerite!"

"Go!" When I didn't budge, she glowered up at me, fangs extended as she snarled, "Go!"

She ran at the woman. I climbed, slower now, fingers trembling, forcing myself to take each step, my gut screaming for me to stop, to go back for her. But I knew she was right. I had no defenses against a gun. She did. I had to get away and trust she'd follow.

When I reached the top, I turned. The first thing I saw was the woman, unconscious on the ground. Then the two men, one holding Marguerite in a head-lock, the other with his gun trained on me. I hesitated. He fired.

The bullet hit the brick below my foot. He lifted the barrel higher. I lunged onto the rooftop, heart thudding. The metal fire escape groaned as someone began to climb it. I scrambled to my feet and took off across the roof.

I got away. As soon as I did, I realized I had to go back.

They'd already tried to kill Marguerite. She was just an obstacle to getting me and, now, a way to get to me, to lure me in. She'd survived being shot, but now that they knew what she was, they'd know how to kill her. I shivered just thinking about how they might try to convince her to give me up. And when they couldn't, they'd kill her. No question.

I gulped icy air as I stood pressed against a wall, catching my breath. Then I closed my eyes and listened. No one was coming. I kept listening, trying to hear the roar of the dam to orient myself. It was close by, just to my right. I turned the other way and started walking.

I found them in the same service lane we'd run into. They'd backed a van in and had the rear doors open as one of the men dragged Marguerite, hands behind her back, gagged and struggling, toward it.

As I strode into the alley, the driver leapt out, raising his gun.

"I come in peace," I said, lifting my fingers in a V.

He paused, half out of the van, his broad face screwing up in confusion.

I raised my hands. "See? No pistol. No switchblade. Not even a ray gun."

The witch I'd taken out earlier came around the other side of the van, approaching slowly. I watched her lips, ready for the first sign of a spellcast.

"I want to make a deal," I said.

She didn't answer, just stopped, her gaze traveling over me like she was looking for a hidden weapon. The driver eased back into the van, door still open, radio going to his lips.

"You can stop looking for her," he said. "She's right here." Pause. "Yeah, it's the O'Sullivan kid. Says she wants to make a deal." His voice dropped. "Better hurry."

The other man resumed dragging Marguerite to the van.

"Uh-uh," I said. "Put her in there and I'm gone. This deal is a trade. You take me and you let her go."

Marguerite shook her head wildly, her eyes blazing. I looked away and focused on the witch.

"You do want me, right?" I said.

"We do."

"And you aren't interested in her."

Her lips twisted with undisguised distaste. Marguerite told me that's how other supernaturals see vampires and werewolves—unnatural and inhuman, worthy only of fear and disgust. They would kill her as soon as they could. I was sure of it now.

I continued, "So you take the prodigal science experiment home to the lab, and the vampire goes free. Fair enough?"

The witch hesitated, then nodded. "Come along then, Kathy."

"It's Kat."

A flicker of annoyance, quickly hidden. "All right then. Kat. Come—"

"I'm not coming anywhere until you release her. She'll walk this way. I'll walk that way. Crisscross. Everyone's happy." *Except me, going back to that horrible place, those awful experiments.* I pushed the thought away. I was valuable, so I'd survive, which was more than I could say for Marguerite if I didn't do this. She'd given up her freedom to look after me. Now it was time for me to do the same for her.

When the witch didn't move, I said, "I'm not going anywhere. You guys have guns, spells, demonic powers, whatever. I have zip. Just let her go, so I'm sure you're holding up your end of the bargain."

Another brief pause, then the witch signaled to the man holding Marguerite. He released her. As she walked toward me, I headed for the witch, my gaze still fixed on her. Out of the corner of my eye, I could see Marguerite pull down the gag, mouthing to me, trying to get my attention, trying to tell me to wait for her signal and then run. I ignored her. I had to go through with this.

I was about five feet from Marguerite when a truck backfired behind me, the sound cracking like gunfire. I jumped and spun. That's *all* I did. I didn't lunge. I didn't run. I didn't even back up. It didn't matter. I'd moved, and when I did, I heard the *pfft* of a silenced shot.

Marguerite screamed. I felt her hit me in the back, the blow so hard it knocked me off my feet, and as I fell, I twisted, and saw her running toward me, still three feet away, too far to have hit me. A spell, it had to be a—

I hit the pavement, flat on my back, blood spraying up from my chest.

Blood. Spraying up. From me. From my chest.

I lifted my head, looking down at myself, and saw—and saw—and saw—

"You shot her!" the witch screeched.

"She was trying to—"

"You were *waiting* for an excuse. You . . ."

She kept shouting as Marguerite dropped beside me, tears plopping onto my face as I lay on the pavement and all I could think was, *I didn't know vampires could cry.*

". . . like Davidoff's going to complain," the man was saying. "I gave him the excuse to test his secret experiment . . ."

The voices drifted away again. Or maybe I drifted. The next thing I knew, I was sitting up with Marguerite's arm around me, her face buried in my hair, tears wet against my scalp as she whispered, "I'm sorry, *mon chaton*. I'm so sorry."

". . . just get the body in the van . . ." the woman was saying.

Body? I jerked up at that, looking around wildly, reassuring myself I was alive. I could still see them, could still hear Marguerite telling me it would be okay, everything would be okay.

Marguerite had me on my feet now, her arm still around me as she whispered, "We're going to run, Kat. We *must* run. Do you understand?"

Run? Was she crazy? I'd been shot. I couldn't—

Everything went black. Then, suddenly, I was on the sidewalk, running as she supported me. The pain in my chest was indescribable. Every breath felt like a knife stabbing through me. Marguerite had one hand pressed to the hole in my chest, trying to keep it closed, but it didn't matter. The blood ran over her fingers, over my shirt, dripping onto the pavement. Yet somehow we ran.

As we stumbled onto the road, a truck horn blasted. We kept going. The truck tried to stop, brakes and tires squealing. We raced past it, so close that the draft from it nearly toppled us. The truck screeched to a halt. The driver shouted. Our pursuers shouted back, but they were stuck on the other side of the vehicle, out of sight.

We ducked into the first alley and kept going.

As we ran, the ground tilted under my feet. I tried to focus, but could see only a haze of dull shapes. Then I heard something. Water. The thunder of the dam, growing closer with each step. I heard Marguerite too, on her cell phone. Emergency. Shooting. The dam. Ambulance. Police. Please hurry.

What was she doing? I couldn't go to a regular doctor. I'd been told that all my life, even before I went away with Marguerite. *In an emergency, call home. Don't let them take you to a hospital.* My parents said it was because they wouldn't understand my condition. True. They just hadn't mentioned that the condition was being a genetically-modified supernatural whose blood tests would make the doctors call the guys in the hazmat suits.

I guess that didn't matter now. I needed immediate medical attention. We'd deal with the fallout later.

The roar of rushing water grew steadily louder. Then another sound cut through it. The wail of sirens. I remembered seeing the police cars downtown. That's why Marguerite had asked for the police—they'd get here quickly, and that would scare off our pursuers. In an emergency, she always said, cause a scene and get the humans involved. No supernatural would risk doing anything with them around.

Marguerite lowered me to the ground, my back brushing against a metal railing. A cold mist of water sprayed my neck. When I blinked, I could focus enough to see we were at the dam. Police lights strobed against the buildings, the sirens deafening now.

There was no sign of our pursuers. This trapped them worse than the truck. They couldn't approach. We were safe.

"Mags," I whispered. I tried to say more, but could only cough, pain ripping through me, bloody spit splattering my clothes.

"Shhh, shhh." She kissed the top of my head, tears raining down her cheeks. "I'm sorry, *mon chaton*. So sorry. I should have told you, should have warned you. You are so young. So young."

Told me what? Young? Too young for what? To die? No. She couldn't mean that. I was fine. The ambulance was coming. I could hear the siren.

Doors slammed, and a police officer shouted for Marguerite to step back. Her trembling fingers fumbled around my neck, finding my necklace. A Star of David. I wasn't Jewish, but we always said I was. Just part of the cover.

When she found it, she breathed a sigh of relief, murmuring, *"Bien, bien."*
Why was that good?

"Step away from the girl," another officer shouted.

"I love you, Kat. You know that, don't you?" She kissed my forehead again. "I love you and I'll never leave you."

She stood then. I tried to call out to her but couldn't. The fog was descending again and it took everything I had just to focus, just to see her, a faint shape in the grayness as the mist from the dam and the fog from my brain swirled together.

"I'll see you on the other side," she whispered. Her fingers grazed my chin as she stepped back.

I twisted my head to watch her as she climbed onto the railing. The police shouted. I shouted, too, but only in my head, shouting her name over and over, telling her to stop, to come back, not to leave me . . .

She blew me a kiss and then back-flipped off the railing. The last thing I saw was Marguerite plummeting down, out of sight, into the river a hundred feet below.

And then . . .

Nothing.

I woke up cold, a chilled-to-the-bone kind of cold, with only a thin sheet pulled up to my chin. Under me, my bed was rock hard. I stretched and my muscles screamed in protest.

Damn, I really needed a workout.

I laughed at the thought. I'd been shot in the chest. Something told me it'd be a while before I was training again.

I inhaled, and resisted the urge to gag as my nostrils filled with the stink of antiseptic and chemicals. The smell of a hospital, bringing back old memories. I shivered. At least I wouldn't be going back to *that* hospital again. Almost worth being shot.

I wiggled my fingers and toes. God, everything ached and I was freezing. Did they have the air conditioning on? My bed was so cold it was like lying on a marble slab.

I rubbed the bed . . . and my fingertips squeaked across the surface. I stopped. Mattresses didn't squeak. Was it covered in plastic? Did it need to be? Had I pissed myself?

I lifted my head. It took some effort—my head was flat on the bed. No pillow? I looked down and caught the flash of my reflection. I was lying on a metal table.

I jumped up so fast I nearly tumbled to the floor. I looked around. Metal. All I saw was metal. Metal table. Metal equipment. Metal trays covered with metal surgical instruments.

Had I woken up in surgery? Oh, God. Had they *finished*? My fingers flew to my chest, finding the spot under my left breast where the bullet had—

There was no bullet hole. No stitches. No bandages.

And no heartbeat.

I shook my head sharply, and pressed my fingers to the spot and closed my eyes, trying to feel . . .

There was nothing to feel. My chest didn't move at all. No heartbeat and no breathing.

As I turned, I caught a glimpse of my reflection in the bank of metal berths behind me. I saw me—just me, same as always, tanned skin, brown hair, green eyes, gold pendant gleaming on my chest.

I caught the pendant and ran my fingers over the points of the star. The Star of David. Now I knew why Marguerite was so happy to see me wearing my pendant. So they wouldn't embalm me.

I heard the words of the man who'd shot me. *Like Davidoff's going to complain. I gave him the excuse to test his secret experiment.*

An excuse to test whether their genetic modification had any effect on my supernatural birthright, my destiny. To die . . . and rise again.

"Katiana."

I glanced over to see Marguerite in the doorway. I couldn't have been asleep long, but she looked like she hadn't fed in weeks. She was pale and unsteady, her eyes sunken and red.

"Guess you were right," I said. "I'm not a werecat."

Her face crumpled. I didn't ask if she'd known I was a vampire. Of course she had. That's why she'd been assigned to me. Why she'd taken me away. I'd always felt like Marguerite was more my family than my parents had ever been. Now I knew why.

I didn't ask why she hadn't told me the truth. I knew. Of every supernatural creature I could have been, this one would be the biggest blow, and she'd wanted to spare me until I was older. I suppose she figured she had plenty of time before I needed to know. Time to let me grow up. Time to let me be normal.

A thought struck. "So, I'm going to be sixteen forever?"

"No, no," she said quickly. "That was one of the modifications, with the experiment. You are supposed to live a normal life, with only the other powers of a vampire."

Supposed to. That was only a theory, of course. No one could know for sure. I'd age or I wouldn't.

"Someone's coming." The words slipped out before I realized I was saying them. I turned toward the closed hall door, but didn't hear anything. Still, I knew someone was there. I could feel him.

A shark's sixth sense.

The perfect predator.

I shivered. Marguerite started to hug me, then lifted her head, catching the same weird sense, and quickly handed me new clothing. I took it and we hurried to the corner. Whoever was coming down the hall passed the room without stopping.

"So what happens now?" I whispered as I dressed. "The Edison Group must know I'm here. They'll be waiting for me to . . . rise."

"They are."

"And when I disappear? They'll know. They'll come—"

"I have made arrangements. Money can buy many things. The records will show you were cremated by accident. You cannot be reborn from that. They will think they have lost you. We are safe." She helped me into my shirt and caught my gaze. "I know you have questions, Katiana. There is so much you must be wondering—"

"Just one thing. Can we go home?"

She nodded. "Yes, we can go home."

"Then, right now, that's all I want."

She nodded, put her arm around me, and led me from the room.

A Haunted House of Her Own

T ANYA COULDN'T UNDERSTAND why real estate agents failed to recognize the commercial potential of haunted houses. This one, it seemed, was no different.

"Now, these railings need work," the woman said as she led Tanya and Nathan out onto one of the balconies. "But the floor is structurally sound, and that's the main thing. I'm sure these would be an attractive selling point to your bed-and-breakfast guests."

Not as attractive as ghosts . . .

"You're sure the house doesn't have a history?" Tanya prodded again. "I thought I heard something in town . . ."

She hadn't, but the way the agent stiffened told Tanya she was onto something. After pointed reminders about disclosing the house's full history, the woman admitted there was, indeed, something. Apparently a kid had murdered his family here, back in the seventies.

"A tragedy, but it's long past," the agent assured her. "Never a spot of trouble since."

"Damn," Tanya murmured under her breath, and followed the agent back inside.

Next, Nathan wanted to check out the coach house, see if there was any chance of converting it into a separate "honeymoon hideaway."

Tanya was thrilled to see him taking an interest. Opening the inn had been her idea. An unexpected windfall from a great-aunt had come right after she lost her teaching job and Nathan's office manager position teetered under end-of-year budget cuts. It seemed like the perfect time to try something new.

"You two go on ahead," she said. "I'll poke around in here, maybe check out the gardens."

"Did I see a greenhouse out back?" Nathan asked the agent.

She beamed. "You most certainly did."

"Why don't you go take a look at that, hon? You were talking about growing organic vegetables."

"Oh, what a wonderful idea," the agent said. "That is *so* popular right now. Organic local produce is all the rage. There's a shop in town that supplies all the . . ."

As the woman gushed, Tanya backed away slowly, then escaped.

The house was perfect—a six-bedroom, rambling Victorian perched on a hill three miles from a suitably quaint village. What more could she want in a bed-and-breakfast? Well, ghosts. Not that Tanya believed in such things, but haunted inns in Vermont were all the rage, and she was determined to own one.

When she saw the octagonal Victorian greenhouse, though, she decided that if it turned out there'd never been so much as a ghostly candle spotted on the property, she'd light one herself. She had to have this place.

She stepped inside and pictured it with lounge chairs, a bookshelf, maybe a little woodstove for winter. Not a greenhouse, but a sunroom. First, though, they'd need to do some serious weeding. The sunroom—conservatory, she amended—sat in a nest of thorny vines dotted with red. Raspberries? She cleaned a peephole in the grime and peered out.

A head popped up from the thicket. Tanya fell back with a yelp. Sunken brown eyes widened, and wizened lips parted in a matching shriek of surprise.

Tanya hurried out as the old woman made her way from the thicket, a basket of red berries in one hand.

"I'm sorry, dear," she said. "We gave each other quite a fright."

Tanya motioned at the basket. "Late for raspberries, isn't it?"

The old woman smiled. "They're double-blooming. At least there's one good thing to come out of this place." She looked over at the house. "You aren't . . . looking to buy, are you?"

"I might be."

The woman's free hand gripped Tanya's arm. "No, dear. You don't want to do that."

"I hear there's some history."

"History?" The old woman shivered. "Horrors. Blasphemies. Murders. Foul murders. No, dear, you don't want this house, not at all."

Foul murders? Tanya tried not to laugh. If they ever did a promotional video for the bed-and-breakfast, she was hiring this woman.

"Whatever happened was a tragedy," Tanya said. "But it's long past, and it's time—"

"Long past? Never. At night, I still hear the moans. The screams. The chanting. The chanting is the worst, as if they're trying to call up the devil himself."

"I see." Tanya squinted out at the late-day sun, dropping beneath the horizon. "Do you live around here, then?"

"Just over there."

The woman pointed, then shuffled around the conservatory, still pointing. When she didn't come back, Tanya followed, wanting to make note of her name. But the yard was empty.

Tanya poked around a bit after that, but the sun dropped fast over the mountain ridge. As she picked her way through the brambles, she looked up at the house, looming in the twilight—a hulking shadow against the night, the lights inside seeming to flicker like candles behind the old glass.

The wind sighed past and she swore she heard voices in it, sibilant whispers snaking around her. A shadow moved across an upper window. She'd blame a drape caught in a draft . . . only she couldn't see any window coverings.

She smiled as she shivered. For someone who didn't believe in ghosts, she was quite caught up in the fantasy. Imagine how guests who *did* believe would react.

She found Nathan still in the coach house, measuring tape extended. When she walked up, he grinned, boyish face lighting up.

"It's perfect," he said. "Ten grand and we'd have ourselves a honeymoon suite."

Tanya turned to the agent. "How soon can we close?"

The owners were as anxious to sell as Tanya was to buy, and three weeks later, they were in the house, with the hired contractors hard at work. Tanya and Nathan were working, too, researching the house's background, both history and legend.

The first part was giving them trouble. The only online mention Nathan found was a secondary reference. But it proved that a family *had* died in their house, so that morning, he'd gone to the library in nearby Beamsville, hoping a search there would produce details. Meanwhile, Tanya would try digging up the less-tangible ghosts of the past.

She started in the gardening shop, and made the mistake of mentioning the house's history. The girl at the counter shut right down, murmuring, "We don't talk about that," then bustled off to help the next customer. That was fine. If the town didn't like to talk about the tragedy, she was free to tweak the facts and her guests would never hear anything different.

Next, she headed for the general store, complete with rocking chairs on the front porch and a tub of salty pickles beside the counter. She bought supplies, then struck up a conversation with the owner. She mentioned she'd bought the Sullivan place, and worked the conversation around to, "Someone over in Beamsville told me the house is supposed to be haunted."

"Can't say I ever heard that," he said, filling her bag. "This is a nice, quiet town."

"Oh, that's too bad." She laughed. "Not the quiet part, but . . ." She lowered her voice. "You wouldn't believe the advertising value of ghosts."

His wife poked her head in from the back room. "She's right, Tom. Folks pay extra to stay in those places. I saw it on TV."

"A full house for me means more customers for you," Tanya said.

"Well, now that you mention it, when my boys were young, they said they saw lights . . ."

And so it went. People might not want to talk about the true horrors of what happened at the Sullivan place, but with a little prodding they spun tales of imagined ones. Most were second-hand accounts, but Tanya didn't care if they were true. Someone in town said it, and that was all that mattered. By the time she headed home, her notebook was filled with stories.

She was at the bottom of the road when she saw the postwoman putting along in her little car, driving from the passenger side so she could stuff the mailboxes. Tanya got out of her own car to introduce herself. As they chatted, Tanya mentioned the raspberry-picking neighbor, hoping to get a name.

"No old ladies around here," the postwoman said. "You've got Mr. McNally to the north. The Lee gang to the south. And to the back, it's a couple of new women. Don't recall the names—it isn't my route—but they're young."

"Maybe a little farther? She didn't exactly say she was a neighbor. Just pointed over there."

The woman followed her finger. "That's the Lee place."

"Past that, then."

"Past that?" The woman eyed her. "Only thing past that is the cemetery."

Tanya made mental notes as she pulled into the darkening drive. She'd have to send Nathan to the clerk's office, see if he could find a dead resident who resembled a description of the woman she'd seen.

Not that she thought she'd seen a ghost, of course. The woman probably lived farther down the hill. But if she found a deceased neighbor with a similar appearance, she could add her own spooky tale to the collection.

She stepped out of the car. When a whisper snaked around her, she jumped. Then she stood there, holding the car door, peering into the night and listening. It definitely sounded like whispering. She could even pick up a word or two, like "come" and "join." Well, at least the ghosts weren't telling her to get lost, she thought, her laugh strained and harsh against the quiet night.

The whispers stopped. She glanced up at the trees. The dead leaves were still. No wind. Which explained why the sound had stopped. As she headed for the house, she glanced over her shoulder, checking for Nathan's SUV. It was there, but the house was pitch-black.

She opened the door. It creaked. Naturally. No oil for that baby, she thought with a smile. No fixing the loose boards on the steps either. Someone was bound to hear another guest sneaking down for a midnight snack and blame ghosts. More stories to add to the guest book.

She tossed her keys onto the table. They hit with a jangle, the sound echoing through the silent hall. When she turned on the light switch, the hall stayed dark. She tried not to shiver as she peered around. *That's quite enough ghost stories for you,* she told herself as she marched into the next room, heading for the lamp. She tripped over a throw rug and stopped.

"Nathan?"

No answer. She hoped he wasn't poking around in the basement. He'd been curious about some boxes down there, but she didn't want to get into that. There was too much else to be done.

She eased forward, feeling the way with her foot until she reached the lamp. When she hit the switch, light flooded the room. Not a power outage then. Good, though it reminded her they had to pick up a generator. Blackouts would be a little more atmosphere than guests appreciated.

"Nathan?"

She heard something in the back rooms. She walked through, hitting lights as she went—for safety, she told herself.

"Umm-hmm." Nathan's voice echoed down the hall. "Umm-hmm."

On the phone, she thought, too caught up in the call to realize how dark it had gotten and flip on a light. She hoped it wasn't the licensing board. The inspector had been out to assess the ongoing work yesterday. He'd seemed happy with it, but you never knew.

She let her shoes click a little harder as she walked over the hardwood floor, so she wouldn't startle Nathan. She followed his voice to the office. From the doorway, she could see his back in the desk chair.

"Umm-hmm."

Her gaze went to the phone on the desk. Still in the cradle. Nathan's hands were at his sides. He was sitting in the dark, looking straight ahead, at the wall.

Tanya rubbed down the hairs on her neck. He was using his cell phone earpiece, that was all. Guys and their gadgets. She stepped into the room and looked at his ear. No headset.

"Nathan?"

He jumped, wheeling so fast the chair skidded across the floor. He caught it and gave a laugh, shaking his head sharply as he reached for the desk lamp.

"Must have dozed off. Not used to staring at a computer screen all day anymore."

He rubbed his eyes, and blinked up at her.

"Everything okay, hon?" he asked.

She said it was and gave him a rundown of what she'd found out, and they had a good laugh at that, all the shopkeepers rushing in with their stories once they realized the tourism potential.

"Did *you* find anything?"

"I did indeed." He flourished a file folder stuffed with printouts. "The Rowe family. Nineteen seventy-eight. Parents, two children and the house-keeper, all killed by the seventeen-year-old son."

"Under the influence of Satan?"

"Close. Rock music." Nathan grinned. "It was the seventies. Kid had long hair, played in a garage band, partial to Iron Maiden and Black Sabbath. Clearly a Satanist."

"Works for me."

Tanya took the folder just as the phone started to ring. Caller ID showed it was the inspector. She set the pages aside and answered as Nathan whispered he'd start dinner.

There was a problem with the inspection—the guy had forgotten to check a few things, and he had to come back on the weekend, when they were supposed to be away scouring estate auctions and flea markets to furnish the house. The workmen would be there, but apparently that wasn't good enough. And on Monday, the inspector left for two weeks in California with the wife and kids.

Not surprisingly, Nathan offered to stay. Jumped at the chance, actually. His enthusiasm for the project didn't extend to bargain hunting for Victorian beds. He joked he'd have enough to do when she wanted her treasures refinished. So he'd stay home and supervise the workers, which was probably wise anyway.

It was an exhausting, but fruitful, weekend. Tanya crossed off all the necessities and even a few wish-list items, like a couple of old-fashioned washbasins.

When she called Nathan an hour before arriving home, he sounded exhausted and strained, and she hoped the workers hadn't given him too much trouble. Sometimes they were like her fifth-grade pupils, needing a watchful eye and firm, clear commands. Nathan wasn't good at either. When she pulled into the drive and found him waiting on the porch, she knew there was trouble.

She wasn't even out of the car before the workmen filed out, toolboxes in hand.

"We quit," the foreman said.

"What's wrong?" she asked.

"The house. Everything about it is wrong."

"Haunted," an older man behind him muttered.

The younger two shifted behind their elders, clearly uncomfortable with this old-man talk, but not denying it either.

"All right," she said slowly. "What happened?"

They rhymed off a litany of haunted-house tropes—knocking inside the walls, footsteps in the attic, whispering voices, flickering lights, strains of music.

"Music?"

"Seventies rock music," Nathan said, rolling his eyes behind their backs. "Andy found those papers in my office, about the Rowe family."

"You should have warned us," the foreman said, scowling. "Working where something like that happened? It isn't right. The place should be burned to the ground."

"It's evil," the older man said. "Evil soaked right into the walls. You can feel it."

The only thing Tanya felt was the recurring sensation of being trapped in a B-movie. Did people actually talk like this? First, the old woman. Then the townspeople. Now the contractors.

They argued, of course, but the workmen were leaving. When Tanya started to threaten, Nathan pulled her aside. The work was almost done, he said. They could finish up themselves, save some money, and guilt these guys into cutting their bill even more.

Tanya hated to back down, but he had a point. She negotiated twenty percent off for unfinished work and another fifteen for the inconvenience—unless they wanted her spreading the word that grown men were afraid of ghosts. They grumbled, but agreed.

The human mind can be as impressionable as a child. Tanya might not believe in ghosts, but the more stories she heard, the more her mind began to believe, with or without her permission. Drafts became cold spots. Thumping pipes became the knocks of unseen hands. The hiss and sigh of the old furnace became the whispers and moans of those who could not rest. She knew better; that was the worst of it. She'd hear a pipe thump and she'd jump, heart pounding, even as she knew there was a logical explanation.

Nathan wasn't helping. Every time she jumped, he'd laugh. He'd goof off and play ghost, sneaking into the bathroom while she was in the shower and writing dirty messages in the condensation on the mirror. She was spooked; he thought it was adorable.

The joking and teasing she could take. It was the other times, the ones when she'd walk into a room and he'd be standing or sitting, staring into nothing, confused when he'd start out of his reverie, laughing about day-dreaming, but nervously, like he didn't exactly know what he'd been doing.

They were three weeks from opening when she returned from picking up the brochures and, once again, found the house in darkness. This time, the hall light worked—it'd been nothing more sinister than a burnt-out bulb before. And this time she didn't call Nathan's name, but crept through the halls looking for him, feeling silly and yet . . .

When she approached the kitchen, she heard a strange rasping sound. She followed it and found Nathan standing in the twilight, staring out the window, hands moving, a *skritch-skritch* filling the silence.

The fading light caught something in his hands—a flash of silver that became a knife, a huge butcher's knife moving back and forth across a whetting stone.

"N-Nathan?"

He jumped, nearly dropping the knife, then stared down at it, frowning. A sharp shake of his head and he laid the knife and stone on the counter, then flipped on the kitchen light.

"Really not something I should be doing in the dark, huh?" He laughed and moved a carrot from the counter to the cutting board, picked up the knife, then stopped. "Little big for the job, isn't it?"

She moved closer. "Where did it come from?"

"Hmm?" He followed her gaze to the unfamiliar knife. "Ours, isn't it? Part of the set your sister gave us for our anniversary? It was in the drawer." He grabbed a smaller knife from the wooden block. "So, how did the brochures turn out?"

Two nights later, Tanya started awake and bolted up, blinking hard, hearing music. She rubbed her ears, telling herself it was a dream, but she could definitely hear something. She turned to Nathan's side of the bed. Empty.

Okay, he couldn't sleep so he'd gone downstairs. She could barely hear the music, so he was being considerate, keeping it low, probably doing paperwork in the office.

Even as she told herself this, though, she kept envisioning the knife. The big butcher's knife that seemed to have come from nowhere.

Nonsense. Her sister *had* given them a new set, and Nathan did most of the cooking, so it wasn't surprising that she didn't recognize it. But as hard as she tried to convince herself, she just kept seeing Nathan, standing in the twilight, sharpening that knife, the *skritch-skritch* getting louder, the blade getting sharper . . .

Damn her sister. And not for the knives, either. Last time they'd been up, her sister and boyfriend insisted on picking the night's video. *The Shining.* New caretaker at an inn is possessed by a murderous ghost and hacks up his wife. There was a reason Tanya didn't watch horror movies, and now she remembered why.

She turned on the bedside lamp, then pushed out of bed and flicked on the overhead light. The hall one went on, too. So did the one leading downstairs. Just being careful, of course. You never knew where a stray hammer or board could be lying around.

As she descended the stairs, the music got louder, the thump of the bass and the wail of the singer. Seventies heavy-metal music. Hadn't the Rowe kid—? She squeezed her eyes shut and forced the thought out. Like she'd know seventies heavy-metal from modern stuff anyway. And hadn't Nathan picked up that new AC/DC disc last month? *Before* they came to live here. He was probably listening to that, not realizing how loud it was.

When she got downstairs, though, she could feel the bass vibrating through the floorboards. Great. He couldn't sleep so he was poking through those boxes in the basement.

Boxes belonging to the Rowe family. To the Rowe kid.

Oh, please. The Rowes had been gone for almost thirty years. Anything in the basement would belong to the Sullivans, a lovely old couple now living in Florida.

On the way to the basement, Tanya passed the kitchen. She stopped. She stared at the drawer where Nathan kept the knife, then walked over and opened it. Just taking a look, seeing if she remembered her sister giving it to them, not making sure it was still there. It was. And it still didn't look familiar.

She started to leave, then went back, took the knife, wrapped it in a dish towel and stuck it under the sink. And, yes, she felt like an idiot. But she felt relief even more.

She slipped down to the basement, praying she wouldn't find Nathan sitting on the floor, staring into nothing, nodding to voices she couldn't hear. Again, she felt foolish for thinking it and, again, she felt relief when she heard him digging through boxes, and more relief yet when she walked in and he looked up, grinning sheepishly like a kid caught sneaking into his Christmas presents.

"Caught me," he said. "Was it the music? I thought I had it low enough."

She followed his gaze and a chill ran through her. Across the room was a record player, an album spinning on the turntable, more stacked on the floor.

"Wh-where—?" she began.

"Found it down here with the albums. Been a while since you've seen one of those, I bet."

"Was it . . . his? The Rowe boy?"

Nathan frowned, as if it hadn't occurred to him. "Could be, I guess. I didn't think of that."

He walked over and shut the player off. Tanya picked up an album. Initials had been scrawled in black marker in the corner. T.R. What was the Rowe boy's name? She didn't know and couldn't bring herself to ask Nathan, would rather believe he didn't know either.

She glanced at him. "Are you okay?"

"Sure. I think I napped this afternoon, while you were out. Couldn't get to sleep."

"And otherwise. . . ?"

He looked at her, trying to figure out what she meant, but what was she going to say? *Have you had the feeling of being not yourself lately? Hearing voices telling you to murder your family?*

She had to laugh at that. Yes, it was a ragged laugh, a little unsure of itself, but a laugh nonetheless. No more horror movies for her, however much her sister pleaded.

"Are *you* okay?" Nathan asked.

She nodded. "Just tired."

"I don't doubt it, the way you've been going. Come on. Let's get up to bed." He grinned. "See if I can't help us both get to sleep."

The next day, she was in the office adding her first bookings to the ledger when she saw the folder pushed off to the side, the one Nathan had compiled on the Rowe murders. She'd set it down that day and never picked it up again. She could tell herself she'd simply forgotten, but she was never that careless. She hadn't read it because her newly traitorous imagination didn't need any more grist for its mill.

But now she thought of that album cover downstairs. Those initials. If it didn't belong to the Rowe boy, then this was an easy way to confirm that and set her mind at ease.

The first report was right there on top, the names listed, the family first, then the housekeeper, Madelyn Levy, and finally, the supposed killer, seventeen-year-old Timothy Rowe.

Tanya sucked in a deep breath, then chastised herself. What did that prove? She'd known he listened to that kind of music, and that's all Nathan had been doing—listening to it, not sharpening a knife, laughing maniacally.

Was it so surprising that the Rowes' things were still down there? Who else would claim them? The Sullivans had been over fifty when they moved in—maybe they never ventured down into the basement. There'd certainly been enough room to store things upstairs.

And speaking of the Sullivans, they'd lived in this house for twenty-five years. If it was haunted, would they have stayed so long?

If it was *haunted*? Was she really considering the possibility? She squeezed her eyes shut. She was not that kind of person. She would not become that kind of person. She was rational and logical, and until she saw something that couldn't be explained by simple common sense, she was sending her imagination to the corner for a time-out.

The image made her smile a little, enough to settle back and read the article, determined now to prove her fancies wrong. She found her proof in the next paragraph, where it said Timothy Rowe shot his father. *Shot.* No big, scary butcher—

Her gaze stuttered on the rest of the line. She went back to the beginning, rereading. Timothy Rowe apparently started his rampage by shooting his father, then continued on to brutally murder the rest of his family with a ten-inch kitchen carving knife.

And what did that prove? Did she think Nathan dug up the murder weapon with those old LPs? Of course not. A few lines down it said both the gun and knife had been recovered.

What if Nathan bought a matching one? Compelled to reenact—

She pressed her fists against her eyes. Nathan possessed by a killer teen, plotting to kill her? Was she losing her mind? It was Nathan—the same good-natured, carefree guy she'd lived with for ten years. Other than a few bouts of confusion, he was his usual self, and those "bouts" were cause for a doctor's appointment, not paranoia.

She skimmed through the rest of the articles. Nothing new there, just the tale retold again and again, until—the suspect dead—the story died a natural death, relegated to a skeleton in the town's closet.

The last page was a memorial published on the first anniversary of the killings, with all the photos of the victims. Tanya glanced at the family photo and was about to close the folder when her gaze lit on the picture of the housekeeper: Madelyn Levy.

When Nathan came in a few minutes later, she was still staring at the picture.

"Hey, hon. What's wrong?"

"I—" She pointed at the housekeeper's photo. "I've seen this woman. She—she was outside, when we were looking at the house. She was picking raspberries."

The corners of Nathan's mouth twitched, as if he was expecting—hoping—she was making a bad joke. When her gaze met his, the smile vanished and he took the folder from her hands, then sat on the edge of the desk.

"I think we should consider selling," he said.

"Wh-what? No. I—"

"This place is getting to you. Maybe . . . I don't know. Maybe there is something. Those workers certainly thought so. Some people could be more susceptible—"

She jerked up straight. "I am not susceptible—"

"You lost a job you loved. You left your home, your family, gave up everything to start over, and now it's not going the way you dreamed. You're under a lot of stress and it's only going to get worse when we open."

He took her hands and tugged her up, arms going around her. "The guy who owns the Beamsville bed-and-breakfast has been asking about this place. He'd been eying it before, but with all the work it needed, it was too much for him. Now he's seen what we've done and, well, he's interested. Very interested. You wouldn't be giving up; you'd be renovating an old place and flipping it for a profit. Nothing wrong with that."

She stood. "No. I'm being silly, and I'm not giving in. We have less than three weeks until opening, and a lot of work to be done."

She turned back to her paperwork. He sighed and left the room.

It got worse after that, as if in refusing to leave, she'd issued a challenge to whatever lived there. She'd now stopped laughing when she caught herself referring to the spirits as if they were real. They were. She'd come to accept that. Seeing the housekeeper's picture had exploded the last obstacle. She'd wanted a haunted house and she'd gotten it.

For the last two nights, she'd woken to find herself alone in bed. Both times, Nathan had been downstairs listening to that damned music. The first time, he'd been digging through the boxes, wide awake, blaming insomnia. But last night . . .

Last night, she'd gone down to find him talking to someone. She'd tried to listen, but he was doing more listening than talking, and she only caught a few *um-hmm*s and *okay*s before he'd apparently woken up, startled and confused. This morning, they'd made an appointment to see the doctor. An appointment that was still a week away, which didn't do Tanya any good now, sitting awake in bed alone for the third night in a row, listening to the strains of distant music.

She forced herself to lie back down. Just ignore it. Call the doctor in the morning, tell him Nathan would take any cancellation.

But lying down didn't mean falling asleep. As she stared at the ceiling, she made a decision. Nathan was right. There was no shame in flipping the house for a profit. Tell their friends and family they'd decided small-town life wasn't for them. Smile coyly when asked how much they'd made on the deal.

No shame in that. None at all. No one ever needed to know what drove her from this house.

She closed her eyes and was actually on the verge of drifting off when she heard Nathan's footsteps climbing the basement stairs. Coming to bed? She hoped so, but she could still hear the boom and wail of the music.

Nathan's steps creaked across the first level. A door opened. Then the squeak of a cupboard door. A *kitchen* cupboard door.

Grabbing something to eat before going back downstairs.

Only he didn't go downstairs. His steps headed for the ones coming upstairs.

He's coming up to bed—just forgot to turn off the music.

All very logical, but logical explanations didn't work for Tanya anymore. She got out of bed and went into the dark hall. She reached for the light switch, but stopped. She didn't dare announce herself like that.

Clinging to the shadows, she crept along the wall until she could make out the top of Nathan's blond head as he slowly climbed the stairs. Her gaze dropped, waiting for his hands to come into view.

A flash of silver winked in the pale glow of a nightlight. Her breath caught. She forced herself to stay still just a moment longer, to be sure, and then she saw it, the knife gripped in his hand, the angry set of his expression, the emptiness in his eyes, and she turned and fled.

A room. Any room. Just get into one, lock the door and climb over the balcony.

The first one she tried was locked. She wrenched on the door knob, certain she was wrong.

"Mom?" Nathan said, his voice gruff, unrecognizable. "Are you up here, Mom?"

Tanya turned. She looked down the row of doors. All closed. Only theirs was open, at the end. She ran for it as Nathan's footsteps thumped behind her.

She dashed into the room, slammed the door and locked it. As she raced for the balcony, she heard the knob turn behind her. Then the creak of the door opening. But that couldn't be. She'd locked—

Tanya glanced over her shoulder and saw Nathan, his face twisted with rage.

"Hello, Mom. I have something for you."

Tanya grabbed the balcony door. It was already cracked open, since Nathan always insisted on the fresh air. She ran out onto the balcony and looked down to the concrete patio twenty feet below. No way she could jump, not without breaking both legs, and then she'd be trapped. Maybe if she could hang from it, then drop—

Nathan stepped onto the balcony. Tanya backed up. She called his name, begged him to snap out of it, but he just kept coming, kept smiling, knife raised. She backed up, leaning against the railing.

"Nathan. Plea—"

There was a tremendous crack, and the railing gave way. She felt herself falling, dropping backward so fast she didn't have time to twist, to scream and then—

—nothing.

Nathan escorted the innkeeper from Beamsville to the door.

"You folks did an incredible job," the man said. "But I really do hate to take advantage of a tragedy . . ."

Nathan managed a wan smile. "You'd be doing me a favor. The sooner I can get away, the happier I'll be. Every time I drive in, I see that balcony, and I—" His voice hitched. "I keep asking myself why she went out there. I know she loved the view, and she must have woken up and seen the moon and wanted a better look." He shook his head. "I meant to fix that balcony. We did the others, but she said ours could wait, and now . . ."

The man laid a hand on Nathan's shoulder. "Let me talk to my real estate agent and I'll get an offer drawn up, see if I can't take this place off your hands."

"Thank you."

Nathan closed the door and took a deep breath. He was making good use of those community theater skills, but he really hoped he didn't have to keep this up much longer.

He headed into the office, giving it yet another once-over, making sure he'd gotten rid of all the evidence. He'd already checked, twice, but he couldn't be too careful.

There wasn't much to hide. The old woman had been an actor friend of one of his theater buddies, and even if she came forward, what of it? Tanya wanted a haunted house and he'd hired her to indulge his wife's fancy.

Adding the woman's photo to the article had been simple Photoshop work, the files—paper and electronic—long gone now. The workmen really had been scared off by the haunting, which he'd orchestrated. The only person who knew about his "episodes" was Tanya. And he'd been very careful with the balcony, loosening the nails just enough that her weight would rip them from the rotting wood.

Killing Tanya hadn't been his original intention. But when she'd refused to leave, he'd been almost relieved. As if he didn't mind having to fall back on the more permanent solution, get the insurance money as well as the inheritance, go back home, hook up with Denise again—if she'd still have him—and open the kind of business he wanted. There'd been no chance of that while Tanya was alive. Her money. Her rules. Always.

He opened the basement door, stepped down and almost went flying, his foot sending a hammer clunking down a few stairs. He retrieved it, wondering how it got there, then shoved it into his back pocket and—

The ring of the phone stopped his descent. He headed back up to answer it.

"Restrictions?" Nathan bellowed into the phone. "What do you mean restrictions? How long—?"

He paused.

"A year? I have to *live* here a year?"

Pause.

"Look, can't there be an exception under the circumstances? My wife died in this house. I need to get out of here."

Tanya stepped up behind Nathan and watched the hair on his neck rise. He rubbed it down and absently looked over his shoulder, then returned to his conversation. She moved back, caught a glimpse of the hammer in his pocket and sighed. So much for that idea. But she had plenty more, and it didn't sound like Nathan was leaving anytime soon.

She slid up behind him, arms going around his waist, smiling as he jumped and looked around.

Her house might not have been haunted before. But it was now.

LEARNING CURVE

An Otherworld Universe Story

"**I**'M BEING STALKED."

Rudy, the bartender, stopped scowling at a nearly empty bottle of rye and peered around the dimly lit room.

"No, I wasn't followed inside," I said.

"Good, then get out before you are. I don't need that kind of trouble, Zoe."

I looked around at the patrons, most sitting alone at their tables, most passed out, most drooling.

"Looks to me like that's exactly the kind of trouble you need. Short of a fire, that's the only way you're getting those chairs back."

"The only chairs I want back are those ones." He hooked his thumb at a trio of college boys in the corner.

"Oh, but they're cute," I said. "Clean, well-groomed . . . and totally ruining the ambiance you work so hard to provide. Maybe I can sic my stalker on them."

"Don't even think about it."

"Oh, please. Why do you think I ducked in here? Anyone with the taste to stalk me is not going to set foot past the door."

He pointed to the exit. I leaned over the counter and snagged a beer bottle.

"Down payment on the job," I said, nodding to the boys. "Supernaturals?"

He rolled his eyes, as if to say, "What else?" True, Miller's didn't attract a lot of humans, but every so often one managed to find the place, though they usually didn't make it past the first glance inside.

I strolled toward the boys, who were checking me out, whispering like twelve-year-olds. I sat down at the next table. It took all of five seconds for one to slide into the chair beside mine.

"Haven't I seen you on campus?" he asked.

It was possible. I took courses now and then at the University of Toronto. But I shook my head. "I went to school overseas." I sipped my beer. "Little place outside Sendai, Japan. Class of 1878."

He blinked, then found a laugh. "Is that your way of saying you're too old for me?"

"Definitely too old." I smiled, fangs extending.

He fell back, chair toppling as he scrambled out of it.

I stood and extended my hand. "Zoe Takano."

"You're—you're—"

"Lonely. And hungry. Think you can help?"

As the kid and his friends made for the exit, one of the regulars lifted his head from the bar, bleary eyes peering at me.

"Running from Zoe?" he said. "Those boys must be new in town."

I flipped him off, took my beer to the bar and settled in.

"How about you try that with your stalker instead of hiding out here?" Rudy said.

"That could lead to a confrontation. Better to ignore the problem and hope it resolves itself."

He snorted and shook his head.

The problem did not resolve itself. Which was fine—I was in the mood for some excitement anyway. It was only the confrontation part I preferred to avoid. Confrontations mean fights. Fights mean releasing a part of me that I'm really happier keeping leashed and muzzled. So I avoid temptation, and if that means getting a reputation as a coward, I'm okay with that.

When I got out of Miller's, my stalker was waiting. Not surprising, really. We'd been playing this game for almost two weeks.

As I set out, I sharpened my sixth sense, trying to rely on that instead of listening for the sounds of pursuit. I could sense a living being behind me, that faint pulse of awareness that tells me food is nearby. It would be stronger if I was hungry, but this was better practice.

Miller's exits into an alley—appropriately—so I stuck to the alleys for as long as I could. Eventually, though, they came to an end and I stepped onto the sidewalk. Gravel crunched behind me, booted feet stopping short. I smiled.

I cut across the street and merged with a crowd of college kids heading to a bar. I merge well; even chatted with a cute blond girl for a half block, and she chatted back, presuming I was part of the group. Then, as we passed a Thai takeout, I excused myself and ducked inside. I zipped through, smiling at the counter guy, ignoring him when he yelled that the washrooms were for paying customers only, and went straight out the back door.

I'd pulled this routine twice before—blend with a crowd and cut through a shop—and my opponent hadn't caught on yet, which was really rather frustrating. This time, though, as I crept out the back door, a shadow stretched from a side alley. I let the door slam behind me. The shadow jerked back. So the pupil was capable of learning. Excellent. Time for the next lesson.

I scampered along the back alley. Around the next corner. Down a delivery lane. Behind a dumpster.

Footsteps splashed through a puddle I'd avoided. Muttered curses, cut short. Then silence. I closed my eyes, concentrating on picking up that pulse of life. And there it was, coming closer, closer, passing the bin. Stopping. Realizing the prey must have ducked behind this garbage bin. Gold star.

A too-deliberate pair of boot squeaks headed left, so I ran left. Sure enough, my opponent was circling right. I grabbed the side of the dumpster and swung onto the closed lid.

"Looking for me?" I said, grinning down.

Hands gripped the top edge, then yanked back, as if expecting me to stomp them. That would hardly be sporting. I backed up, took a running leap and grabbed the fire escape overhead. A perfect gymnast's swing and

I was on it. A minute later, I was swinging again, this time onto the roof. I took off across it without a backward glance. Then I sat on the other side to wait.

I waited. And I waited some more. Finally, I sighed, got to my feet, made my way across the roof, leapt onto the next and began the journey home.

I was peering over the end of a rooftop into a penthouse apartment, eyeing a particularly fine example of an Edo-period sake bottle, when I sensed someone below. I glimpsed a familiar figure in the alley. Hmmm. Lacking experience, but not tenacity. I could work with this.

I leapt onto the next, lower rooftop. Then I saw a second figure in the alley with my stalker. Backup? I took a closer look. Nope, definitely not. We had a teenage girl and a twenty-something guy, and they were definitely *not* together, given that the guy was sticking to the shadows, creeping along behind the girl.

The girl continued to walk, oblivious. When she paused to adjust her backpack, he started to swoop in. Her head jerked up, as if she'd heard something. He ducked into a doorway.

Yes, you heard footsteps in a dark alley. Time to move your cute little ass and maybe, in future, reconsider the wisdom of strolling through alleys at all.

She peered behind her, then shrugged and continued on. The man waited until she rounded the next corner and slid from his spot. When he reached the corner and peeked around it, I dropped from the fire escape and landed behind him.

He wheeled. He blinked. Then he smiled.

"Thought that might work," I said. "Forget the little girl. I'm much more fun."

He whipped out a knife. I slammed my fist into his forearm, smacking it against the brick wall. Reflexively his hand opened, dropping the knife. He dove for it. I kicked it, then I kicked him. My foot caught him under the jaw. He went up. I kicked again. He went down.

I leapt onto his back, pinning him. "Well, that was fast. Kind of embarrassing, huh? I think you need to work out more."

He tried to buck me off. I sank my fangs into the back of his neck and held on as he got to his feet. He swung backward toward the wall, planning to crush me, I'm sure, but my saliva kicked in before he made it two steps. He teetered, then crashed to the pavement, unconscious.

I knelt to feed. I wasn't particularly hungry, but only a fool turns down a free meal, and maybe waking up with the mother of all hangovers would teach this guy a stalking lesson he wouldn't soon forget.

"Die, vampire!"

I spun as the teenage girl raced toward me, wooden stake on a collision course with my heart. I grabbed the stake and yanked it up, flipping the girl onto her back.

"That's really rude," I said. "I just saved your ass from a scumbag rapist. Is this how you repay me? Almost ruin my favorite shirt?"

She leapt to her feet and sent the stake on a return trip to my chest. Again, I stopped it. I could have pointed out that it really wouldn't do anything *more* than damage my shirt—vampires only die by beheading— but I thought it best not to give her any ideas.

She ran at me again. I almost tripped over the unconscious man's arm. As I tugged him out of the way, she rushed me. I grabbed the stake and threw it aside.

She lifted her hands. Her fingertips lit up, glowing red.

"Ah, fire half-demon," I said. "Igneus, Aduro or Exustio?"

"I won't let you kill him."

"You don't know a lot about vampires, do you? Or about being a vampire hunter. First, you really need to work on your dialogue."

"Don't talk to me, bloodsucker."

"Bloodsucker? What's next? Queen of Darkness? Spawn of Satan? You're running about twenty years behind, sweetie. Where's the clever quip? The snappy repartee?"

She snarled and charged, her burning fingers outstretched. I sidestepped and winced as she stumbled over the fallen man.

"See, that's why I moved him."

She spun and came at me again. I grabbed her hand. Her burning fingers sizzled into my skin.

"Fire is useless against a vampire, as you see," I said. "So your special power doesn't do you any good, which means you're going to have to work on your other skills. I'd suggest gymnastics, aikido and maybe ninjitsu, though it's hard to find proper ninjitsu outside Japan these days."

She wrenched free and backed up, scowling. "You're mocking me."

"No, I'm helping you. First piece of advice? Next time, don't telegraph your attack."

"Telegraph?"

"Yelling, 'Die, vampire' as you attack from behind may add a nice—if outdated—touch, but it gives you away. Next time, just run and stab. Got it?"

She stared at me. I retrieved her stake and handed it over. Then I started walking away.

"Second piece of advice?" I called back. "Stay out of alleys at night. There are a lot worse things than me out here."

I spun and grabbed the stake just as she was about to stab me in the back.

I smiled. "Much better. Now get on home. It's a school night."

Keeping the stake, I kicked her feet out from under her, then took off. She tried to follow, of course. Tenacious, as I said. But a quick flip onto another fire escape and through an open window left her behind.

I made my way up to the rooftops and headed home, rather pleased with myself. We'd come quite a ways in our two weeks together, and now, having finally made face-to-face contact, I was sure we could speed up the learning curve.

The girl was misguided, but I blamed popular culture for that. She'd eventually learn I wasn't the worst monster out there, and there were others far more deserving of her enthusiasm.

Even if she chose not to pursue such a profession, the supernatural world is a dangerous place for all of us. Self-defense skills are a must, and if I could help her with that, I would. It's the responsibility of everyone to prepare our youth for the future. I was happy to do my part.

THE SCREAMS OF DRAGONS

A Cainsville Universe Story

"And the second plague that is in thy dominion, behold it is a dragon.
And another dragon of a foreign race is fighting with it, and striving to
overcome it. And therefore does your dragon make a fearful outcry."
—*Cyfranc Lludd a Llefelys*, translated by Lady Charlotte Guest

WHEN HE WAS YOUNG, other children talked of their dreams, of candy-
floss mountains and puppies that talked and long-lost relatives bearing
new bicycles and purses filled with crisp dollar bills. Bobby did not have
those dreams. His nights were filled with golden castles and endless meadows
and the screams of dragons.

The castles and the meadows came unbidden, beginning when he was
too young to know what a castle or a meadow was, but in his dreams he'd
race through them, endlessly playing, endlessly laughing. And then he'd
wake to his cold, dark room, stinking of piss and sour milk, and he'd roar
with rage and frustration. Even when he stopped, the cries were replaced by
sulking, aggrieved silence. Never laughter. He only laughed in his dreams.
Only played in his dreams. Only was happy in his dreams.

The dragons came later.

He presumed he'd first heard the story of the dragons in Cainsville. Visits
to family there were the high points of his young life. While Cainsville had

no golden castles or endless meadows, the fields and the forests, the spires and the gargoyles reminded him of his dreams, and calmed him and made him, if not happy, at least content.

They treated him differently in Cainsville, too. He was special there. A pampered little prince, his mother would say, shaking her head. The local elders paid attention to him, listened to him, sought him out. Better still, they did not do the same to his sister, Natalie. The Gnat, he called her—constantly buzzing about, useless and pestering. At home, *she* was the pampered one. His parents never seemed to know what to make of him, his discontent and his silences, and so they showered his bouncing, giggling little sister with double the love, double the attention.

In Cainsville the old people told him stories. Of King Arthur's court, they said, but when he looked up their tales later, they were not quite the same. Theirs were stories of knights and magic, but lions too, and giants and faeries and, sometimes, dragons. That was why he was certain they'd told him this particular tale, even if he could not remember the exact circumstances. It was about a British king beset by three plagues. One was a race of people who could hear everything he said. The second was disappearing foodstuffs and impending starvation. The third was a terrible scream that turned out to be two dragons, fighting. And that was when he began to dream of the screams of dragons.

He did not actually *hear* the screams. He could not imagine such a thing, because he had no idea what a dragon's scream would sound like. He asked his parents and his grandmother and even his Sunday school teacher, but they didn't seem to understand the question. Even at night, his sleep was often filled with nothing but his small self, racing here and there, searching for the screams of dragons. He would ask and he would ask, but no one could ever tell him.

When he was almost eight, his grandmother noticed his sleepless nights. She asked what was wrong, and he knew better than to talk about the dragons, but he began to think maybe he should tell her of the other dreams, the ones of golden palaces and endless meadows. One night, when his parents were out, he waited until the Gnat fell asleep. Then he padded into the living room, the feet on his sleeper whispering against the floor. His grandmother didn't notice at first—she was too busy watching *The Dick Van Dyke Show*. He couldn't understand the fascination with television. The moving pictures were dull gray, the laughter harsh and fake. He supposed they were for those who didn't dream of gold and green, of sunlight and music.

He walked up beside her. He did not sneak or creep, but she was so absorbed in her show that when he appeared at her shoulder, she shrieked and in her face, he saw something he'd never seen before. Fear. It fascinated him, and he stared at it, even as she relaxed and said, "Bobby? You gave me quite a start. What's wrong, dear?"

"I can't sleep," he said. "I have dreams."

"Bad dreams?"

He shook his head. "Good ones."

Her old face creased in a frown. "And they keep you awake?"

"No," he said. "They make me sad."

She clucked and pulled him onto the chair, tucking him in beside her. "Tell Gran all about them."

He did, and as he talked, he saw that look return. The fear. He decided he must be mistaken. He hadn't mentioned the dragons. The rest was wondrous and good. Yet the more he talked, the more frightened she became, until finally she pushed him from the chair and said, "It's time for bed."

"What's wrong?"

She said, "Nothing," but her look said something was very, very wrong.

For the next few weeks, his grandmother was a hawk, circling him endlessly, occasionally swooping down and snatching him up in her claws. Most times, she avoided him directly, though he'd catch her watching him. Studying him. Scrutinizing him. Once they were alone in the house, she'd swoop. She'd interrogate him about the dreams, unearthing every last detail, even the ones he thought he'd forgotten.

On the nights when his parents were gone, she insisted on drawing his baths, adding in some liquid from a bottle and making the baths so hot they scalded him and when he cried, she seemed satisfied. Satisfied and a little frightened.

The strangest of all came nearly a month after he'd told her of the dreams. She'd made stew for dinner and she served it in eggshells. When she brought them to the table, the Gnat laughed in delight.

"That's funny," she said. "They're so cute, Gran."

His grandmother only nodded absently at the Gnat. Her watery blue eyes were fixed on him.

"What do you think of it, Bobby?" she asked.

"I . . ." He stared at the egg, propped up in a little juice glass, the brown stew steaming inside the shell. "I don't understand. Why is it in an egg?"

"For fun, dummy." His sister shook her head at their grandmother. "Bobby's never fun." She pulled a face at him. "Boring Bobby."

His grandmother shushed her, gaze still on him. "You think it's strange."

"It is," he said.

"Have you ever seen anything like this before?"

"No."

She waited, as if expecting more. Then she prompted, "You would say, then, that you've never, in all your years, seen something like this."

It seemed an odd way to word it, but he nodded.

And with that, finally, she seemed satisfied. She plunked down into her chair, exhaling, before turning to him and saying, "Go to your room. I don't want to see you until morning."

He glanced up, startled. "What did I—?"

"To your room. You aren't one of us. I'll not have you eat with us. Now off with you."

He pushed his chair back and slowly rose to his feet.

The Gnat stuck out her tongue when their grandmother wasn't looking. "Can I have his egg?"

"Of course, dear," Gran said as he shuffled from the kitchen.

The next morning, instead of going to school, his grandmother took him to church. It was not Sunday. It was not even Friday. As soon as he saw the spires of the cathedral, he began to shake. He'd done something wrong, horribly wrong. He'd lain awake half the night trying to figure out what he could have done to deserve bed without dinner, but there was nothing. She'd fed him stew in an eggshell and, while perplexed, he had still been very polite and respectful about it.

The trouble had started with telling her about the dreams, but who could find fault with tales of castles and meadows, music and laughter?

Perhaps she was going senile. It had happened to an old man down the street. They'd found him in their yard, wearing a diaper and asking about his wife, who'd died years ago. If that had happened to his grandmother, Father Joseph would see it.

Certainly, he seemed to, given the expression on Father Joseph's face after Gran talked to him alone in the priest's office. Father Joseph emerged as if in a trance, and Gran had to direct him to the pew where Bobby waited.

"See?" she said, waving her hand at Bobby.

The priest looked straight at him, but seemed lost in his thoughts. "No, I'm afraid I don't, Mrs. Sheehan."

Gran's voice snapped with impatience. "It's obvious he's not ours. Neither his mother nor his father nor any of his grandparents have blond hair. Or dark eyes."

Sweat beaded on the priest's forehead and he tugged his collar. "True, but children do not always resemble their parents, for a variety of reasons, none of them laying any blame at the foot of the child."

"Are you suggesting my daughter-in-law was unfaithful?"

Father Joseph's eyes widened. "No, of course not. But the ways of genetics—like the ways of God—are not always knowable. Your daughter-in-law does have light hair, and I believe she has a brother who is blond. If my recollection of science is correct, dark eyes are the dominant type, and I'm quite certain if you searched the family tree beyond parents and grandparents you would find your answer."

"I have my answer," she said, straightening. "He is a changeling."

Two drops of sweat burst simultaneously and dribbled down the priest's face. "I . . . I do not wish to question your beliefs, Mrs. Sheehan. I know such folk wisdom is common in the . . . more rural regions of your homeland—"

"Because it *is* wisdom. Forgotten wisdom. I've tested him, Father. I gave him dinner in an eggshell, as I explained."

"Yes, but . . ." The priest snuck a glance around, as if hoping for divine intervention—or a needy parishioner to stumble in, requiring his immediate attention. "I know that is the custom, but I cannot say I rightly understand it."

"What is there to understand?" She put her hands on her narrow hips. "It's a test. I gave him stew in eggshells, and he said he'd never seen anything like it. That's what a changeling will say."

"I beg your pardon, ma'am, but I believe that's what *anyone* would say, if given their meal served in an egg."

She glowered at him. "I put him in a tub with foxglove, too, and he became ill."

"Foxglove?" The priest's eyes rounded again. "Is that not a poison?"

"It is if you're a changeling. I also gave him one of my heart pills, because it's made from digitalis, which is also foxglove. My pill made him sick."

"You gave . . ." For the first time since he'd come in, Father Joseph looked at Bobby, really looked at him. "You gave your grandson your heart medication? That could *kill* a boy—"

"He isn't a boy. He's one of the Fair Folk." Gran met Bobby's gaze. "An abomination."

Now Father Joseph's face flushed, his eyes snapping. "No, he is a *child*. You will not speak of him that way, certainly not in front of him. I'm trying to be respectful, Mrs. Sheehan. You are entitled to your superstitions and folksy tales, but not if they involve poisoning an innocent child." He knelt in front of Bobby. "You're going to come into my office now, son, and we'll call your parents. Is your mother at work?"

He nodded.

"Do you know the number?"

He nodded again.

The priest took Bobby's hand and, without another word, led him away as his grandmother watched, her eyes narrowing.

That was the beginning of "the bad time," as his parents called it, whispered words, even years later, their eyes downcast, as if in shame. The situation did not end with that visit to the priest. His grandmother would not drop the accusation. He was a changeling. A faerie child dropped into their care, her real grandson spirited away by the Fair Folk. Finally, his parents broke down and asked the priest to perform some ritual—any ritual—to calm his grandmother's nerves. The priest refused. To do so would be to lend credence to the preposterous accusation and could permanently scar the child's psyche.

The fight continued. He heard his parents talking late at night about the shame, the great shame of it all. They were intelligent, educated people. His father was a scientist, his mother the lead secretary in her firm. They were not ignorant peasants, and it angered them that Father Joseph didn't understand what they were asking—not to "fix" their son but simply to pretend to, for the harmony of the household.

They took their request to a second priest, and somehow—for years afterward, everyone would blame someone else for this—a journalist got hold of the story. It made one of the Chicago newspapers, in an article mocking the family and their "Old World" ways. His family was so humiliated they moved. His grandmother grumbled that his parents made too big a fuss out of the whole thing. It didn't matter. They moved, and they were all forbidden to speak of it again.

That did not mean no one spoke of it. The Gnat did. When she was in a good mood, she'd settle for mocking him, calling him a faerie child, asking him where he kept his wings, pinching his back to see if she could find them. When she was in a rare foul temper, she'd tell him their grandmother was right, he was a monster and didn't belong, that their parents only had one real child. And even if it was all nonsense, as his mother and father claimed, *that* part was true—he no longer felt part of the family. They might not think him a changeling, but they all, in their own ways, blamed him. His parents blamed him for their humiliation. The Gnat blamed him for having to leave her friends and move. And his grandmother blamed him for whatever slight she could pin at his feet, and then she punished him for it.

He came to realize that the punishments were the purpose of the accusations rather than the result. His grandmother wanted an excuse to strap him or send him to bed without dinner. At first, he presumed she was upset because no one believed her story. That did not anger him. Nothing really angered him. Like happiness, the emotion was too intense, too uncomfortable. He looked at his sister, dancing about, chattering and giggling, and he thought her a fool. He looked at his grandmother, raging and snapping against him, and thought her the same. Foolish and weak, easily overcome by emotion.

He did not accept the punishments stoically, though. While he never complained, with each hungry night or sore bottom, something inside him hardened. He saw his grandmother, fumbling in her frustration, venting it on him, and he did not pity her. He hated her. He hated his parents, too, for pretending not to see the welts or the unfinished dinners. Most of all, he hated the Gnat, because she saw it all and delighted in it. She would watch him beaten to tears with the strap, and then tell their grandmother that he'd broken her doll the week before, earning him three more lashes.

While there was certainly vindictiveness in the punishments, it seemed his grandmother actually had a greater plan. He realized this when she decided, one Sunday, that the two of them should take a trip to Cainsville. He even got to sit in the front seat of the station wagon, for the first time ever.

"Do you think I've mistreated you lately?" she asked as she drove.

It seemed a question not deserving a reply, so he didn't give one.

"Have you earned those punishments?" she said. "Did you do everything I said you did? That Natalie said you did?"

He sensed a trick, and again he didn't answer. She reached over and pinched his thigh hard enough to bring tears to his eyes.

"I asked you a question, parasite."

He glanced over.

"You know what that means, don't you?" she said. "Parasite?"

"I know many words."

Her lips twisted. "You do. Far more than a child should know. Because you are not a child. You are a parasite, put into our house to eat our food and sleep in our beds."

"There's no such thing as faeries."

She pinched him again, twisting the skin. He only glanced over with a look that had her releasing him fast, hand snapping back onto the steering wheel.

"You're a monster," she said. "Do you know that?"

No, you are, he thought, but he said nothing, staring instead at the passing scenery as they left the city. She drove onto the highway before she spoke again.

"You don't think you deserve to be punished, do you? You think I'm accusing you of things you didn't do, and your little sister is joining in, and your parents are turning a blind eye. Is that what you think?"

He shrugged.

"If it is, then you should tell someone," she said. "Someone who can help you."

He stayed quiet. There was a trick here, a dangerous one, and he might be smart for a little boy, as everyone told him, but he was not smart enough for this. So he kept his mouth shut. She drove a while longer before speaking again.

"You like the folks in Cainsville, don't you? The town elders."

Finally, something he could safely answer. She could find no fault in him liking old people. With relief, he nodded.

"They like you, too. They think you're special." Her hands tightened on the wheel. "I know why, too. I'm not a foolish old woman. I'm just as smart as you, boy. Especially when it comes to puzzles, and I've solved this one. I know where you came from."

He tried not to sigh, as the conversation swung back to dangerous territory. Perhaps he should be frightened, but after months of this, he was only tired.

"Do they ask you about us?" she said. "When they take you off on your special walks? Do they ask after your family?"

He nodded. "They ask if you are all well."

"And how we're treating you?"

He hesitated. It seemed an odd question, and he sensed the snare wire sneaking around his ankle again. After a moment, he shook his head. "They only ask if you're well and how I'm doing. How I like school and that."

"They're being careful," she muttered under her breath. "But they still ask how he is. Checking up on him."

"Gran?"

She tensed as he called her that. She always did these days and it was possible, just possible, that he used it more often because of that.

"You understand what honesty is, don't you, boy?"

He nodded.

"And respect for your elders."

It took him a half-second, but he nodded to this as well.

"Then you know you have to tell the truth when an adult asks you a question. You need to be honest, even if it might get someone in trouble. Always remember that."

While he liked all the elders in Cainsville, Mrs. Yates was his favorite, and he got the feeling he was hers, too. There had been a time when his grandmother had seemed almost jealous of her, when she would huff and sniff and say she thought Mrs. Yates was a very peculiar old woman. His parents had paid little attention—Gran had made it quite clear she thought everyone a little peculiar in Cainsville.

"There are no churches," she'd say. And his mother would sigh and explain—once again—that the town had started off too small for churches and by the time it was large enough, there was no place to put them, the settlement being nestled in the fork of a river, with marshy ground on the only open side. People still *went* to church. Just somewhere else.

It was his mother whose family was from Cainsville. Gran only accompanied them because she didn't like to be left out of family trips. She didn't like the town and she certainly didn't like Mrs. Yates. But that day, as she went off to visit his great-aunt, Gran sent him off with two dollars and a suggestion that he go see what Mrs. Yates was up to. Just be back by four so they could make it home in time for Sunday dinner.

He went to the new diner first. That's what everyone in Cainsville called it. The "new" diner, though it'd been there as long as he could remember. It still smelled new—the lemon-polished linoleum floors, the shiny red leather booths and even shinier chrome-plated chairs. The elders could often be found there, sipping tea by the windows as they watched the town go by. "Holding court," his grandmother would sniff, saying they were watching for mischief and waiting for folks to come by and pay their respects, like they were lords and ladies. He didn't see that at all. To him, they were simply there, in case anyone needed them.

Today, he found Mrs. Yates in her usual place. He thought she'd be surprised to see him, but she only smiled, her old face lighting up as she motioned him over.

"Mr. Shaw said he spotted your car coming into town," she said. "But I scarce dared believe it. Did I hear the rest right, too? Your gran brought you?"

He nodded.

"Does she know you're here?"

"She said I could come talk to you if I wanted."

Then he got his look of surprise, a widening of her blue eyes. "Did she now?"

He nodded again, and he expected her to be pleased, but while her eyes stayed kind, they narrowed too, as she surveyed him.

"Is everything all right, Bobby?"

He nodded without hesitation. Gran thought she was clever in her plan, that he would tattle on her to Mrs. Yates without realizing that's exactly what she wanted. He had no idea what she hoped to gain, but if Gran wanted it, he wasn't doing it.

"Are you sure?" Mrs. Yates said, those bright eyes piercing his. "Nothing is amiss at home?"

He shrugged. "My sister's annoying, but that's old news."

He thought she'd laugh, pat his arm and move on. That's what other grown-ups would do. But Mrs. Yates was not like other grown-ups, which was probably why he liked her so much. She kept studying him until, finally, she squeezed his shoulder and said, "All right, Bobby. If that's what you want. Now, do you have your list of gargoyles?"

He pulled the tattered notebook from his back pocket. He'd been working on it since he was old enough to write. Cainsville had gargoyles.

and tried to pretend he wasn't different. She acknowledged it and understood it and made him feel better about it.

"Do you want to go play with the girls?"

He nodded. He *did* like the girls—Hannah, at least. What bothered him was the prospect of sharing Mrs. Yates with them later. But it would make her happy, and he was still her special favorite, so he shouldn't complain.

"Off you go then. Come to the diner later and we'll have those milk-shakes."

Mrs. Yates said Hannah and Rose were in the small park behind the bank. They were often there on the swings, and when he rounded the corner, that's where he expected to see them. The swings were empty, though. He looked around the park, bordered by a fence topped with chimera heads. Walkways branched off in every compass direction. He heard Rose's voice, coming from the one leading to Rowan Street.

The girls crouched beside a toppled cardboard box. Hannah was reaching in and talking. He liked Hannah. Everyone liked Hannah. His mother said she reminded her of the Gnat, but she couldn't be more wrong. Yes, Hannah was pretty, with brown curls and dark eyes and freckles across her nose. And, like the Gnat, she was always laughing, always bouncing around, chattering. But with Hannah, it was *real*. The Gnat only acted that way because it tricked people into liking her.

Rose was different. Very different. She was a year younger than Bobby and Hannah, but she acted like a teenager, and she looked at you like she could see right through you and wasn't sure she liked what she saw. She had black straight hair and weirdly cold blue eyes that blasted through him. She wasn't pretty and she never giggled—she rarely even laughed, unless she was with Hannah.

Rose saw him coming first, though it always felt like "saw" wasn't the right word. Rose seemed to sense him coming. She stood and when she fixed those blue eyes on him, he quailed as he always did, falling back a step before reminding himself he had done nothing wrong. Rose only tilted her head, and when she spoke, her rough voice was kind.

Lots of them. For protection, the old people would say with a wink. Every year, as part of the May Day festival, children could show the elders their lists of all the gargoyles they'd located, and the winner would take a prize. If you found all of them, you'd get an actual gargoyle modeled after you. That hardly ever happened—there were only a few in town.

It sounded easy, finding all the gargoyles, and it should be, except many hid. There were ones you could only see in the day or at night or when the light hit a certain way or, sometimes, just by chance. He'd been compiling his list for almost four years and he only had half of them, but he'd still come in second place last year.

"Let's go gargoyle hunting." Mrs. Yates got to her feet without groaning or pushing herself up, the way Gran and other old people did. She just stood, as easily as he would, and started for the door. "Now remember, I can't point them out to you. That's against the rules." She leaned down and whispered, "But I might give you a hint for one. Just one."

Behind them, the other elders chuckled, and Bobby and Mrs. Yates headed out into town.

He found one more gargoyle to add to his list, and he didn't even need Mrs. Yates's hint, so she promised to keep it for next time. They were going back to the diner and the promise of milkshakes when Mrs. Yates glanced down the walkway leading behind the bank.

"I think I hear the girls," she said. "Why don't you go play with them a while, and then bring them to the diner and we'll all have milkshakes."

He hesitated.

"You like Rose and Hannah, don't you?"

He nodded, and her smile broadened, telling him this was the right answer, so he added, "They're nice," to please her.

"They're very nice," she said. "It's not easy for some children to find playmates. Some boys and girls are different, and other children don't always like different. You'll appreciate it more someday, when being different helps you stand out. But children don't always want to stand out, do they?"

He shook his head. She understood, as she always did. His parents lied

"Are you okay, Bobby?"

"Sure."

Her lips pursed, as if calling him a liar, then she waved for him to join them. As he stepped up beside the girls, he was chagrined to realize that as much as he'd grown in the last few months, Rose had grown more. She might be only seven and a girl, but he barely came up to her eyebrows. She moved back to let him stand beside Hannah.

"See what we found?" Hannah said.

It was a cat, with four kittens, all tabbies like the momma, except the smallest, which was ink black.

"Show him what you can do," Rose said.

Hannah glanced up, her forehead creasing with worry.

"Go on," Rose said. "Bobby can keep a secret. Show him."

He looked at Rose, and she nodded, giving him a small smile—a sympathetic smile, as if she knew what he was going through and wanted Hannah to share her secret to make him feel better. He bristled. He didn't want Rose's sympathy. Didn't need it. But he did want the secret, so he let Rose cajole Hannah until she blurted it out.

"I can talk to animals." Hannah paused, face reddening. "No, that doesn't sound right. It's not like Dr. Dolittle. I don't hear them talk. Animals don't talk. But they do . . ." She turned to Rose. "What's the word you used?"

"Communicate."

Hannah nodded. "They communicate. I can understand them, and they can understand me."

He must have seemed skeptical, because her cheeks went the color of apples in autumn.

"See?" she hissed at Rose. "This is why I can't tell anyone. They'll think I'm crazy."

"I don't think you're crazy," he said. "But you're right—you probably shouldn't tell anyone else."

Hannah's gaze dropped, and he felt bad. Like maybe he should tell her about the dreams and how he admitted it to Gran, and what happened next.

Did they know what happened? His grandmother always said Cainsville was a "backwater nowhere" town, where they acted as if they weren't sixty miles from one of the biggest cities in America. Gran said they were ignorant, and they liked it that way. They didn't read newspapers, didn't listen to the news or even watch it on television. That wasn't true. He'd once told Mrs. Yates about going to the site of the World's Fair, and she'd known all about it. She'd told him stories about the fair, the sights and sounds and even the smells. He'd gotten an A on his paper and his teacher said it was almost like he'd been there. He'd asked Mrs. Yates if *she'd* been there, and she'd laughed and said she wasn't *that* old. No one was. So people in Cainsville weren't ignorant, but he supposed that knowing about the 1893 World's Fair wasn't the same as knowing what his teacher called "current events."

"You shouldn't tell *everyone*," Rose said to Hannah. "Definitely not anyone outside Cainsville. But no one here will think you're crazy." She nudged Hannah with her sneaker. "Tell him about the black kitten."

Hannah took more prodding, but when Bobby expressed an interest, she finally stood and said, "He's sick. Momma Cat is worried he's going to die. He doesn't get enough to eat because he's smaller than the others."

"He's not that much smaller."

"He's different," Rose said. "That's why they won't let him eat very much. I think he's a matagot. That's what we were talking about when you came up."

"A matagot?"

"Magician's cat," Rose said, as matter-of-factly as if she'd said the cat was a Siamese. "It's a spirit that's taken the form of a black cat."

"They say that if you keep one and treat it well, it will reward you with a gold piece every day," Hannah said.

"Gold?" he said.

Something in his tone made Rose tense—or maybe it was the way he looked at the black kitten. Hannah only giggled.

"It's not true, silly," Hannah said. "Magic doesn't work that way. Not real magic."

"What do you know about real magic?"

She shrugged. "Enough. I know it can make gargoyles disappear in daylight and tomato plants grow straight and true. I know it can let some people read omens—like old Mrs. Carew—and some see the future, like Rose's Nana Walsh."

He turned to Rose. "Your grandmother can see the future?"

"Futures," she said. "There's more than one. It's all about choices."

He didn't understand that but pushed on. "If I asked her to see my futures—"

"You can't," Hannah cut in. "Not unless you can talk to ghosts. I'm not sure anyone can talk to ghosts. If there are ghosts." She turned to Rose, as if she was the older, wiser girl.

"There are," Rose said. "Those with the sight sometimes say they see them. Others can, too. But most times when a person says they're seeing ghosts it's their imagination. Even if you can talk to them I'm not sure why you'd want to."

Hannah nodded, and his gaze shot from one girl to the other, unable to believe they were talking about such things seriously. Kids at school would call them babies for believing in magic. His parents would call it ungodly. His grandmother would probably call them changelings.

"About the cat. The . . . matagot." He stumbled over the foreign word.

"We don't know if it is one," Rose said. "Hannah says his mother thinks he's strange. She still loves him, though."

"As she should," Hannah said. "There's nothing wrong with strange."

Rose nodded. "But we're worried."

"Very worried." Hannah knelt beside the box where the mother cat was licking the black kitten's head. "Momma Cat is even more worried. Aren't you?"

The cat *mrrow*ed deep in its throat and looked up at Hannah. Then she nosed the kitten away from her side.

"I think she's going to drive it off," Bobby said. "They do that sometimes. With the weak, the ones that are different."

Hannah shook her head, curls bouncing. "No, she's asking me to take it."

"You should," Rose said. "Your parents would let you."

"I know. I just hate taking a kitten from its mother."

The cat nosed the kitten again and meowed. Hannah nodded, said, "I understand," and very gently lifted the little black ball in both hands. The cat meowed again, but it didn't sound like protest. She gave the black kitten one last look, then shifted, letting its siblings fill the empty space against her belly.

"You'll need to feed it with a dropper," Rose said. "We can get books at the library and talk to the veterinarian when she comes back through town."

Hannah nodded. "I'll take him home first and ask Mom to watch him."

They got to the end of the walkway before they seemed to realize Bobby wasn't following. They turned.

"Do you want to come with us?" Hannah asked.

He did, but he wanted the milkshake with Mrs. Yates too, and if the girls were busy, he'd get the old woman all to himself.

"I told Mrs. Yates I'd meet her at the diner," he said, not mentioning the milkshakes.

Rose nodded. "Then you should do that. We'll see you later."

"Is your family coming for Samhain?" Hannah asked.

"I think we are."

Hannah smiled. "I hope so."

"Make sure you do," Rose said. "It's more fun when you're here."

He couldn't tell if she meant it or was just being nice, but it felt good to hear her say it and even better when Hannah nodded enthusiastically. He said he'd be back for Samhain, and went to find Mrs. Yates.

On the way home, his grandmother asked about his visit with Mrs. Yates. She was trying to get him to admit that he'd tattled on her. Even if he had, he certainly wouldn't admit it. His grandmother might say he was too smart for his age, but sometimes she acted as if he was dumber than the Gnat. Finally, she pulled off the highway, turned in her seat and said, "Did Mrs. Yates ask how things were at home?"

"Yes."

"And what did you tell her?"

"That they were fine."

She put her hand on his shoulder. It was the first time since he'd admitted to the dreams that she'd voluntarily touched him, except to pinch or slap.

"You know it's a sin to lie, Bobby."

"I do."

"Then tell me the truth. Did you say more?"

He hesitated. Nibbled his lip. Then said, "I told her Natalie was being a pest."

Her mouth pressed into a thin line. "That's not what I mean."

"But you asked—"

"Did you say *anything* more?"

"No." He hid his smile. "Not a word."

A month later, as Samhain drew near, he mentioned it over dinner.

"We aren't going," his mother said quietly.

"What?"

"Gran feels Cainsville isn't a good influence on you right now."

He shot a look at his grandmother, who returned a small, smug smile and ate another forkful of peas.

"Remember what happened when you visited last month?" his father said. "You came home and you were quite a little terror."

That was a lie. His grandmother had punished him twice as much after they got back, making up twice as many stories about him misbehaving. He'd thought she was just angry because her plan—whatever it had been— failed.

Gran's smile widened, her false teeth shining as she watched him.

"I don't care," the Gnat said. "I hate Cainsville. It's boring."

His grandmother patted her head. "I agree."

He shot to his feet.

"Bobby . . ." his father said.

"May I be excused?" he asked.

His father sighed. "If you're done."

Bobby walked to his room, trying very hard not to run in and slam the door. Once he got there, he fell facedown on his bed. The door clicked open. His grandmother walked in.

"You're a very stupid little beast," she said. "You should have told the elders. They'd take you back."

He flipped over to look at her.

"If you're being mistreated, they'll take you back," she said. "But you didn't tell them, so now we have to wait for them to come to us. I'll make sure they come to us."

His grandmother soon discovered another flaw in her plan. Two, actually. First, that whoever she thought would "come for him" was not coming, no matter how harsh her punishments. Second, that his parents' blindness had limits.

As the months of abuse had passed, he'd come to accept that his parents weren't really as oblivious as they pretended. Nor were they as enlightened as they thought. Even if they'd never admit it, there seemed to be a part of them that thought his grandmother's wild accusation was true. Or perhaps not that they actually believed him a changeling faerie child, but that they thought there was something wrong—terribly wrong—with him. He was different. Odd. Too distant and too cold. His sister hated him. Other children avoided him. Like animals, they sensed something was off and steered clear. Perhaps, then, the beatings would help. Not that they'd ever admit such a thing—heavens no, they were modern parents—but if he didn't complain, then perhaps neither should they.

They did have limits, though. When the sore spots became bruises and then welts, they objected. What would the neighbors think? Or, worse, his teachers, who might call children's services. Hadn't the family been through enough? Gran could punish him if he misbehaved, but she must use a lighter hand.

That did not solve the problem, but it opened a door. A possibility. That door cracked open a little more when his mother received a call at work from one of the elders, who wondered why they hadn't seen the Sheehan family in so long. Was everything all right? His mother said it was, but when she reported the call at home, over dinner, his grandmother fairly gnashed her teeth. His mother noticed and asked what was wrong, and Gran said nothing but still, his mother *had* noticed. He tucked that away and remembered it.

Christmas came, and he waited until he was alone in the house with his mother, and asked if they'd visit family in Cainsville. His mother wavered. And he was ready.

"Your grandmother doesn't think you're ready," she said as they sat in front of the television, wrapping gifts.

"I've been much better," he said.

"I'm not sure that you have."

He stretched tape over a seam. "I don't think I'm as bad as Gran says. I think she's still mad at me because we had to move."

A soft sigh, but his mother said nothing. He finished his package and took another.

"I think she might exaggerate sometimes," he said quietly. "I think Natalie might, too. I get the feeling they don't like me very much."

Of course his mother had to protest that, but her protests were muted, as if she couldn't work up true conviction.

"If you don't see me misbehaving, maybe I'm not," he said. "I do, sometimes. All kids do. But maybe it's not quite as much as Gran and Natalie say."

He worded it all so carefully. Not blaming anyone. Only giving his opinion, as a child. His mother went silent, wrapping her gift while nibbling her lower lip, the same way he did when he was thinking.

"I have friends in Cainsville," he said. "Little girls who like playing with me. They're very nice girls."

"Hannah and Rose," his mother said. "I like Hannah. Rose is . . ."

"Different," he said. "Like me. But she's not mean and she doesn't misbehave. She hardly ever gets in trouble. Even less than Hannah."

"Rose is a very serious girl," she said. "Like you. I can see why you'd like her."

"I do. I miss them. I promise if we go to Cainsville, I'll be better than ever." He clipped off a piece of ribbon. "And *your* family is there. You want to see them. Gran never liked Cainsville, so she's happy if we don't go."

"That's true," his mother murmured, and with that, he knew he'd won an ally in his fight to return to Cainsville. But as he soon learned, it hardly mattered at all. His mother had a job, just like a man, but she didn't make a lot of money, and his father always joked that it was more a hobby than an occupation, which made his mother angry. That meant, though, that his father was the head of the house. As it should be, Gran would say, and she could, because there was only one person his father always listened to—his own mother, Gran. If Bobby's grandmother said no to Cainsville, then they would not be going to Cainsville and that was that.

Gran said no to Cainsville.

No to Cainsville for the holidays. No to Cainsville for Candlemas. No to Cainsville for May Day.

It was the last that broke him. May Day was his favorite holiday, with the gargoyle hunt contest, which he was almost certain to win this year, according to Mrs. Yates.

He *would* go to Cainsville for May Day. All he had to do was eliminate the obstacle.

Everyone always told him how smart he was. Part of that was his memory. He heard things, and if he thought they might be important, he filed the information away as neatly as his father filed papers in his basement office. A year ago, his grandmother had admitted to feeding him one of her heart medicine pills. Father Joseph had been horrified—digitalis was foxglove, which was poison. Bobby had mentally filed those details and now, when he needed it, he tugged them out and set off for the library, where he read everything he found on the subject. Then he began stealing pills from Gran's bottle, one every third day.

After two weeks, he had enough pills. He ground them up and put them in her dinner. And she died. There were a few steps in between—the heart attack, the ambulance, the hospital bed, his parents and the Gnat sobbing and praying—but in the end, he got what he wanted. Gran died and the obstacle was removed, and with it, he got an unexpected gift, one that made him wish he'd taken this step months ago, because as his grandmother breathed her last and he stood beside her bed, watching, he finally heard the screams of dragons.

It started slow, quiet even. Like a humming deep in his skull. Then it grew and the humming became a strange vibrating cry, somewhere between a roar and a scream. Finally, when it crescendoed, he couldn't even have said what it sounded like. It was *all* sounds at once, so loud that he burst out in a sob, hands going to his ears as he doubled over.

His mother caught him and held him and rubbed his back and said it would be okay, it would all be okay, Gran was in a better place now. Yet the dragons kept screaming until he pushed her aside and ran from the hospital room. He ran and he ran until he was out some back door, in a tiny yard. Then he collapsed, hugging his knees as he listened to the dragons.

That's what he did—he listened. He didn't try to block them, to stop them. This was what he'd dreamed of and now he had it, and it was horrible and terrible and incredible all at once. He hunkered down there, committing them to memory as methodically as he had the dreams of golden palaces and endless meadows. Finally, when the screams faded, he went back inside, snuffling and gasping for breath, his face streaked with tears. His parents found him like that, grieving they thought, and it was what they wanted to see, proof that he was just a normal little boy, and they were, in their own grief, happy.

He waited until three days after the funeral to broach the subject of Cainsville. He would have liked to have waited longer, but it was already April 27, and he'd given great thought to the exact timing—how late could he wait before it was too late to plan a May Day trip? April 27 seemed right.

After he'd gone to bed, he slipped back out and found his parents in the living room, reading. He stood between them and cleared his throat.

"Yes, Bobby?" his mother said, lowering her book.

"I've been thinking," he said. "Natalie's so upset about Gran. We all are, of course, but Natalie most of all."

His mother sighed. "I know."

"So I was thinking of ways to cheer her up."

As he expected, this was about the best thing he could have said. His mother's eyes lit up and his father lowered his newspaper.

"It's May Day this weekend," Bobby said. "I know Natalie thinks Cainsville is boring, but she always liked May Day."

"That's true." His mother snuck a glance at his father. "Last year, she asked if we were going before Bobby did."

"I thought we might go," he said. "For Natalie."

His father smiled and reached to rumple Bobby's hair. "That's a fine idea, son. I believe we will."

Rose knew what he'd done. She saw it in her eyes as he walked over to her and Hannah, cutting flowers before the May Day festivities began. Rose saw him coming and straightened fast, fixing him with those pale blue eyes. Then she laid her hand on Hannah's shoulder, as if ready to tug her friend away.

Hannah looked up at Rose's touch. She saw him and grinned, a bright sunshine grin, as she rose and brushed off the bare knees under her short, flowered dress. Rose kept hold of her friend's shoulder, though, and squeezed. Hannah hesitated.

He stopped short. Then he glanced to the side, pretending he'd heard someone call his name, an excuse to walk away. He headed toward one of the elders, setting out pies. The pie table was close enough for him to hear the girls.

Rose spoke first. "I had a dream about Bobby," she whispered.

Hannah giggled. "He is kind of cute."

"Not like *that*."

Hannah went serious. "You mean one of *those* dreams?"

"I don't know. There were dragons."

He stiffened and stood there, blueberry pie in hand, straining to listen to the girls behind him.

"Dragons?" Hannah said.

"He was hunting them."

"I bet they were gargoyles. He's really good at finding them. He has twice as many as I do, and he doesn't even live here."

"He killed one," Rose said.

"A gargoyle?"

"A dragon. An old one. She was blocking his way, and he fed her foxglove flowers, and she started to scream."

His stomach twisted so suddenly that he doubled over, the elder grabbing his arm to steady him, asking if he was all right, and he said yes, quickly, pushing her off as politely as he could and taking another pie from the box as he struggled to listen.

"That's one freaky dream, Rosie," Hannah was saying.

"I know."

"I think it just means he's going to win the gargoyle contest."

"Probably, but it felt like . . ." Rose drifted off. "No, I'm being dumb."

"You're never dumb. You just think too much sometimes."

Rose chuckled. "My mom says the same thing."

"Because she's smart, like you. Now, let's go ask if Bobby wants to come see Mattie."

The *tap-tap* of fancy shoes. Then a finger poked his back.

"Bobby?"

He turned to Hannah, smiling at him.

"We're glad you came," she said. "We missed you."

He nodded.

"It's not time for the festival yet. Do you want to come see Mattie?"

"That's what she named the kitten," Rose said, walking up behind her friend. "Short for matagot."

"No, short for Matthew."

Rose rolled her eyes. "Whatever you say."

Hannah pretended to swat her, then put her arm through Bobby's. As she did, Rose tensed and rocked forward, like she wanted to pull Hannah away. She stopped herself, but fixed him with that strange look. Like she knew what he'd done. With that look, he knew Rose had a power, like Hannah. And him? He had nothing except taunting dreams of castles and meadows, and the screams of dragons, fading so fast he could barely remember the sound at all.

"Smile, Bobby," Hannah said, squeezing his arm. "It's May Day, and we're going to have fun." She grinned. "We'll always have fun together."

He won the gargoyle hunt that year. The next year, too. They went to Cainsville for all the festivals and sometimes he and his mother just went to visit. Life was good, and not just because Gran was dead and he'd gotten Cainsville back, but because he'd learned a valuable lesson. He did not have magic powers. He would likely never have them. But he did have a power inside him—the screams of dragons.

He would admit that when he killed his grandmother, he thought he'd suffer for it. He'd be caught and even if he wasn't, it would be as Father Joseph preached—he would be forever damned in the prison of his own mind, tormented by his sins. Father Joseph had lied. Or, more likely, he simply didn't understand boys like Bobby.

No one ever suspected Gran died of anything but a natural death, and his life turned for the better after that. He learned how to win his parents' sympathy if not their love. To turn them, just a little, to his side, away from the Gnat. He learned, too, how to deal with his sister. That took longer and started at school, with other children, the ones who bullied and taunted him.

He decided to show those children why he should not be bullied or taunted. One by one, he showed them. Little things for some, like spoiling their lunches every day. Bigger things for others. With one boy, he loosened the seat on his bike, and he fell and hit his head on the curb and had to go away, people whispering that he'd never be quite right again.

Bobby took his revenge, and then let the children know it was him, and when they tattled, he cried and pretended he didn't know what was happening, why they were accusing him—they'd always hated him, always mocked and beat him, and the teachers knew that was true, and his tears and his lies were good enough to convince them that he was the victim. Each time he won, he would hear the dragons scream again, and he'd know he'd done well.

Once he'd perfected his game, he played it against the Gnat. For her eighth birthday, their parents gave her a pretty little parakeet that she adored. One day, after she'd called him a monster and scratched him hard enough to draw blood, he warned that she shouldn't let the bird fly about, it might fly right out the door.

"I'm not stupid," she said. "I don't open the doors when she's out." She scowled at him. "And you'd better not either."

"I wouldn't do that," he said. And the next time she let the bird out, he lured it with treats to his parents' room, where the window was open, just enough.

He even helped her search for her bird. Then she discovered the open window.

"You did it!" she shouted.

She rushed at him, fingers like claws, scratching down his arm. He howled. His parents came running. The Gnat pointed at the window.

"Look what he did. He let her out!"

His father cleared his throat. "I'm afraid I left that open, sweetheart."

"You shouldn't have let the bird out of her cage," his mother said, steering the Gnat off with promises of ice cream. "You know we warned you about that."

The Gnat turned to him. He smiled, just for a second, just enough to let her know. Then he joined them in the kitchen where his mother gave him extra ice cream for being so nice and helping his little sister hunt for her bird.

The Gnat wasn't that easily cowed. She only grew craftier. Six months later, their parents bought her another parakeet. She kept it in its cage and warned Bobby that if it escaped, they'd all know who did it. He told her to be nicer to him and that wouldn't be a problem. She laughed. Three months later, she came home from school to find her bird lying on the floor of its cage, dead. His parents called it a natural death. The Gnat knew better, and after that, she stayed as far from him as she could.

While his life outside Cainsville improved, his visits to the town darkened, as if there was a finite amount of good in his life, and to shift more to one place robbed it from the other.

He blamed Rose. After her dream of the dragon, she'd been nicer to him, apparently deciding it had been no more than a dream. Unlike Hannah's power, Rose's came in fits and starts, mingling prophecy and fantasy.

But then, after he did particularly bad things back home—like loosening the bike seat or killing the bird—he'd come to Cainsville and she'd stare at him, as if trying to peer into his soul. After a few times, she seemed to decide that where there were dragons, there was fire, and if she was having these dreams, they meant something. Something bad.

Rose started avoiding him. Worse, she made Hannah do the same. He'd come to town and they'd be off someplace and no one knew where to find them—not until it was nearly time for him to go, and they'd appear, and Rose would say, "Oh, are you leaving? So sorry we missed you."

Soon, it wasn't just Rose looking at him funny. All the elders did. Mrs. Yates stuck by him, meeting him each time he visited, taking him for walks. Only now her questions weren't quite so gentle. *Is everything all right, Bobby? Are you sure? Is there anything you want to tell me? Anything at all?*

It didn't help that he'd begun doing things even *he* knew were wrong. It wasn't his fault. The dreams of golden castles and endless meadows had begun to fade. It did not directly coincide with the first screams of the dragons, but it was close enough that he'd suspected there was a correlation. When he stopped tormenting his tormenters and let the screams of dragons ebb, the dreams of the golden world continued to fade, until he was forced to accept that it was simply the passing of time. As he aged, those childish fancies slid away, and all he had left were the dragons. So he indulged them. Fed them well and learned to delight in their screams as much as he had those pretty dreams.

There were times when he swore he could hear his grandmother's voice in his ear, calling him a nasty boy, a wicked boy. And when he did, he would smile, knowing he was feeding the dragons properly. But they took much feeding, and it wasn't long before no one tormented him and there were no worthy targets for his wickedness. He had to find targets and, increasingly, they were less worthy, until finally, by the time he turned twelve, many were innocent of any crime against him. But the dragons had to be fed.

That summer, his mother took him to Cainsville two days after he'd done something particularly wicked, particularly cruel, and when he arrived at the new diner, the elders were not there. Even Mrs. Yates was gone. He'd walked to her house and then to the schoolyard, where they sometimes sat and watched the children play. He found her there, with the others, as a group of little ones played tag.

When she saw him, she'd risen, walked over and said he should go to the new diner and have a milkshake and she'd meet him there later. She'd even given him three dollars for the treat. But he'd looked at the children, and he'd looked at her, standing between him and the little ones, guarding them against him, and he'd let the three bills fall to the ground and stalked off to talk to Rose.

He found her at her brother's place. Rose was the youngest. A "whoops" everyone said, and he hadn't known what that meant until he was old enough to understand where babies came from and figured out that she'd been an accident, born when her mother was nearly fifty. This brother was twenty-nine, married, with a little girl of his own. That's where Rose was—babysitting her niece.

Bobby snuck around back and found the little girl playing in a sandbox. She couldn't be more than three, thin with black hair. He watched her and considered all the ways he could repay Rose for her treachery.

"What are you doing here?" a low voice came from behind him. He turned to see Rose, coming out of the house with a sipping cup and a bottle of Coke. Like Mrs. Yates, she moved between him and the child. Then she leaned over and whispered, "Take this and go inside, Seanna. I'll be there in a minute, and we'll read a book together."

She handed the little girl the sipping cup and watched her toddle off. Then she turned to him. "Why are you here, Bobby?"

"I want to know what you told the elders about me."

"About you?" Her face screwed up. "Nothing. Why?"

He stepped toward her. "I know you told them something."

She stood her ground, her chin lifting, pale eyes meeting his. "Is there something to tell?"

"No."

"Then you don't have anything to worry about."

She started to turn away. He grabbed her elbow. She threw him off fast, dropping the bottle and not even flinching when it shattered on the paving stones.

"I didn't tell anyone anything," she said. "I don't have anything to tell."

"Bull. I've seen the way you look at me, and now they're doing it, too."

"Maybe because we're all wondering what's wrong. Why you've changed. You used to be a scared little boy, and now you're not, and that would be good, but there's this thing you do, staring at people with this expression in your eyes and . . ." She inhaled. "I didn't tell the elders anything."

"Yes, you did. You had a vision about me. A fake vision. And you told."

"No, I didn't. Now, I can't leave Seanna alone—"

He grabbed her wrist, fingers digging in as he wrenched her back to face him. "Tell me."

She struggled in his grip. "Let me—"

He slapped her, so hard her head whipped around, and when it whipped back, there was a snarl on her lips. She kicked and clawed, and he released her fast, stepping back. She hit him then. Hit him hard, like a boy would. Plowed him in the jaw and when he fell, she stood over him and bent down.

"You ever touch me again, Bobby Sheehan, and I'll give you a choice. Either you'll confess it to the elders or I'll thrash you so hard you'll wish you *had* confessed. I didn't tattle on you. Now leave me alone."

"You think you're so special," he called as she climbed the back steps. "You and your second sight."

"Special?" She gave a strange little laugh, and when she turned, she looked ten years older. "No, Bobby Sheehan, I don't think I'm special. Most times, I think I'm cursed. I know you're jealous of us, with our powers, but you wouldn't want them. Not for a second. It changes everything." She glanced down at him, still on the ground. "Be happy with what you have."

He was not happy with what he had. As the year passed, he became even less happy with it, more convinced that Rose and the elders were spying on him from afar. Spying on his thoughts. This was not paranoia. Twice, after he'd done something moderately wicked, his mother got a call at work. Once from Mrs. Yates and once from Rose's mother.

"Just asking how you are," his mother said over dinner after the second call. She slid him a secret smile. "I think Rose might be sweet on you. She seems like a nice girl."

"Her family's not nice," the Gnat said as she took a forkful of meatloaf. "Her one brother's in jail."

His mother looked over sharply. "No, he isn't. He's in the army. Don't spread nasty gossip—"

"It's not gossip. I heard it in town. He's in jail for fraud, and so was Rose's dad, for a while, years ago, and no one thinks there's anything weird about that. I overheard someone say the whole family is into stuff like that. They're con artists. Only people act like it's a regular job." She scrunched up her freckled nose. "Isn't that freaky? The whole town is—"

"Enough," his mother said. "I think someone's pulling your leg, young lady. There is nothing wrong with Rose Walsh or her family. They're fine people."

For once, he believed the Gnat. He'd wondered about Rose's brother ever since he took off a few years ago and Rose said he'd joined the army to fight in Vietnam, but he'd been over thirty, awfully old to sign up.

Con artists. That explained a lot. Rose was conning the elders right now, telling them stories about him. Trying to con him, too, into not wanting powers. He did. He wanted them more than anything. And he was going to find a way to get them.

He spent months researching how to steal powers and learned nothing useful. It did not seem as if it could be done, and the more he failed to find an answer, the more the jealousy gnawed at him, and the harder it was to focus on keeping the dragons fed and happy. He had to do worse and worse things, and it made him feel even guiltier about them. Together with the jealousy, it was like his stomach was on fire all the time. He couldn't eat. He started losing weight.

He had to go back to Cainsville. At the very least, the visit would calm the gnawing in his stomach and let him eat. He would talk his mother into a special trip to Cainsville and he would go see Hannah. Not the elders. Not

Mrs. Yates. Certainly not Rose. No, he'd visit Hannah. She'd help him set things right.

His plan worked so beautifully that he felt as if the success was a sign. His luck was turning. He asked his mother to go and off they went that Sunday. He arrived to hear that Rose was in the city, and he found Hannah in the playground, tending to an injured baby owl.

"Did a cat get it?" he asked as he walked over.

She'd started at the sound of a voice, and he expected that when she saw it was him, she'd smile. She didn't. She scooped up the owl and stood.

"Bobby," she said. "I didn't know you were coming today."

"Surprise." He grinned, but she didn't grin back. Didn't even fake it. Just watched him as he opened the gate and walked in. "Is the owl all right?"

She hesitated, then shook her head. "Something got him. Maybe a cat. He's dying." Another pause. "That's the worst part. When they're hurt and I can't help."

"You can put it out of its misery."

She almost dropped the fledgling. "What?"

"I'll do it. Mercifully. Then you won't need to feel bad because you can't help."

She stared at him like he'd suggested murdering her mother for pocket change. One of the dragons roared, a white-hot burst of flame that blazed through him.

"I'm thinking of you," he said, glowering at her.

"And I'm *not*. That isn't how it works. Rose said you . . ." she trailed off.

"Rose said *what*?" He stepped forward.

Hannah shrank, but only a little, before straightening. "That you don't understand about the powers. You think they're this great gift. There are good parts, sure, but bad, too. Lots of bad. I woke up in the middle of the night last week because a dog had been hit by a car. I ran out of the house and my mom helped me take it to the vet's, but there was nothing we could do. It was horrible. Just horrible. And I felt it—all of it. But the only thing that made that dog feel better was having me there through the whole thing, no matter how hard it was. So I did it. Because that's my responsibility."

Then you're a fool, he thought. *The dog wouldn't have helped you. It would have left you by the road to die.* He didn't say that, because when he looked at her, getting worked up, all he could think was how pretty she'd gotten. Prettier than any girl in his class, and he wanted to touch her, and when the impulse came, it was like throwing open a locked door. This was how he could steal her power. Touch her, kiss her . . .

He bit his lip and rocked back on his heels. "I'm sorry, Hannah. I wasn't thinking. My dad always said a quick death is better than suffering, and that's what I meant. Help you *and* help the baby owl." He met her gaze. "I'm sorry."

She nodded. "It's all right. I'm just feeling bad about it." She set the fledgling back on the ground.

"I know." He stepped closer. "I wish I could make you feel better."

Another nod, and in a blink, he was there, his arms going around her, his lips to hers. It wasn't the first time he kissed a girl. He'd done more than kiss them, too. Sometimes that was him being wicked, but most times, he didn't need to be—he knew how to say the right things. *A little charmer*, that's what his mother called him, obviously relieved that her sullen boy had turned out so well.

So he kissed Hannah. It was a good kiss. A sweet and gentle one, for a sweet and gentle girl. But she jerked back and pushed him away hard, as if he'd jumped on her.

"I-I'm sorry, Bobby," she said. "I have a boyfriend."

He was about to say "Who?" when he saw her expression.

Liar.

The dragon whipped its tail inside him, lighting his gut on fire. He forced it to settle. He wouldn't be wicked with Hannah. He just wouldn't. Not unless he had to.

"It's Rose, isn't it?" he said, stepping back, looking down at his sneakers. "She doesn't like me. She has dreams about me—about a dragon. She told me that, but I don't understand what it means."

"She doesn't either. What did she tell you?"

He shrugged and continued the lie. "Something about a dragon. That's all I know."

"It's two dragons. She dreams they're fighting over you and screaming awful screams. Then one wins and it . . . it . . ."

"It what?"

"Devours you," she blurted. "We don't know what it means."

"What do the elders say?"

"Elders?" She frowned at him. "We didn't tell the elders. Rose looked it up in books. She has lots of books from her Nana. Some talk about the sight and dreams, but she can't figure this one out."

"So she's never told the elders? About me?"

"Of course not. What's there to tell?"

He bit his lip. "I get the feeling Rose doesn't like me very much anymore." He lifted his gaze to hers. "I get the feeling you don't either."

"I . . ." She swallowed. "I'm fine, Bobby, I just—"

He grabbed her around the waist and kissed her again. This time when she struggled he held on, kept kissing her, and the more she fought, the more certain he was that this was the answer. She had the power. Touch her. Kiss her—

She kneed him between the legs.

He gasped and fell back. "You little—"

"What's happened to you, Bobby?" she said as she scooped up the bird and backed away. "You never used to be like this."

"I just wanted to kiss you. You didn't need to—"

"That wasn't kissing me. That was hurting me. You want to know why I don't like you as much?" She held up the owl. "Because they don't. The animals. You scare them and you scare me."

She cradled the fledgling against her chest and ran off, leaving him there, gasping for breath in the playground.

He started walking, not knowing where he was going, spurred by the fire in his gut, a fire that seeped into his brain, blinding him. When the rage-fog cleared, he found himself on Hannah's street. And there, crossing the road, was what he'd come to find, though he only knew as he saw it.

The black cat. Hannah's matagot kitten. A middle-aged cat now, slinking arrogantly across the street without even bothering to look, as if no car would dare mow it down.

He followed the beast, waiting for it to get to a secluded spot. In Cainsville, though, there weren't any secluded spots. When he'd been young, he'd felt as if he was being merely observed, someone always watching over him, keeping him safe, and he'd loved that. Now it felt as if he was being spied on, judgmental eyes tracking his every move. As he moved, he'd sometimes see someone peek out from a house, but they'd only smile and nod. He might be thirteen, but here he was still a child, innocently out playing hide-and-seek or tag with his friends. He could cut through yards and steal behind garages and no one would ever come out to warn him off as they would in the city.

Eventually, the cat stopped prowling, and did so in one of the rare secluded spots—the yard of an empty house. Cainsville had a few of them, not abandoned but empty. This one was surrounded by a solid fence for privacy, and once Bobby was in that yard, he was hidden. That is where the beast stopped to clean itself, proving that whatever airs cats might put on, they were very stupid beasts.

As he crept up behind the cat, his hands flexed at his sides. He had to grab it just right or it would yowl. Pounce and snatch. That was the trick. Scoop it up by the neck, away from scrabbling claws and then squeeze. It was simpler than one might think, particularly when the beast was so preoccupied that it didn't turn even when his foot accidentally scraped a paving stone.

He got as close as he dared. Then he sprang.

The cat whipped around and leaped at him. The shock of seeing that stopped him for a split second, and before he could recover, the cat was on him, scratching and biting, and it was like Rose and Hannah all over again, fighting like wild animals, only this animal had razor claws and fangs, and when he finally threw the beast off, blood dripped from his arms and his face.

He ran after the cat, but it bounded away, leaped onto the fence and turned to hiss at him, almost half-heartedly, as if he wasn't worth the effort. He glowered at the beast, then stomped toward the gate. When he swung it open, someone was standing there. Three someones. Mrs. Yates and two of the other elders.

"What have you done, Bobby," Mrs. Yates said, her voice low.

"Me?" He lifted his blood-streaked hands. "Ask that damned cat. I was trying to rescue it for Hannah."

"No," she said. "That isn't what you were doing at all."

"I don't know what you mean. If Hannah told you—"

"Hannah told us nothing. She doesn't need to. We know."

He looked at her, and then at the other two elders, and *he* knew, too. Knew the truth he hadn't dared admit. The girls weren't tattling on him. It was the elders, burrowing into his head, reading all his most wicked thoughts, seeing all his most wicked deeds.

He managed to pull himself up straight and say, "You're all crazy." Then he pushed past them and raced back to his mother.

It was the old story. The one where he'd first heard about the screams of dragons. It was coming true. All of it. First the dragons. Then his stomach, twisting and hurting so much these days that he couldn't eat—just like the king couldn't eat because his food went missing. Now the people who could hear everything. The elders and Rose. They knew what he was doing even when he didn't speak a word. He could not escape them, again like the king in the story.

That's why he used to dream of castles. He wasn't a changeling child. He was a king—or he had been—and the old story was replaying itself, consuming him and his life.

After that last trip to Cainsville, the elders were no longer content with the occasional call to check on him. Twice they'd shown up at his house. His *house*. Mrs. Yates had taken him aside and tried to talk to him, prodding him hard now with her questions, telling him she was worried, *so worried*. If only he'd talk to them, they might be able to help.

Liar.

They didn't care about him. They came as a warning. Letting him know they were in his head, watching and judging. Letting him know they were going to win. He was still a little boy. He would be consumed by them—the dragons—as Rose's dreams predicted. It all made sense now, or it did, the more he thought about it, obsessed on it, dreamed of it. It was like a puzzle where the pieces don't seem to fit, but you just had to be smart and twist them around until they did.

He went to the library and dug until he found the story in an old book of legends. He'd vaguely recalled that the king had stopped his enemies by feeding them something. According to the book, he'd fed them food made from very special insects. Bobby read that, and he went home to sleep on it, and when he woke, he knew exactly what he had to do.

It was May Day again. This year, the Gnat had decided not to come. She'd been at a friend's place and called to say she was spending the night and skipping the trip. He'd given the news to his parents when they returned from a bridge party.

The next morning, his mother started fussing, worrying that the Gnat would change her mind as soon as they'd left for Cainsville.

"She'd call before that," his father said. "She's a big girl."

"I can phone and ask if you want," Bobby said.

"Would you? That's sweet." She patted his back as he walked past. "Whose house did you say she was at again?"

He answered from the next room, his reply garbled, but his mother only said, "Oh, that's right. Now, does anyone know where we left the tanning lotion? I want to get started early this year. Wait, I think Natalie had it . . ."

A few minutes later he found her in his sister's room. "She's not there. I remember her saying something about going to the roller rink."

His mother sighed. "I wish she wouldn't. Those places seem so unhealthy for girls, with the lights all off and so many boys . . ."

"I can talk to her about it tomorrow if you're worried."

Another pat as she zoomed past, tanning lotion in hand. "Thank you, dear. You're a good brother, even if she doesn't always appreciate you. Did you pack that pie you made?"

"Pie?" His father appeared in the doorway. "Bobby made pie? Apple, I hope."

"Shepherd's pie," his mother said. "He made it last night while we were out. Didn't you notice the mess when we got home?" She glanced over. "So you *did* find hamburger meat in the freezer."

"One last package, like I said."

"I was so certain we'd run out." She headed for the hall. "All right. Time to go."

The waitresses at the new diner let him warm his casserole in the oven. He was sitting in the back, watching the timer, when the door swung open and Rose burst in, Hannah at her heels.

"That smells good," Hannah said. "Is it true? You made pie?"

"Shepherd's pie. I hope you're not still mad at me. I'm . . ." He lowered his voice as he walked toward her. "Sorry about the last time. That's why I made the pie. For you and Rose. To say I'm sorry. For the elders, too. I don't want anyone to be mad at me." He gazed into her eyes. "I hope you'll have some."

She seemed nervous, but forced a smile. "Sure, Bobby. And I'm sorry, if I overreacted. You scared me and—"

"What have you done?"

It was Rose. She hadn't spoken since she'd entered. He hadn't even glanced her way, seeing only Hannah. Now he looked over to see her standing in front of the oven, staring at it. When she turned to him, her face was even paler than usual, her blue eyes bulging.

"What have you done, Bobby?" she whispered.

"Done? What—"

"I had a dream," she said. "Last night."

"More dragons," he scoffed. "Dreams of me and screaming dragons."

"No." Her horrified gaze never left his. "It wasn't dragons I heard screaming."

"Whatever." He turned away. "You're crazy. Your whole family is crazy."

"Where's your sister, Bobby?"

He shrugged, his back still to Rose. "She stayed home."

"Where is your sister?" She said each word slowly, carefully, and he was about to reply when the door opened again. He turned as Mrs. Yates and

two of the elders walked in. They seemed concerned. Only that. Then they stopped, mid-stride. They inhaled, nostrils flaring, and when they turned to him again, horror filled their eyes, the same horror that crackled from Rose's wide-eyed stare.

"Bobby," Mrs. Yates said. "What have you done?"

He wheeled and raced out the back door.

Before he knew it, he found himself back where he'd been the last time, in the backyard of the empty house. He looked around wildly, saw a break in the lattice work under the deck, and crawled through, wood snapping as he pushed his way in, splinters digging in, blood welling up.

When he got inside, he turned around and huddled there, hugging knees that stank of dirt, his arms striped with blood.

Blood.

He remembered the blood.

He shot forward, gagging, stomach clenching, head pounding, the images slamming against his skull. He kept gagging until he threw up. Then he sat there, hugging his legs again as the tears rolled down his face.

Gran was right.

I am a monster.

And I don't even know how it happened.

"Bobby?"

It was Mrs. Yates. He scuttled backward, but she walked straight to the hole and bent to peer in. She smiled, but it was such a terribly sad smile that he wished she'd scowl instead, scowl and rage and call him the monster he was.

"I am so sorry, Bobby," she said. "I don't know . . ." She inhaled. "I won't make excuses. We could tell things weren't . . . We had no idea how bad . . ." Another inhalation, breath whistling. "I'm so, so sorry. I wish I'd known. I wish I could have helped."

He said nothing, just kept clutching his knees.

"I can't stop what's going to happen now, Bobby. I wish I could. I would give anything to fix this. But I can't. I can only make it easier."

He started to shake, holding his legs so tight his arms hurt.

"I read those newspaper articles," she said. "About your grandmother. What she said. Your dreams. We should have talked about that. Perhaps if we'd talked . . ." She shook her head, then peered in at him. "You dreamed of golden castles, didn't you? Castles and meadows and streams."

"And dragons," he whispered.

She went still. Completely, unnaturally still. "Dragons?"

He nodded. "I dream of dragons screaming. And then I wasn't dreaming and they still screamed."

"You should have told—" She cut herself short, chin dipping. "Let's not talk about the dragons. You won't hear them anymore. I promise. But the castles. You liked the castles?"

He nodded.

"Would you like to see them?"

"They're gone. They went away."

She inched a little closer to the gap in the lattice. "I can bring them back. Back as bright as they ever were. Castles and meadows, cool breezes and warm sunshine. Laughter and play, music and dancing. Is that what you remember?"

He nodded.

"Would you like to go there?"

"Yes."

She ducked her head and crawled under with him. In one hand, she held a bottle. She pulled out the stopper and held the bottle out to him. The liquid inside seemed to glow, and when he looked up at her, she seemed to glow, too, the wrinkles on her face smoothing.

"Do you trust me, Bobby?"

He nodded.

"Then drink that. Drink it, and you'll see the castles again. You'll go there, and you won't ever need to come back."

He took the bottle, and he drank it all in one gulp. As soon as he did, the dragons stopped screaming, and he saw Mrs. Yates, glowing, every inch of her glowing, like sunlight trapped under her skin, her eyes filling with it, drawing him in as she reached out to hug him. He fell into her arms, and the glow consumed everything, the world turned to gold, and when he opened his eyes, he was sitting on sun-warmed grass, staring up at a castle, and a girl laughed behind him and said, "Come and play, Bobby." He turned, and she looked like Hannah but not quite, and she smiled at him, the way Hannah used to smile at him. He pushed to his feet and raced after her as she ran off, laughing.

And that was where he stayed, just as Mrs. Yates promised. Endless days in a world of gold and sunshine, days that ran together and had no end. Every now and then he would fall asleep in a lush meadow or in a chamber in the beautiful castle, and when he did, his dreams were terrible nightmares, where he was bound to a hospital bed, screaming about dragons. But the nights never lasted long, and soon he was back in his world of castles and meadows, running, chasing, playing, dancing until he forgot what the screams of dragons sounded like, forgot he'd ever heard them and forgot everything else—his grandmother, his sister, his parents, the girls, Mrs. Yates—all of it gone, wisps of a dream that faded into nothing, leaving him exactly where he'd always wanted to be.

THE KITSUNE'S NINE TALES

An Age of Legends Universe Story

"**D**OES HE SEEM resigned to his fate?"

Senri stood in the small tea room over the Gate of the Crimson Phoenix as he looked down on the crowd thronging the Imperial Way below. Imperial guards led a man through the shouting onlookers in a slow march to the dungeons. The prisoner was taller than most, his dark skin shining under the summer sun, perspiration making the green eyes on his fox tattoos gleam. More sweat dripped, and blood too, where the manacles dug in. He shuffled along, his gaze down, letting the crowds pelt him with rotten fish and cries of "Coward!" and "Traitor!" and nodding with each, as if accepting it as his due.

"Does he seem resigned to his fate?" the man behind Senri asked again.

"He does."

"He is not."

Senri turned to the man. Broad-shouldered but not tall. Dark hair frosted with white. Dressed in a formal robe, which he'd pushed askew like a too-tight tunic. He'd shoved up his sleeves, and Senri could see battle scars dissecting the dragon tattoos that covered his arms.

Emperor Jiro Tatsu. Ruler of the largest empire the world had ever known.

"Who is he?" the emperor said, waving at the prisoner below.

Senri frowned, thinking he'd misheard. Otherwise, the question was ridiculous—there could scarcely be a peasant child who'd not know the answer, and Senri was a warrior from a line stretching back beyond the First Age.

"Who is he?" Emperor Tatsu asked again, patiently.

"Alvar Kitsune. Former marshal of the imperial army."

"More than that."

"He's a traitor. A coward who—"

"No, no." The emperor waved a hand, as if that was inconsequential. "Who *was* he?"

"As marshal? The leader of the largest army in the world. The second most powerful man in the empire after your imperial highness."

"Yes, but more. To me. Who was he?"

Senri faltered again. Was this a trick? Emperor Tatsu was not known for them. A blunt man, he was reputed to have little patience with the intricate machinations of court life.

The young warrior replied carefully. "He was, I believe, your friend. That is, you knew him well, if you would not necessarily count him as—"

"He *was* indeed a friend. The best I have ever known and, I fear, the best I ever will know. We grew up together. We won this empire together. We—"

Footsteps tripped up the stairs outside the tea room. Too light to be a warrior's tread. Too quick to be a woman's. When no one appeared, the emperor sighed.

"I would suggest, Tyrus, that you not consider a career as a court spy."

"I wasn't spying, Father." It was a child's voice and, a moment later, a young boy appeared in the doorway. "I was waiting for a break in the conversation before I intruded."

"Yet you would still intrude." The emperor tempered the rebuke with a smile as he beckoned the boy in.

The child looked about seven summers of age. He was clearly his father's son, though slighter of build and softer of face, a child more handsome than his sire, undoubtedly taking after his mother, whoever she might be. That was what Senri paused to decide—the maternity of the child before him. It was not an easy task. The emperor had two wives, three official concubines and five master courtesans, most of whom he'd fathered children on. The answer came when the boy smiled, a blazing grin that brought to mind the lovely First Concubine, Maiko. One of the bastard princes, then. Pity. Male imperial bastards had a habit of dying young, usually under mysterious circumstances.

"What is so urgent that you had to interrupt my meeting?" the emperor asked.

"I apologize." The boy bowed. "But it *is* urgent. Marshal—I mean, former marshal—Kitsune will be exiled to the Forest of the Dead tonight, and Gavril wishes to see him."

Emperor Tatsu had not shown a flicker of emotion as he named Alvar Kitsune to Senri as his dearest friend, but now, while his face remained impassive, pain flickered through his eyes.

"He isn't down there, is he? Gavril?"

Tyrus hesitated, as if considering a lie, but he nodded, and the two men walked to the window again. Senri saw the boy in a sweep. He was hanging back, dressed in a cloak with the hood pulled up. Half a head taller than Tyrus, though they seemed of an age. The boy watched as his father was paraded down the Imperial Way, his young face as stony as the emperor's, until he reached up to push back a stray braid. Even from where Senri stood, he could see the boy's hand shaking. The braid fell forward again and the boy scowled, shoving it back angrily now.

"Did Gavril ask to see his father?" Emperor Tatsu asked.

"He wouldn't," Tyrus said.

"I know," the emperor murmured. "So you ask on his behalf. You're a good friend, Tyrus. Gavril will need that now."

"He will need to see his father," the boy said, his voice firm but his gaze lowered. "One last time."

The emperor sighed. "Bring him around to the prison gate. We'll figure out how to do this." He looked at his son. "Discreetly."

The boy looked offended. "Of course."

"Off with you now. I'll be there soon."

Once Tyrus was gone, Emperor Tatsu turned back to Senri and seemed, for a moment, to forget why he was there, before shaking his head sharply.

"Yes, as I was saying, I know Alvar Kitsune better than I know any man alive. I am entrusting you to escort him to the Forest of the Dead and ensure he does not escape. It will be the most difficult task you will ever face, because Alvar will not meekly walk into that forest and accept his fate. You know his clan's totem?"

"The nine-tailed fox."

"Yes. The kitsune. The trickster. There are many ways Alvar will attempt to escape, and before you leave, I am going to tell you every one."

Their destination was not called the Forest of Exiles. Or the Forest of Permanent Imprisonment. It was the Forest of the Dead. One could claim it was so named because it had been, in past ages, used for elder abandonment, but few truly believed that. Yes, the forest itself was dead—devoid of life—but that was only another excuse for the name. Excuses for those who liked to think their empire did not practice primitive customs. They were civilized. Their criminals were not forced to kneel, head on a block, before a sword sliced it from their neck. No, their worst criminals were merely exiled for the winter to a forest . . . one surrounded by an insurmountable wall of lava rock, infected with swamp fever, containing neither game nor clean water.

Senri could not recall the last time an exile had walked out of the Forest of the Dead come spring. Yet, like most, he had no qualms over the punishment. It was, in many ways, worse than a quick death, and the prospect of such exile would give even the most hardened criminals pause. Those who committed their crimes despite the risk deserved the punishment.

And Alvar Kitsune? Did he deserve it? That was the question that Alvar raised once they entered the Wastes, as Emperor Tatsu had warned he would.

A five-day hard walk across lava fields separated the forest from the rest of the empire. The Wastes were a remnant from the Age of Fire, when two volcanoes had erupted, wiping out entire villages. In fact, the only thing left standing in the entire region was the forest. The lava had seemed to rise up around it, as if stopped by the force of the spirits within, later hardening into a wall that encircled the Forest of the Dead.

The armed escort and the prisoner set out into that wasteland, tramping across the uneven lava rock, peering into a landscape without a single tree or bush to enliven the view. They'd been walking half a day before Alvar Kitsune spoke his first words since leaving the imperial city four days earlier.

"You do not truly think I did it," he said, his face forward, as if he addressed the wind whipping past, burning their faces. "You seem a bright young man. I hope you understand what has happened here."

Senri said nothing. The three other guards glanced over. Alvar's voice was loud enough to carry, intentionally so. *He will single you out as the leader,* the emperor had said. *But he will appeal to all four.*

"I hope every warrior in the empire understands what happened here," Alvar continued. "Two decades of power has dulled his wits. He's so arrogant he didn't even bother to trump up plausible charges against me. Fleeing a losing battle? Abandoning my men under cover of magic? I don't know which is more outrageous: accusing me of cowardice or sorcery." He looked at Senri. "As for the latter, I trust you are no superstitious peasant."

He was not. Yet one had only to look into Alvar's green eyes to consider the possibility. Sorcerer's eyes. Unnatural in color.

"As for cowardice?" Alvar shook his head. "You have not served directly under me, boy, or I'd remember you. But I'll presume you have served in an army I've led into battle."

"I am not yet battle-tried," Senri said. "None of us are."

The former marshal looked at the four young men, and Senri was certain he cursed under his breath. Emperor Tatsu was no fool—he'd chosen loyal and distinguished guards, but ones too young to have served in battle, ones who knew Alvar Kitsune only as a distant figure at the head of victory parades. Ones who would have no reason to believe him innocent of the charges.

Senri smiled to himself, and they continued on in silence.

Their second day in the Wastes brought the former marshal's second attempt to win his freedom.

It was an ice-cold morning, one that would soon turn into a blistering hot day made worse by the black lava under their feet, reflecting the sun's rays back on them. For now, Senri walked with his cloak pulled tight. One of the other men tugged up his hood. Senri grunted at him and the young warrior lowered it. Nothing could impede their vision on this journey.

He will have hired men to waylay you, the emperor had said. *But I doubt they will attack. They will see I have men of my own following at a distance, ready for trouble. Take care, though. Sleep in shifts and keep your eyes open.*

Indeed, that very morning Senri spotted a distant mercenary scout . . . And saw an arrow fly as if from nowhere and take the man down. No other scouts appeared. The second play had failed.

"Are you married?" Alvar asked that afternoon as they walked.

Senri shook his head. The former marshal gave a wry smile. "I presume none of you are?"

"That is correct."

"Naturally. Old enough to be trusted with my care, but not old enough to have wed. Children, then?"

"I am not wed."

A sly grin. "One is not required for the other."

"I have no children."

None of them did. Again, the emperor had taken precautions, knowing what tactic Alvar would use next.

"Brothers? Sisters?"

Senri shook his head, and when he did, he saw those green eyes gleam, the fox spotting a mouse peeping from its hole.

"You are an only child then. I know what that is like. I myself have two brothers, but only one child. My son, Gavril. Perhaps you've seen him."

Do not lie, Emperor Tatsu had said. *He will smell a lie.*

"I have. He is a fine-looking boy."

"Indeed he is." A wide grin. Then he lowered his voice. "I only wish his mother was more . . . capable. She was my third wife. Young and pretty, well-born, and at the time that was all that mattered. She has lived a pampered life and I fear, in my absence, my son will suffer."

"You said you have brothers."

The faintest flicker of chagrin, as if Alvar wished he had not mentioned that. "True, but neither is posted in the imperial city, and both have sons of their own. Many sons."

Senri shrugged. "They are still his uncles. Nothing is more important than family, particularly for warriors. Your brothers will watch over him and train him, and he will have a good life. The emperor has made it clear that your wife and son will not suffer for your crimes."

"And you take him at his word?"

"I do."

"Then you are a fool."

None of the other guards fell for that "think of my son" ploy. Alvar did not surrender the cause there, naturally. He had more angles, each one following exactly as the emperor had predicted. Nine tales, Emperor Tatsu had said. Like his clan totem. Each was subtly done, half a day passing between, the former marshal gradually becoming more talkative, as if not only resigned to his fate, but determined to make the most of his final days, enjoying what little company he had. He would raise topics that were simply conversational, and then take advantage of useful ones that rose naturally.

Senri was from the Inugami clan—that was obvious from his dog tattoos. But who was his father? No, Alvar admitted, he did not know him, but did his father not have a brother who'd served as a palace guard? Yes, Alvar knew *him* very well. How was his uncle's daughter? Alvar recalled that she had been ill, and his own wife had sent ointments. Had they helped? Senri had heard nothing of it? Oh, well, still, was the child well? She was? Excellent.

And another guard, Hiraku, was from the Tanuki clan. Did he know Iwao Tanuki? A cousin? Wonderful. Alvar recalled the veteran warrior fondly. They had fought side by side with the emperor at the battle of Ashawan. Ah, there was a battle. They had freed the locals from the tyranny of a mad warlord, and the people had been so grateful that Alvar and Emperor Tatsu had scarcely been able to take a step without some noble or peasant offering his pretty daughter. They'd been young then, both of them, and yes, they had indulged, perhaps more than they ought. To be so young again. Young and strong and healthy. Rich, too. Wealth and power. What every young man dreamed of. These young warriors did, did they not? No? Well, they should, and they would be wise to snatch any opportunity.

The four ignored Alvar's hints. When they finally reached the end of the Wastes, the same could not be said for one particular guard in the village of Edgewood.

As the name suggested, Edgewood guarded the only break in the wall surrounding the Forest of the Dead. It was the only settlement in the Wastes and the last stop on their journey. Traditionally, convicts spent their last night in Edgewood's livestock enclosure. Alvar seemed to expect better. He got better, of a sort. He did not need to stay with the animals. Their group wasn't stopping in the village.

Give your regrets to the commander of Edgewood, the emperor said. *But do not overnight there. Do not speak to the villagers. In particular, do not allow anyone to bring the Seeker and Keeper to bless Alvar, though he will request it. They are but children, yet he is not above using them to his advantage. Refuse his request, then move quickly or he will find a guard willing to accept a very generous bribe.*

Alvar did humbly request a final blessing from the young Seeker. The request was refused.

Then, before they entered the forest, Senri turned to the youngest warrior in their party. Odon was barely into his second decade, but a renowned swordsman and son of the captain of Emperor Tatsu's private guard.

"You will stay here. The village will deal with you."

He did not feel pity as Odon sputtered in panic, asking what he had done, please tell him what he had done. The answer was, simply, nothing. Senri had spoken privately to the commander and no punishment awaited the young warrior. Emperor Tatsu had insisted on the ruse for two reasons. First, it would put the other guards on alert, warning them not to succumb to Alvar's final pleas. Second . . . Well, there was another reason, more personal, and while the emperor had not given it, Senri had understood.

They paused only briefly to replenish supplies. As they prepared to part from the village guards who'd escorted them to the second tower, Senri saw one secret a dagger to Alvar.

Senri walked over and held out his hand. Alvar gave the dagger to Senri, who in turn passed it back to the village warrior. The man hesitated only long enough for Senri to draw his sword. He did not wave it in threat. That was not its purpose. When Senri withdrew it, the village guard nodded, satisfied. Then he knelt and plunged his dagger into his gut. Senri swung his sword and cut off the man's head, granting him mercy as swiftly as possible.

They left Edgewood's guards standing—some stone-faced, others shame-faced—beside the headless corpse of their traitorous comrade, as Senri escorted his remaining two men and Alvar Kitsune into the forest.

When you enter the forest, he will become desperate. He will no longer attempt to befriend or bribe you. Like a fox in a trap, he will do what it takes to escape, bite any hand that tries to ease his situation. The curses will come then, as he finally admits to sorcery—true curses, against you and your family. He will rage and he will threaten, and that is the time when you must watch your men most closely, when they are most likely to break.

True. All of it. It was a two-day walk to the center of the forest, and on the dawn of the second day, when Alvar cursed their ancestors, swore his magic would damn them to the nether regions, the stronger of Senri's two remaining comrades broke. He turned on his fellow guards and Senri cut him down with a single stroke. Then, calmly, he continued on.

The forest was a spirit-forsaken place. For two days, they'd tramped through absolute silence. Senri had experienced nothing like it, not even in the Wastes. This was a thick, almost sticky silence that threatened to draw the very life from their bones.

It was as they finally neared their destination that Alvar Kitsune made his eighth play for freedom. His eighth tale.

He will know what truly lies in store for him. He knows what I will do because it is exactly what he would do, and what I have learned of treachery, I have learned from him.

"He's going to kill me, you know," Alvar said to the last guard, Hiraku.

He said it conversationally, more calm than he'd been since leaving the village gates.

When Hiraku frowned, Alvar nodded toward Senri. "Your silent leader there is under orders to kill me when we reach our destination. Murder me, then turn his blade on you before he takes his own life. That is why young Odon was left behind. Rescued from his fate because Jiro does not dare kill the son of his head guard. He is fond of the man, and too sentimental by far. Yet that sentimentality no longer extends to his oldest friend."

Hiraku shook his head. "Execution is not permitted—"

Alvar cut him short with a laugh. "*Public* execution is not permitted. Private, though? Oh yes. Certainly. I am a threat to your emperor. He could have had me assassinated, but that would compel my men to avenge me, to carry on my efforts and depose the despot in my stead. No, Jiro had to take away the most precious thing a warrior has. My honor. Label me coward, have me convicted as one, and exile me . . . then kill me here, where no one will see. The village commander has been told not to send a search party after us when you fail to return. In the spring, the Seeker will find our bodies, and it will seem that I tried to escape and we all perished in the attempt."

Hiraku turned on Senri. "Tell me he is wrong."

Senri opened his mouth to say so, but he was a moment too slow, and in his hesitation, Hiraku had his answer. Hiraku pulled his sword—he was too slow, too, and perhaps he knew it, preferring to die with his blade in his hand. He barely had time to get it from his belt before his head lay at his feet.

"Well done," Alvar said, stepping forward and clapping Senri on the back. "An admirable job all around."

"Thank you, my lord." Senri bowed, and as he rose, he took the dagger from his own belt and presented it to Alvar. The former marshal—and future emperor—took it with a grin.

"There's nothing like an empty belt to make a warrior feel naked," Alvar said, sticking the dagger into his sash. "Now tell me, because I really must ask. Did I do exactly as Jiro claimed I would? All my attempts to escape?"

All but one, Senri thought. But he'd dismissed the last. The ninth tale. So he only said, "You did."

"In the order he said I would do them?"

"Yes, my lord."

Alvar threw back his head and laughed. "I don't know if I should be flattered that he studied me so well or insulted that I was so predictable. I'll miss him. I truly will. Even as I cut the head from his neck, I will feel regret. We get few enough friends in this life, and fewer still as good as Jiro Tatsu."

"My lord, we need to—"

"Yes, yes. Stop talking and start acting. First, grab the boy's blades. I won't take your sword, but I'd like his, and you ought to have a dagger."

Senri bent to retrieve Hiraku's blades. As he straightened, cold sliced through him. A blade between his ribs, driven straight into his heart. He hung there, impaled on his own dagger, and Alvar leaned over to whisper, "There was one more tale, was there not? Please tell me there was. I would be disappointed if Jiro missed it."

Emperor Tatsu had not missed it. There was indeed a ninth tale, this one stark and unembellished. It had come as Senri had left that tea room, the emperor taking his arm and saying, "One more. The most important of all . . ."

Take it from one who knows—if you place your trust in Alvar Kitsune, he will put a dagger in your back. Do not ever doubt that.

Yet he had. One last tale, the gravest and the truest, and Senri had ignored it.

Alvar yanked out the blade, and the young warrior collapsed to the cold forest floor.

Last Stand

If you had to make a last stand for the survival of your race, Monica supposed there were worse places to do it. As she gazed out over the fort walls, she could imagine fields of green and gold, corn stalks swaying in the breeze.

How long had it been since she'd tasted corn? Monica closed her eyes and remembered August backyard barbecues, the smell of ribs and burgers on the grill, the chill of an icy beer can as Jim pressed it to her back, the sound of Lily's laughter as she darted past, chasing the other children with water balloons.

Monica opened her eyes and looked out at the scorched fields. She'd been the one who'd given the order to set the blaze, but there hadn't been corn in them, not for years. Only barren fields of grass and weeds that could hide the enemy, best put to the torch.

"Commander," a voice said behind her.

She turned and a pimply youth snapped his heels together and saluted. The newer ones did that sometimes, and she'd stopped trying to break them of the habit. They needed to believe they were in a proper army, with proper rules, even if they'd never worn a uniform before. It was what kept them going, let them believe they could actually win this war.

"Hendrix just radioed," the youth said. "He's bringing in the latest group of prisoners."

Monica nodded and followed him off the ramparts. They passed two teenage girls in scout uniforms who nodded, gazes down as they murmured polite greetings. Monica hid a smile, thinking that, once upon a time, she'd have killed to get that respect from girls their age, back when she'd stood at the front of a classroom.

She thought about all the kids she'd taught. Wondered where they were now, how many were Others, how many were dead . . . Too many in the last category, she was sure. What would they think, seeing their chemistry teacher leading the last band of resistance fighters? Could they ever imagine it? She couldn't imagine it herself some days.

As she followed the youth into the fort, Gareth swung out from the shadows. He fell into step beside her, his left foot scraping the floor—a broken leg that never healed quite right.

Before he could say a word, she lifted her hand.

"Objection noted, Lieutenant."

"I didn't say a word, Commander," he said.

"You don't need to. You heard we're bringing in a fresh lot, and you're going to tell me—again—that we can't handle more prisoners. The stockade is overcrowded. We're wasting manpower guarding them. We're wasting doctors caring for them. We should take them out into the field, kill them and leave the corpses on spikes for the Others to see."

"I don't believe I've suggested that last part. Brilliant idea, though. I'll send a troop to find the wood for the poles—"

She shot him a look. He only grinned.

"We aren't animals, Lieutenant," she said. "We don't stoop to their level."

Of course he knew she'd say that, as well as she knew his complaint. Gareth just liked to voice his opinion. Loudly and frequently. She'd answered only for the sake of the new recruit leading them.

When they reached the main hall, she heard the cry: "Prisoners on the grounds!" For the newer soldiers, it was a warning and they scattered in every direction. Monica never tried to make them stand their ground. She understood too well where that fear came from, those years of hiding, watching, waiting to run again. She did, however, ask her officers to take note of those who fled and, later, they'd be taken to the stockades, so they could see that the Others weren't the all-powerful demons of their nightmares.

Once they were convinced, they'd react to that cry very differently. They'd join the other soldiers now lining Stockade Walk to watch the parade of prisoners. They wouldn't jeer, wouldn't say a word, would just stand firm and watch, the hatred so thick you could smell it, heavy, suffocating.

As they walked into the main hall, already choked with soldiers, Gareth said, "You can watch from the second floor, Commander."

"Like hell."

A wave went through the assembled men and women, grunts and nods of approval from those who'd overheard, whispers going down the line to those who hadn't. *Yet another crowd-pleasing routine,* she thought wryly. Gareth won approval for the suggestion and she for refusing.

As they entered the hall, Gareth's shoulders squared, pulling himself up to his full six-foot-five, his limp disappearing. The crowd of soldiers parted to let them through. Those who didn't move fast enough earned a glower from Gareth, and scrambled aside so fast they tripped. Him, they feared and respected. Her, they loved and respected. Yet another of their routines.

Monica took up her usual position at the first corner. When the prisoners walked into the hall, she'd be the first one they saw, waiting at the end.

She could hear them outside the doors now. This was the toughest part. Nearly every man and woman in this hall had been in this same situation, waiting in their hideouts, hearing the Others approaching, praying they passed. *Oh God, praying they passed.*

Gareth moved up behind her. Out of sight of the soldiers, he rubbed the small of her back.

When the footsteps stopped at the door, a few soldiers broke ranks and, shame-faced, bolted back to their bunks. It was still too much for them, the memories too fresh.

The door started to open. Monica's own memories flashed. In that first moment, she didn't see soldiers and prisoners. She saw the gang of Others who'd burst into her own hideaway ten years ago. She heard Jim's shout of rage as he rushed forward to protect them, yelling for Monica to take Lily and run. She heard his screams as they fell on him. She heard Lily's screams as she saw her father torn apart. She heard her own screams as she grabbed Lily and ran for the basement, as they caught her, ripping Lily from her arms. Her screams for them to show mercy—Lily was only a child, only a little girl. They hadn't.

Gareth moved closer, letting her rest against him. He leaned down to murmur reassurances in her ear, then, as she relaxed, the reassurances turned to reminders. *Stand tall. You're in charge now. You own their asses. Don't let them forget that.*

Now she saw prisoners, strangers, not the monsters who'd slaughtered her family and tortured her. Broken and cowed and filthy, they shuffled along the gauntlet of soldiers.

Gareth tensed. Monica looked up sharply, gaze tripping over the prisoners, trying to see which one had triggered his old cop instincts. Sure enough, there was one at the end, long greasy hair hanging in his face, but not quite hiding the furtive looks he kept shooting her way.

She stood firm, gaze on the prisoner. He looked away as he passed. Then he wheeled and lunged at her.

Gareth leapt forward so fast all Monica saw was a blur and a flash of silver. The prisoner's head sailed from his shoulders. It hit the floor with a dull thud and rolled. When it came to rest at a soldier's feet, the young woman kicked it. A cheer started to surge, choked off at a simple, "No," from Monica.

She motioned for someone to clean up the mess. The procession of prisoners continued on. None even gave any sign they'd seen what happened. They just trudged along, gazes down, until they disappeared from sight.

Word came next that the scouts had been spotted. They were moving fast, meaning they were bringing bad news. She left the hall with Gareth and headed for the meeting room to await their arrival.

As they passed the lecture hall, Monica could hear the teacher giving a history lesson for the children, all born after the Great Divide.

Three flu epidemics had threatened the world in the decade preceding the Great Divide. As they'd escaped each relatively unscathed, experts swore they'd only dodged one bullet to put themselves in the path of a bigger one.

The virus had started in Indonesia, with sporadic outbreaks downplayed by authorities until they could announce a vaccine.

Their salvation turned into their damnation. Some said the vaccine had been deliberately tampered with. Others blamed improper testing. They knew only that it didn't work.

No, that wasn't true. If the goal was to ensure that people survived the flu, then it worked perfectly. People were vaccinated, they caught the virus, they died, and they rose again.

Even before they rose, though, they'd carried a virus of their own, unknowingly spreading it through lovers, drug use, and blood donations. By the time officials realized the problem, a quarter of the population was infected. After the vaccinations stopped, another quarter died from the influenza itself. Both viruses continued to spread.

That was the Great Divide. The human race sliced in two, one side fighting for supremacy, the other for survival.

The world will end, not with a bang, but with a sniffle.

Or, to be precise, with the risk of a sniffle.

After Monica escaped her captors, her only thought had, indeed, been survival. Her own. But as she ran from the hordes, she'd picked up others like a magnet attracts iron filings. Everyone was alone. Everyone needed help. As a mother, she wanted to protect them. As a teacher, she wanted to guide them. Within a year, she found herself leading twenty survivors. Then they found Gareth.

He'd been in the middle of what had once been a town square, fighting a half-dozen of the Others, a roaring whirlwind of blood and steel, fighting valiantly, but wounded and outnumbered.

They'd rescued him. His story was one of the simpler ones—no family slaughtered before his eyes, just one guy, living a normal life until the day he wasn't. He'd tried to stick to what he knew—being a cop, protecting the innocent, which these days meant roaming the countryside, fighting bands of Others so survivors could escape. A noble plan, if not terribly efficient. Monica had suggested that, if he really wanted people to protect, he could look after them.

And so it began. Ten years later, they were here, commanding what might well be the last of their kind, awaiting a final battle. A battle they knew they couldn't win.

The scouts' news was exactly what she'd expected. The Others were amassing just beyond a forest to the east, the only place for miles that couldn't be seen from the ramparts. When she'd ordered her troops to raze the fields, they'd started cutting down the forest, then realized the task was beyond them. Besides, she'd reasoned, that meant the Others would pick that spot for their camp, so she could concentrate their surveillance there.

Surveillance. It sounded so strategic, as if they were fully prepared to meet the enemy, simply biding their time, when the truth was that they were foxes backed into a den, waiting for the wolves to arrive.

She hadn't brought them here to die. She'd hoped by running so far, they'd send a message to the Others: "Look, you've won. We've holed up here in this wasteland and here we'll stay. Now just leave us alone. *Please* leave us alone."

One last plea for mercy. It was, she realized as the scouts gave their report, too much to hope for. Deep down, she'd always known it was.

"Prepare a reconnaissance team," Monica said as she rose from the table. "We'll leave at the first night bell."

Two of the trained scouts exchanged uneasy looks. They'd come from the true military teams, long since disbanded, where commanding officers stayed behind the enemy lines. They glanced at Gareth, as if hoping he'd advise her to stay behind.

"You heard Commander Roth," he said. "Get that team ready."

Monica was back on the ramparts, looking out over the barren fields, waiting for the team to convene below. The scrape of Gareth's dragging boot told her he was coming, but she didn't turn, just stood at the railing, looking out until she felt his arms around her waist.

"We knew this was coming," he said.

"I know."

"We're as prepared as we're ever going to be."

"I know."

"There's still one more option," he said.

"No."

"Just saying . . ."

"And I'm saying that I know it's an option. I'll remember it's an option. But—"

She inhaled and shook her head. He pulled her back against him, chin resting on her head, and she relaxed against the solid wall of his chest.

She felt his head turn, as he made sure there was no one around before he leaned down and kissed her neck, his lips cool against her skin. Those who'd been with them a long time knew they were lovers, had been for years. As discreet as they were, it was hard to hide something like that, living in close quarters. They were still careful, though, for the sake of those, like the scouts, who'd come from the troops, where such a thing would be a serious concern.

There weren't many of them left—true soldiers, trained ones. "Military commander" had never been Monica's role. Years ago, when they'd started meeting up with other groups of survivors, she'd made it clear that she wasn't cut out for that. She'd take charge of the civilians. Gareth had been invited to lead a military division, but he'd stayed with her, trained the civilians to protect themselves. Then, one by one, the troops had fallen, the few survivors making their way to Monica's group, until they were all that remained. Now they looked to her to protect them, and she wasn't sure she could.

By the time they left, night had fallen. That wasn't an accident. They traveled at night when they could, moving silently across the burned fields. The same open land that protected them from sneak attacks made them prisoners during the daylight.

It was an hour's walk to the forest's edge. They'd just drawn within sight of it when they heard a barely muffled gasp of pain ahead. They'd split up, Gareth and Monica proceeding, the others fanning out.

The stifled whimpers came from just past the first line of trees. It sounded like a child, but they continued ahead with caution, Gareth in the lead, machete drawn. Those were the best weapons they had—knives and spears and makeshift swords. They had guns, too, but without ammunition, they were little more than clubs. The Others were no better off. This was a primitive war of tooth and claw and steel, as it had been for years, the munitions factories among the earliest targets.

Monica's weapon of choice was a throwing knife, and she had one in each hand as she followed Gareth. At the rustle of undergrowth, he stopped, and she peered around him to see a figure rising between the trees.

"Oh, thank God," a girl's voice said. "Oh, thank *God*."

The figure wobbled, then dropped with a cry. They found her on the ground, clutching her leg as she lit a lantern. She was no more than eighteen, thin-faced and pale.

"I thought you were the Infected," she said, her voice breathy with relief. "They got the rest of my troop. I-I tried to fight—"

"Shhh," Monica said, moving closer.

The girl looked up at them. Seeing Gareth's scarred face, she gave a start, but Monica nudged him back. He slid into the shadows.

"They took the others," the girl said. "They took them all."

Monica crouched beside the girl. "We'll get you back to your camp. We just arrived ourselves. Reinforcements." She offered her most reassuring smile. "You'll have to show us the best way to go. In case more of them are out here."

The girl nodded and reached up. Monica tucked the throwing knives into her waistband halter and tried to take the girl's arm, but the girl clasped hers instead, fingers biting in as she rose slowly.

Then she yanked Monica toward her. Silver flashed as the girl's free hand pulled a knife from under her jacket. Monica's foot expertly snagged the girl's "wounded" leg and she went down, the knife flying free. Monica kicked it out of the way as the girl grabbed for it. Another kick to the girl's stomach and she fell, doubled-over and gasping.

"Did you really think I didn't know what you are?" the girl snarled between gasps. "Did you think I couldn't *smell* what you are?"

"No," Gareth said, stepping forward, machete whispering as it brushed his leg. "And did you really think we wouldn't smell an ambush?"

He swung the machete as the forest around them erupted, Others lunging out from their hiding places. The girl tried to scuttle back, but he was too fast. Her head flew from her shoulders. Blood jetted up, her body convulsing in death. The Others stopped, all frozen in mid-step, staring.

"What?" Gareth boomed, bloody machete raised. "Isn't that what you do to us? Lop off our heads? The only way to be sure we're dead? Well, it works for you, too." He smiled, his scarred face a pale death mask against the night. "Any volunteers?"

"You may want to consider it," Monica said, her quiet voice cutting through the silence. "Because, if you look over your shoulders, you'll see we aren't alone. And they won't kill you. They'll turn you." She looked around, her perfect night vision picking out each face, her gaze meeting each set of wide eyes. "They'll infect you."

Gareth roared, giving the signal for attack and the forest erupted again as their soldiers leapt from the undergrowth and swung from the trees. In that first wave of attack, some of the Others bolted. More ran after a few half-hearted swings of a blade. She had invoked the greatest weapon they possessed: fear.

Fear of becoming Infected. *Fear of becoming like us.*

Without that weapon, they'd have been massacred. Even with it, the fight was long and bloody. Finally, they were left standing among bodies, some their own, but most not and that was really all they could hope for.

They continued on. They'd come to see the Others' camp and they weren't turning back. It was a slower walk now, trudging through the forest, some of them wounded. Nothing was fatal—few things were for them—but injuries healed slowly and imperfectly, like Gareth's broken leg and scarred face. It was, as with everything about their condition, a trade-off, in some ways better than life before, in others worse.

As a teacher, Monica had been one of the first to be inoculated, along with her family. One of the first vaccinated, one of the first infected, one of the first to die. The virus had hit with lightning speed, leaving her writhing with pain and fever, listening to her daughter's screams, unable to get to her.

Then, a miracle. Or so it seemed at the time. Death and rebirth.

Before they could even decide what to do, the soldiers came, the first squads deployed with orders to annihilate the Infected. They'd gone into hiding, staying one step ahead of the death squads, squatting in abandoned homes, certain if they could just wait it out, the authorities would realize their mistake and *help* them. But the order to kill all Infected stayed. Then came the bounty. Then the gangs of blood-crazed bounty hunters. They'd escaped the death squads, but not the gangs.

Jim had blamed zombie movies. When the dead rose again, people were sure they knew what they faced—an undead scourge that would end life as they knew it.

Some of the old stories were true. The Infected could not be easily killed. They carried the pallor of death, the faint smell of rot. Their bite could infect the living. They fed on meat, preferably raw, and while they had no particular hunger for human flesh, it was true that, if driven mad with hunger, they had been known to do what they would otherwise never consider.

But, unlike the zombies of legend and lore, they were still alive in every way that counted, still cognizant, and they could be reasoned with. The same could not be said for the living—for the Others.

The Infected had been hunted to near extermination and now, when Monica finally set eyes on the Others' camp, those seemingly infinite tents, she knew their end was at hand.

"We can't fight this," she whispered to Gareth.

"But we will."

And that was what it came down to. They *would* fight, hopeless or not.

They started back for the fort. She let Gareth take the lead, her mind whirring with everything she needed to do. She didn't notice when she veered slightly off course. Didn't notice the tripwire. Didn't notice until her foot snagged it and she heard Gareth's shout and saw him diving toward her, shoving her out of the way, heard the explosion, saw the flying debris and saw him sail backward, hitting the ground hard enough to make the earth shake.

She raced over and dropped beside him.

"Shit," he said, rising on his elbows to look down at his chest, his shirt shredded, the flesh below shredded, too, a mangled, cratered mass. "That's not good."

She let out a choking sound, meant to be a laugh, but coming out as a sob. It'd been a small blast, a homemade bomb designed to do nothing more than shoot shrapnel, but all that shrapnel had slammed into Gareth's chest. If he hadn't been Infected, he'd have been dead before he hit the ground.

She waved the medic over, but one look at his face told her all she needed to know. They could recover from most injuries, but if the damage was too great, too extensive . . .

Oh God. Not Gareth. Please, not Gareth.

She stayed beside him as the medic took a closer look. The soldiers ringed around them, solemn-faced, a few shaking, arms around each other.

When the medic looked up to give his report, Gareth waved the soldiers back out of earshot. They hesitated, but obeyed at a growl from him.

"I can make him comfortable," the medic murmured. "Get him back to the fort . . ."

"Waste of time," Gareth said. "Someone's bound to have heard that blast. Get them moving before—"

"No," Monica said. "You're coming if I need to carry you myself."

She expected him to argue, but he gave a slow nod. "You're right. They don't need this. Not now. Take me back, tell them I'll pull through."

That wasn't what she meant at all, but he had a point. Their best warrior— a man who'd single-handedly annihilated mobs of Others—killed by a simple tripwire bomb? That was a blow to morale they could ill afford.

The medic bound Gareth's chest while the soldiers fashioned a make-shift stretcher from branches and clothes, and they took Gareth back to the fort.

Monica stood on the guard's balcony overlooking the stockade crammed with Others. Prisoners of war. That had been her policy from the start. Leave as many of the enemy alive as possible. Bring them here. Keep them alive and comfortable. Use them as bargaining chips and as proof to the Others that they weren't monsters.

It hadn't mattered. Her missives to the government had gone unanswered, as they always had.

For years, she'd tried to reason with the Others. First to negotiate, then, as their numbers dwindled, to beg for mercy. She understood that they posed a threat. So they'd go away, far from the living.

The Others might as well have been getting letters from a colony of diseased rats. Eventually, she'd realized that was exactly how they saw the Infected—diseased rats that somehow had the power of communication. Sub-human. Dangerous. A threat requiring swift and thorough extermination.

She looked out at the Others and thought of what Gareth had said. The final option. Back when she'd first started arguing for the taking of prisoners, the other commanders had seen the possibilities. Horrified, she'd fought until the option was off the table. Only it wasn't really. It never had been.

She left the guardroom and walked through the fort. She passed the rooms of soldiers playing card games, of civilians mending clothing and preparing meals, of children listening to stories at the feet of the old ones. Everywhere she looked, people were carrying on, hiding their fear, laughing and talking, just trying to live.

Just trying to live. That's all they'd ever asked for, and that was all she ever wanted for them. So how far was she willing to go? Not to save them—she wasn't sure that was even possible anymore—but to give them every possible chance for survival.

How far would she go? As far as she could.

Three days later, she was back on the balcony overlooking the stockade. Gareth was beside her.

"I need to be there," he'd said. "They need to see me standing there."

So the doctors had done what they could, binding him up, and she'd done what she could, washing away the worst of the stink of rot that had set in. They'd cleared the hall and carried him on a stretcher to the stockade door. He'd taken it from there, finding the strength to walk up to the guard post. He stood in front of a pillar and she knew he leaned against it, but to those below, their champion was back on his feet. And, now, with this new hope she'd given them, so were they.

Once again, she looked out over the men and women packed into the room below. Only this time, they looked back at her. More than one hundred and fifty trained soldiers on their feet, watching her.

In those faces, she saw fear and uncertainty. She saw hate, too, but less of that, surprisingly less.

Guards ringed the room. Civilians walked up and down the aisles with trays of meat. Cooked meat because, for now, that would make them comfortable. They gave the hostages as much as they wanted. That would help. So, too, would the doctors slipping along, silent as wraiths, watching for signs of trouble, others in the back room, dosing the meat with mild sedatives.

The transition had gone smoother than she'd expected. The doctors assured her it would, but she'd seen one too many hellish deaths and rebirths to truly believe them. They were right, though. After all these years, the virus had mutated, ensuring its own survival by making the process faster, less traumatic. One shot of the virus. Then a death-inducing dose of sedative. Within a day . . . rebirth. And now, two days later, an army to command.

She started her speech with a history lesson. How the Others had driven them to this place. How they'd fought the sporadic incursions, killing only those they could not capture. How they'd treated the prisoners of war humanely. Every man and woman there could attest to that. But now, with the wolves at their door, refusing to negotiate, they'd been forced to do the unthinkable.

"We need soldiers to fight," she said, her voice ringing through the stockade. "Right now, I'm sure you don't feel much like helping us. But you won't be fighting for us, you'll be fighting for yourselves. You are us now. You are Infected. Every one of you is now free to walk out our front gates. But you won't. Because you know they won't let you. Your brothers-in-arms, your friends, your families—everyone one of them would lop off your head if you walked into that camp because you are no longer human. You are Infected."

She paused to let her words sink in. Behind her, Gareth shifted, struggling to stay on his feet. She glanced at him. He smiled and whispered that she was doing fine.

She turned back to the troops. "To everyone you left behind, you are now dead. Do you feel dead?"

They shuffled, the sound crossing the stockade in a wave.

"To everyone you left behind, you are now a monster. Do you feel like a monster?"

More shuffling, sporadic grunts.

"To everyone you left behind, you have no right to live."

Another glance at Gareth. He stood straighter, chin lifting. He was dying. They all were and this was how they had to face it: stand tall and refuse to let Death win so easily. They'd cheated it before. Now they had to cheat it again.

She turned back to the crowd below. "Do you want to live?" She paused. "Are you willing to *fight* to live?"

The answer came softly at first, her own troops calling back. Gradually, more voices joined them, the new soldiers joining in, their shouts boosting the confidence of the others until the cry ran through the fort.

Gareth moved up behind her, his fingers sliding around her waist, his touch ice-cold now.

"You gave them hope," he said. "You gave them a chance."

She nodded. It wasn't much, but it was the best she could do. Maybe, just maybe, it would be enough.

BAMBOOZLED

An Otherworld Universe Story

Dakota Territory, 1877

"Are you sure she can do it?" the boy asked Nate as he watered their trio of horses.

Lily could have pointed out that she was standing right beside him and had both a name and ears. But she knew the boy—Will—wasn't trying to be rude; he was simply like most of the young men they recruited: rarely set foot off his family homestead, rarely seen womenfolk other than his momma and sisters. And frontier mommas and sisters did not look like Lily.

Even now, as Will talked about her, he couldn't look her way—as if merely to glimpse her might damn his mortal soul. Lily could point out that his soul ought to be a lot more worried about the thieving that was coming, but to a boy like Will, that was part of life. Pretty girls with painted faces were not.

Lily's face was, of course, not painted right now. She was dressed in breeches, boots, and an overcoat, with her hair pushed up under her hat. It didn't matter. Will still wouldn't look.

"Can she do it?" he asked again. "I mean no offense—"

"Then stop giving it," Nate growled.

Lily noticed a cloud of dust cresting the rise beside them. "I do believe my wardrobe has arrived."

Emmett and Levi rode up, their horses run hard, flanks heaving. They had arranged to meet at midday and the sun had passed its zenith a while back.

"Had some difficulties," Emmett said as he nudged his horse to water.

"That it?" Nate pointed at the wrapped parcel behind Levi's saddle. When Levi nodded, Nate took it and said to Lily, "Come on."

Lily let Nate lead her behind an outcropping of rock. Emmett and Levi knew better than to sneak a look while she was dressing, and Lily was quite certain Will wouldn't dare, but Nate believed in coppering his bets. Otherwise, things would get messy. Nate didn't take kindly to trespass of any sort.

"We cutting the boy loose after the job?" he asked as they walked.

She nodded. "That's best. It's not working out. You promised Wilcox you'd try him. You did."

Nate grunted and handed her the parcel. As she untied it, she snuck a peek at him. Six feet tall. Well built. Rough featured, but not in a way that was displeasing, at least not to her. What she noticed most, though, was what she'd noticed about Nate from the start: the uncanny way he carried himself. When he moved, he was like a catamount on the prowl. Yet most of the time he wasn't moving at all, standing so still he seemed a statue, his gaze scanning the landscape.

It wasn't natural, that complete stillness, that constant alertness. She wondered why others never thought it peculiar. She had right from that first time, seeing him across the saloon. He'd noticed her, too, but not in the way men usually did. He'd only stared, no expression, no reaction. Yet his gaze hadn't left her as she'd taken a table with the rest of her acting troupe.

The trouble had begun later that evening, when a gambler made the mistake of equating actresses with whores. It was a common misconception. Lily couldn't even properly blame the man, considering that her two companions had already accepted paid invitations. The acting life required a second income; Lily made hers with light fingers.

She'd told the gambler she wasn't for sale, but he'd thought she was only haggling. That was when Nate had come over. He'd asked the gambler to let Lily be. When the man laughed, Nate fixed him with a stare as cold as a Nebraska winter. It hadn't taken long for the gambler's nerve to crack. He'd gone for his Colt; Nate broke his arm. Just like that. Lily saw the gambler reach for his piece and then he was screaming like a banshee, his arm snapped, bone sticking out, blood gushing. That's when she realized Nate wasn't quite human.

Now Nate turned his gaze on Lily as she undressed. Lily was used to men staring at her. They'd been doing it since she was fourteen, which was when she discovered it was so much easier to pick a man's pocket if he was gaping at her bosom. Nate wasn't like that. He gazed at her with what seemed like his usual expressionless stare, but Lily had learned to read deeper, and what she saw there now was hunger. He didn't move, though, not until she adjusted the dress and twirled around.

"How do I look?" she asked.

Nate growled an answer and, before she could blink, he was on her, one hand behind her head, the other at her rear as he pulled her into a deep kiss.

"I really ought not to have bothered putting on the dress," she said as she broke for air.

Nate chuckled and hoisted her onto the nearby rocks.

They rode into town after sundown. That was best. There were many variations on their game, but in each they'd learned the value of a late approach. By morning, the town would be buzzing with rumors of the party that arrived under the cover of night. A slip of a girl, bundled in an overcoat but riding a fine horse and wearing a fine dress. A proper young lady, escorted by a surly uncle and three young gunmen.

As the day passed, the story grew. The girl's uncle kept her under close watch at the inn, but they'd had to venture out, as she was in need of a new dress. And what a pretty thing she was, with yellow hair, green eyes, and the sweetest French accent.

The girl was shy, the uncle taciturn, and no one in town learned much from either, but the young fellows with them were far more talkative, especially after a drink or two. They said the girl came from New Orleans. Her parents were in California, expanding their empire. Shipping or railroad, no one was quite sure which, but they were powerfully flush. A suitor waited in California, too. A rich man. Very old, nearing sixty. The uncle was taking the girl to her parents and her fiancé and her new life. They'd been diverted here by news of Indian trouble and were waiting until the army had it in hand. Until then, the party would pass the time in their little town.

Lily's mark came at dinner. It was earlier than they'd expected—most men didn't like to seem eager. But it was said that John Anderson was keen to wed. Or wed again, having recently lost his young wife in a tragic accident. It was also said that "accident" might not have been quite the proper word to use. Anderson hadn't been as pleased with his bride as he'd hoped. Her daguerreotype had sorely misrepresented her and she had not cared for ranch life. She'd also objected to her husband's ongoing association with the town's whores and his penchant for bringing them home. Women could be quite unreasonable about such things. So Mrs. Anderson had perished and her grieving husband was impatient for a new bride.

Lily and Nate were dining at the inn. They'd barely taken their seats when Nate made a noise deep in his throat, too low for others to hear. He kept his attention on the wall-posted menu while Lily glanced over to watch their mark stroll through the door. They said John Anderson was a handsome man, but she couldn't see it. Or perhaps it was simply everything else she'd heard about him that tarnished her opinion. She did, however, watch him until he looked squarely in her direction. Then her gaze darted away as she clutched her napkin and cast nervous glances at her "uncle."

Anderson stopped at their table, took off his hat with a flourish and introduced himself. Gaze lowered, Lily waited for her uncle to reciprocate. He didn't.

"I see that you have not yet begun to dine," Anderson said after an awkward silence. "May I invite you both to join me at my table?"

"No," Nate said.

"Does that mean I may not ask or you will not join me?"

Anderson's lips curved in the kind of smile that would warn another man off. Nate only stared at him.

"No."

"All right then. May I ask—?"

"No."

Lily simpered and shot looks at Anderson, her eyes pleading with him to excuse her uncle's behavior.

"I see," Anderson said. "Well, then, perhaps I'll have the pleasure of seeing you both around town."

Nate's answering snort said, "The hell you will." Anderson nodded stiffly and retreated to his table.

They had been in town for nearly a fortnight. During the course of it, Lily found increasingly more opportunities to see John Anderson. It was a difficult wooing with her uncle so determined to keep the rancher away, but they met in furtive assignations that grew ever more daring until Anderson finally extended the required invitation to visit him at home. Not that he was quite so forward. He simply said he had a hound dog with pups that would surely delight Lily and he wished for her to see them. Naturally, it would have to be at night—*late* at night, after her uncle was abed. But Anderson would send his foreman to accompany her so she would be safe. At least until she arrived.

And so the foreman—a man named Stewart—arrived at the appointed hour of midnight. Lily informed him that her uncle was deeply asleep, having been aided by a draught of laudanum. They set off into the night.

Nate and the boys followed.

Lily slowed outside the big ranch house and looked about nervously.

"It is dreadfully dark, monsieur," she said.

"Mr. Anderson is right there, miss." Stewart pointed at the lit front window. "Waiting in the parlor."

She gave a sheepish smile. "I am sorry to be such a child. I have not visited a man's home without an escort." She dipped her gaze. "And I have *never* visited at night."

"There's nothing to worry about, miss. Mr. Anderson is a proper gentleman. You have my word on that."

Lily continued to stall. Nate insisted on scouting before she ventured inside. Finally, she caught sight of Nate's distant figure, poised in the side yard, gazing about, face lifting slightly to sniff the breeze. He motioned to say that he'd circled the homestead and all was well.

"I am ready to go in, monsieur," she murmured to Stewart, and he took her up to the front door.

An hour later, Anderson lay passed out on the parlor settee. He looked very peaceful, Lily thought as she knelt beside him. He would not be nearly so happy when he woke, but even without his odious reputation, Lily would not have regretted bamboozling him. Men like Anderson were no better than bunko artists themselves—seducing young women in the expectation the ruined girl would be rejected by her suitor and then she, and her inheritance, would be handed to him by parents hoping to make the best of a bad situation. It proved such men were not as worldly as they believed or they would know it was a ruse unlikely to succeed. This was not English society where one eager bride could easily be exchanged for another. Out on the frontier, a good woman was like a fine horse or pair of boots: you hoped they'd be pleasing and well-formed, but you expected they'd been used a time or two, which only saved the fuss of breaking them in.

Anderson hadn't even won a flash of bared ankle. Lily was adept at the art of the tease, a skill she'd learned as an actress. In cities, she was expected to perform in actual plays, but out in the Territories, men just came to see pretty girls in pretty dresses teasing and dancing and warbling on stage.

Other women who worked this game would be required to lie with the mark, even if she had a beau in the gang. Out here, a girl was lucky if her lover didn't toss her garter onto the poker table and give her away for a night when his luck soured. With Nate, Lily didn't need to worry about that.

Once she'd confirmed that Anderson was out cold, she dashed through the house to be sure it was empty. When she'd arrived, she had Anderson take her on a tour of his "lovely home." He'd dismissed the help, as men usually did. She still checked, in case a maid or hired hand had snuck in the back. The house was clear.

Lily brought Nate and the boys in and gave them quick instructions on where to find the best goods. Emmett and Levi needed little guidance and Will would simply follow them. The five worked together on the parlor and adjoining rooms. Then Nate told the boys he was taking Lily outside to "scout for trouble." Will looked confused. Levi smiled and shook his head. Emmett winked and told Nate to have fun. Nate grabbed a parcel he'd left by the door and off they went.

Naturally, Nate and Lily were not heading outside to scout. This, too, was part of the routine, and Emmett and Levi seemed to think it was quite reasonable that the boss would whisk his girl off mid-job for a roll in the hay barn. After all, they'd been forced to sleep apart for a fortnight now. Could anyone blame him? Well, yes, they could, but the boys never seemed to realize it was the least peculiar. With Nate, they were accustomed to peculiar.

"Did it go all right?" he asked as they slipped around the house.

Obviously it had, if Anderson was asleep and the boys were emptying the home, but Lily knew that wasn't what Nate meant. "He didn't lay a finger on me."

"Good."

As Lily walked, she unfastened her dress, keeping to the shadows of the house. That took a while, and she didn't stop moving until she had to wriggle out of it. She glanced over to see Nate watching her.

"No," she said, waggling her finger.

He growled deep in his throat. She laughed and took the parcel from his arm.

"Don't grumble," she said. "You know it's better if we wait."

Another soft growl, this one less complaint than agreement. She laughed again and tugged on her breeches, shirt, and boots. Her pistol was there, too—a little derringer that tucked neatly under a shirt or a dress.

"Did you find him?" she asked when she'd finished.

"Out back. Farthest building from the house."

She smiled. "That ought to make it easy."

Lily peered through the open window. Stewart was at his kitchen table, playing solitaire while drinking whiskey straight from the bottle.

Growing up in New Orleans, Lily had been subjected to more church-going than any child ought to be, which had much to do with her running off at fourteen. Too many gospel mill lessons pounded in with a strap. From what she'd learned there, the nature of demons was quite clear. They were hideous beasts with wings and scales and horns. They did not, in short, look like Theodore Stewart. But as she'd come to understand, most church lessons were less than useful in the real world.

Stewart was a demon. Or a half-demon, fathered by one of those unholy beasts whom, Lily was quite sure, hadn't borne scales and horns when he seduced Stewart's momma. Stewart had, however, inherited his father's pre-dilection for hell-raising, which was why they were there.

While their thieving provided a handsome income, it was merely a front. The real prize sat at that table, drinking himself to sleep. This was the world Nate had introduced her to, one filled with creatures that the church deemed "monstrous aberrations." Half-demons, witches, sorcerers, vampires, werewolves, and others. Monsters? Perhaps. Monstrous? She glanced at Nate, peering through the window, sharp gaze assessing his prey. No, not always. But they did cause trouble with somewhat more regularity than average folk, which meant there were plenty with a price on their heads, like Stewart.

Nate leaned over and whispered into her ear, so Stewart couldn't hear through the open window.

"I'll go in here. Can you take the front?"

She nodded.

"Be careful," he murmured.

She nodded again, but there was rarely any need for her to be overly cautious. While she had starred in the opening acts of this performance, Nate took that part now. Like the understudy for an actor who never took sick, Lily's new role was rather dull. In all their jobs together, only once had a mark even noticed Nate, and that was only due to an unfortunately-placed looking glass. Even then, Nate had taken their mark down before he reached the door.

Lily still undertook her role with caution, derringer in hand as she crept around the tiny house to the front door. There she found a suitably shadowy place to wait.

When she heard a faint noise to her left, she wheeled and swung her pistol up, her eyes narrowing as she strained to see—

Cold metal touched the back of her neck. "Don't move."

She calmly assessed the voice. Did it sound firm? Confident? Or did it waver slightly, suggesting a man uncomfortable with pointing a gun at a girl of twenty? And perhaps even less comfortable with the prospect of pulling the trigger.

"Lower the gun," he said.

She recognized the voice now, though the tone was not one she'd ever heard him use. She cursed herself—and Nate—under her breath.

"Will?" she said.

"I told you to lower—"

"Please don't hurt me, Will." She raised her voice a little, knowing Nate's ace hearing would pick it up. "If you want a bigger share, I'm sure we can manage it. P-please don't—"

He kicked her legs out from under her. She tried to twist as she fell, but he'd caught her by surprise. Will grabbed her gun arm. Before she could throw him off, his fingers burned so hot she gasped as agony ripped through her forearm and Will plucked the derringer from her grasp.

So Will was a fire demon, like Stewart. They'd been euchred.

"William!" a voice called from the cabin. "Bring her in."

Will grabbed Lily by the hair and dragged her to the cabin door. He pulled it open and shoved her through, his gun at her neck.

Nate and Stewart faced off inside. Nate glanced at Lily. Then he looked away.

"Seems we have your girl," Stewart said.

Nate grunted.

"William here tells me you're fond of her," Stewart continued. "That you would, I presume, not wish to see any harm befall her."

Another grunt.

"I'll take that as a yes. Now, as I'm sure you know, there's many a man who'd pay handsomely to mount Nathaniel Cooper's head on his wall. But I have a buyer who'd prefer you alive. He's quite interested in your special skills. There aren't nearly enough of your kind out here. So here's what I'll do. You come with me and we'll take the girl, too. None of my men will harm her. And, yes, I have men. Or half-men, half-demon." Stewart raised his voice. "Bob? Jesse?"

Two answering shouts came from outside. Nate took advantage of the pause to glance at Lily again. She held his gaze before he turned away.

Stewart continued, "As you see, there is little sense in running, although I'm quite certain you won't attempt it, so long as we have your pretty mate—"

Nate spun and fired . . . right at Lily's chest. She managed only a strangled gasp of shock before slumping to the floor.

Theodore Stewart stared down at the girl's body, her shirt bloody, limbs akimbo, sightless eyes staring up.

In the world of supernaturals, it was generally accepted that Nathaniel Cooper was a bastard. That was true of most of his breed—violent, unsociable loners. But even among them, Cooper was renowned as a heartless son of a whore. Still, William had said he was fond of the girl. *Very* fond of her.

Apparently, William had been mistaken.

Stewart crouched to close the girl's eyes. He ought to have foreseen this. William was but a boy and didn't understand the ways of men. And yet Stewart had still been caught unaware by Cooper's move, which was exactly what the bastard intended. He'd killed the girl and then fired off a second round at Stewart as he bolted out the door.

As Stewart rose, the door banged open and William strode in.

"You get him?" Stewart asked.

"Not yet. Jesse and Bob are tracking him. I reckoned I ought to make sure he didn't circle back and try to collect on his bounty." William walked to the girl. "Damnation. She was a pretty painted cat. I was really hoping to get a poke." He nudged the girl's arm with his boot. Then he bent and touched it. "She's still warm." His gaze traveled over the body. "You think it'd be all right if I—"

"No. Get outside and scout."

Stewart waited until William left. Then he looked down at the girl. The boy was right. She was finer than anything he'd seen in a while.

He fingered the bottom of her shirt. He wouldn't do *that*, of course. That was disgusting. But there was nothing wrong with taking a look.

Stewart unfastened her bottom button and then the next one, slowly peeling back her shirt. Out of the corner of his eyes, he caught a movement, but before he could lift his head, a hand grabbed him by the throat and threw him across the room.

Lily reflected that this was perhaps not the most opportune moment to end her performance. Yet she wasn't about to play dead while he disrobed her.

Her side blazed as she sprang to her feet. Bullets hurt, no matter how good a shot Nate was and how careful he'd been to hit her where there wasn't risk of serious injury. Her eyes stung, too, from staring at the ceiling until Stewart had done the Christian thing and closed her eyelids. She supposed she ought to have shut them herself, but she knew that open eyes would be the most damning proof of her death, and she was a fine enough actress to manage it.

Stewart was still lying on the floor, dazed, trying to figure out how he'd arrived there, clear across the room. When he saw Lily coming at him, he only gaped.

Lily yanked Stewart's gun from his holster and tossed it aside. Only then did Stewart snap out of it. He caught her by the arm, his fingers flaring red-hot, fresh pain scorching through her already-burned arm. She ignored it and grabbed him by the neck. His eyes bulged as she squeezed. They bulged even more as her hand began to change, palm roughening, nails turning into thick claws.

"You didn't expect this?" she said as she lifted him from the floor. "You *did* call me his mate."

"No. You can't be—"

"Do you smell that?" Lily turned her face, nose lifting. "I do believe we're about to have company."

The door flew open and Will stumbled in.

"Cooper," he said, panting. "It's Cooper. He's . . ."

He saw them, her hand around Stewart's throat. His mouth worked. He had one hand still on the door. Then it crashed open, sending Will scrambling out of the way as a massive wolf charged in. The beast's nostrils flared. Its gaze swung to Lily. Then, with a grunt, the beast tore after Will as he dashed for Stewart's gun, his own obviously lost.

Will made it halfway across the room before the wolf leaped on him. He hit the floor and rolled onto his back. His hands shot up, fingers blazing. The wolf's jaws swung down and ripped out his throat.

"No," Stewart whispered as Will's life's blood spurted onto the floorboards. His gaze shifted to Lily. "I have money."

"And so will we, when we collect the bounty on you."

"Whatever they said I did, it isn't true. I have enemies. Lying sons of whores—"

"A Kansas wagon train two years back," she said. "A train full of settlers massacred and left for the buzzards, after your gang had some sport with the womenfolk."

"I . . . Wagon train? No. That wasn't . . ." He trailed off. "I have money. More than any bounty—"

"I'll take the bounty," she said and snapped his neck.

"Stop grumbling," Lily said as Nate daubed her bullet wound with a wet cloth. "I told you to shoot me."

Which she had, mouthing it when he'd glanced at her during the standoff. That did not, she understood, make him feel any better about the situation.

"It passed clean through," she said. "We heal quickly. I won't want to shift for a few days, but I'll be fine otherwise."

He still grumbled. She leaned forward and brushed her lips across his forehead.

"I need to be more careful," he said.

"We both will be."

"That boy . . ." A growl as he glanced at Will's body. "I ought not to have been duped."

"We both were. We'll have a talk with Wilcox about this. He was the one who asked us to take the boy. And he was the one who set us on Stewart."

Another growl.

"We'll have satisfaction," Lily murmured. "In the meantime, presuming those half-demons were from Stewart's old gang, we ought to be able to collect bounties on them, too."

Nate grunted. The prospect, she knew, did not cheer him immediately, but it would, after she'd recovered and he'd finished chastising himself for letting them be bamboozled.

"You did well," he said as he dressed her wound.

"I've not forgotten how to act," she said with a smile. "And you gave me all the other skills I required."

It had taken work to convince him to share his curse with her. Eventually, he'd come to realize that the only way a werewolf's mate could be safe was if she was truly his mate. The process, as he'd warned, had not been easy. The life, too, was not easy. But she would never regret it. Lily knew what she wanted—the man, the life, the person she wanted to be. And she had it. All of it.

"We ought to hurry," she said. "The boys will be waiting back at the inn by now." She paused. "Do you think they heard anything before they left?"

Nate snorted.

Lily laughed. "Yes, they're not the cleverest of lads. Which is the way we like them." She got to her feet. "Let me find a clean shirt."

She looked at him, still naked after shifting back from wolf form. "And we'd best find your clothing. Although . . ." Her gaze traveled down his body. "The boys *are* very patient. I suppose they wouldn't mind waiting a mite longer."

Branded

A Darkest Powers / Darkness Rising Universe Story

THERE'S NOTHING AS BORING as civics class, and in the fortress, that's saying something. Still, monotony can be good, if the alternative is fighting for survival every second of every day until you die a horrible, violent death, your bones gnawed and sucked clean by scavengers, not all of them animal. That's the message of civics class, and students get it every six months to remind us how good we have it in the fortress. After seventeen years, I could recite it in my sleep.

As the minister droned on, Priscilla elbowed my ribs. "Braeden keeps looking at you, Rayne."

I glanced over. Braeden smiled. He mouthed something, but I didn't catch it—I was too busy looking at that sad twist of a smile. Maybe there was still time. Maybe I could—

But I couldn't. It was done.

The minister had now begun the history lesson, just in case we'd somehow forgotten how we all got here.

"The end began when the world discovered the existence of supernatural beings. Witches, sorcerers, vampires, werewolves, and others, all living among us. When they were revealed, the natural order was destroyed forever, and the very earth revolted. Famines, earthquakes, tsunamis. . . .

"Then those supernatural beings decided that infiltrating our world was not enough. They needed to infiltrate our very selves. They convinced scientists to modify ordinary humans with supernatural DNA, promising superior soldiers for our wars against those who sought to take our food supplies and our habitable land.

"And so we took refuge in our fortresses, where we continued to live as civilized beings, protected from the Outside. Yet even here, we are constantly under siege from another threat, equally dangerous: overpopulation. That is why—"

The classroom door flew open. Two regulators burst in, one armed with a cudgel; the other, a syringe.

"Braeden Smith," barked the cudgel-welding one.

Every kid surrounding Braeden stumbled over himself getting away—chairs toppling, desks scraping the wooden floor—until Braeden was alone. He rose slowly, hands instinctively going to the pockets of his grease-and-soot-streaked trousers, then thinking better of it and lifting them.

"Is this about the Fourth's horse?" he asked. "He says my father didn't shoe it properly but—"

"Braeden Smith." The regulator with the cudgel walked toward Braeden. "You are hereby charged with breaking the First Law of the fortress." The whispers and gasps of the students almost drowned out his next words. "You have been accused of having supernatural blood. Werewolf blood. You will be taken to the stocks, and watched for signs—"

"What? No! I'm not a—"

The regulator grabbed Braeden by the arm and twisted it, but Braeden broke free. He looked around, as if lost, then his gaze fell on me. He let out a snarl and flew at me. I stood my ground as Priscilla and the other girls ran, shrieking.

"You did this!" Braeden said as he charged. "You treacherous bitch!"

I made a move to dive for safety, but he grabbed me in a headlock, still ranting as I struggled. The regulator with the syringe crept up behind Braeden. As he injected him, Braeden stiffened. His hand dropped to mine. A quick squeeze. Then he hit the floor, unconscious.

———

A day later, they had their proof. Braeden had transformed into a wolf. We'd known he would. Braeden had grown up on the Outside and knew the gene ran in his family. As with most supernatural powers, it left whole generations untouched. We had hoped it would pass Braeden. It didn't.

On the day of his branding, nearly everyone in the fortress crowded into the square. I read once about hangings in the Old World, how people would watch with great delight and baskets of food. There was no joy here, certainly no feasting. We came because if we did not, then someone—a regulator, a minister, a prefect—might notice our absence and decide we were not as committed to the laws as we should be. Or, worse, that we had cause to fear the same fate for ourselves.

They'd given me a place of honor, on the raised platform with the First's and Second's families. As Priscilla clutched my hand, I noticed her mother frown, but Priscilla's chin shot up in a rare show of defiance, and she held my hand tighter. Her father noticed and nodded, first at me, then at her. She glowed at his approval.

Priscilla and I had always been schoolmates, but now that she believed I'd informed on a werewolf, I had risen to the status of friend. Friends with the Second's daughter. How my mother would laugh if she were here to see it. No, she wouldn't laugh. She'd rub her hands and plot how to use it to her advantage. That's what it was all about in the fortress—getting ahead, surviving and thriving.

For my mother, surviving had meant accepting life as a whore. It's a real job in the fortress, just like a blacksmith or a doctor or a farmer, and it's considered just as necessary for the stability of the community. She accepted it. I wouldn't. There were other ways to survive, if you were willing to take chances, including the chance that you *wouldn't* survive.

They led Braeden out. He'd been stripped to the waist, his feet bare, his trousers even filthier than they had been when the regulators had taken him in. His face was unshaven, dark shadow on his cheeks; his hair unwashed, falling over his face. Making him look like an animal. *See? This is what we saved you from.*

I looked at his chest—the lean muscles, the old scars, the healed burns— and remembered all the nights lying in our cubbyhole, touching him, whispering with him. There were new marks now, lash welts crisscrossing every inch of bare skin.

"They'll beat me, Rayne," he'd warned. "You need to be ready for that."

"I know."

I tried not to see the welts, but of course I did, and the rage built inside me until Priscilla's hand twisted in mine. I realized I was clutching too tight and loosened my grip.

Taking deep breaths, I forced myself to look at the figure on the stage and see another Braeden. To see the boy who'd been bought from the Outsiders to replace the blacksmith's dead son.

In the fortress, couples are allowed only one child. If that child dies, they can have another baby, but that isn't a solution for someone like the blacksmith, who needed a replacement for the strong, healthy ten-year-old son who'd been his apprentice.

The day that Braeden had first been brought in, everyone had found an excuse to be in the square. They'd ogled the boy, who'd looked much as he did now—barefoot and filthy. They'd whispered about his eyes, how savage he looked, how angry, how dangerous. But I hadn't seen anger—I'd seen terror.

I remembered him again, at twelve. A prefect's son and his friend had cornered me behind the schoolhouse and decided that since I was going to be a whore someday, I should be willing to take off my shirt for a credit, and if I wasn't, then they'd take it off for free. Braeden came around the corner and sent them scattering with an ease that made my weak kicks and punches look like the struggles of an infant. I'd asked him for lessons in fighting and said I'd pay. He'd said he didn't need that kind of pay and I'd lost my temper, snarling that I wasn't a whore and when I said pay, I meant credits. He'd been amused, I think. But he agreed. Only he wouldn't trade for credits—he wanted me to teach him something: how to read and write.

When they lifted the brand, I was thinking of Braeden again, at fourteen, the first time he kissed me. I tried to focus on the memory, but I could smell the fire and see the glowing metal.

"The brand is nothing," he'd said. "I've had worse burns. You know that."

I'd seen those burns. Some accidental. Some not. Mr. Smith might call

Braeden his son, but he slept in the barn and worked from sunrise to sunset, and if he didn't do a good-enough job, he'd be beaten, sometimes burned.

Yet this was different. I saw that glowing metal coming toward Braeden's back, and I had to drop Priscilla's hand before I squeezed hard enough to break bones. I gripped my legs instead, my fingers digging in.

The brand sizzled as the metal touched his back. His body convulsed. I swore I smelled the stink of burning flesh. He didn't cry out, though. They always cried out, even the grown men, sometimes dropping to their knees, howling and weeping. But after that first flinch, Braeden stood firm, gaze straight ahead, biting his lip until blood trickled down his chin.

Next the regulator pressed soot into the wound. That's when Braeden almost lost it. His eyes bulged with agony and tears streamed down his cheeks. His gaze rolled my way. His eyes met mine and he mouthed, "Just a burn," before looking away again.

"He saw you," Priscilla whispered. "He said something."

"Cursing me to a thousand hells, I'm sure," I said, my voice thick.

She put a thin arm around my shoulders. "You did the right thing. Can you imagine if no one had discovered him? A werewolf?" She shuddered. "The last one in the fortress ate three children before he was caught."

I doubted it. I'd been with Braeden when he changed to a wolf, and he'd never even nipped at me. Priscilla's story was an old one, passed down as an example of how horrible supernaturals could be and why they must be rooted out at all costs. There probably *had* been a werewolf. And children might have died in the years leading up to his discovery, but that was hardly unheard of in the fortress. Disease and death stalked the young and old here. It grew worse with every passing year, as supplies and food sources dwindled.

There were no words after the branding. The charges and the sentence had been read beforehand. Now all that remained was the final part of that sentence. The casting out.

A horse-drawn cart waited beside the stage. The regulators prodded Braeden toward it. When he gazed about, as if blinded and befuddled by pain, they gave him a tremendous shove off the stage and he hit the cart with a thud, crumpling at the bottom. A regulator jumped in after him and forced him to stand. It took a moment for Braeden to get himself steady—

there was a post in the cart, where they often had to tie the convicted to keep him upright—but Braeden managed it and stood there as he had on the stage, gaze forward, expression blank.

The crowd followed in a procession behind the cart. Now there was a little spring in their steps. This was the part they looked forward to, as they jostled and jockeyed for a spot near the front. Not to watch a convict cast out. Again, that struck a little too close to everyone's gravest fear. But they were about to see a sight they'd talk about for days. The Outside.

The cart rolled along the dusty streets, past the wooden buildings. Children too young to watch the branding leaned out the open windows. Mothers tugged at the children, but only halfheartedly. It wasn't a sight for a child, but fortress life would be better and easier if they understood the alternative.

The cart stopped at the gates, and the regulator took longer than necessary fussing with the locks, making people stamp and twitch and whisper with excitement. I pulled my gaze from Braeden's whip-striped back and looked up at the structure that kept us safe.

The walls of the fortress stretched twenty feet in the air. Our buildings might rot and list, but no expense would be spared for this wall. Voyager parties traveled for days and lost members to the hybrids and the tribes, all to bring back wood to repair the wall. Sixteen feet up there was a platform that stretched around the perimeter. Guards patrolled it at all times. One was permanently stationed at the gates, bearing one of the few guns we still had from the Old World.

As the gates began to open, Priscilla gripped my arm, her hands trembling. "Don't be afraid," she whispered. "We're safe here."

That was the point. That was what this drama was all about. As those gates swung open, there was a collective gasp. A few women who'd fought to the front now shrieked and pressed back into the crowd. Men snorted at their cowardice, but even they shrank as the gates swung open to reveal. . . .

Nothing.

That's what you saw at first. That's what was so terrifying. The gates opened and you looked out to see miles of barren, rock-strewn dirt, stretching in every direction.

The sun beat down, baking and cracking the earth. It was so bright that it took a moment for your eyes to adjust. Then you noticed the plain was not empty. Far to the left, there was a mountain, dark with trees and capped with snow. To the right rose a thin ribbon of smoke. You didn't need to wonder what was at the base. Not a bonfire—no Outsider would be so foolish as to announce his presence with that much smoke. It was a camp, now burning. Torched.

Braeden told me once about coming across a burned camp, back when he was with the tribe. They'd seen the smoke and gone to it, holding back and sending scouts until they were sure the raiding party had left. Then they'd swooped in for the scraps the raiders hadn't wanted, bits of fur or wood left unscorched. They'd ransacked the bodies, too, taking whatever they could from the corpses of those too proud or too foolish to flee when the raiders sounded their horn.

"We didn't take the bodies," Braeden had said. "Sometimes the elders argued about that. Other tribes took them. For meat."

I remembered how disgusted I'd been. I remembered how angry Braeden got.

"You don't understand what it's like out there, Rayne. You do what you have to. I really don't want to eat another person, but if it was that or starve. . . ."

He was right, of course. Later I found out that, sometimes, in the long winter, when someone died in the fortress, their body wasn't taken out to be burned. People did what they had to, and it was no different in here than it was out there.

There were piles of bones on the landscape, too. We sent out voyagers to scavenge those when one of the craftsmen needed material, but we didn't bother storing any. The piles weren't going anywhere, and space inside was already at a premium.

Off to the far left there was a body not yet reduced to bones. Carrion eaters attempted to remedy that, silently ripping flesh from the corpse. From the looks of the body, it had been a hybrid. I could no longer tell what kind. Maybe part bull or part bear or part cat. Those were common ones.

The hybrids were the end result of the overreaching ambition that began with the supernaturals. The minister taught us that supernaturals had convinced us to use their DNA, but Braeden's family told him it had been the humans' idea. They'd rounded up the supernaturals and taken that DNA. The scientists had started with careful, controlled studies, but then the wars for food and land broke out, and there wasn't time for caution.

Eventually they decided there was no need to limit themselves to creating ultrapowerful werewolf soldiers or spell-casting assassins. If they could use the DNA of supernaturals, could they use animals, too? That was near the end of the Old World, when the situation was so dire that no one cared about limits. So they created hybrids. Then the Great Storms came and the Final War came, and when it ended, the hybrids and modified supernaturals broke out of captivity and fought back. It took only a few years for the first fortress to rise, shielding a small group of uninfected humans against that endless wasteland overrun with hybrids and roving bands of survivalists.

That's where Braeden was born. Out there. When he was five, his parents had been killed by hybrids. He'd survived and been found by a tribe of wanderers. They'd taken him in—as a slave whose job was to roam from camp and attract any nearby hybrids so that his tribe could kill them for meat.

So Braeden knew the hybrids better than any fortress dweller. We were told they were just animals with humanoid features, but he said they could be as cunning as humans, setting traps and raiding camps. Some even had language. The point of the lie was to convince us they weren't human so that we wouldn't feel guilty when we slaughtered and ate them.

The hybrid rotting outside our gates hadn't accidentally perished there. I'd heard the shot two days ago. It had ventured too close to the fortress and a guard had killed it. The carcass would warn others away. To me, that proved the hybrids had some human intelligence.

When the gates opened, the regulators drove the cart through, then stopped just past the walls. By now, Braeden had recovered enough to walk on his own. Once he was out of the cart, the driver led the horses to the side, and two regulators flanked Braeden as the First stepped from the edge of the crowd and solemnly walked toward him. A young prefect followed.

The elderly First stopped in front of Braeden.

"Braeden Smith," he said in his reedy voice. "You have been found to possess werewolf blood, which has been proven to manifest itself in the form of a physical transformation. For this, you must be cast from the fortress. However, in recognition of the fact that you have been an otherwise loyal and productive member of the community—and that this curse comes through no fault of your own—this is not a sentence of execution. We hope that you will find your place in the Outside. To that end, we will provide you with the tools necessary to do so."

He motioned to the young prefect, who stepped forward and handed him a dagger, the metal flashing in the sunlight.

"A weapon for defense."

He dropped it at Braeden's feet. A small bow followed.

"A weapon for hunting."

A filled skin and a bound package.

"Water and food."

Another parcel.

"Clothing and shoes."

Finally, a bag.

"And a pack with which to carry it. You are young and strong, Braeden Smith, and I trust that you will not perish in this harsh land. Go forth with our gifts. And do not return."

Everyone waited for the inevitable final outcry from the convicted. Some attacked the First, and their exile turned into a speedy execution. Some raged and had to be forcibly dragged into the Outside. Most dropped to the First's feet, wailing and begging, promising anything, should they be permitted to stay.

Braeden bent and picked up the shoes first. He put them on. Then he stuffed the food, the waterskin, and the rest of the clothing into the pack. He slung the bow over his shoulder. When he reached for the knife, the First tensed, but he could not recoil, could not show fear. Braeden picked up the knife, thrust it into the sheath, fastened it to his belt, and hefted the pack. Then, without a glance at the First or the fortress, he began to walk into the Outside, bloody soot falling from his brand in a trail behind him.

The gates closed as soon as the cart was brought back in. I left then, mumbling apologies to Priscilla as she told me again how brave, how terribly brave, I'd been. Before I could escape, her father clamped a hand on my shoulder and said I must come to dinner soon, that the fortress needed more young women like me.

If only he knew.

I got away, then raced to the smithy. Braeden's "father" wasn't there. He hadn't gone to the ceremony, more out of shame than because he couldn't bear to watch his boy branded and cast out. I made my way through the stables, past the horses that were the fortress's most valuable commodity. That's what Mr. Smith had used to buy Braeden—a horse. The tribe wanted it because horses were the only way to cross the barren lands one step ahead of the predators, human and otherwise. As Braeden said, though, he doubted their foresight had lasted past the first harsh winter, when they'd have looked at five hundred pounds of meat and decided having a horse really wasn't that important after all.

When I ducked out the stable's back door, the smell hit me, like it always did. The dung heap. Almost as valuable as the horses themselves—or it would be, once it rotted into fertilizer for the forest garden's near-barren soil. Given the stench, this was one treasure everyone steered clear of. It was Braeden's domain, one he never argued about, because that dung heap kept everyone from discovering his cubby.

The wall was actually two layers with empty space between. In other parts, the space was used for storage. Here, because of the dung heap, it was left empty. Years ago Braeden had cut through a board behind the heap and made a narrow door. I had to twist out a nail to get the board free. Then I swung it aside and squeezed in.

There used to be straw here, covering the ground and masking some of the smell, but a drought two years ago meant Braeden couldn't afford to steal enough from the barn to replace it, so I'd brought rags instead. As for the smell, you got used to it.

On the other wall Braeden had carved out a peephole. He'd covered it with a nailed piece of old leather, in case light from inside the fortress revealed the hole at night. I pulled the leather off and peered through. Braeden was a distant dot on the horizon now. It was still daylight, and the hybrids rarely came out then, but I knew they were there, hiding in the outcroppings of rock or the rare stand of scrubby bush. Braeden knew too, and steered clear of all obstacles.

"I know how to survive out there, Rayne," he said when he came up with the plan.

"You were ten."

"But I survived. And I've been out with the voyagers. I'll be fine." He'd paused then, peering at me through the dim light in the cubby. "It's you I'm worried about."

"You've taught me well."

"I hope so," he'd whispered, and kissed me, a long, hungry kiss as we stretched out on the rags and told ourselves everything would be all right.

I stared out at his distant figure.

"Everything will be all right," I whispered. But I didn't quite believe it. I don't think either of us did.

I fell asleep in the cubby that night. I knew I shouldn't—it was risky. But I had to trust that everyone in the whores' dormitory would think I was just too upset to come back. Why did I stay? I don't know. I guess it made me feel like, if things went wrong, and Braeden came back, I'd know and I could save him from the guard's bullets. I couldn't, of course. If he returned, even pursued by a pack of hybrids, he'd be shot.

When I woke to the sound of voices, I bolted up so fast I hit the wall and froze. Then I heard another whisper—a male voice, from outside—and I scrambled over to the peephole. I couldn't see anything. It was night and pitch-black. Then, slowly, I made out figures moving along the wall. More than one. Not Braeden. I started to exhale, then stopped.

There were figures. Outside the wall. That *wasn't* a cause for relief.

I crept toward the door, to race out and warn the guards that we were under attack. Then I heard a child's voice.

"Are we going to live in there, Momma?"

"Shh!"

"But—"

A man's voice. "We will . . . if you can be quiet, child. Just for a while longer." A pause as they continued creeping along the wall, then he said, "Do you remember what we told you, child? What you need to say? It is very important."

"Yes," the girl lisped. "I am to say that I am hungry and cold, that I do not eat very much but I am a good worker, like my mother and my father. Then I am to cry. If I do not, you will pinch me."

"Only to make you cry, child. It is very important that you cry. They will not listen otherwise."

I cursed under my breath. Outsiders, coming to try to persuade the Six to let them into the fortress. It happened nearly every moon cycle. They came and they begged and they pleaded, and their cries fell on deaf ears.

It had been a generation since our fortress accepted refugees. Yet the desperate still came, only to be refused and sometimes. . . .

I shook off the thought and reached for the cubby door. It was not my business. It could not be my business.

And yet. . . .

Any other time, even the child's voice wouldn't have moved me. You learn not to be swayed by useless emotions like mercy and pity. But tonight, listening to the child, I thought of Braeden, alone out there, and I thought of the branding, and I thought of what would happen if these Outsiders approached the gate and refused to leave.

I returned to the peephole and pulled back the leather.

"You there!" I whispered.

It took a moment for me to get their attention, but when I did, they came over and gaped around, as if the very wall had spoken.

"You need to leave," I whispered. "Now."

"What?" the girl said. "We have walked—"

The woman reached out, scowling, and pulled her daughter closer. "Ignore her, child. It is only a fortress girl, not wanting to dirty her pretty town with the likes of us."

The man stepped forward. "There is no need to fear us, girl. We are hard workers, and your town needs hard workers, so you do not need to dirty and callous your pretty hands."

I looked at my already dirty and calloused hands and bit back a bitter laugh. What did they imagine when they pictured life in the fortress?

"I don't fear you," I said. "I'm trying to warn you. Whoever told you this town takes refugees has lied. It hasn't taken one in my lifetime, and it does not take kindly to those who ask."

The girl whimpered. Her mother pulled her closer, scowl deepening.

"It is you who lie, girl. We know what you fear. That we will take some of your precious milk and your honey and your fresh water. You want it all for yourself."

Milk? They'd killed the cows decades ago, when they realized the milk was no longer worth the cost of supporting them. We had goats now, but their milk was reserved for children and, on special occasions, made into cheese. As for honey, the bees had started dying almost from the start, and the few that remained were coddled like princesses, because if they perished, the crops would no longer be pollinated. We would never risk disturbing them by removing honey from their hives.

Water was another matter. We did have it. Every fortress was built around a spring, encompassing just enough land to grow crops and keep livestock and support the community forever. A noble dream. After generations, though, the water didn't flow as freely as it once did. And the land? There must have been no farmers among the early settlers, or they would have warned that you could not keep using the same land year after year and expect bountiful crops.

"We have nothing to spare," I said. "We have too many to support as it is."

We're dying. Don't you get it? We're all dying. Out there. In here. It makes no difference.

I didn't say that—I didn't want to scare the little girl—but she started to cry anyway.

"They won't take us, Momma. You promised they would—"

"They will," the woman said. "Do not listen to that foolish girl. She is greedy and wants it all to herself. Come. We will speak to the guard."

"If you try, then you are the fool," I whispered, my voice harsh, anger rising. "I only hope you are not fool enough to persist when the guard tells you to begone, or you will see your daughter's blood stain the—"

"Enough!" the man roared, and he leaped forward, challenging the very wall itself. Behind him, the little one began to sob. "You are a wicked girl, and you had best hope I do not find you when I am in there, or I shall teach you a lesson."

"Come," his wife whispered. "While the child cries. It will soften their hearts."

Nothing will soften their hearts, I wanted to rage. *You don't get it. You really don't get it. We have nothing to share. We are dying. Every third moon, the Six meet to assess the food supply and discuss new ways to decrease the population. They don't just cast out the supernaturals anymore. The smallest crime is weighed against your contribution to the community, and if the balance is not in your favor, you are exiled.*

Nothing I could say would stop them. They were determined to make a better life for their child, which only made me all the more angry, because it made me feel pity. That love of parent for child was nothing I'd ever known. My mother had cared for me, in her way, but thought more of what I could do for her, the credits I could bring if my looks blossomed while hers faded.

When she'd died three years ago, she'd been pregnant. For that, she was executed. Those in the fortress were allowed only one child, and in trying to secretly have a second, she'd committed high treason. She'd begged for mercy, pleaded and wept that she had been blinded by maternal instinct, which would have been much more touching if I hadn't known the truth—she'd promised the child to the doctor for an outrageous sum. His wife was barren, and the new population rules did not allow adoption. They'd conspired to pretend the doctor's wife was pregnant, while hiding my mother's condition. It failed. She died. A community that would kill one of its own for the crime of attempting to bear a second child was not about to admit three strangers.

I stayed where I was and strained to listen. They hadn't even reached the gate before a patrolling guard tramped over, platform boards shuddering.

"Who goes there?" the guard called.

I could hear the parents prompting the child to speak, but she was too distraught, crying loudly now.

"I asked who goes there!"

"We . . . we are refugees," the woman said. "Our tribe was raided by the Branded. We are the only survivors. We throw ourselves on your mercy and—"

The child cut in, finding her voice. "I am hungry and cold, sir. I do not eat very much, but I am a good worker, like my mother and my father." She snuffled loudly.

"There is no room for refugees here," the guard said. "Begone."

"Where?" the woman said. "There is no place for us to go."

"Find a place. Now leave."

"We'll leave," the woman said. "Just take our child. She's strong and she's healthy and she'll be no bother at all. She'll prove her worth. Just take—"

"We have more than enough children of our own. We need no extra mouths to feed. Now, begone!"

He cocked his gun, the metal clank ringing out in the silence. The woman started to wail as her husband begged the guard to take their daughter. Another guard joined the first and ordered them to leave.

"Yes, all right," the man said. "We are going, but we will leave the child."

"You will not—"

"Stay there, child," he said. "Just stay there." To his wife: "Come. We will leave. They will take her."

"No, we will not," the guard said, his voice growing louder as the parents' footsteps tramped over the hard earth. "Come back and get the child or you are leaving her for the hybrids."

The girl wailed. I heard her try to run, but her father caught her and forced her back, whispering, loud enough for the guards to hear, "You will be fine. No one would be so cruel." His voice rose another octave. "No one would be so cruel."

His footsteps retreated.

"Come back for the girl!" the guard shouted.

"You would not—"

"If I open this gate to your child, my own life is forfeit. If you do not take her, there is only one way for me to show mercy: kill her before the hybrids do."

"You would not—"

"I would! Now get back here and take your child and begone before—"

"You will not. I know you will not."

"I must! Are you a fool? A monster who would sacrifice his own child?"

The guard continued to rant, his voice growing louder, his partner joining in, entreating the parents to come back, do not do this, come back. Inside the fortress, people began to stir, doors opening, then closing quickly as they realized what was happening. Stopping up their ears because they knew what was coming. What had to come.

A shot.

A single shot, barely audible over the guard's voice, choked with rage and grief as he cursed the parents to deaths in a thousand hells. The father shrieked and raged, and his wife wailed, and they raced back to their dead child, and the guards told them no, they must go, leave her, she was gone and the scent of the blood. . . .

The parents didn't listen. I could hear them still sobbing and cursing as they carried their child's body into the wasteland.

Then, reverberating through the night air, a growl. Joined by a second. I opened the peephole to see eyes reflecting in the darkness.

"Drop the child!" the one guard shouted, his voice raw. "Drop her and run!"

The guard continued to shout as his partner tried to quiet him, to tell him it did no good. The growls continued, seeming to come from every direction. And then, as if answering some unknown signal, feet and paws thundered across the baked earth, coming from the left, from the right, too many to count.

The woman screamed. She didn't scream for long.

Growls. Snarls. Roars. The wet sound of ripping flesh.

I stumbled from the peephole, fumbled open the door, and raced back to my quarters.

For two nights, I scarcely slept, racked by nightmares of the child at the gate, the creatures beyond, those eyes, those snarls, that horrible ripping sound. I thought of that and I thought of Braeden. Out there. Alone.

"It's the smell of blood that draws them out, Rayne," he'd said.

"But the branding. There will be blood—"

"The soot does more than mark the brand. It covers the blood. As long as I take shelter at night, the only hybrids who will attack are the ones who are starving. Easily fended off with a blade."

He was right. The hybrids hadn't attacked until the child was killed. They must have heard and smelled the three refugees, but they were still human enough to have learned lessons about attacking healthy targets.

At least ones who were in groups.

Braeden was alone.

He'll be fine. He'll be fine. He'll be fine.

And if he wasn't? This fate had been chasing him from the day he began his first transformation. He couldn't have hidden that forever. Either way, he would have been cast out, and all we could do was take control of the situation. Make plans.

Plans.

The morning after Braeden was cast out, Priscilla had come to the livestock barns, where I was tending to the chickens. Except for civics class, most children stopped school as soon as they were old enough to work. My true "job" might be six months away, but that didn't mean I could laze around until then. I had chores that paid for my room and board, and I worked extra tasks for credits that could be bartered for everything from shoes to rations. These days, for most people, credits went to rations, which only drove the price higher, until it was a rare night you went to bed with a full stomach.

Priscilla had asked me to lunch in the dining hall of the Six, and I'd come away sated for the first time in memory. There'd been extra tasks I'd planned to do that afternoon, but she had wanted to spend the time with me, and I knew that was more valuable than any paper token in my pocket.

In another life, would Priscilla and I have become friends? Probably not. She was sweet and kind, but too timid by far. As hard as I struggled to remind myself that she had not chosen her place in the world, I couldn't help but feel guilty niggles of contempt when she twittered about the refugees at the gate, telling me they had escaped into the night, as her father told her.

For the next three days, I accepted all her invitations, both to meals and quiet times together. Did she see me as a friend? Perhaps. But I think, in truth, I was more of a pet. An exotic pet in a world where children made cages for mice because anything larger was a source of food, not companionship.

On the third evening, when I was supposed to meet her in the square to watch a rare dramatic performance, I did not show up. She found me in tears behind my quarters. Hearing her, I leaped up and wiped my cheeks.

"Wh-who's there?" I squinted into the twilight. "Oh, Priscilla. What are you doing—?" My eyes widened, mouth dropping open. "Oh! I was supposed to—" I looked up at the stars. "The performance. I missed it." I hurried over to her, tripping as I did. "I'm so sorry."

"What's wrong?"

"Wrong?" Another wipe of my eyes as I cleared my throat. "Nothing. I was just"—I pointed up—"admiring the night sky."

"You've been crying."

I denied it. She pushed. I continued to deny. This went on for a few minutes before I blurted, "I heard a rumor."

Thus far in our relationship, while Priscilla was the Second's daughter, she'd treated me as an equal, more recently as someone she looked up to. I was a year older. I was more mature. I was certainly more worldly. And then, of course, there was the matter of my recent estimable "bravery." When I said this, though, she pulled herself up tall and smiled, shaking her head as a mother might with her child.

"There are always rumors, Rayne. You can't pay them any mind."

"But this—this was about Braeden."

"Oh." She paused, as if uncertain how to react, then reached to grip my hands. "I know you must feel some guilt, but you shouldn't. You really and truly shouldn't. You did the right thing, and I'm sure he's fine. He grew up Outside, remember?"

"It—it's not that."

"I know it is." She enunciated each word carefully, as if I truly were a child. "You did the right thing."

"I didn't do any—" I sucked in breath. "It doesn't matter. What I heard was about the interrogation. When they forced him to transform." I paused. "Who witnesses that?"

She frowned. "Hmm?"

"When an alleged supernatural is forced to reveal his or her powers, who is there to witness it? Is one of the Six present?"

"Oh, no."

"So it's just a prefect."

"And a regulator, of course," she said.

"But no one else?"

"No. Why?"

"I heard—" I stopped myself. "Nothing. I heard nothing. I'm sorry."

I broke from her grip and fled into my quarters.

I avoided Priscilla for the next two days. It wasn't easy, but I stuck with others or in places where I knew she wouldn't follow, like the whores' quarters. Then on the second evening, I was playing ball with a group of young people in the square. Priscilla was there, watching us. Partway through the game, I started hesitating, as if overcome by my thoughts. Finally, I made my excuses and fled. She followed.

I raced behind the dining hall to a stairway that led to the wall platform. This section was blocked off—it had been unstable for years, and we couldn't yet retrieve enough material to fix it. I climbed over the barrier and ran up the stairs. At the top, I grabbed the wall and stood there, leaning out.

"No!" Priscilla shrieked.

Her dainty boots tapped across the platform as she ran.

I turned and waved her back frantically. "It's not safe!"

She kept coming. "Whatever you're thinking of, Rayne, don't do it. Please don't do it."

"Don't. . . ?" I looked down and stepped back with a wry smile. "It's twenty feet, Priss. At most, I'd twist my ankle. I wasn't going to jump." I took another step from the wall to reassure her. "I was just. . . ." I looked out at the setting sun. "Thinking, I guess. Of him. Of what I did."

I stared out until she got a little closer, then wheeled and blurted, "I didn't turn him in. Not on purpose." I took a deep breath. "Braeden and I. He was. . . ."

"Your boyfriend."

I nodded. "One night, we were out together, and he told me that there were werewolves in his family. I—I went a little crazy. We'd been together for years and he'd never said a word, and now he tells me he could turn into a wolf? That we could be alone together, and he could suddenly transform? Kill me? Eat me? He insisted it was no big deal—it might never happen. Might? Might?"

I stopped and gulped breath.

Priscilla came over and patted my back. "That must have been terrible."

I nodded. "It was. We fought. Really fought. I yelled at him and I think—" Another gulp of air. "I think someone heard. Someone told the regulators."

"But not you."

I shook my head. "No. But when they came, I didn't . . . I didn't stand up for him. I didn't defend him. I knew it was right—that he needed to be taken. To be tested."

Lies. All of it. I'd known about the werewolf blood since Braeden and I became more than friends. I had been the one who'd informed on him—as part of the plan, our plan.

"I thought—I thought he'd be fine. I told myself that he needed to know for sure. Then . . . when they said it was true—he did transform—I knew there was nothing I could do, nothing I should do. He had to leave. For the sake of everyone, he had to leave."

"Of course. A werewolf cannot be allowed—"

"But he's not a—" I clamped my hand over my mouth, eyes going wide. "I-I'm sorry. I shouldn't say anything. Just . . . just leave me, Priss. I know you mean well, but I can't involve you in this."

"What did you hear?"

"Hear?" More feigned terror and horror. "I didn't hear anything."

Once again, I let her press, and I pretended to resist until I finally blurted,

"They say he didn't transform. That the prefect lied. I overheard the regulator—the one who was with Braeden—and he said that after the last two accusations, when they didn't find anything, some of the Six were angry. They thought the prefect wasn't doing his job right. So he . . . he lied."

"But if Braeden didn't transform, he would have said something."

"Accuse a prefect of lying? What good would that do? Every accused denies they manifested powers. They're beaten for the lie, then cast out." I looked beyond the wall. "I need to get to him."

"What?"

I turned back to her. "I need to get Braeden and bring him back. I could tell what I heard, but they wouldn't believe me. I need proof. I need Braeden."

"You—you—" She sputtered for a minute, unable to find words, then took my arms again. "You'd never find him out there, Rayne."

"No, I can. I know where he'd go. We talked about that, in case something ever happened to either of us. Where we'd go. What we'd do. How we'd survive. We had a plan. It made us feel safer."

She looked confused.

"Everyone has a plan, Priss. Everyone who isn't the Second's daughter. What they'd do if they were accused of having supernatural blood. If they were accused of a crime. If they were cast out. How they'd kill themselves quickly or how they'd survive. Braeden used to live out there, and he traveled with the voyagers, so he had a good plan. He told me about a spring where I could camp and wait for a tribe to come by, then join them. That's where he'll be—until a tribe comes. Which is why I have to go now."

"Go?" Again she sputtered. "Go how? You can't go out there. You'd never survive."

"Not alone."

Her eyes shot wide. "You—you want me—"

"No, of course not. I'd never ask anyone to do that. I meant a horse. I could do it with a horse. I just need help—"

I stopped, and now it was my eyes widening in horror. "I don't mean—I shouldn't ask—I'm sorry. I just. . . ."

I turned back to the wall and looked out, pouring every ounce of despair into my expression, imagining Braeden out there, alone, waiting for me, and I never came. That must have done the trick because Priscilla reached for me. I sidestepped, then feigned a stumble and let myself collapse in a heap on the platform, tears starting to stream.

"I just—I love him so much. He's the only boy I've ever loved. The only one I will ever love."

I continued in that vein for a while. It was, in some ways, more of a struggle than the lies. It shouldn't be, because this part was true, but to pour my heart out in such melodrama felt like a mockery of the truth. I loved Braeden. I wanted to spend my life—any life—with him. But, to me, love isn't mooning and moaning—it's taking action to protect the one you love. Deed, not word. Priscilla needed words. She was still very much a child, a princess locked in a tower, dreaming of her prince. She actually did have one—she'd been betrothed to the Third's son for a decade. But he was still a gangly, pimple-faced youth of thirteen, and she was a pretty young woman noticing all the handsome young men around her, and knowing she couldn't so much as share a lingering glance with one.

She might never have read a romantic story, but she still yearned for what I had. Or a prettied-up, fantasy version of what I had, in which the young couple wouldn't set off to a harsh life together in the bleak wasteland, but would ride home, victorious and vindicated, living happily ever after within the safe bosom of the fortress.

So she promised to do whatever was in her power to make this dream come true. I argued, of course, but the more I fought, the more resolved she became. She would aid in the cause of truth and true love, whatever the cost. She would be brave, too.

Finally I agreed, on one condition.

"You must tell them I tricked you," I said.

"Tricked me?"

I nodded. "I set you up. I used you. You considered me a friend, and I abused your trust and tricked you into helping me escape with a horse. Then they cannot punish you."

"But then I won't seem brave; I'll seem a fool."

I took her hands. "Don't think of that. Remember that this might not work. I might be killed. Braeden might have already been killed. Even if we return, they might not permit him to stay."

"They will. I know they will. I heard Father telling the First how sorry he was to lose Braeden. He was strong and healthy and already a skilled blacksmith, and now another will need to be trained, and the smith is an old man. That prefect is old, too, and it is not the first time he has given my father reason to doubt his loyalty. They will exile the prefect and welcome Braeden back, and hail you as a hero." Her eyes clouded. "But I will be seen as a fool."

I told her we'd work that out, that I'd be sure to give her credit when I returned—if I returned. She wasn't happy, but she saw my point, and turned instead to excitedly planning my trip, as if I were heading off on some grand adventure.

I was leaving that night. When I told Priscilla, I panicked her a little, and I began to think I'd miscalculated, but when I said I had my bag ready, she agreed tonight was best. And it was—not giving her time to rethink everything I'd said and realize that, as stories went, it was rather ludicrous: "I think my boyfriend was wrongly accused, so I'm going to ride to near-certain death to bring him back, and hope the Six will believe a blacksmith and a future whore over a prefect and a regulator." But it was heroic and it was romantic, and that was all that mattered, so long as I didn't give her too much time to ponder it.

Getting the horses was easy. They weren't guarded—the penalty for disturbing one was exile, and you couldn't exactly ride through the fortress without anyone noticing. Or you couldn't unless you were the Second's daughter, in which case they'd notice but wouldn't dare stop you. The Six and their families were allowed to exercise the horses between their rare forays into the Outside. So too were the blacksmiths, which was how I'd learned to ride.

When Priscilla arrived at the stables, I was filling the saddlebags with goods Braeden and I had been saving for weeks. She'd brought more—as much as I had two times over, all gathered easily in the space of an hour or two.

We each selected a mount. If anyone challenged us, she would say she was treating her friend to a midnight ride, as was her prerogative.

We headed along the lane of shuttered homes to the gates. The main gates were enclosed in a courtyard, for added security from the Outside. The gates into the courtyard were simply latched. Not much need for added security from our side—no one in their right mind would sneak through.

I unlatched the gate, and Priscilla rode through first. I followed and closed it behind us. The gate guard noticed, of course, and started down from his post. Priscilla swung off her mount and raced up the stairs to meet him, breathless, as if she'd run the whole way. I moved my horse into position alongside the main gate, where I could reach the locks.

"Father needs you," Priscilla panted. "He needs every regulator he can find. It's—it's—"

The guard made her slow down. As he focused on her, I began undoing the locks.

"It's the regulator who guarded Braeden Smith," Priscilla said. "The werewolf bit him and he didn't tell anyone and now he's transforming and Father needs help—"

The regulator started down the steps again, faster now, then stopped. "The gate—"

"Father is sending someone. He says not to wait."

As the regulator raced down, I stopped working on the locks and moved the horse in front of them. He cast a quick glance my way, but didn't pause when he saw me. Everyone in the fortress knew I was the new pet of the Second's daughter. He didn't question Priscilla's words. Why would anyone lure him from his post? No one ever left the fortress. No one ever tried to sneak someone in—the fortress wasn't large enough to hide a stranger. So he saw me, gave a curt nod, and hurried off.

"Quickly!" Priscilla said as soon as he was gone. "The patrol will come soon."

I'd timed the patrols of the night guard and knew we had only a few moments before one reached the gate.

I was on the last lock when I heard the thump of boots.

"Hurry!" Priscilla whispered.

I resisted the urge to glower at her and tugged at the lock. It was sticking. It'd been the first I'd tried to undo, but when it didn't come easily, I'd moved on and now I was back to it, and it hadn't magically popped open in the interim.

I yanked at it as Priscilla urged me to hurry and the guard's boots came ever closer until—

It came free. By the time it did, my hands were shaking so badly, I could barely grab the rope to pull the door open. I fumbled, then caught it and yanked. It barely budged. Priscilla rode over and took the end from me and I held the middle and we pulled.

The gate swung open.

"Go!" Priscilla whispered.

I wasted only a moment to whisper back a thank-you. Then I rode, heels knocking my horse's flanks to spur her ever faster. I listened for the shouts of the guard or a shot from the gun, but none came. He'd still been too far away. I kept straining, but all I could hear was the thunder of hooves. Then, as I passed the first outcropping of rock, a dark shape leaped out. I passed it easily, but as I did, I heard a shriek from behind me, and turned to see Priscilla on her horse, fifty feet back.

I spurred my horse around. Another dark shape raced on all fours across the baked earth. I caught a glimpse of fur and fangs as my horse passed it, and I circled back to Priscilla.

"Ride!" I shouted. "Just ride!"

The first hybrid snarled up at me and I could see it now, a hairless, naked bearlike thing with tiny eyes and claws as long as my fingers.

I pulled something from my pocket. A hunk of dried meat, put there for just such a purpose, as Braeden had advised. I held it out. The hybrid lunged for it. I spurred my horse, meat still held out, leading the beast away from Priscilla. Then I threw the meat and jammed my heels into the horse's sides. She didn't need the encouragement—the moment I gave her rein, she was off, following Priscilla's horse across the wasteland.

I didn't stop riding until I reached the first waypoint. When Braeden and I had planned our escape, he'd mapped out every step of it for me. The first waypoint was a large outcropping of rock five miles from the fortress.

"Don't stop until you reach it," he'd said. "If you do, the hybrids will come out."

So I couldn't pause long enough to say anything to Priscilla, let alone try to send her back. We rode until I saw the outcropping, then veered toward it, my horse breathing hard now, sweat rippling down her neck.

"Leave the horse outside," Braeden had said. "She's been trained to defend herself. The hybrids will eventually work themselves up to attacking, but you'll both have time to rest."

I did as he'd instructed. Priscilla stayed mounted, waiting for me to speak. I ignored her, filled the horse's water bag, and headed into the cave-like outcropping. It was dark, but I could see a pile of brush at the mouth. Dried brush. Left for me. When I saw that, I let out a sigh of relief so hard it was more of a sob. I quickly lit the fire, then hurried into the cave. There, on the wall, he'd written with a flint rock: "Be safe." I smiled, struggling not to choke again, then quickly wiped the note off as Priscilla approached the fire at the cave's mouth.

"Rayne?" she said, her voice nearly a whisper.

"Get in here," I said. "Past the fire. Before you attract a hybrid."

"I—"

"Did you water your horse? Did you even bring water?"

"I—I did."

"Had it all planned then, did you?" I glowered at her as she carefully stepped around the tiny blaze. "Because, really, this wasn't going to be difficult enough for me. Now I have the Second's daughter to look after. What did you think you were doing?"

"Helping. You can't do this alone. Even you said—"

"If you're saying I asked—or even hinted—"

"No, you didn't, but it was the right thing to do." Her chin shot up. "I wasn't going to stay behind and pretend you tricked me. I'm tired of being treated like a fool. I can be brave, too. I just never get the chance. This is my chance."

I argued, but there was little to be done. She couldn't go back now.

"Have a drink," I said. "We can't stay here long. Now that I have the Second's daughter with me plus two horses, they'll have a search team out already."

"I . . . I didn't think about that."

I grumbled and scowled. Yes, they'd come looking, but the ground was baked hard, no tracks left behind, and it was hours until daylight. The fortress had no experience tracking people in the Outside. For a horse, they'd come. For two horses and the Second's daughter, they'd definitely come. But they'd be ill-equipped for the task. As long as we kept moving, we'd be fine. As for the part where Priscilla thought we were "rescuing" Braeden and bringing him home? That could be dealt with later.

We stopped at two more posts that night. As long as it was dark, we had to keep the horses moving fast, which meant they needed regular breaks with water. Braeden had planned for that. I found his messages at the next two posts, telling me he'd gotten at least that far. As for the rest. . . ?

At dawn I let the horses slow. Daylight would not keep all hybrids away, but now I could see them coming and kick the horses to a gallop.

Soon we came into a field of rock and upturned earth, the scars left by earthquakes a century ago. It went for miles in each direction, and we had to pick our way through it.

"This will be the most difficult part," Braeden had said. "You'll feel more secure, because you aren't on the plains, but if you feel sheltered, so does everything else. Get through it as fast as you can and back out to the plains where you can see again."

I looked around. Twisted earth and upheaved rocks turned the land here into something almost beautiful. Hills and fissures, overhanging rocks, even patches of green where the upheaval had brought underground springs closer to the surface. It smelled of water, too, a rich scent, like lush crops in the rare year when the baking sun didn't stunt their growth.

Behind me, Priscilla was lagging, and I had to keep waving for her to catch up. She was sulking because when she'd seen the greenery, with its promise of fresh water, she'd wanted to stop. I'd explained why we couldn't, but it didn't matter. She was tired and aching and wanted rest, and I wasn't giving it to her.

When I looked back again, I caught a flicker to the east, where the sun was, already so bright it hurt. I squinted and shielded my eyes. The landscape was empty. I'd seen something, though. A dark shape against the gray-and-beige rock.

As I motioned Priscilla forward, I caught another movement, almost directly to my left. A figure perched on a furrow of upturned earth. A human figure. When I turned, it dived for cover.

I frantically waved for Priscilla. She pretended not to notice me. Another figure climbed over a rock to my left. My horse whinnied and sidestepped. I jabbed my finger at the figures, but when Priscilla looked, they were gone, and she just kept trudging along.

I measured the distance between us. Too far for me to whisper a warning without the watching figures knowing they'd been spotted.

"Outsiders won't attack like hybrids," Braeden had said. "The horse is too valuable to risk killing. They'll follow you and wait until you dismount, but if they know they've been seen, they'll swoop in."

I'd stopped looking around now, but could catch glimpses of movement in every direction as our pursuers crossed the rough landscape, drawing closer. I tried to turn my horse around and go back to Priscilla, but we'd been traveling down a narrow path between a fissure and a line of rock, and while there was room to turn, my horse disagreed, whinnying and balking, hooves stamping the hard earth.

I waved for Priscilla. She pulled her horse up short and sat there, scowling.

"I can't go any faster," she called, ignoring my frantic gestures for silence. "My horse is tired and the rocks hurt his hooves and I don't understand why we can't just—"

A stone hit the ground, right at her mount's front hooves. He reared up.

"Priscilla!"

I yanked the reins, hard enough that my horse finally started to turn. Priscilla managed to stay on her mount, but one foot fell from the stirrups and she clung there, leaning over the beast, reins wrapped around her hands, eyes wide. Another rock struck near the horse's rear hooves. Then another hit his flank, hard enough that I heard the impact. The horse bucked. Priscilla flew off. The Outsiders charged, seeming to rise from behind every outcropping of rock, swarming toward us.

My horse tried to twist and run. I held the reins tight and spurred her on. I reached Priscilla before the Outsiders did. I grabbed her outstretched arms and heaved her up, nearly unseating myself. I managed to haul her on just as an Outsider leaped. He caught her foot. The horse's back hoof kicked him in the stomach, and he sailed through the air, spitting blood.

I righted myself in the saddle. We were surrounded. Eight Outsiders. All men. They were filthier than the refugees who'd come to the fortress, some wearing ragged clothing, some wearing only a loincloth, one wearing nothing but a bluish paint streaked across his body. Their hair was as long and matted as their beards. Savages, ultimately not much more civilized than the hybrids. But they were human enough to keep their gazes half-fixed on the riderless horse, now snorting and pawing the ground.

I looked for an escape route. There wasn't one, and even if they were watching the horse, making sure they didn't lose it, the other half of their attention was on us and the second horse. I pulled my dagger from my boot. One saw it and snarled. He charged, but I was already in motion, spurring my horse toward her stablemate.

"What are you—?" Priscilla began.

As we closed in on the horse, I raised my knife.

"No!" she shrieked, both hands clutching me, fingers digging into my sides.

I slashed the knife and caught the other horse in the flank. He let out a scream. Then he bolted. Seeing their prize escaping, six of the Outsiders tore after it. The oldest one shouted and snarled and waved, as if trying to call some back, but none listened.

I gave my horse full rein then, and she galloped back the way we'd come. An arrow whizzed past. A second caught the folds of my shirt. But they didn't dare risk hurting the horse—or wasting arrows—so after two shots, they settled for chasing us, howling and raging as they fell ever farther behind. Twice the horse stumbled on the rocky ground. Once, I thought she was going down, but I managed to rein her in, slowing her enough to get her footing and keep it, and we continued on through the rocky divide.

When we reached the other side, I took us a little distance out onto the plain, then stopped my horse and slid off.

"You don't need to do that," Priscilla said. "We can both ride."

I certainly was not walking so that she could ride. I resisted the urge to snap that and said, "You need to get off, too, before the horse keels over from exhaustion."

"O-out here?" She looked around. "It's not safe."

"That looks like a sheltered spot over there," I said, pointing to a pile of stone, oddly out of place in the empty plain.

It was the next stop on the mental map Braeden had given me. He'd called it something I hadn't quite understood—an Outsider term. As I drew closer, I realized it was a pile of ruins. The remains of a building from the Old World. There weren't many of them left—they'd been scavenged decades ago. But this one was a twisted mass of man-made rock and metal rods that looked as if it had been fused together in a giant oven.

"Wh-what is it?" Priscilla asked as we drew closer.

"A building from the Old World," I said. "Destroyed by some kind of bomb, I think."

"Bomb?" She said the unfamiliar word like I must have repeated Braeden's Outsider term. If you hadn't read every book in the fortress's collection a few times, there were a lot of words you wouldn't know—ones that had dropped from our vocabulary because we had no use for them. Even I wasn't sure exactly what a bomb was or whether one had done this.

I crawled through what must have been a doorway. Inside, it was hushed and cool. I picked my way through the rubble until I saw Braeden's message: "Soon." I wiped it away quickly, but there was no rush—Priscilla was still outside.

"Get in here," I said. "We need to rest, and this is safer than any pile of rock. We can stay here for a while."

She finally came in. She didn't look around, just walked straight into the main room, stretched out gingerly on the ground, and laid her head on her arm. As she rested, I continued poking about.

When I first heard the growl, I was near the back wall, in a separate room. I wheeled, ready to race back to Priscilla, but the rational part of my brain said it was only the wind whistling past. A real growl meant hybrids, and if one got anywhere near the ruins, the horse would have let us know. But when the growl came again, closely followed by Priscilla's shriek, I stumbled back to her so fast I reached the main room only to trip on the rubble and fall face-first, barely catching myself as I hit the ground.

As I lifted my head, Priscilla raced over to help me.

"It's okay," she whispered. "I think it's Braeden."

I looked up to see a massive black wolf in the doorway. Saliva dripped from its open mouth. Blue eyes held mine. Human blue eyes, one of them filmed over, as if blind.

"It's a werewolf," I whispered. "But it isn't Braeden."

"How would you know?"

I didn't answer. I'd seen Braeden in wolf form. His dark eyes stayed the same and his fur matched his hair—medium brown. This wolf was almost black, with grizzled gray around his mouth. Older. Bigger, too. A lot bigger.

"Don't break eye contact," I whispered. "We're going to back up—"

"To where?" Panic edged into her voice.

I reached out and gripped her arm, my gaze still holding the wolf's. "We'll find another way out."

There wasn't one. Not that I had seen. But she nodded and rose to her feet.

"Don't break eye—" I started.

The wolf growled, the sound reverberating through the hushed room, and Priscilla leaped up to run. The wolf lunged. I dived out of the way. Priscilla flew into the wall, as if the wolf had hit her, but he was still running. I looked up to see a man in the doorway, his hands lifted, fingers sparking.

A woman appeared behind the man, pushing past as the wolf brought Priscilla down. I started to run to Priscilla, but the first man hit me with magic, knocking me off my feet. I saw Priscilla twisting under the wolf as she tried to fight it off. The woman said something—words I didn't understand— and Priscilla stopped. Just froze.

Something hit my side. I caught a flash of fur, felt claws scrape my leg. I tried to rise, tried to drag myself away, but a second wolf had me. Still I fought. Then fangs clamped down on the back of my neck, pinning me to the ground, and I stopped struggling.

"The Branded," Priscilla whispered. "We're dead now. Worse than dead."

She moaned and huddled on the dirt floor of the hut. Our attackers had brought us there, thrown us in, and left us. It felt like half a day had passed, just sitting there in the dark, waiting, listening to Priscilla.

When the door flap opened, the sudden blast of sunlight was so strong it blinded me. I felt fingers grip my forearms. Someone yanked me to my feet. Priscilla screamed at them to leave us alone, that she was a Second's daughter, and her father would hunt them to the ends of the earth if she were harmed.

The man who held me only laughed and kicked at her when she tried to attack. Then he dragged me out, stumbling, into the bright midday sun. As he led me, I blinked hard and looked around. I'd been blindfolded when they brought us in. Now I saw that we were in a camp filled with leather tents. People milled about, mostly men, a few women, no children or elders. A raiding party. Some looked over at me as I passed. Most continued with their tasks—sharpening weapons, cooking food, tending to the small herd of horses tied nearby, my own mount now among them.

My captor said nothing, just led me along, one hand on my arm. When we reached another tent, he opened the flap and prodded me inside.

Again, I was blinded, this time by the sudden dark, and I stumbled. Fingers gripped my arms and steadied me. They pulled me inside, and the door flap closed. Then arms went around me, lips coming to mine in a deep kiss.

"You did it," Braeden whispered when he pulled back.

I blinked. There was a small lantern blazing, and after a moment, I could see him in the dim light. His cheek was cut, healing now, along with a blackened eye. I hugged him, tight and fierce, and when he stiffened a little, I remembered his back, whipped and branded. I tried to pull away, whispering an apology, but he hugged me again.

"You really did it," he whispered.

I looked up at him. "We did it."

A smile. A kiss. Then he led me to a blanket, where dried meat and water waited. I took the water first, gulping it.

"You weren't hurt?" he said.

I shook my head.

"You knew it was me, didn't you?" he said. "The wolf that took you down? I thought you would, but then I wasn't sure you did."

"I knew," I said. "I'm just a good performer." Another gulp of water. "So it worked? The Branded took you in?"

"I had to fight a few rounds to prove my worth, but they can always use werewolves, and young and healthy is even better. It doesn't hurt that they lost their blacksmith last year."

"Good. So now. . . ."

I took a deep breath. My heart hammered so hard my hands shook. Braeden squeezed them.

"It'll work. The hard part is over. Now we just need to—"

The tent flap opened, and in walked a massive man with grizzled black hair and blue eyes, one cloudy and sightless.

"So, girl," the man said. "What are we going to do with you?"

The Branded. That's what those in the fortress called them, in hushed tones with averted gazes. They might fear the hybrids and the tribes, but it was the Branded they invoked to frighten children. The greatest danger in the Outside, one the fortresses themselves created by casting out those with supernatural powers and branding them. Did they not realize that those branded outcasts would find each other? That they'd create their own tribes, more organized, more powerful, and more dangerous than anything in this barren world?

This was why I had informed on Braeden, rather than just helped him sneak over the wall. He needed that brand. While not every branded Outcast was accepted—those rejected were killed on the spot—we knew he'd be a prize recruit. As long as he bore the mark.

A mark I did not bear.

"The boy tells me you have no powers," the grizzled man said. "You're certain of that?"

"As far as I know." If I had, this would have been much simpler. I didn't say that, of course, only dropping my gaze respectfully.

"That's a shame. You would have made a good addition to our tribe."

Beside me, Braeden stiffened. "She brought you—"

I quieted him with a hand on his arm. I tried to be discreet, but the man noticed and laughed.

"He said you were a smart one," he said. "I see he's right. I'm well aware of what she brought, boy. Reminding me is not appreciated."

"I'm young and strong and healthy," I said. "I can read and write. I can cook. I can sew. I can farm. I can tend livestock. I can fight, too. With weapons or without. I can ride. I can hunt. I can slaughter and skin. I can do anything the tribe requires of me."

"*Almost* anything," Braeden said, his voice a growl as he gripped my hand.

"Put your back down, boy," the man said. "You've made the situation clear, and I don't need that reminder either."

The man circled me, his gaze critical, assessing my health, my strength.

"Anything I don't know, I can learn," I said.

"I'm sure of that. Braeden tells me this plot was your idea?"

Not entirely true, but it did me no good to be modest, so I nodded.

"I don't know what you're expecting, girl, but life here isn't going to be as easy as it was in the fortress."

"No life is easy," I said. "It's just a different kind of hard."

"True." He looked toward the door. "It's a good horse. We were hoping for two, but we can raid those that stole the other one. About the girl, though. . . . You're sure her father wants her back? She's not a son."

"Yes," I said, "But without a son, she's the only way he can hold on to power and pass it along to his kin. The First is old. He will die before next winter ends. Everyone is certain of it. He has no living child. Both the Second and Third will want the position, and they know that an alliance is the best way to solve the problem. If Priscilla marries the Third's son, both can rest assured of their legacy. They will each move up one post with the promise that the son will become First after Priscilla's father."

The grizzled man shook his head. "It's all too complicated for me. But that's the fortress way, and if you're as smart as you seem, you'd know that your gift is useless if they don't want her back."

"They will."

"You took a big risk, expecting her to follow you. Would have been easier just to take her."

"I knew she'd come, and it worked better if she thought it was her idea. Also, this way, the fortress will never know I betrayed her, so they won't have the excuse to exile my friends."

The man smiled. "Good. Loyalty is important here. All right then. We accept your gifts. Welcome to the Branded, girl. There's just one more thing we need to do. . . ."

I stood by the fire. There was no crowd here. No onlookers at all. Only those who needed to attend. Everyone else continued with their work.

It was Braeden who held the brand in the fire. The camp had been using the stable master as a smith, and the grizzled man—the camp leader—offered to have him do it, but Braeden said no. The leader seemed surprised, but I understood. Braeden didn't trust anyone else to do it right.

Braeden gave me a piece of leather to bite down on. I didn't refuse it. I couldn't start my life here screaming in agony.

"If you have to cry out, they'll understand," he whispered as he took out the brand.

"I won't." I smiled back at him. "It's only a burn."

"I wish I didn't have to—"

"I trust you."

"I mean I wish it wasn't necessary."

"It is."

He moved me into position, lying flat on my stomach, which he said would be easier. I lifted my head and looked at Priscilla's tent. If I strained, I could hear her crying. Did I feel guilty for what I'd done? Yes. Did I wish

I hadn't? No. I knew what I had to do, and I did it. Sometimes, that's the only choice you have.

Braeden lowered himself to one knee beside me, and I could feel the heat of the brand over my shoulder.

"I'm sorry," he whispered.

"I'm not," I said, and closed my eyes as the metal seared into my flesh.

THE LIST

An Otherworld Universe Story

E VERYONE STARTED LAUGHING when I walked into Miller's bar. Never a
good way to start an evening out.

Randy waved for me to ignore them and join him at his table. He had
my beer waiting. There would be a list of supplies he needed me to steal,
too, but that wouldn't come out until later in the evening. Don't ask me
where he learned such good manners. Certainly not from his half-brother,
Rudy, who was snickering and whispering behind the bar.

"Ignore them, Zoe," Randy said, popping the top from my bottle.

"What's going on?"

"You don't want to know."

Whatever it was, it was bringing a much needed air of liveliness to the
place. Miller's might not be the worst dive in Toronto, but don't tell Rudy
or he might decide he can skip the monthly cleaning.

It isn't even a bar really, just a dark cave of a room off an alley, with a
Miller's Beer sign in the window. The sign used to flash, until Rudy realized
it was attracting patrons and unplugged it.

There's no rule against outsiders, but the ambiance stops them better than
a three-hundred-pound bouncer. It's a racially-segregated club. Sorcerers,
half-demons, witches and necromancers are all welcome. As for vampires,
only one is allowed. I'd feel a lot more special about that if I wasn't the only
vampire in town.

"How's the clinic going?" I asked.

Randy made a face, which meant "the usual." Chronically under-funded and in danger of closing, which is why I stole medical supplies for him.

"I had an interesting case today," he began. "This guy—"

"Hey, Zoe!" Rudy called. "Come here. Got something to show you."

"Don't do it," Randy murmured.

I walked over to the bar, reached across and snagged a beer bottle from the ice.

"Uh-uh," Rudy said. "You haven't paid for your first one yet."

"And I don't plan to pay for this one either. So what's up?"

The guy on the stool beside me leaned over. I resisted the urge to lean back. One advantage to not breathing? You don't need to smell anything you don't want to. As for the guy's name, it was either Dennis or Mo. I'd known them both for years. Still can't tell them apart. Both on the far side of sixty. Both missing half their teeth. Both half-demons. Or so they claimed. I've never seen them demonstrate any powers beyond the ability to sleep on rotting bar-stools.

For simplicity, I usually call them both Dennis. Neither complains. Most times, they're past the stage of remembering their names anyway.

"You are not a real vampire," Dennis said.

I sighed. "This again? Fine. In the morning, I'll go drain the blood of a few virgins, okay?"

"Real vampires don't go out in the morning."

"Hey, I agreed to the slaughter of innocents. Don't push it. And don't ask me to pretend I can't see my reflection in a mirror, either, or I'll never look good enough to get those virgins back to my place."

"Can you sparkle?" someone across the room called. "I hear that's what real vampires do these days."

"Oh, I can sparkle. Just not for you."

A round of laugher. I headed back to our table.

"We got confirmation, you know," Rudy called after me.

I turned. "Confirmation of what?"

"That you're not a real vampire." He picked up a folded newspaper from the bar. "You aren't on the list."

I returned and took the paper from the bar. Two papers, actually. The first was the *Toronto Sun*, our daily tabloid. The other was an underground rag.

I read the *Sun* headline. *Researcher Claims Twenty-Four Vampires Living in Toronto.*

"Cool," I said. "Add me and we can field our own baseball team."

I skimmed the article. The researcher was an anthropologist who specialized in vampire lore—its origins and its connection to modern life. He'd compiled a list of people suffering from porphyria and deemed them "real vampires." The underground paper had reportedly found and printed his list as twenty-four vampires living in Toronto.

"It's a known medical condition," I said. "You need to drink blood and you have an aversion to sunlight, which means, when it comes to 'real' vampires, it's only half-right."

"Or maybe you're half-wrong," Dennis said.

"No, Zoe's all sorts of wrong," Rudy said. "Which is why she isn't on the list. Meaning she's not a real vampire. Meaning I win a whole lotta bets."

I flipped him the finger and took the *Sun* back to our table to finish the article.

"Hey, look, the guy's giving a lecture tomorrow at U of T," I said.

"Don't even think of going, Zoe," Randy said.

"Why would I do that? To mock the guy when he doesn't recognize a real vampire? That would be very immature."

I ripped out the article and pocketed it. Randy sighed again.

I took Brittany the Vampire Slayer to the lecture. At seventeen, she's waffling about post-secondary education, so I'm trying to convince her that university is not as boring as she thinks. And that vampire hunting really isn't a viable career goal. There are only about a dozen of us in North America. In five years, she'd have slaughtered the lot, and then what?

"I am not a vampire hunter," she grumbled as she trudged along beside me. "And why can't we take the subway?"

"Because walking is good exercise. A vampire hunter must be in excellent physical—"

"I'm not—"

"But you were. Remember how we met? You running at me with your garden stake, yelling, 'Die, bloodsucker.'"

She reddened. "That was last year, okay? I don't know why you have to keep bringing it up."

"Because it was adorable. And Brittany the Vampire Slayer rolls off the tongue much better than Brittany the Former-Vampire-Slayer-Who-Now-Just-Wants-to-Hunt-Bad-Guys-in-General."

"Not 'in general.' Not 'bad guys' either. That sounds so lame. I'm going to join the interracial council and hunt supernaturals who misuse their powers."

"See, now that's what I mean about redefining goals. That's very specific and feasible. However, working for the council is a volunteer position. You need to plan for a long-term, satisfying career."

"I could work with you. Become a thief."

"The income stream is too erratic. But if you'd find that sort of work satisfying, we could look at something in the financial sector. For starters, though, you're going to attend public lectures with me, get a feel for a university education."

"And for each lecture, I get one shopping trip."

"That was the deal."

When I met Brittany, she had little appreciation for the finer things in life, like clothing. In a year, I've weaned her out of her track pants, sneakers and hoodies. I'm very proud of that. Of course, I'm also proud of the advances she's made in stalking and fighting, under my direction, but I believe that just because a girl can kick ass, doesn't mean she shouldn't look good doing it.

The lecture was very educational. I say that with scarcely a drop of sarcasm. I'm always fascinated by vampire lore. It's like when I was a young girl in Imperial Japan and my grandfather would recount our family's storied past, as samurais and shoguns, and while we knew less than half of it was true, it was enthralling nonetheless. Vampire folklore is the same—thrilling, vaguely accurate accounts of my race's history.

Dr. Adair himself was far less interesting, as such people usually are. A round little man with a shock of white hair, his saving grace as a speaker was his passion for his subject. Even Brittany stopped squirming after a few minutes. By the end, she was so enrapt that as others rose to leave, she still sat there, leaning forward, hoping for more.

"That was actually interesting," she said as we pulled on our leather jackets. "Like history and mythology and science all mixed together."

"If you enjoyed it, I could introduce you to an anthropologist," I said. "He's a werewolf."

"Oh?" A slight arch of the brows, a blasé gesture that I'd learned, in teen body language, marked genuine interest. Brittany had never met a werewolf. They were almost as rare as vampires, and there were none living in Toronto.

"His mate's a delegate on the interracial council."

I got a "Seriously?" and a genuine grin for that. I was going to have to remember to name-drop more often. As we walked out, she checked her school calendar, to see when we might be able to squeeze in a werewolf visit. I didn't mention that her parents might not let her go off to New York State with me. She wouldn't ask; they wouldn't care.

"Miss?" called a voice as we crossed the front of the room. "Miss?"

I turned to see Dr. Adair waving me back.

"Uh-oh," Brittany whispered. "He's made you, Zoe. You're in trouble now."

I rolled my eyes, but I'll admit to a spark of concern as I walked to the podium.

"Do you know a good place to get a drink?" he asked

"Drink?"

"Oh." He flushed and looked from me to Brittany. "I'm sorry. I thought you were old enough. My mistake."

"Believe me, I'm old enough."

I glanced at the crowd of people streaming out. Seemed odd to single me out. I certainly didn't look like an alcoholic. Just your typical college-age girl. Maybe that's why he was asking—horny old guy hoping to hook up with a fan. Or maybe he really did know something and by drink he meant my kind of beverage. The red stuff.

"What sort of . . . bar are you looking for?" I asked.

He leaned over and lowered his voice. "Not one most of these folks would frequent."

I glanced at the attendees again. Lots of Goths and vampire wannabes.

"Ah," I said.

"Yes. You looked . . . normal."

Brittany choked on a laugh.

I gave him directions to a neighborhood pub that profs frequented. As I wrote it down for him, a girl in a leather corset and black lipstick started sighing impatiently.

When Brittany and I finally left, Goth Girl muttered, "Finally. Fucking mundanes. Aren't you missing *American Idol*?"

"Aren't you missing the muzzle to go with that dog collar?" Brittany shot back. "Better yet, do us all a favor and get one that covers your whole face."

I took her by the arm and steered her out as Goth Girl shouted profanities.

"Did you hear what she called us?" Brittany said. "Mundanes. Do you know what that means?"

"People who are not members of her subculture. Which we are not. Unless you want to be part of a group that thinks fishnets go with army boots."

"She's not going to leave that poor guy alone, you know," she said, as Goth Girl tagged along after Adair. "She'll be onto him like a leech for the rest of the night. We can't let that happen."

"Yes, I believe we could."

"We shouldn't. It's wrong."

I shook my head. "All right. We'll follow them as a stalking lesson. But no fighting. If she won't leave, I'll cut in and distract her, and you'll lead him away."

Brittany sighed. "You know, for a vampire, Zoe, you can be killer dull."

"So I've been told."

As we stalked Adair and Goth Girl, I pondered the political correctness of my label. Did they still refer to themselves as Goths? That seemed very 1985. I was sure the terminology had changed. I'd have to check up on that. If you're going to blithely slap labels on people, you should at least know the right one. For now, Goth Girl she was.

She wasn't pestering Dr. Adair overly much. Just walking with him, asking him questions, which he seemed happy enough to answer. There's a certain ego appeal to having someone hanging on your every word. It didn't hurt that—once you got past the bad dye job and worse fashion sense—the girl was actually cute. Not my type—I prefer blond hair and pink lipstick—but I couldn't blame Dr. Adair for enjoying her company. I had a feeling she'd be joining him for that drink. Maybe more. Whatever the end result, Brittany was getting a hunting lesson, and that was always worthwhile.

Goth Girl and Dr. Adair were heading for the parking building, where he said he needed to drop off his bag. The girl suggested a short cut, in a way that had him trotting after her.

I tugged the back of Brittany's jacket. "You're too young for that kind of lesson."

"I'm seventeen, Zoe. I know all about sex."

"Sex, yes. Screwing behind buildings with strangers, no."

"I'll stop watching when clothing starts coming off."

Considering Goth Girl was wearing a mini-skirt, the removal of clothing would not be necessary. But before I could say so, Brittany took off, creeping along as Goth Girl and Dr. Adair cut between two buildings.

"Can I ask you a question about the list?" Goth Girl's voice drifted back.

"Of course."

"Why didn't I get on it?"

"Hmm?"

"I sent you my qualifications. You rejected me."

"It's not a rejection, my dear. There are very strict criteria for the list. While there are thousands of adherents to the basic tenants of vampirism—avoiding the sun and drinking blood—the list only contains those who are medically—"

"I sent you a doctor's note."

"And I'm sure I attempted to verify it. Having met you, though, I'm happy to review—"

"I want on that list, Doctor. I'm a vampire. And I can prove it."

A shriek from Adair. Brittany was already running. I raced after her.

Goth Girl had Adair up against the wall and was going for his jugular with her fangs. Fangs that flashed silver in the moonlight.

Brittany charged and hit her in the side. Goth Girl went flying. She hit the ground and lay there, in a huddle, whimpering. I motioned for Brittany to watch her as I helped Adair to his feet. He'd slid to the ground when the girl released him and was sitting there, staring in shock. As I bent over him, Brittany turned her back on the girl. Before I could say anything, the girl yanked out a weapon from her boot. A knife.

Goth Girl leapt at Brittany. I shoved my protégé aside and told her to get Adair out of here. I kicked Goth Girl's feet from under her. She stumbled, but didn't go down. When she spun, knife out, she nearly nicked Adair. That got him moving. Got Brittany moving, too, hustling him to open ground.

Goth Girl ran at me. I waited until the last second before spinning out of the way. My jacket caught on the tip of her blade. Put a nice hole in the leather. I stopped playing then, and took her down with a high kick to the chin. Another kick sent the knife flying.

When she fell, I dropped onto her and pinned her. She snarled and thrashed and tried to bite me with a set of really awkward silver teeth.

"I hope you didn't pay much for those," I said.

"It's not fair," she howled. "I belong on that list."

"Yeah? Well, so do I." I curled back my lip and let my fangs extend. "And I've got a lot more right to be there than you."

I didn't hurt the girl. No reason to. I wasn't hungry. I gave her a stern warning about curses and revenge and the incredible psychic powers that would tell me if she spoke of this to anyone or contacted Adair again. Total bullshit, but if you're crazy enough to believe in vampires, you're crazy enough to believe that crap, too.

She ran off after that. Probably to change her panties. The smell was . . . not good. And suggested she'd had enough of unholy bloodsuckers to last her a lifetime.

Next I found Brittany with Adair and gave him a stern warning, too. If he was going to work in this field, he really needed to be more careful about following people into dark alleys. A can of pepper spray might be wise, too.

"Y-you're right," he said, as he rose unsteadily from the bench. He looked around, blinking. "Now I really need that drink. Do you know anyplace quiet? Out of the way? Where I won't bump into anyone like . . ." He shuddered. "That?"

"I know just the place," I said as I took his arm, Brittany falling in step beside me. "It's called Miller's . . ."

YOUNG BLOODS

An Otherworld Universe Story

THE MAN ON THE SUBWAY CAR was dead. He looked like he was just passed out drunk, but Roger wasn't fooled.

The dead man slumped against the window, eyes closed. His mouth hung open, one cheek damp with drool. A teenage girl started to slide in beside the dead man, then stopped, nostrils flaring as the stink of BO and booze hit her. She quickly moved on.

The man hadn't been dead long. The blood dripping down his neck still glistened. Three drops of it had fallen on his dingy white shirt, forming an ellipse. To be continued, the mark said. Fate's idea of a joke, Roger supposed.

When Roger saw the twin puncture wounds on the dead man's neck, he'd thought of finding another seat. But by then, the vampires had spotted him, and he'd had to sit down. Pretend he didn't realize the old man was dead. Pretend he didn't know they were there.

Roger never doubted that they were vampires. He knew what those neck wounds meant. Any fool should. The fact that the local media failed to draw the same conclusion about two other blood-drained corpses proved his suspicions regarding their collective IQ level.

He supposed the real question should be: How did vampires manage to drain a man's blood on the subway? A tragic reflection on modern society. The bigger tragedy was that Roger wasn't surprised.

He looked around at his fellow commuters. The teenage girl had taken a seat across the car, earbuds planted, music blasting, gaze fixed on the nothingness zooming past her window. Opposite Roger, a businesswoman's fingers flew over her cell phone keyboard. A man in a coal-gray suit was trying to catch her attention, a mission as futile as flirting with the metal pole between them. Two more men sat farther down, hidden behind their newspapers. They shared a subway car, but they might as well have been in hermetically sealed pods for all the attention they paid to their surroundings.

The only ones who were paying attention were the vampires. Two of them. Neither looked like he'd passed his twentieth birthday. Both were dressed in leather jackets, motorcycle boots, worn jeans and tattoos. Their fingernails were clean though, even their beard stubble carefully cultivated. Wannabe thugs, the kind you could find on any city street corner, attracting girls who thought they'd be a safe walk on the wild side. All bark, no bite. These boys, though, had plenty of bite.

He'd known they were the vampires the moment he'd realized what happened to the old man. It wasn't the flush of color on their pale cheeks. It wasn't even the faint smear of blood in the corner of the older one's mouth. It was the eyes of the younger. Hard, vacant, empty eyes.

The train slowed for the next stop. A transfer station. The businesswoman snapped her phone shut and walked past, giving Roger an appraising glance that earned him a glower from the would-be suitor dogging her heels. The other two men got off, too. Roger didn't. That would be the smart thing, he supposed, under the circumstances, but that would mean leaving the teenage girl alone with the vampires. So he'd stay.

As the train pulled from the station, the younger vampire said, "What are you looking at, old man?"

Roger glanced over his shoulder, thinking someone else must have gotten on.

"I mean you, old man."

He turned and met the boy's empty eyes. *Old man?* He could have laughed at that. The businesswoman certainly didn't seem to think he was old. But, he supposed, to this boy, he was.

"I asked what you're looking at."

Roger thought of saying "not much," but it didn't seem wise. Nor did denying that he'd been looking. So he murmured an apology and fixed his gaze on the dead man, then quickly shifted it to the window.

The seat beside Roger squeaked. He glanced over to see the older vampire sitting there, arms crossed, staring at him.

Roger nodded. The vampire scowled, and thumped his leg down on the seat opposite them, blocking Roger's exit and smirking a challenge. Roger nodded again and returned to gazing out the window.

"That old guy's really tired, huh?" the vampire beside him said.

Roger considered pretending not to hear him, but settled for a vague, "Hmm?"

The vampire waved at the old man slumped in his seat. "Dead to the world."

Roger managed a small laugh. "Looks that way."

"Maybe he's not sleeping."

Roger peered at the old man. "I think you're right. From the smell of him, he's passed out drunk."

The vampire caught his eye. "Should I check?"

Roger shrugged. "If you like."

The vampire didn't like that. He said nothing, though, just squirmed in his seat, glancing over and then, waiting for Roger to realize he was sitting across from a dead man.

Roger took out his calendar and flipped through it, checking his appointments for the week.

"You'd better not be planning to get off anytime soon," the vampire said.

"I'm not."

A pause, then the vampire called to his friend across the aisle. "Tasty, isn't she?"

Roger glanced over to see the younger vampire sitting beside the teenage girl. She was still staring out the window, music cranked up, oblivious.

"Very tasty." The younger vampire leaned over and inhaled. "She even smells good."

Roger returned to his calendar. Out of the corner of his eye, he watched the younger vampire poised over the girl, his gaze shunted Roger's way, waiting for a reaction. When none came, he growled and the older vampire snatched the calendar from Roger's fingers.

"You won't be needing this." He tore the book in half and dropped it on the subway floor. "Something tells me there won't be any more appointments in your future, old man."

The younger vampire laughed. The train slowed, pulling into a station.

"Actually, I believe this is my stop," Roger said, standing.

The vampire put his feet up on the seat, blocking Roger's path again. "No, I believe it isn't. You're going all the way to the end of the line, old man." He flashed a smile, fangs extending.

Roger froze. He glanced out the window and waited until the train stopped, doors opening. Then he scrambled over the blond vampire's legs. The younger vampire lunged, but Roger dodged and made it out the doors, the vampires on his heels.

As the door closed behind them, the younger vampire let out a string of curses, realizing he'd lost the girl. Roger barreled through the sleepy late-evening commuters. A guard shouted. Roger glanced over, but the man's gaze was fixed on the vampires behind him—the thugs chasing the middle-aged businessman through the station.

Roger broke into a jog and raced out the exit as the guard called for backup.

Roger made it to the road, only to find he'd exited into a section of down-town that had closed hours ago. Office buildings lined the road, only the occasional lighted window suggesting signs of life.

He looked up and down the empty street.

"No cabs out here, old man," a voice called.

He turned to see the two vampires sauntering toward him, teeth glittering under the sickly glow of the streetlights.

"No cabs, no buses, no cops . . ." the younger one said. "Guess you should have stayed on the subway. Let me finish the girl. Maybe I'd have let you go. Now I'm hungry. And the more you make me run, the hungrier I'm going to get."

Roger took off.

After ten minutes of running, Roger began to reflect that he really needed to add a workout routine to his daily schedule. Seemed those boys were right. He really was getting old.

He veered down another back road. His shoes thumped against the pavement, as loud as a locomotive chugging along the tracks, the sound echoing through the emptiness.

That was the only sound he heard, though. Had he lost them? He turned into an alley, gaze fixed over his shoulder, watching and listening for—

A thump in front of him. He spun to see the older vampire standing there, the fire escape overhead still vibrating from his leap.

"Gotcha," the vampire said, flashing his fangs.

"Actually, no. To get me, you needed to jump down after I passed you and found myself trapped in a dead-end alley."

The vampire frowned, momentarily thrown. He recovered with a grin. "Maybe I don't want to trap you. Maybe I like running."

"True, but I don't. Getting old, as you so graciously pointed out. Which is why I appreciate what you've done—trapping *yourself* between me and that dead end."

Roger smiled. A wide, teeth-baring smile.

The vampire blinked. "What the—?"

He didn't get a chance to finish the sentence.

Roger crouched on the fire escape. He could hear the younger vampire stomping along the empty street, calling to his buddy, his tone taking on a crackly edge of worry.

Roger stomped on the fire escape floor. The metal twanged, and the boy raced into the alley, then stopped and looked around.

"Tim?" he said.

Roger dropped from the fire escape. He didn't thump when he hit the pavement. You don't reach his age by being noisy and careless.

"Tim?" the boy called, louder.

"Over there," Roger said.

The boy whirled, stumbling. Seeing Roger, he tried to find a suitably menacing glower, but couldn't quite manage it.

"Over there." Roger pointed at the trash bags littering the end of the alley. A boot stuck out from behind one. "And over there." He pointed to a lock of blond hair peeking from behind another. "I think there's part of a hand over there, too, but that was an accident. Getting old. The reflexes are the first thing to go."

The boy looked from body part to body part, then turned to stare at Roger.

"You know what else happens when you get old?" Roger continued. "You get comfortable. Set in your ways. You find a city like this." He waved around them. "You settle in. You make it your own. And you really, really hate it when some young bloods waltz in and crap all over the place." He ran his tongue over his teeth, letting his fangs extend. "It's very inconvenient."

The boy backed up. "I—I didn't know . . ."

"But you should. It's basic respect. You don't have it and, I'm sorry to say, it doesn't look like anything you're capable of learning. Now I need to clean up the mess you made."

The boy bolted. He managed to dodge Roger and raced onto the road. But he didn't get far.

Roger was finishing up when his cell phone rang. He checked the call display. Leslie.

"Please tell me you're on your way," she said when he answered.

"On my way. . . ?"

"To Fresno's? For drinks? At eleven?"

He swore.

"Forgot, didn't you?" she said with a chuckle. "You're getting old, Roger."

"So I've been told." He sighed and finished tucking the young vampire's body behind the trash bags. "So I've been told."

The Door

H ER EARLIEST MEMORY was of the door.

She'd woken in the night, hearing a noise, and padded into her parents' room to see her mother sound asleep. Then the noise came again, a bang from the front of the house. From beyond the door.

She crept down the hall, through the living room and into the kitchen. The door was there. She inched closer, barely daring to breathe.

What if it opened?

What if something was on the other side trying to get in. Some monster from her fairy-tale books. An ogre or a troll or a wicked witch.

The house was so silent she could still hear her mother breathing. Then the noise came again.

She swallowed and wrapped her arms around herself.

Something *was* there. Beyond the door.

She was not supposed to open the door. That was the rule. The only real rule she'd ever known. Do not open the door. Never open the door.

But if a monster was out there . . .

She had to peek. Just a peek to be sure before she ran and woke her mother.

She slid toward the door, one stockinged foot and then the other, making as little noise as possible. Then she gripped the knob and turned.

The door opened easily. On the other side . . . Well, she knew what was *right* on the other side, because she'd caught glimpses before. It was a tiny room with boots and shoes and other stored items. And a second door. When Momma or Daddy went out, they'd go through the first one, and then they'd close it before she'd hear them open the other. That was the real door. The one that led to terrible things, and she had no idea what those things were, nor had her parents even said they were terrible, but she knew. She just knew.

The noise came again and she struggled for breath and then continued her sliding walk toward that second door—

It opened and a figure filled it. A huge figure carrying a huge bag, and she had one brief flash of all the monsters it could be—all the trolls and the ogres—and then she heard, "Oh! What are you—?" and it was her father's voice, and he hurried in and quickly shut the door and put down the bag before scooping her up. "What are you doing here, sweetheart? You know you aren't supposed to open the door."

"I heard a noise."

"Ah, well, that would be me, very happy to be home. I didn't mean to get in so late. But I brought you treats. Lots of treats."

With the bag dragging from his other hand, he carried her through the inner door and kicked it shut behind them. Then he set her on the table and opened the sack. Inside she saw food. He dug down and pulled out a long box covered in bright pictures.

"Do you know what this is?" he asked.

She shook her head.

"Candy Land. It was my first game when I was your age. Now it's yours. And to go with it . . ." He dug deeper and pulled out something that made her squeal, and he chuckled and handed her the red lollipop. "Candy Land and candy. The perfect match. And books, too. I brought lots of books. Now, let's find one, and we'll read it while you eat that lollipop, and then you'll be ready to go back to bed. We have a big day tomorrow, putting away all the food. I have more on a wagon outside. I'll bring it all in while you find a book you like."

———

That was her first memory. Her first game, too. The first of many. Many games and many days spent playing them, the three of them. Even more than the games, her father brought books. He'd read them to her or her mother would, and soon, she could read them to herself, at least the easy ones.

There were toys, too. Action figures and stuffed animals and building blocks, and she'd act out the scenes from the books, sometimes by herself, sometimes for her parents.

Her mother would tease that Daddy brought back more books than food. Once, when she was supposed to be asleep, she heard Momma doing more than teasing about it, talking to her father in a low, anxious voice.

"She doesn't need so much. The toys, the books, the games. Not if it means you have to stay out there longer."

"I'm fine," he said. "And if it makes her happy, it makes me happy."

They were happy. Just the three of them, in their house. There was a yard, too. In books, every house had a yard, and theirs was no different. A backyard with a swing and a slide and grass and a fence, and she was not supposed to climb the fence, but she could lean against it and gaze out at the endless blue sky, the sun shining down from above.

Then, when she was old enough to read all the books, she got a surprise. They all got a surprise, or so it seemed from her parents' whispered conversations. A baby. A girl. A little sister. Then it was the four of them, and it was as if everything started over again. Out came the baby books, with her reading them to her sister, and then Candy Land, pulled up from under the house where they'd stored it.

Some of the old toys and games and books—the ones she'd outgrown— would go away with Daddy, but the ones she couldn't bear to part with were still there, in the storage space under the house and, later, piled up outside along the fence. She remembered once, after reading about a storm, her sister had panicked on seeing the piles of books and games along the fence.

"We have to bring them in!" she said. "They'll get wet when it rains."

She'd laughed at that, laughed and scooped her sister up. "Have you ever actually seen it rain, silly?"

"Well, no, but it must, right? When we sleep?"

She shook her head. "Rain is only in books. Like snow and storms and polar bears. Now, speaking of polar bears, there's a book over here that I think you'll like . . ."

It was not long after that that Daddy got sick. The arguments, still quiet ones, held behind their parents' closed bedroom door happened more often.

"I'll go out instead now," their mother said. "It's my turn. You're sick and—"

"—and I will not get any less sick by staying indoors. I'll do it for as long as I'm able, gather as much as I can, while I can. You'll need to go out soon enough."

Momma cried at that. Cried so softly that she had to put her head against the door to hear the quiet sobs and their father's equally quiet voice, soothing her, calming her, until the bed creaked and there were more whispers and sighs and then all went quiet.

Their father did not go out for as long after that. Short trips, but more of them, until the space under the house was teeming with more food than she'd ever seen. And then he could not go out, could barely leave the couch, and they'd take turns sitting with him and reading to him, or just playing and reading in the same room until, one morning, he did not wake up.

"But we'll see him again, won't we?" she said to their mother, after the days of crying, of grief. "That's what the books say. That we'll see him when we go wherever he is."

"That sounds about right," their mother said and hugged her hard.

Time passed. Their mother went out now, often for days on end, and despite what she'd said about their father bringing back too many books and games and toys, she did the same.

Her sister was old enough to read all the books when their mother took ill. It was as it had been with their father, a slow progression of wasting, with more frequent but shorter trips out as she filled the stockpile below the house.

When their mother became too sick to leave her bed, she stayed with her, bringing food and books and games. Then came the night when their mother woke her and motioned not to wake her sister, sound asleep on the other side of the bed.

"I have one more book for you to read," Momma said, her voice a papery whisper, so soft that she had to bend to hear her.

Momma pressed a thin leather journal into her hands. "I wrote this for you. It explains everything—what happened here, what you'll need to do, how to get food and water." Momma took her hands and wrapped them around the book. "You will need to make a decision when you read it. What to do about the door. For your sister."

She nodded.

"Your father did all this for you," Momma said. "He loved you so much. We both did." A moment's pause and then, "Were you happy?"

She frowned, not understanding the question.

"Were you happy? Here? Like this?"

"Of course."

Momma took her face in her hands and kissed her forehead, her lips so light she barely felt them. "I hope you still can be. I hope you both always can be. We were. In spite of everything."

Momma lay down and rested and then, as dawn's light slipped into the room, she gave a long rattling sigh, and her chest stopped rising and stopped falling.

She leaned over their mother and kissed her cheek. Then she carried her sister into the living room and put her on the couch. Once her sister was tucked in, she retrieved the book from her mother's bedside and headed for the kitchen.

The door.

She'd not seen it in so long. The inner one would open and close, and she would not even bother trying to peek through anymore. She didn't care what was out there.

Yet now . . .

She looked down at the book. She could read it first. Get answers that way. But she set it on the kitchen table and walked to the door instead. She opened the inner one. Then she moved through the tiny room that still held their father's shoes and jacket.

There was a lock on the outer door, up high where the children could not reach it. But she wasn't a child anymore, and when she stood on her tiptoes, she could turn it easily. She did, and she pulled open the door and stepped out.

Light. That was the first thing she saw, and it was all she saw, the light so bright it hurt and she doubled over, shielding her eyes. At first it seemed to come from everywhere. As her eyes slowly adjusted, she realized that the light came from an opening nearly as tall as her. She could see nothing except that opening. She walked toward it and ducked and went through it and—

Her stockinged toes touched down on nothing, and she pulled back quickly. She put her hands over her eyes to block the light, and then peered through her fingers. She saw . . . sky. That was all. Sky. Except it didn't look like the sky behind the house. This blue was pale, almost white, and the clouds moved. She blinked hard and stepped back, and when she did, her gaze dropped and she saw a city.

She knew it was a city from pictures in her books. A city below, sprawled out beyond the forest.

A dead city.

That was the phrase that sprang to her mind. She didn't know from where until a memory flashed, of her father speaking to her mother long ago.

"It's a dead city now," he'd said. "Everyone who could leave is gone. Everyone who stayed . . . The radiation . . ."

"Is it safe to even be going there?"

"Do we have a choice?"

She could only vaguely recall reading about radiation in a book and knew nothing more about it. Her mother's journal would explain. For now, she understood this—that the food and water they needed to survive was out there, where it wasn't safe, but there was nothing they could do about that except not eat, not drink.

Her eyes had adjusted enough that she could look around and when she did, she saw that she was standing in the mouth of a cave high above the city. A cave in a mountainside.

She looked behind her, and there was their house. Built inside a cave. She walked back through the hole, exhaling in relief as the light dimmed and she could see better.

She looked at the walls, painted bright blue. Her sky. She glanced down to see the green underfoot, not like the green beyond the cave's mouth at all, but short and prickly and never growing any longer. Her grass. Her gaze turned up to see a hole in the roof of the cave, with light streaming through. Her sun.

She heard a click and then the padding of feet in the small room and a voice calling her name. With a gasp, she raced to the door and through it, and scooped up her sister as she pulled the door shut behind her.

"And what are you doing, missy? You know you aren't supposed to open the door."

"I heard a noise. And Momma won't wake up."

Grief surged as she buried her face in her little sister's hair. "I know. We'll talk about that. First, though, don't ever open the door. There's no reason to. Everything you need is in here."

And with that, she made her decision. Without even considering an alternate choice, she made it.

She put her sister down and prodded her into the kitchen. "Let's go play a game. Maybe Candy Land. I know it's a baby game, but I feel like playing it today. Later, we'll have breakfast and talk about Momma. In a few days, I'll need to go out, like Momma and Daddy did. But not yet. Not just yet."

She stepped into the tiny room and locked the outer door. Then she walked into the kitchen, shut the inner door firmly behind her and went to play Candy Land with her sister.

Dead Flowers by a Roadside

THE HOUSE IS DAMNABLY SILENT.

I sit in the middle of the living room, furniture shoved out of the way, one chair tipped over where it fell, pushed too hard in my haste. Shards from a broken vase litter the floor. One is inches from my hand.

Amy would panic if she saw it. I close my eyes and imagine it. Her gasp from the doorway. The patter of her stockinged feet. The soft click of the piece against the hardwood as she snatches it up. Her voice as she tells me not to move, she'll clean the mess, I need to be more careful—really, I need to be more careful. What if I'd cut myself? What if Clara had run in?

In my mind, her voice is not quite right. The cadence, the tone are fading already. Amy's voice. Clara's voice. How much longer before they slide from memory altogether? Before I'm reduced to playing old videos that don't sound like them, not really, and telling myself they do, just so I can still hear their voices in my head.

I open my eyes and look at the ancient book lying open in front of me. Spidery writing, water-smeared ink, barely legible. The air smells faintly of acacia. That's critical, the book says. The dead will not speak without the scent of acacia to pull them through the ether.

Not true.

I know it is not true because I have seen the dead. Heard the dead. All my life they've been there, flitting past, whispering in my ear. Never once have they needed acacia.

Yet for three months, I've been trying to contact them. My wife. My child. I beg, I plead, I rage and shout for a sign, any sign. Comfort, any comfort. In desperation I turn to the books, to the acacia. But I hear only silence. Damnable silence.

I look down at the shard of glass by my hand.

Daydreaming again, weren't you? Amy laughs. *Always dreaming. Always distracted. One of these days, you're going to hurt yourself.*

I run my finger along the edge of the shard. As sharp as her ceramic knives, the ones I bought for her birthday, kept in the cupboard so Clara wouldn't mistake the white blades for plastic.

And don't you use them either, she'd said to me. *Please.*

Worried about me. About us. That was her nature. Double-checking door locks. Double-checking the stove. Double-checking Clara's car seat. Even if she'd done it herself, she always double-checked. If Clara or I so much as stubbed our toes and yelped, Amy would come running.

She'd always come running.

I take the shard, pinch it tight between thumb and forefinger. Drag the edge along my arm. Blood wells up.

"Amy?"

I cut deeper. Blood drips onto the dirty pages of the useless book.

"Amy? I need you."

Damnable silence. Always silence.

Crouched at their graves. Talking until I realize I'm only speaking to fill the silence, and I stop. I touch the marble. Cold. Always cold, even now with the late winter sun beating down.

No flowers. I took them away as soon as they started to wither. Dead flowers by a grave seems wrong. Left and forgotten. Nothing here should be forgotten.

I bring new mementos every week. Something small. Something meaningful. A franc from our honeymoon. A seashell from our last vacation. A button from Clara's first communion dress. A cat's-eye marble from Amy's childhood collection. Indestructible. As memories should be.

I come here twice a week to talk to them. I know they won't hear me, but I hope others will. Other ghosts. I can see them flitting past the graves. Wandering, endlessly wandering, looking for someone to take their message to the world beyond.

That someone used to be me. I couldn't set foot in a cemetery without being besieged by the dead. Now they give me wide berth. They know I come with a plea of my own. Find my wife. Find my daughter. Tell them I need to see them. Need to speak to them.

I want something from the ghosts, so they'll have nothing to do with me. I sit here and I talk to my wife and child, and I pray my words will thaw the hearts of those shades. I pray one will finally approach and say "I'll do this." They don't. They keep their distance and they wander in silence. Always silence.

The doorbell rings. I hear it through the garage walls. Someone on the front porch. Someone come to call. I ignore it and keep working on the car.

Three months, and it's almost finished. The windshield replaced. The engine repaired. The dents pulled out.

There's one thing I can't fix. The blood on the passenger's seat. No longer red. Faded to rust brown. But still blood. Undeniably blood.

The insurance company didn't want me to have the car. Too badly damaged, they said. We've paid you, now let us dispose of it. I'd pulled out my contract and showed them the clause where I could buy back the wreck for a few hundred dollars. At least let us remove the seat, they said. No one needs to see that. But I do.

"Hello!" a voice calls.

I stay crouched by the front of the car, replacing the cracked headlight. The door opens.

"Hello?"

It isn't anyone I know. I can tell by the voice. I consider staying where I am, but that's childish. I stand and wipe my hands on my jeans.

"Can I help you?"

It's a portly man, smiling that desperate, too-hearty smile of the salesman. I let him talk. I have no idea what he's saying, what he's selling. Just words, fluttering past.

"I'm not interested," I say.

He sizes me up. I wonder how I look to him. Unshaven. Bleary-eyed. Worn blue jeans. Grease-stained T-shirt. A drunk? An addict? Can't hold a job? Explains why I'd be home in the middle of the day. Still, it's a decent house, and he's desperate.

He sidles around the front of the vehicle.

"Nice car," he says.

It isn't. Even before the accident, it was a serviceable car, nothing more. Amy had wanted something newer.

Not fancier, she said. *Just safer, you know. For Clara.*

I hear BMWs *are safe,* I said. *You're a lawyer's wife now, not a law student's. You need a BMW.*

She laughed at that. Said I could buy her one when I made partner. I played along, but secretly made phone calls, visited dealers, planned to buy her a BMW or a Mercedes, whichever would make her feel safer. It was to be a Christmas gift.

Christmas.

That's what we'd been doing three months ago. Christmas shopping. The mall busy, the shoppers cranky, we'd left later than we expected, past dark. Cars were still streaming into the lot, circling for spots. A woman saw me putting bags in our trunk. She asked if we were leaving and I said we were. When I got in the car, Amy was still standing by the open rear door, trying to cheer up Clara, fussing, her nap missed.

Hon, there's a lady waiting for our spot.

Whoops. Sorry.

She fastened Clara's chair and climbed into the passenger seat. I started backing out.

*Wait! I need to double-check the—*She glanced back at the car waiting for our spot. *Never mind. I'm sure it's fine.*

"You restoring it?" the salesman's voice jerks me from the memory and

I glower at him. I don't mean to. But for a second, I'd heard Amy's voice, clearly heard it. Now it was gone.

"Yes," I say. "I'm restoring it."

"Huh."

He struggles for a way to prolong the conversation. I bend and continue tinkering with the light. He stands there a moment. Then the silence becomes too much and he leaves.

A week later, the car is roadworthy. Barely. But it will make it where I want to go, all the bits and pieces intact, no chance of being pulled over.

The roadside.

I pull to the shoulder. It's dark here, just outside the city. An empty snow-laced cornfield to my right, a bare strip of two-lane highway to my left. In front of the car, a crooked cross covered in dead flowers. More dead flowers stuck in a toppled tin can. I didn't put them there. I don't know who did. Strangers, I suppose. Heard of the tragedy and wanted to mark the place. I'd rather they hadn't.

I didn't need that wretched memorial to remind me where it happened. I would know the exact spot without any marker, the image burned into my memory.

Coming back from Christmas shopping. Dark country road. The car quiet. A good silence. A peaceful silence. Clara asleep, Amy and me being careful not to wake her. Snow falling. First snow. Amy smiling as she watches the flakes dance past.

A pickup ahead of us. A renovation company. Boards and poles and a ladder piled haphazardly in the back.

Oh, Amy said. *That doesn't look safe. Could you. . . ?*

My foot was already off the gas, our car falling behind the truck until all we could see was its rear lights through the swirling snow.

She smiled. *Thanks.*

I know the drill.

She reached over to squeeze my leg, then settled back to snow-watching silence.

Another mile. I'd crept up on the truck, but was still far enough back, and she said nothing. Then I saw it. A figure walking down the other side of the road. A woman in a long, red jacket.

I looked over. Ghost, I told myself, and I was quite certain it was, but I'd hate to be wrong and leave someone stranded. I squinted through the side window as we passed and—

Watch—!

That was all she said. My head whipped forward. I saw the ladder fly at us. I swerved to avoid it. The car slid, the road wet with snow. An oncoming car. I saw the lights. I heard the crunch of impact. Then . . . silence.

Now, three months later, I sit by the side of the road and I hear her voice.

Always dreaming. Always distracted. One of these days, you're going to hurt yourself.

Yes, I hurt myself. More than I could have ever imagined possible.

I get out of the car. The tube is in the trunk. I fit it over the exhaust pipe, and run it through the passenger window. Then I get inside and start the engine.

Does it take long? I don't know. I'm lost in the silence. There's a momentary break as a car slows beside me. The driver peers in, thinks I'm dozing, revs the engine, keeps going. The silence returns. Then I begin to drift . . .

I wake up. The car has stopped running. I check the fuel gauge. Half-full. I try to start the car, but the engine won't turn over. I slump onto the dashboard, defeated.

Then I hear . . . something. A bird call? I look out the windshield. Fog, so thick I can't see anything else.

I get out of the car. The hinges squeak. I leave the door open behind me and walk around the front. The memorial cross is there, but it's been replaced, the flowers fresh and white, the can beneath them upright and filled with daisies.

Clara loves daisies. I smile in spite of myself and walk to the flowers. More scattered around it. Still more trailing off toward the field.

As I follow them, I stumble through the fog. That's all there is. Fog.

Rolling across the field. I look down at the flowers, crushing beneath my feet. I keep going, following them.

Another noise. Not a bird call. It sounds like . . .

"Amy?" I call. "Clara?"

A voice answers. Then another.

The silence ends.

Suffer the Children

Addie

Addie slid through the forest as silent as a lynx, her beaded moccasins muffling her footfalls. The young stag wasn't as quiet. When it vanished from sight, she could track it by the crackle of autumn leaves under its hooves. Finally, it stopped to feed and she closed the gap between them until she could see it, small antlers lowered as it tugged at a patch of grass not yet brown and withered.

Addie eased the bow from her back, notched an arrow, and took aim. The buck's head jerked up. She loosed the arrow, but it was too late—the buck was in flight. Addie fired a second but too quickly, spurred by frustration and anger, the arrow lodging in a nearby maple.

When the crash of the fleeing deer subsided, she peered around the dawn-lit forest. Something had startled the beast and it hadn't been her. She would never have been so careless.

Addie pulled her coat tighter against the chill. The jacket was too small for her now—she'd grown nearly a half foot in the past year—but she refused to let Preacher and Sophia buy one from the traders. She wanted to make one exactly the same way, doing everything from killing the deer and mink to curing the leather to sewing the cloth. There was not another twelve-year-old in Chestnut Hill who could claim the same. Not a *girl* of any age. Her parents may not have given her much, but they'd taught her to look after herself.

They'd also taught her—unintentionally—how to sense danger. So now, after the buck had bolted, she went still and listened. She paid particular attention to noises from the north, upwind of the deer, presuming it was a scent that had startled it. After a few moments, she heard the tramp of boots on a well-packed path.

Addie eased her bow onto her shoulder and pulled her skinning knife from its sheath. Then she slunk soundlessly through the woods. She knew exactly where to go—there was only one trodden path in the area, used by the villagers to get to the lake. When she was near enough to see figures, she crouched behind a low bush.

It was two men. One was middle-aged, perhaps thirty, the other so ancient that even with a cane and the younger man's arm, he shuffled along. Neither was from the village. A hundred people lived in Chestnut Hill and Addie knew every one. The only travelers they saw were trappers and traders, and precious few of either so deep in the forest, three days' ride from Toronto. These men were neither traders nor trappers. Settlers, then? Lured north by the promise of land or work on the railroad or in the mines? Settlers needed supplies, though, and these men carried only packs on their backs. No wagon. No cart. Not even horses.

And where had they come from? The road lay on the other side. The men headed toward town on a path that only led from the lake. Trappers did come through the forest, but she saw no sign of such gear on these men. They hadn't come *across* the lake—it was too small, with no settlements nearby save Chestnut Hill.

Addie slipped through the forest to get a closer look. Both men had short hair and neatly trimmed beards. Though they wore long coats, she could see their clothing underneath. White shirts and black trousers. They looked as if they were heading to church.

Missionaries. Perhaps they'd been traveling on foot from Greenville, ten miles away, and gotten lost in the forest, taking the first well-trodden path they saw. It didn't matter *where* they had come from, only that they were heading to Chestnut Hill.

How would Preacher feel about other men of faith in his town? She ought to warn him. With any luck, they'd just be passing through. Chestnut Hill might not even allow them to stay, given that it still reeled from the tragedy that had Addie out in the woods, avoiding the glowers and glares of villagers, blaming her for the simple fact that she lived. That she'd survived.

She was about to start back when the younger man looked straight at her. She froze, telling herself she was mistaken; there was no way he could have heard her, no way he could see her now, dressed in brown behind the dying leaves of a cranberry bush. But he didn't simply glance her way. His eyes bore straight into hers, and when they did, she swore her heart stopped.

"You there," he called. "Girl."

How could he tell she was a girl? She was dressed as a boy, in trousers, her dark hair pulled back.

"Girl," he called again. "We're heading to Chestnut Hill. Is this the way?"

Her parents had taught her to look after herself because no one else would do it for her. She knew now they'd been wrong—and so she did try to be kind, to be helpful as Preacher and Sophia counseled. Yet even as she spurred herself to step from behind the bush and lead this man to Chestnut Hill, she looked into his eyes and she could not move, could not speak.

The man released his grip on his elder's arm and started toward her.

"We're here to help, child," he said, his voice low and soothing, like Preacher coaxing Sophia's cat from under the porch. "We know what Chestnut Hill has suffered and we wish to—"

Addie bolted from her hiding place, running back toward the village like she had a black bear on her tail.

PREACHER

Preacher was taking confession behind the village outhouse. As the wind sliced through the weathered boards, bringing a blast of the stench from within, he reflected that this might not be the place to conduct such a holy endeavor.

He also reflected that it was rather a fitting choice, given the astounding inappropriateness of the entire situation. He was as suited to the position as the location was to the task.

He'd come to Chestnut Hill to teach, along with his wife, Sophia. They'd been doing so in Toronto together, and when this offer came, Sophia begged him to consider it. They'd been wed six years, and she had yet to conceive, a situation that bothered her far more than it did him. She'd begun to wonder if it was the noisy and noisome city affecting her health. The job in Chestnut Hill seemed the best way to test such a theory. Preacher didn't care much where they lived, as long as she was happy, and off they went.

They'd arrived in Chestnut Hill to find the local priest had been taken by the same influenza as the schoolteacher. So the council had made a decision. Two teachers was a luxury, one they were willing to bestow on their beloved children, but it seemed equally important that they be reared as proper Christians. Sophia would teach and her husband would take the priest's place.

Preacher had argued most strenuously against this arrangement. He was not a man of the cloth. That was all right, the council had replied—they'd never really wanted a papist anyhow and the good father had simply been the only man who'd take the position. Preacher could obviously read the Bible. That was enough.

It was not enough. He knew that, felt the deception in his gut every day. He was not a God-fearing man. He wasn't even a God-loving man. Sophia was the churchgoer, though he'd attended when he could, to please her. She'd offered to take the position instead, but the council had been aghast at the suggestion. Men taught the word of God. Even, it seemed, wholly unsuitable men.

So, from that moment on, he was Preacher. Despite his best efforts to retain his name, only Sophia called him Benjamin. To everyone else, he was Preacher. The false servant of God.

Now he sat straddling a wooden bench, his back to old Millie Prior, listening to a litany of offenses too trivial to be called sins, as he tried not to inhale the stench of the outhouse. As for why he held confession here, it was the village's decision—not a commentary on his ability but based, like all their choices, on simple convenience and expediency. Even if it was a papist custom, the people still expected confession, and the outhouse was discreetly removed from the village, used only when folk were out and about and couldn't get home to utilize their own facilities. It had a bench, in case people had to wait their turn during a festival or such. It made sense, then, to have the priest—and now the preacher—hold confession there.

As he listened to Millie admit to envying her sister-in-law's new dress, a commotion sounded in the woods behind him. When he saw who it was, he had to blink, certain his vision was impaired. His foster daughter never made a noise, and here she was, barreling toward him like a charging bull, dead leaves and branches cracking underfoot.

"Preacher!" Addie said, stumbling forward. "There's men—"

As Millie glared over, Preacher said, "I'm sorry, child. I'm hearing confession. You'll need to leave." Then, behind Millie's back, he motioned for Addie to simply step to the side and pantomime the news, which she did, mouthing that she'd seen missionaries heading to town as he gave Millie two Hail Marys and absolved her of her sins.

"But I'm not done, Preacher," Millie said. "I still—"

"We ought not to take up too much of the Lord's time, Miz Prior. If you need unburden yourself of more, we can do it at your next confession."

She grumbled, but there was no rancor in it. Everyone knew God was a busy man—she simply thought she deserved more of his time than others. Once she was gone, Preacher strode over to Addie. She was obviously agitated, but he knew better than to offer any of the usual parental comforts, like a hug or even a squeeze on the hand.

When he was a boy, he'd found a dog half-dead in an alley and though he'd nursed it back to health, it was never quite right, always wary, always expecting the worst. His mother said someone had beaten it when it was a pup, and he ought to do his best to be kind to it, but he ought never to expect too much. It would always cower at a raised hand, anticipating a beating, no matter how often it got a pat on the head. Addie never cowered, but she had that same look in her eyes, always wary, always expecting the worst.

"Missionaries, you said?" he whispered as he walked over to her, hiding in the forest until Millie was gone.

"Two men. I don't like the looks of them."

"Indigent?" he said. When she looked confused, he said, "Vagrants?"

"No, they were dressed as fine men. I just . . . I didn't like their looks. They said they were coming to help us. After . . . what happened."

Preacher sucked in breath. "Snake-oil salesmen."

"Yes!" Addie said. "That's what they put me in mind of. Peddlers. We had some a few years back, when they were thinking of putting the railroad through here. They sold my ma a cream that was supposed to make her look young again and it didn't work and my pa got so mad . . ." She trailed off, her gaze sliding to the side. "It wasn't good."

No, Preacher was certain it wasn't. Not much had been "good" in Addie's young life. Sometimes, the wilderness did things to people, especially those like her folks who stayed out there, away from the villages. People weren't supposed to live like that. It was as if the forest got into their blood, leached out the humanity. He'd been there when they'd found Addie's parents. You'd have thought a wild creature broke in. That's what they told Addie anyway. Whether she believed it . . .

Preacher looked down at his foster daughter, holding herself tight as she peered into the forest, watching for trouble. No, he hoped she'd believed them, but he doubted it.

"I'll go warn the mayor," he said. "No one needs the kind of comfort they're selling. Perhaps we can stop them before they reach the village. Can you run home and tell Sophia? She might hear a commotion, and she ought to stay inside and rest."

"Is she still feeling poorly?"

He nodded. "But if anyone asks, she's busy writing lessons for when school starts again."

Addie gave him a look well beyond her years. "I know not to tell anyone she's unwell, Preacher."

He apologized and sent her off, watching her go, bow bobbing on her thin back. Their house was across town; it was quicker cutting through the village, but she always took the forest. Once she disappeared, he headed into town.

Sophia was indeed unwell, yet it was no grave cause for concern. Celebration, actually. After three years in Chestnut Hill, her dream had been realized. She was with child. And it could not have come at a worse time.

Preacher strode toward the community hall. That's where the mayor and his wife would be. Where *he* ought to have been, even though it wasn't Sunday. For the past month, he'd spent more time in the hall—which doubled as the church—than he had at home. Tending to the living. Tending to the dead.

So many dead.

These days, the only villager as busy as Preacher was the carpenter, building coffins. Tiny coffins, lined up in the community hall like props for some macabre play—a tragedy unlike anything the Bard himself would have dared put to paper.

Thirty-six dead in a month. One-third of the entire village. Eight elderly men and women had passed, but the rest were children. In September, twenty-four children had trooped to Sophia's class for the year. When they reopened the school, she'd have six. And there would be no little ones starting for years after that. No child below the age of five had survived.

Diphtheria. Not that anyone other than Preacher and Sophia used the word. Here, it was simply "the sickness," as if there were no other that mattered.

What had Chestnut Hill done to deserve this? How had they offended God?

They had not. Preacher knew that. He'd gone to university. He knew about Louis Pasteur and the role bacteria played in disease. That was why Sophia had disbanded school as soon as they realized it wasn't merely children's coughs and colds. That was why they had urged the town to quarantine the sick. They had not listened, of course. Everyone knew the way to treat ailments of the chest was with hot tea, a little whiskey, and plenty of prayer.

Except that God was not listening, and the more their preacher insisted that this tragedy was not a punishment from on high, the more they became convinced that Preacher himself had done something wrong. Displeased the Lord. Failed to make some proper . . . Well, they weren't sure what— only heathens offered sacrifices, but they were convinced he'd failed to do *something*.

Or perhaps he *had* done something . . . for his own child. For his foster daughter. Addie had lived, hadn't she? Preacher could point out that Addie had been on one of her hunting trips when the diphtheria broke out, and as soon as she returned, they'd sent her back into the woods with supplies, to stay another week. Also, she was twelve, past the age of most victims. It didn't matter. The preacher's daughter had lived where their children had perished. And now his wife was pregnant? That would only seal the matter, which was why Preacher and Sophia had agreed to not breathe a word of it until they had to, hopefully months from now.

"Preacher?" a voice called as he stepped into the village lane. "Where are you off to in such a hurry?"

He turned. It was Mayor Browning, helping his wife into the community hall, where their son lay in one of those small coffins, the last victim of the outbreak.

"May I speak with you?" Preacher said. "I know it couldn't be a worse possible time but—"

A commotion sounded at the end of the road. Someone calling a welcome. Someone else ringing a bell, telling the town that visitors had come, an occurrence rare enough to bring everyone out, no matter how dark the mood.

He was too late. The strangers had arrived.

ADDIE

Addie raced home through the woods. As she did, she tried not to look at the houses that backed onto the forest, tried not to remember the children who'd lived there. She hadn't known most of them very well. She'd not even gone to school until her parents passed and she came to live with Preacher and Sophia. Still, she had known the children, and there'd been many times she'd come this way and seen them. Sometimes, if Addie felt Sophia's invisible hand prodding her, she'd even call a hullo.

When she reached the mayor's house, she circled wide into the forest, so she wouldn't need to see it at all. Not that it helped, because her path ended up taking her by the fallen oak tree where she'd last seen Charlie Browning, the mayor's son. They'd been tramping around in the woods before her hunting trip, before the sickness came. Just tramping around and talking, as they usually did. Then they came to the fallen oak and sat and kept talking. It'd been night, and she'd leaned back to look at the stars, her hands braced against the log. Her hand had brushed his, and he'd laid his on hers, and when she'd looked over, he'd given her a smile that was shy and nervous and not like Charlie at all.

She'd seen that smile and she hadn't pulled her hand away, even if she thought perhaps she ought to, and now . . . Now she wasn't sure if she wished she had or not. She thought of that summer night, and she was glad he'd been happy that last time they'd been together, but . . . perhaps it would have been easier if he hadn't been. If she hadn't been. If they'd fought and now she could look back and say she hadn't liked him very much, that they hadn't been very good friends after all. It hurt too much otherwise.

They hadn't even let her see him after he'd gotten sick. Preacher and Sophia said it would have been all right, if it was a short visit and she didn't touch him. But Mayor Browning and his wife wouldn't let her, not even when she heard Charlie in the sickroom, coughing and calling for her. Perhaps tomorrow, they said. When he was feeling better. Only there was no tomorrow. Not for Charlie.

Addie circled the mayor's house and continued on until she reached the little clapboard cabin she shared with Preacher and Sophia. It was one of the smallest homes in town, only four rooms. Addie had her own bedroom, and it didn't matter if it was half the size of Charlie's; it was hers, something she'd never had at her parents' house, where she'd slept by the fire. Sophia assured her that when the baby came, it would sleep in their room, and they'd build a new house before it was old enough to need its own. Addie had said it didn't matter, not really. It did, though, and she was glad they understood.

Addie went in the door and found Sophia at the kitchen table, composing lessons. Sophia wanted to reopen school in a week. She said the children needed to be reassured that life would return to normal. But Addie had heard people saying they weren't going to send their children back. Perhaps next year. Getting an education wasn't all that important in Chestnut Hill. It wasn't as if you would do anything with it. Wasn't as if you were going anywhere else.

Addie didn't plan to tell Sophia there'd be no school. Her foster mother needed to get back to normal too, perhaps more than anyone else. Each death had been a blow that Addie swore she could see on Sophia's fragile body. There'd been days when it was all she and Preacher could do to make Sophia eat. That's when Preacher told her about the baby, so she'd understand how important it was for Sophia to be healthy. Addie had already known. Her mother had lost three babies after Addie, and she'd recognized the signs of pregnancy. She'd kept quiet, though, until they'd seen fit to tell her. Now she guarded that secret as ferociously as a bear with a single cub. It was theirs, and it made them a family—truly a family, trusting one another with their deepest secret. No one was going to take that away from her.

"Addie," Sophia said, rising with a smile. "What did you catch?"

"Nothing."

Alarm filled Sophia's pretty face, and Addie could have laughed, as if returning empty-handed portended the end of the world. Sophia knew she always caught a deer or a few rabbits and if she hadn't, then something was wrong. Having a person know you that well . . . it felt good.

"There's men coming," she said. "Preacher says they're snake-oil peddlers, on account of the deaths."

The alarm on Sophia's face grew. "Oh my."

"It's all right. Preacher will stop them. He just wanted me to tell you. Are you feeling poorly?"

A wan smile. "Better today. Let me make you some breakfast—"

"I already ate. Took biscuits this morning before I left." Addie paused, still just inside the door. "Can I go back? Help Preacher if he needs me? He seemed mighty worried."

"Go on, then. I'll stay inside. Last thing anyone needs is hearing me tell those peddlers where they can put their wares."

"You can tell me," Addie said with a grin.

Sophia laughed. "Go on, now. Tell Benjamin I'm feeling fine. I'll make a hot lunch for both of you."

When Addie headed back out, she could hear a hullabaloo down the road and knew Preacher hadn't been able to stop the peddlers. Addie blamed Millie. True, the old woman had left as soon as Preacher asked, but Addie blamed her anyway, for taking up his time with something as silly as confession when he had so much else to attend to these days. Addie believed in God; Sophia said she ought to, so she did. She just didn't figure He had time to be listening to old gossips confess their sins. Not if He obviously hadn't had time to listen to Addie's prayers and save Charlie.

Addie stayed in the forest as she circled around to the commotion. People were spilling out of their houses now. Eager for the distraction. As she drew close, she could hear the whispers starting already. The men were doctors. No, they were undertakers. No, they were from the government, putting the whole village under quarantine.

The advantage to moving through the woods was that Addie could get a lot closer to the situation than those who'd just come out their doors. Someone had brought the two men straight to Preacher and the mayor, down by the community hall, so she was able to creep alongside it and hear everything unfolding.

"We'd like to have a word with you, Your Worship," the younger stranger was saying, and Addie figured that meant Preacher, but it was the mayor who answered.

"Whatever you're selling, we aren't interested."

"I'm sorry," Preacher said. "It's been a very hard month for us. We really would prefer to be left alone in our time of crisis. We'll certainly provide a hot lunch, though, and replenish any supplies you need before you go on your way."

"I understand your hesitation," the younger man said. "But I can assure you that we did not come to profit from your tragedy. Instead, we offer . . ." He cleared his throat. "I hesitate to say more in public, Your Worship. Please, grant us a few minutes of your time. After hearing what we offer, if you wish us to move on, I assure you, we will, without another word to anyone."

Mayor Browning clearly wanted the men to leave. He was a brusque man by nature. Now his only child had just passed, and he had no patience for intrusions, no more than he'd had when Addie tried to visit Charlie. Yet Preacher took him aside, pulling him closer to where Addie hid.

"Let's allow them to have their say," Preacher said. "They're here now. If we refuse, they may try to sell their snake oil on the side. We'll hear them out, refuse their offer, and escort them, politely, from town."

Mayor Browning allowed that this was probably the most expedient way to deal with the situation. When he went back and told the strangers to have their say, though, they insisted on having the whole town council present at the meeting. That led to more discussion, but finally the mayor broke down again. There were only two others who made up the council and they were there, anyway, listening in. He'd bring them all inside and get this over with, so he could return to his grieving wife.

Addie went in the back door of the community hall. It led to a small kitchen, where they would lay meals for a festival or other special occasions. Now the table was covered in food brought for the bereaved, most of it left untouched for days and starting to stink.

She could hear Mayor Browning in the next room, asking his wife to leave for a few minutes. She argued—her child would be in the ground soon enough and she wanted to spend every last moment at his side. But the mayor was firm. She ought to go, but only briefly. Leave out the back door and take some air. He'd call her back when he could.

Addie quickly retreated and hid herself under the porch as Mrs. Browning left. Then she crept inside again.

The hall had two main rooms with a wall between them, which could be removed for large gatherings. During the funerals, they'd kept the wall up— bodies would be laid out in the back room, while service for one victim would take place in the front. From the voices, Addie could tell that the men were holding their meeting in the front room, so she slipped into the back one.

As soon as she saw the open coffins, she went still. She'd just finished thinking that this was where they kept the bodies and yet she hadn't really thought about it at all.

He's here. Charlie's here.

I won't look. I won't. I'll just walk—

Walk across to the other wall. Where his coffin lay. She couldn't see Charlie, nestled too low, but she could tell it was his by the items laid on the table. All the parents had done that—set out small personal belongings that would be laid to rest with the child. Things that mattered to them. Things that mattered to Charlie.

An American coin from a trader who told wild tales of life in the South. A ribbon from a parade in Toronto, on his trip there five years past. A drawing of a pure black Arabian horse, the sort of fine mount he dreamed of owning. Finally, an eagle feather, from last summer, when they'd climbed the bluffs together. He'd wanted her to have it, but she'd found one for herself. Now she wished she'd taken his gift. Something to remember him by.

She could still take it.

Steal from the dead? What would Preacher say?

Addie swallowed and yanked her gaze from the feather. She could hear voices settling in the next room as the introductions finished. This was what she'd come for—to hear what the strangers wanted. Not to lose herself in grief and wicked thoughts.

She hurried to the wall and pressed her ear against it.

Preacher

Preacher tried not to pace as the other members of the town council intro-duced themselves. It was not a quick process. While there were only four, including himself, explaining their positions took some time. No one in Chestnut Hill held a single occupation, not if they participated in public life. The village was simply too small for that.

To supplement his own income, Preacher hired himself out as a scribe, composing letters for the largely illiterate population. He helped Sophia with the garden and chickens. He rode four hours a week to retrieve the village mail. And he'd begun letting Addie teach him to trap, though that was primarily an effort to participate more fully in his foster daughter's life.

The mayor also ran the trading post out of a room in his house. The blacksmith covered any issues of law enforcement. The doctor raised cattle and hunting dogs. And, of course, when each explained his council position, he had to make it sound more important than it was, necessitating further pointless delay.

"And my name is Eleazar," the younger stranger said as the council finally completed their introductions.

"Eleazar? Is that French?" the blacksmith—Dobbs—asked.

"It's biblical," Preacher said. "The first son of Aaron."

"Yes," Eleazar said. "It is a foreign name to you, I'm sure, but my family has been in this country since before the war with the Americans. My colleague's roots go back even further." A smile flickered on the man's face. "Rene is indeed French, though I hope you will not hold it against him."

The old man gave a creaky laugh. Preacher marveled that he managed to stay on his feet, let alone that he had traveled here on foot. Rene had to lean against Eleazar even now, and as much as Preacher hated to draw this meeting out any further, he could no longer watch the old man teeter.

"Please," he said. "Have a seat. We don't have much time to spare, but your walk must have been long. Rest your feet."

"Thank you, Benjamin," Eleazar said.

Preacher stiffened at the use of his Christian name. He could tell himself it was too familiar and they ought to use his surname. But the truth was that after three years of lamenting the fact that he seemed to have lost his name, lost his identity, he took offense now. It felt disrespectful, as if the man was refusing to acknowledge his place as the village's spiritual representative. Which was ridiculous, of course. Preacher was just being testy.

Eleazar continued. "I understand you have suffered a great tragedy. Diphtheria, wasn't it?"

The men nodded.

"And, if I may ask, how many were lost?"

"Thirty-six," Preacher said. "We lost thirty-six souls."

"Most of them children?"

Preacher tried not to squirm. None of the men sitting here needed each fact recited, every reminder thrown in his face. He could tell by Eleazar's soft tone that he didn't mean it that way, but that was what it felt like. Each of these men had lost someone—the blacksmith his eight-year-old son and toddling daughter, the doctor two grandchildren, and the mayor his son. The pain of waking daily to a world without them was reminder enough.

"Yes," Preacher said. "Mostly children. I'm sorry to be blunt, but if you would like a fuller explanation, I would happily provide that in private. I don't think we all need to be part of such a conversation, not when Mayor Browning's boy lies in the room behind us."

Preacher kept his voice low, but he would admit that was a little sharper a rebuke than a man of God ought to give.

"Your Worship," Eleazar said to the mayor. "I apologize. I did not realize—"

"There was no way you could," Preacher said. "However, under the circumstances, you can see why we're being more abrupt than is Christian. If you could please tell us what you want, so we can return to grieving for our children . . ."

"What if you didn't have to grieve?"

Preacher's head whipped up as his eyes narrowed. "What?"

Eleazar leaned forward. "We are here to offer life, my friends. Renewed life. The resurrection of your children."

Preacher shot from his seat so fast that it crashed over behind him. "You would dare—" He struggled to get the words out. "I have seen peddlers prey on the fears and misfortunes of others, but I have never, in my life, heard anything as outrageous or egregious—"

"We are not peddlers, Benjamin. We are, like you, men of God—"

"You are not."

"Preacher," the doctor murmured. "Let the man finish."

Preacher glanced over at Doc Adams, normally the most levelheaded and reasonable of the group. The old sawbones held himself very still, giving no reaction, but deep in his gaze Preacher saw something terrible. He saw hope, and he wanted to stamp it out, no matter how cruel that might seem, because this was the wrong sort of hope, the absolutely wrong sort.

"There's no harm in letting him finish," Mayor Browning said, his voice uncharacteristically quiet.

Yes, Preacher wanted to say. *There is harm. Great harm. He's offering you the thing you want most. The thing you know you cannot have. You must resist the temptation by refusing to listen.*

Yet how could he say that? These were grown men, not schoolchildren to be lectured by a teacher—or a preacher. If he suggested that they were not capable of seeing through lies to truth, he would insult them. Which he'd gladly have done, to be rid of these hucksters, but it was too late. They'd already heard the insidious whisper of the serpent. They would find a way—any way—to listen to the rest.

"Please proceed," Preacher said stiffly as he righted his chair. "Forgive my interruption."

Eleazar waited until Preacher was seated again. Then he folded his hands on his lap and said, "This is no snake oil, my good men. I would not exploit your tragedy that way. When my ancestors came from the old country, they brought with them special knowledge. Great knowledge. Passed on from God himself."

The man glanced at Preacher, as if expecting another interruption. Preacher clenched his teeth to keep from saying anything. He'd not give Eleazar the satisfaction. He had to trust that the village men were not fools. Let them listen and recognize lies.

"You are familiar, I'm sure, with the story of Lazarus? Raised from the dead by the Holy Son, Christ Jesus?"

"I can assure you we are," the mayor said.

"Mr. Dobbs mentioned that my name seems odd. It is my family name, and it has a meaning that is indeed biblical. It's another form of Lazarus. My ancestor was that poor man, raised from the dead, taught the art of resurrection by Christ Jesus himself."

"No," Preacher said, rising. "I'm sorry, gentlemen. I can't countenance this. To say this stranger is descended from Lazarus is one thing. Even to say he can raise the dead is merely preposterous. To claim that Jesus taught his ancestor the skill? That is blasphemy."

The others had to know that. They took their faith more seriously than he. All of them, as much as it pained him to admit it. Yet not one even looked his way. They kept their gazes averted, and when he saw that, he knew that they recognized the blasphemy. And they chose to ignore it.

"Is it not . . . possible?" Doc Adams said.

Preacher turned to stare at him. The doctor? He was the most educated among them. The one who made his living following the natural science of the world. Who knew that dead was dead.

"It can happen, can't it, Doc?" Dobbs asked. "I mean, I've heard of things like that."

Doc Adams nodded. "And I've seen it. A man on the dissection table at the university. We cut into him, and he started awake."

"Because he *wasn't* dead," Preacher said.

Mayor Browning turned to him. "Are you saying that the doctor who pronounced him so was wrong?"

"Yes, that is exactly—"

"I am surprised you would be the one arguing most vehemently, Benjamin," Eleazar said in his soft voice. "A man of faith ought to believe in miracles. In the mercy of God." He paused and looked Preacher in the eye. "Unless you are not such a man of faith."

Preacher blanched. He was certain the barb was thrown wild, that Eleazar did not truly see into his heart, and yet, with his reaction, he confirmed it. And in Eleazar's response, a faint smile, Preacher knew he was lost.

"Our preacher is a good man," Doc Adams said. "If he is skeptical, it's because he . . ." The doctor seemed to struggle for a way to put it.

"He doesn't have a dog in this fight," Dobbs said.

The doctor flinched and Dobbs flushed. "That didn't sound right," the blacksmith said. "But they know what I mean. He hasn't lost anyone. His wife lives. His daughter lives."

"Foster daughter," Doc Adams corrected.

"It's the same thing," Preacher said. "While you all know how I feel about the loss of our children, I would not dare match my grief to yours. So I take and concede the point. However, my having not lost anyone means that I'm the only one who can see this clearly and—"

"Preacher?" Mayor Browning turned to him. "I'm going to ask you to step outside. We want to hear what these gentlemen have to say."

Preacher forced a nod. "All right then. I will remain silent—"

"No." The mayor met his gaze. "I don't believe you will. I am asking you to leave. Please don't make me insist."

Preacher looked into the mayor's face, the set of his jaw, the flint in his gaze. Dobbs rose to his feet, squaring his thick shoulders, as if he were a tender of bar, ready to throw an unruly patron through the door. Doc Adams shrank back, taking great interest in a mark on the wall.

No one here would take Preacher's side. They wanted to hear what the men had to say. They needed to. His job was to counsel them to make wise and spiritual decisions, but if their ears were stopped, he must leave them to make their own mistakes. He could hope they'd hear the lies for what they were but, at worst, they would lose only coin and pride.

"All right," Preacher said. "If anyone needs me, I'll be home with my wife. Good day, gentlemen."

BROWNING

Preacher left without argument. Which the mayor took to mean he wasn't as strenuously opposed to the idea as he pretended.

Their preacher was an odd duck. A fine enough man—he just had odd ideas. City ideas. Dobbs thought him soft, and while it was true that he wasn't like the men who'd lived out here all their lives, the preacher held his own. He just spent more time in his head than a man ought to. Worried more than a man ought to.

That was, Browning decided, what had happened here. Preacher felt obligated to object to anything that might smack of dark arts, but it was only a perfunctory objection. A strong perfunctory objection, Browning would give him that, and yes, the man had seemed genuinely upset, but . . . well, he'd left, hadn't he? If Browning wanted to see that as a sign that his protest lacked conviction, then he could and he would.

Besides, this wasn't the dark arts. It was faith. Eleazar was right—the Lord Jesus Christ had raised a man from the dead. It was right there in the Bible. That made it a miracle. A gift from God, not the Devil.

"Go on. Tell us more," he said when Preacher had left.

"Thank you, Your Worship. We can return the living, but only if they have been dead four days or less, like Lazarus. I presume there are children that meet that criterion?"

"My son," Browning blurted.

There were others, of course, but in that moment, he did not even pause to consider them. They did not matter. His son—his only child—lay dead twenty feet away, behind the wall. What would he give to see the boy alive again? There was part of him that dared not even ask the question because the answer terrified him.

"And my granddaughter," Doc Adams said. "And Mr. Dobbs's son and—"

"My daughter died five days ago," Dobbs said. "Is that—"

"No," Eleazar said softly. "It is too long."

"Like my grandson," Doc Adams said. "Gone a week now."

Eleazar nodded.

"My daughter was wee still," Dobbs said. "My wife can have others. My son was growing into a strong lad. If you could return him . . ."

He said it so casually, Browning marveled. *If you could return him.* As if asking for a simple favor. *If you could bring a pie on Sunday, that would be lovely.* Browning knew Dobbs loved his boy. But it was not the same as his own situation. Dobbs had two other children and apparently planned others to replace those lost. Browning's wife had lost their first two in infancy, to influenza. She was past the age of bearing more. Without their son, they had nothing. No child. No grandchildren. No great-grandchildren. Only the two of them, growing old in their loneliness and their grief.

"Tell us more," Browning said again.

"There is a price," Doc Adams said. "Surely there must be a price."

Eleazar looked uncomfortable. "Yes, I fear there is. I cannot perform this miracle often. That was the stricture given by the Lord Jesus Christ. We must be very careful imparting our gift, so as not to disrupt the natural order of things. I search out tragedies, such as yours, where it can be of most use. That means, however, that there is a cost, to allow my assistant and me to live frugally and continue our work."

"How much?" Dobbs asked.

"My normal rate is one thousand dollars for a resurrection."

Doc Adams inhaled sharply. Dobbs looked ill. Browning began quickly calculating. He had money and a few items he could sell. Yes, he could manage it. When he looked at the faces of the others, though, he felt a slight pang of guilt. A thousand dollars would be impossible for them. Men at the mines bragged of earning that much in a year.

"Most of us would not be able to afford that," Browning said, quickly adding, "Though a few could scrape it together."

"Understandable," Eleazar said. "And while that is my fee, normally I am performing a single resurrection, so I require an exorbitant amount, as it is all I may earn for a year or more. However, as there are multiple resurrections required here, I did not intend to charge so much for the good people of Chestnut Hill. How many children would there be, if price were no object?"

"Seven," Doc Adams said. "I pronounced seven poor children dead in the last four days."

"Then my fee would be three hundred dollars apiece."

Doc Adams exhaled in relief. Browning knew he could afford that with ease. He glanced at Dobbs as the younger man counted on his fingers.

"Would you require cash?" Browning asked. "Or would goods be sufficient?"

"If they are easily transported goods—horses, jewelry, furs—yes, we would take them for market value."

Dobbs nodded, a slow smile creasing his broad face. He could manage that. Most could. It was not a small amount—one could purchase three good horses for as much. But at least half of the families would be able to get by and there were enough wealthier folks in town to lend the rest. That would be important, he realized. He could imagine the rancor it would bring to Chestnut Hill if there were parents unable to afford the fee. Best to lend it to them, at a reasonable rate.

"We could manage it," Browning said. "For all seven."

"But we'd need the children back first," Doc Adams cut in. "What you're offering is, as you said, a miracle, and those are few and far between. We cannot simply trust you can do as you claim."

A kernel of panic exploded in Browning's gut. He wanted to shush the doctor. Tell him not to insult this man, who was offering a dream come true, lest he take that dream and vanish whence he came.

As soon as he thought it, though, he was shamed. Was this not what Preacher had warned of, when he said the men were coming? *They'll want to prey on our tragedy, Mayor. They'll offer us impossible things for our hard-earned cash, and I fear the village folks are too grief-stricken to think straight.*

Browning had agreed wholeheartedly . . . when he thought the men might only be selling some elixir of youth or happiness. Instead, they offered something even more unbelievable, and here he was, ready to leap on it without a shred of proof.

"The doctor is right," Browning said. "We'll need the children resurrected before we pay the full cost. We can arrange something, of course—a contract or such."

Eleazar smiled. "I doubt any court would recognize a contract to raise the dead, but yes, of course I do not expect you to pay us without the children. In fact, I do not expect you to even agree to pay us without proof. That is why I will resurrect one child first, free of any charge. In demonstration." He turned to Browning. "You said you had a son newly passed?"

Browning's heart pounded so hard he could barely force a nod.

"May I ask his age?"

"He just passed his thirteenth birthday."

"A boy on the cusp of becoming a man. I am particularly sorry for your loss then. I know the disease usually affects only the very young and the very old."

"He was the eldest of the victims," Doc Adams said. "He'd suffered a cold this summer—a serious one that affected his lungs. While he seemed quite recovered, I believe it must have made him vulnerable."

"Indeed." Eleazar glanced at the old man, Rene. "Then with my assistant's aid and the mayor's approval, I will return this boy to life."

"When?" Browning blurted.

Eleazar smiled, indulgent. "He will be back in time for your wife to serve him dinner." The smile faded, his gaze growing troubled. "There is, however, one other—"

Eleazar stopped, looking sharply toward the door at the back of the room.

"Sir?" Doc Adams said.

"I thought I heard something. Is anyone back there?"

Browning shook his head. "My wife left that way before we began. The room was empty."

"So there is a door?" Eleazar rose and walked to it, swinging it open fast and peering in as the others scrambled to their feet.

As Eleazar strode through, Browning hurried after him. He found the man in the back room, looking about. Browning could see into the kitchen, where the rear door was closing.

Someone *had* been there. Eleazar hadn't noticed it, though, and Browning didn't point it out. Browning was not about to do anything to upset him. Not after what he'd just said about . . .

Charlie.

Browning's gaze swung to the coffin, the largest in the room, two chairs placed in front of it, where he and his wife had spent the night.

His wife. Dorothy. What would she say? Her heart might break with joy.

Eleazar strode over, scattering Browning's thoughts.

"There's no sign anyone was here," Browning said. "Perhaps mice? Or coons in the eaves."

"I'm sure it was nothing," Eleazar said. "I'm a touch anxious about what I have to say next. My fears likely got the best of me."

"What you have to say?" Browning paused. "Yes, you were saying there was something else." His heart thudded anew. *No, please, nothing else.* Nothing that would stop this man from bringing Charlie back.

Eleazar was walking again, moving to Charlie's coffin.

"Is this him, then?" he asked. "Your boy?"

Browning stayed where he was. He wasn't looking in that coffin. If there was a chance he could see his son alive, he didn't wish to see his corpse.

Was there a chance?

Dear God, let it be possible. Let his boy rise from that coffin, not the pasty-faced child with the mottled lips and eyelids, that sick child, that dead child. Let him rise as Browning remembered him.

Browning cleared his throat. "Yes, that's Charlie."

Eleazar smiled. "He's a fine boy. Well-formed. Don't you agree, Rene?"

Browning had not even noticed the old man there. Rene leaned over the coffin, and something in his face made Browning go cold. He wanted to leap forward. Yank the old man back. He swallowed hard. Rene nodded, jowls bobbing.

"You have a fine boy, sir," Rene said, and there was nothing in his clouded old eyes but kindness.

"Thank you." Browning turned to Eleazar. "You said there was more?"

Eleazar nodded. "Another price, I fear. One that cannot be negotiated." He walked back to Browning. "I said earlier that I use my powers sparingly because that is the Lord's will. There is another reason. The second price. Unlike our Lord, I am but a mortal man. I cannot return the soul to a body for nothing, as he did. There must be an exchange."

"Exchange?"

"A soul for a soul."

Browning blinked. "I . . . I don't understand."

"I do," said a voice behind him.

Browning turned to see Doc Adams in the doorway, looking ill.

"Yes," Eleazar said. "Our good doctor understands. I cannot steal a life from heaven, like a base thief. I take a soul for you, I give a soul to Him. For a child to live again, someone must die."

PREACHER

Preacher was poring over a Latin book with Sophia. The words . . . well, as he'd joked to her, they could have been Greek for all he understood of them. He knew Latin, of course. At this moment, though, his mind was otherwise too occupied to translate them to English. He was trying to distract himself from what was happening at the community hall and it was not working.

His wife was also trying to distract him, and had been since he'd explained when he came home.

"You can do nothing about it," Sophia said. "They must make their own choices and their own mistakes."

Which is what he'd told himself. Yet he could not shake the feeling that he ought to have done more.

"You cannot," his wife said, as if reading his thoughts. "You dare not, under the circumstances."

Again, she spoke true. His position was precarious enough of late, worse now with the baby on the way. If he were to argue against listening to these men when his daughter had survived and his wife was with child. . . ? Who knew of what they might accuse him.

"I'm going to start teaching Latin to the younger children," Sophia said, thumbing through a well-used book. "Simple words, as I do with French. The names of animals and such."

What younger children? he wanted to ask. The three below the age of eight who'd survived? He knew they could not think like that. Better to focus not on the loss but on those that remained, on how the smaller class would mean more attention for each pupil, more work they could do, such as starting Latin sooner.

Preacher was saying just that when the front door banged open, Addie rushing in, words spilling out so fast that they couldn't decipher them. Both Preacher and Sophia leaped from the table and raced over, thinking she was injured.

"No," Addie said. "I'm well. It's the men, what they're offering. To bring back the children."

"Yes, we already know," Sophia said, leading the girl inside. "It's terrible and—"

"Terrible?" Addie pulled from her grasp. "It's wondrous."

Sophia winced.

Preacher moved forward, bending in front of the girl. "Yes, it would indeed be wondrous . . . if it was possible. It's not. They're taking advantage of our grief. Promising the impossible because they know we're desperate enough to pay the price."

"You're wrong," Addie said, backing away.

"So they aren't charging a fee?" Preacher asked softly.

Addie said nothing.

"Adeline?" Sophia said, her voice equally soft but firm. "Did they say there would be a cost?"

"Yes, but they're reducing it, on account of there being so many children—"

"How much?"

She hesitated. "Three hundred apiece."

"My Lord," Sophia breathed. "That's . . ."

"Exactly the right price," Preacher said grimly. "As much as they can charge and still have people pay it . . . with everything they own." He turned to the girl. "You see that, Addie, don't you? These families have lost their children and now they may lose everything else, in a desperate and hopeless attempt to regain them."

Addie shook her head. "It's not like that. He's going to do a demonstration. Free of charge."

"What? That's not poss—" Preacher began.

"It's a hoax, Addie," Sophia said, laying her hand on the girl's arm. "Swindlers have many of them. They'll conjure up some trick and—"

"And what if it's real?" Addie said, crossing her arms. "You don't know that it isn't. You don't."

"Yes, we do, sweetheart. They cannot—"

"You're wrong," Addie said. "They're going to do the demonstration. They'll bring Charlie back. And I'll be there to see it."

She turned and raced out the door as Sophia and Preacher stared at one another.

"Charlie?" Sophia said finally. "Oh, Benjamin. Of all the children . . ."

"I know," he said. "She does not need that. I'll go and be there for her when she's disappointed."

"Not disappointed," Sophia said. "Heartbroken. I'll go with you, too. I'm well enough, and I ought to be there for her."

He nodded and gathered her bonnet and coat.

BROWNING

Someone must die.

You knew there was a trick, Browning told himself. There had to be.

No, it wasn't a trick. It was a hitch. He ought to have known it couldn't be as easy as paying cash on the barrel. A life given for a life returned. That was how it worked, and he ought to have been relieved, now that it made sense.

Relieved? Someone has to die for Charlie to live.

His wife would do it. That was the first thing he thought, even as the idea horrified him. Dorothy would gladly give her life for her son's. Yet that didn't help at all. What would the boy do without his mama? What would Browning do without his wife? Their family would be torn asunder as much as it was now.

I could get another wife. I can't get another son.

Again, his mind recoiled, but again, it didn't quite drop the idea. Dorothy was a good housekeeper and a fine cook. He would not wish to lose her. But if he had to choose . . . and if the decision was hers, made on her own, without his prodding . . .

"You cannot expect us to do that," Doc Adams was saying. "While there are those who would give their lives for the children, we would again need proof before such a decision could be made. No one will sacrifice himself on such a chance."

Browning turned sharply on his heel, to motion for the doctor to be silent, not to give offense, but again Eleazar seemed to take none, only nodding in understanding.

"The good doctor is right," Eleazar said. "Normally, there would be someone near death willing to offer his or her life—eager, even, to leave this world of pain and pass into the kingdom of heaven. But you have lost all your elderly and infirm in the same tragedy that claimed the lives of the young. There is but one elder remaining."

"No," Doc Adams said. "I fear there is not."

"Oh, but there is." Eleazar motioned to his assistant. "Rene has offered himself for this demonstration."

"What?" Dobbs said, stepping forward.

Browning made a move to shush him as his heart filled with hope again.

"It's all right," Rene said in his creaking old voice. "A man as young as your blacksmith cannot understand what it is to wish his life done. I pray that he may never know the horrors of age. My body has failed me, and yet it stubbornly clings to life. I cannot end it myself or I would be damned. So I offer it to this village, to the mayor's young son. I will die so he may live."

That was the end of the discussion. It had been decided, apparently, even before the men arrived in Chestnut Hill. The old man would die so the younger one could prove his skill. With Charlie. Browning's son would live again, and there would be no price to pay. None at all. Of course, he would not tell the others that. He'd pretend that he'd paid his three hundred to help cover the cost of others. As for the other price . . .

How will I tell them? Where will we find volunteers?

Did it matter? Charlie was coming back. The others could deal with that choice themselves when the time came.

Eleazar killed his assistant in the back room.

There was no hesitation, no preparation. He didn't even say what he was doing, only asked Dobbs and Browning to take Charlie's coffin out the front, where the villagers could see. They were not to say what was to come—it must be a surprise. As they'd told him, they didn't want to raise hopes unnecessarily. Take the coffin out and make some excuse, and he'd be there in a moment. Doc Adams ought to speak to anyone still outside. With that, Eleazar and the old man disappeared into the kitchen.

Browning was still carrying Charlie's coffin to the door when Eleazar appeared.

"Rene has passed," he announced.

"What?" Dobbs nearly dropped his end of the coffin.

"It was swift and merciful. Doctor, could you please confirm it is done? He's resting in the back."

Doc Adams did as he was asked, while Browning and Dobbs carried the coffin outside.

Most people had gone home now, content to wait and hear what the mysterious men wanted. Some had lingered, though, and when they brought out the coffin, a gasp went up.

"All is fine," Doc Adams assured them as he came out. "All is fine. The men have asked us to bring one of our dearly departed into the sunlight, so they might better see his condition."

Whispers snaked through the smattering of people. The men were doctors then, or scientists. A few left in disappointment.

As Browning stepped away from his son's closed casket, he caught sight of a man striding along the road, a slender woman beside him, her blond hair pushed up under a bonnet.

Preacher. Bringing his schoolteacher wife to chastise them.

He's going to stop this. Take away your chance. Take away your Charlie.

The warnings seemed to slide around him, whispers like . . .

The voice of God. That's what it was. Resurrection was God's work, and now this "preacher" thought he'd stop it. The preacher who hadn't stopped Charlie from dying. The preacher whose own daughter lived. A girl who'd wanted to see his son before he passed.

The voice whispered, *You know there's a reason she lived. And a reason your son died. A strong, healthy boy, older than the rest, contracts the illness after the rest? It's unnatural.*

Browning shoved past the villagers, ignoring their grunts of surprise. He bore down on Preacher. The schoolteacher started forward, chin raised, eyes flashing, but her husband pulled her back with a whispered word. He strode forward to meet Browning.

"If you dare—" Browning began.

"Dare what? Dare stop you from something we both know will fail?" Preacher said, lowering his voice. "If I thought it would do any good, I'd try, but your course is clearly decided. Nothing will help now but for you to *see* failure, however hard that will be for all of us."

Browning clenched and unclenched his fists. The rage still wound around his gut like a cyclone.

Hit him. Show him who's the mayor.

But he's given me no cause.

Hit him anyway. Drive him off. Tell him begone. He's a doubting Thomas. He'll spoil everything.

"If you'll excuse us," the schoolteacher said, elbowing between the men. "Addie is here somewhere, and we'd like to find her."

Browning looked down at the woman. It took a moment for his gaze to focus, the rage still nearly blinding him. He felt his fists clench again. Felt them start to rise. Then he realized what he was doing, whom he was about to hit, and they dropped quickly, and he stepped back.

"Thank you," the schoolteacher said.

"Your Worship?" It was Eleazar, calling to him. "We're ready to begin."

ADDIE

Addie could see Charlie's closed coffin, out in front of the community hall. She could also see Preacher and Sophia, searching for her in the small gathering. She started scooting around the building, but her foster parents were splitting up now, one heading for each side, knowing if she wasn't in the crowd, she was still in the forest.

She raced to the back porch and swung onto the railing, then up to the roof.

Like Charlie taught me to do.

While Addie was an expert tree climber, she would never have considered using those skills to sneak around town. Spying on folks wasn't right. As Charlie said, though, "When you're a child, no one tells you anything, so you need to eavesdrop sometimes, to know what's going on." They'd tried listening in on the town meetings through the chimney, but it didn't really work. So they mostly just climbed up here to get a better view of anything taking place in the village square.

Like bringing a boy back to life.

Bringing Charlie back to life.

She crawled across the roof carefully, slipping a little as she went but always catching herself in time. Below, she could hear Preacher asking someone if they'd seen Addie. They hadn't. No one had.

If Addie went down there, she wasn't sure that Preacher would stop her

244

from watching. He probably wouldn't. He and Sophia really were teachers, right down to their bones. They'd explain why she ought not to watch, but if she insisted, they'd let her, believing it was always best to see a thing for yourself. To learn a lesson for yourself.

She didn't care. She wasn't going to watch this with them standing beside her, suffocating under the weight of their disapproval. Even recalling their expressions when she told them made her want to scream. Made her want to charge back home, grab her belongings, leave, and never come back.

They'd betrayed her. That's what she felt, and it hurt worse than any of her dead father's beatings. Eleazar had promised to bring Charlie back, and they wouldn't even consider that he might be able to work miracles. Sophia and Preacher—the very people who'd taught her about God.

She took a deep breath and calmed herself as she crept to the front. She stretched out there, then inched forward until she could peer down.

Below was Charlie's coffin. Still closed. Eleazar knelt beside it. Addie couldn't see the old man—Rene. He must have stayed inside, where it was warm.

Mayor Browning stood at the foot of the coffin. Dobbs and Doc Adams flanked him. All three stared at the coffin as if mesmerized. The other spectators milled about, peering over and then whispering to themselves, as if wondering what the fuss was about. They hadn't been told. Good. If people knew, they'd all come running and they'd crowd around and Addie wouldn't see the miracle. Wouldn't see Charlie rise.

If she listened closely, she could hear Eleazar talking. She couldn't understand what he was saying, though. It wasn't English.

Because Christ didn't speak English. That's what Sophia told her when she'd asked why the Bibles were translated. Jesus spoke another language and so did the people who wrote the Bible. Hearing Eleazar speaking in a foreign tongue proved he was no fraud.

He finished the words, and then he reached for the coffin lid. Addie held her breath, her heart beating so hard it hurt.

What if Preacher and Sophia were right?

When were they ever wrong? When had they been cruel to her? Misled her?

"No," she breathed. "They *are* wrong. They must be."

As Eleazar opened the wooden lid, Addie squeezed her eyes shut, prayed as hard as she could.

Please, God, let him live. I know you didn't listen before. I know why—

Addie's heart clenched, and she couldn't hold her breath any longer, panting for air as pain filled her.

I know why you didn't listen. I was evil. I was wicked. I . . . I . . .

She couldn't even form the words in her head. What she had done. The sin for which God had punished her.

I deserve that punishment. But Charlie doesn't. Please let him come back.

She heard a gasp from below and her eyes flew open. *He's alive. He's really . . .*

Addie stared down. Charlie's coffin was almost exactly under her perch, and when she opened her eyes, she saw his face. His pale, dead face. His sunken, closed eyelids.

No, he is alive. That's why they gasped.

Only it wasn't. She looked at the faces of the villagers, the women shrinking back, and she knew the sound came from them, a simple reaction to seeing the poor dead boy. She had but to see Mayor Browning's expressionless face to know Charlie did not live.

Yet the mayor's face *was* expressionless. It did not crumple with grief and disappointment. He stood there, resolute. Waiting.

Eleazar bent over the coffin. He lifted his fingers to Charlie's face and traced them over his pale forehead. When he pulled them back, there were three red lines left there.

"Is that blood?" someone whispered.

"Of course not," another hissed back.

Eleazar spoke again, in that foreign tongue, touching his fingertips to Charlie's eyelids, his nostrils, and then his lips. When he reached the lips, he held his fingers there, his head bent, words flowing faster until . . .

Eleazar stopped abruptly, as if in midsentence. His head jerked up. His fingers pulled back and . . .

Charlie's lips parted. Or they seemed to, opening so little that Addie was certain she'd blinked, certain she was seeing wrong, that his lips had been like that already or were moved by the man's fingers.

Yes, moved by the man's fingers. A trick. Isn't that what Sophia warned of? Charlie's lips moved by chicanery and—

His eyes opened. Addie stopped breathing.

Trick. It's a trick.

Charlie sat up and looked about. His gaze lit on Mayor Browning and he smiled, and Addie knew there was no trick.

Charlie lived.

After Charlie sat up in his coffin, the village erupted like a volcano in one of Sophia's books. Some people ran shrieking that the dead had risen. Others fell and gave thanks to God for his infinite mercy. And still others barely drew breath before demanding to know why Charlie had been resurrected—why him, why not their child.

"Charlie was returned to us as proof of this man's holy power!" Browning's voice boomed over half the town. "I offered my own child to be tested, as is only right. As your mayor, I must take that risk for my family, before asking you to take it for yours!"

"Is he truly alive?" Millie Prior pushed through and peered at Charlie as Doc Adams examined him. When she reached to poke him, Eleazar grabbed the old woman's hand hard enough to make her shriek.

"Please," Charlie said, his voice low and rough with disuse. "She meant no harm."

"He speaks," Millie breathed.

He speaks, Addie thought. *But he doesn't sound like—*

She bit her lip, as if that could stopper her thoughts.

"Yes," Charlie said. "I can speak, but barely. I feel . . ." He gripped Eleazar's hand for support.

"He's very weak," Eleazar said. "I'm sorry if I startled you, my good woman. I do not wish him to be poked and prodded about during his recovery. Your doctor is examining him now."

Doc Adams rose. "The boy lives. He breathes. He speaks. His heart beats. His blood flows."

Millie dropped to her knees. "Praise be. Dear Lord, thank you . . ."

As she continued, Doc Adams explained which children could be resurrected. Eleazar took Charlie's hand and helped him from the coffin. He told Mayor Browning to fetch his wife and then announced that he would take Charlie inside to rest. Addie waited until they were gone, then scampered back across the roof.

Addie eased open the back door to the community hall. Inside, she could hear Eleazar talking to his assistant. She closed the door silently behind her. While Eleazar was occupied, she'd speak to Charlie. Yes, he was weak, but she'd take up none of his time or his strength. She simply wanted to . . .

She didn't know what she wanted. What she expected. Only that she'd been robbed of the chance to see him before, and she would get it now. No one would take that from her now, and if something went wrong—

It won't. He's back.

If something went wrong, at least she wouldn't lie awake, wishing she'd seen him one last time. So she crept into the community hall while Eleazar spoke to Rene.

She hadn't even reached the kitchen door, though, before the conversation stopped.

"I need to rest now," Charlie said, and she realized Eleazar hadn't been talking to his assistant, Rene, at all.

This would make things more difficult. Eleazar and Charlie were both in the front room, and the assistant was here somewhere, too.

It didn't matter. She *would* see Charlie.

She peered into the back room before she slid through. There were three coffins now, the fourth gone. Something caught her attention on the floor. An eagle's feather, under the table where Charlie's coffin had lain. When they'd picked it up, they'd let his treasures scatter.

Anger darted through her. Those things of Charlie's had been so important to his parents after he'd died. Now they were as they'd been in his life—useless clutter. How many times had his mother tried to throw out that eagle feather, saying it was filthy? It was treasured only after he was gone, like Charlie himself. His father had paid him no mind when he was alive—

Addie wiped the thoughts from her mind. *Unchristian,* Sophia would say.

She paused again, caught on that new thought. Preacher and Sophia. She hadn't even seen them after the resurrection. They'd been there, lost in the crowd. Were they regretting their hasty judgment? Looking for her to apologize?

Stop thinking. Start moving. Or you'll lose your chance.

She stepped into the room, gaze fixed on that feather, to retrieve it for Charlie. She picked it up and as she rose, she caught sight of a figure and stifled a yelp as she wheeled. It was Rene. He sat in front of one of the other coffins, with his back to her. His head was bowed. Asleep.

Addie exhaled in relief. She ought to be more careful. She'd been checking the room for him when she'd gotten distracted by the feather. She tucked it under her jacket now and silently tiptoed to the door joining the two rooms. He never stirred.

The adjoining door was closed tight. Addie turned the handle as carefully as she could and then eased it open. Through the crack she could see Charlie. He sat in a chair, leaning back, his eyes closed, looking like . . .

Well, looking like Charlie. Exactly like the Charlie she knew, his color coming back, the swelling fading. His dark hair hung in a cowlick over one eye, and Addie smiled, expecting him to reach up and push it impatiently aside, as he always did. He seemed too tired for that, though, and just sat there, slouched in the chair.

Eleazar was across the room, rummaging in his pack. He muttered to himself as he did, doubling the noise.

"Charlie?" Addie whispered.

No response.

A little louder. "Charlie?"

His eyelids flickered. Then they opened, and she was looking straight into those eyes she knew so well, gray-blue, like the sky on a windy day. She looked into them and saw . . .

Nothing. Not a flicker of recognition.

Because he can barely see me through this crack in the door.

She glanced at Eleazar. He was still retrieving things from his pack, turned away enough not to see her. She inched the door open until her face fit in the gap. Then she grinned at Charlie and, in her mind, she saw him grin back, as he always had, ever since the first time they met, when her ma brought her to town for supplies. Charlie had been in his father's shop room, and he'd snuck a licorice whip from the jar for her. That's who Addie saw in her mind—that boy, that grin—and it took a moment before she realized she wasn't seeing it in front of her.

Charlie wasn't even smiling. He looked right at her and that expression in his eyes never changed.

He doesn't know me.

Because he's tired. He's confused.

She lifted the eagle feather and waggled it. He frowned.

Addie glanced at Eleazar. He was reading a book, muttering to himself as he turned the pages. Addie opened the door a little more and slipped through. Charlie sat barely three paces away. She crossed the gap and held out the feather. He only stared at her. She laid it on his blanket-draped lap.

"Here," Eleazar said. "I've found that—" He looked up and saw her. "Who are you?"

"I-I'm Addie. Adeline. I came to see—"

"He's not ready to see anyone. Begone, girl."

She backed up to the doorway. Charlie didn't look down at the feather, as if trying to remember where it came from. He didn't look at her either. He closed his eyes as if she'd already left.

"Charlie?"

His eyelids flickered open, and he glanced over with annoyance.

"He needs his rest, child," Eleazar said, striding toward her. "He's not himself yet. You need to leave."

She retreated through the door into the rear.

"No!" Eleazar said, raising his voice. "Not that way."

But she was already through, already racing across the room. As she reached the kitchen door, she heard Charlie's voice, and she thought he was calling her back, telling Eleazar he remembered her now. She turned, and as she did, she saw the assistant, Rene, saw his face now as he sat there, head bowed. Saw the bruises around his neck. Saw his eyes. Open. Bulging. Dead.

Addie spun and bolted out the kitchen door.

BROWNING

Mayor Browning's wife was home now with Charlie. When he'd left, she'd been sitting at their son's bedside, watching him sleep, looking very much as she had the night before, sitting at his coffin's side. She'd even had the same look on her face, anxious and afraid.

When he'd first told her the news, she'd shouted at him, for the first time in their marriage. She'd even thrown something—a plate she'd been washing, shattering it against the wall as she cursed him. She seemed to think he was pulling a prank. Yes, he'd been known to make them. Yes, sometimes, perhaps, they bordered on cruel, but this was not one he'd ever have attempted. He'd struck her, another first for their marriage. Struck her full across the face, bellowing at her that she was an ungrateful wretch, that he'd done this for her—brought back her boy—and this was how she treated him.

She'd raced out of the house then, not even pausing for a bonnet or a cloak, gathering her skirts and running like a girl through the streets, graying hair streaming behind her.

Now they were home. Her boy was home. Yet she was not beside herself with joy. Not falling to her knees to thank the Lord. She hovered over Charlie, pushing his cowlick aside, tentatively, as if the slightest touch might send him back to the other side. It was not what Browning expected. Not what he wanted. But he supposed it might take time for her to accept the miracle as real.

Eleazar had summoned him back to the community hall. Yes, *summoned* him, as if he were a common innkeeper. That rankled, but Browning reminded himself of the incredible debt he owed the man. Eleazar wished to speak about the other children, and he had a right to be somewhat abrupt—time was wasting, the children were wasting.

So Browning returned to the community hall. Doc Adams and Dobbs were already inside with Eleazar.

"How is Charlie?" Dobbs asked.

"Tired. Sleeping."

"That's to be expected," Eleazar said. "I fear he will not be his usual self for several days. He will require sleep, and he may be somewhat confused. His memory is weakened also. Do not overtax him."

"We won't," Browning said.

"Now, on to the matter at hand—the rest of the children. Doctor? As I was saying, I'll ask that you go round the parents up now. I'll need them all here to discuss my fee."

"About that," Doc Adams said. "I've been thinking on the . . . other part. I-I'm not certain how to tell—"

"You won't. Just bring them here. I'll discuss the rest with these two gentlemen."

As the doctor left, his words repeated in Browning's mind. *The other part.* How would they tell people that to bring their children back, they had to pay a life? Before Charlie was resurrected, it had seemed simple enough. Of course people would pay that price, terrible though it was. This was their children. His own wife would have gladly given her life for their son.

Except, now, having seen Charlie return, Browning wasn't as certain. No, in fact, he was quite sure that if he'd told Dorothy the cost, she'd have flown at him like a harpy, as she'd done when he said Charlie was back. She'd never have believed him. She certainly wouldn't have offered to die for the chance to resurrect their son. She'd have thought him mad.

It is madness. Desperate madness. How had they ever agreed—

No, not madness. Charlie was alive.

"How're we gonna do it?" Dobbs asked, and when Browning looked over, the blacksmith was sitting down, his face pale.

"Strangulation," Eleazar said. "That is the swiftest and cleanest way."

Dobbs raised his gaze to the man, his eyes filling with horror. "I only meant finding volunteers. We don't need to . . . to . . . *take* them, too, do we?"

"Do you expect me to?" Eleazar's eyes flashed with annoyance. "I took Rene's life because I owed him as much, for his years of service. He trusted me to be swift and kind. It is still an unpleasant task, one I don't intend to repeat six more times."

Dobbs looked as if he might be sick. Browning's mind reeled. *Six times.* Strangle six people. Take six lives. How had this seemed simple before?

"Now, you must do it quietly," Eleazar said. "You cannot announce this price or you will have chaos. Even if you get your volunteers, there will be resentments and rancor for years."

"Even if we get our volunteers?" Browning turned to the man. "I thought . . . You've done this before. People must have volunteered."

"Certainly. If, as I said, they are ill or elderly and wish to escape this life. Sometimes, though, that is not the case, which is what it seems here."

"Then how. . . ?" Browning swallowed. "You brought Charlie back in front of them. Now the doctor is out telling them they can have their children back for three hundred dollars. If they arrive and we say it's not true . . ."

"It damned well better be true," Dobbs said, pushing to his feet. He turned on Browning. "You tricked me."

"What—"

"Your son was the demonstration. He's alive, and you didn't have to pay anything for it. No money. No life. Now my boy lies in his coffin, and you're telling me he's not going to come back unless I kill someone?"

"I never said—I didn't volunteer Charlie. Mr. Eleazar asked for him. You were sitting there when he did. You heard everything."

Browning turned to Eleazar and the man nodded, but his agreement seemed a moment too slow.

"You two made a deal," Dobbs said to Browning. "On the side, before Doc and I arrived."

As Browning sputtered, Eleazar rose, shaking his head. "That's ridiculous. His Worship heard the plan when you did."

The words were the right ones, but something in Eleazar's tone didn't properly support them. Browning could see it as Dobbs's meaty face mottled with fury.

They won't believe me, no matter what Eleazar says. They'll think I used my position to strike a bargain.

"I'll pay," Browning said quickly. "I will donate my three hundred to help anyone who falls short, at no rate of interest."

"And the rest?"

"I had nothing to do with the rest. Mr. Eleazar offered his assistant. Everyone else will have to find a suitable volunteer."

"How?" Dobbs's voice rose. "My wife? Myself? Bring back one child and leave the rest with no one to raise them? No one to support them? Another of my children? Pick the one I like least? How is a father supposed to do such a thing? There is no one else. We have no other family in Chestnut Hill."

Perhaps you ought to have thought of that before you agreed. That's what Browning wanted to say as his guilt turned to outrage at the injustice of it all. He hadn't offered Charlie. He hadn't brokered a special deal.

Browning squared his shoulders. "If you cannot pay, then perhaps—"

The mayor never saw the blow coming. He felt Dobbs's fist hit his jaw, sending him reeling back. He recovered and swung at Dobbs but missed, the younger man grabbing his arm and wrenching, sending him flying into the wall.

"Gentlemen," Eleazar said. "Really. Must it come to this?"

He sounded almost bored, and Browning turned on him, the outrage filling him as pain coursed through his jaw. They were turning on each other now, and Eleazar was to blame. Eleazar had brought this to Chestnut Hill. He'd—

Resurrected Charlie. This was the man who'd granted his fondest wish.

Browning's fists dropped to his sides.

"There are other ways," Eleazar said. "They may be distasteful, but given the alternative of not returning the children . . ."

"What do you propose?" Browning asked.

Eleazar took a seat again. "In every village, there are . . . those who are not fully contributing to community life."

The blacksmith's face screwed up in confusion. "What do you mean?"

"I mean those who live on the outskirts, both physically and metaphorically. Those living outside the village. Those who drink more than they ought. Perhaps aren't quite as intelligent as others. Perhaps not as mentally sound. Perhaps don't fit in—the native population and such. Are there any of those around Chestnut Hill?"

"Some," Dobbs said. "There were little Adeline's parents, but they're dead now. There's others too. Old man Cranston and his wife. They're crazy, both of them. Trapper Mike. He's half-Injun, with a squaw wife. Timothy James, another trapper, when he's not too drunk to remember to empty his traps."

"See, there's five, with only a few moments of thought. I'm sure there are more."

Dobbs nodded, thinking it through. Dear God, was he really thinking it through? No, he couldn't be. Not that way. He was seeing a solution and seizing it, with no thoughts except how this brought his boy back.

"You're . . . you're suggesting we commit murder," Browning said slowly.

"Hardly. I'm suggesting you remove an unproductive segment of the local population. A potentially dangerous segment. Have any of these people ever caused problems for you?"

Dobbs nodded. "Timothy James went after one of Millie Prior's grand-daughters a few years ago. Grabbed her in the forest and touched her before she got away. Old man Cranston shoots at anyone who steps on his property. He doesn't even *have* property. No one knows what he considers his, on account of him being crazy. And Trapper Mike? Folks around here swear he steals from their traps. Never caught him, but he's sneaky. I don't doubt he does it. Then there's Paul over by the lake. Won't tell nobody his last name. I hear he's a fugitive. I've been trying to get an accounting from the Mounties, but they haven't come by Chestnut Hill in near on a year."

"Because you aren't on the railroad route," Eleazar said. "The authorities are ignoring you. Leaving you to defend this town all by yourself . . . Sheriff. I'd say it'd be your God-given right to go talk to those folks, and if they give you any trouble, well, I think you've had enough trouble from them. Who knows what they'll do next? You need to look after your town."

Dobbs nodded. "I do. Look after my town and its children."

"Now, you, Mayor Browning." Eleazar turned to him. "I'd say it's your responsibility to accompany the good sheriff." He paused. "If your people don't get their children back after you got Charlie. . . ? I've seen some ugly things in these wilderness towns. Folks can go a little wild out here. A mob is a wicked thing, Mayor."

Browning looked from Eleazar to Dobbs. And he knew he didn't have a choice. This was the cost of bringing his boy back. The real cost.

ADDIE

Addie raced all the way home. She got there just as Preacher and Sophia arrived. Any other time, walking together, they would have been talking or whispering, and Preacher would have had his hand on Sophia's arm. Today it was as if each walked alone, silent and stone-faced with shock.

Preacher saw Addie first. He seemed to take a moment to recognize her. Then he said, "Adeline," and Sophia started from her stupor.

"You were there," Sophia said. "You saw."

Addie nodded.

"I—we don't know how to explain it," Sophia said. "It is . . . beyond reckoning."

"There must be something to it," Preacher murmured, as if to himself. "Some science. Perhaps the boy was not dead. I've read of such things. Perhaps it's not diphtheria but some new disease. These men pretend to raise the dead, but they know the children were never truly gone, so . . ." He shook his head. "No, I don't see how that's possible. Doc Adams would have noticed."

They reached the porch. Preacher ushered them inside. Neither seemed to have noted that Addie hadn't breathed a word. As soon as the door closed, she said, "Something's wrong with Charlie."

Preacher blinked, as if waking from sleep. "Wrong. . . ?"

"Besides the fact that he's been raised from the dead?" Sophia stopped and her cheeks flushed. "I'm sorry, Addie. I don't mean to be sharp. I'm still trying to reconcile what I saw. That a boy could rise—"

"It's not Charlie."

She got them into the living room, prodding them along as if they were the children. "I went inside to see him. Whoever—whatever—is inside Charlie, it's not him. Or he's wrong. Very wrong. He didn't know me at all."

Preacher lowered himself into a chair. "Eleazar said he'd be exhausted—"

"It was more than that. He had no idea who I was. He didn't recognize a feather that he wore in his cap for half a year. He didn't care to *try* to recognize it. Or me. It was not Charlie."

"But that's . . ." Sophia trailed off and shook her head. "I'm not sure if that's more or less incredible. How would it not be him? Who would it be?"

"*What* would it be," Addie said, correcting her. "Eleazar has summoned a demon into Charlie's body. He is possessed."

Preacher and Sophia didn't much like Addie's possession notion. It seemed quite reasonable to her. She'd grown up in a world where monstrous things happened, and rather than run from the idea, she'd always embraced it. Nothing thrilled her so much as stories of hags and squonks, loup-garous and wampus cats.

She knew all about possession. It was right there in the Bible. And it was real, too. Millie Prior's cousin up in North Bay had been possessed, and they had to bring a priest all the way from New York City to exorcise her. If priests did it, then it must have been real. Addie didn't see how you could argue with that. Preacher still did.

Eventually, they seemed to accept that something might be wrong with Charlie.

"If he was brought back, it would make sense that he'd be . . . not right," Sophia said. "It's unnatural. It's not the work of God. I know that."

"The work of the Devil," Addie said.

She could tell Sophia didn't like that idea much either. If Addie found herself pulled toward demons and evil, Sophia sought out angels and goodness. That's the way she was. As for Preacher, Addie figured he didn't quite believe in angels *or* devils—he just knew this was wrong. The dead ought not to come back, however much one might wish it.

"His assistant is dead, too," Addie said.

Sophia stared at her for a moment, then managed to say, "His. . . ?"

"Rene," Preacher murmured. "Or Mr. Rene. I'm not sure if it was a Christian name or family."

"There is no Christian in these men," Sophia muttered. "You mean the old one, then? He was the assistant? And you say he's . . . he's . . ." She couldn't seem to finish.

"Dead. I saw him at the hall. I thought he was asleep, but his eyes were open and . . . he was dead. I'm sure Eleazar has killed him."

She went still. Preacher did too, and Addie could tell they were processing the shock of her news.

"But why?" Sophia said finally. "Why bring him here, only to kill him?"

"I'm going to find out," Preacher said, rising. "Addie? Stay with Sophia and watch out for her. I'll return as soon as I have answers."

PREACHER

When Preacher said he was going to get answers, he didn't mean to find out why Rene had been murdered and what was "inside" Charlie Browning. The first step was confirming that what Addie said of Rene was true. Not that he suspected her of lying. She'd never do so on such a grand scale.

No, Addie believed what she said to be true. While he could not take her claims as truth, he had been a teacher long enough to know that you did not doubt a child to her face. Few things eroded her confidence more. You accepted the truth of what she said and quietly investigated on your own. As he was doing now.

When he arrived at the community hall, Doc Adams was coming out. Preacher stopped on the road, behind a cluster of people. Through the open door, he could catch a glimpse of Eleazar with the mayor and Dobbs.

Another meeting. He wouldn't be welcome there. He watched Doc Adams hurry away, fending off questions from those gathered outside. Of the other council members, the doctor would be most likely to speak to Preacher, but he was clearly on a mission. Preacher was too—a mission that involved finding answers, not asking for them.

Once the doctor had left, Preacher retreated two houses over and cut through to the forest. He came out behind the community hall and entered through the back door. As he walked through the kitchen, he could hear Dobbs shouting about something, but the walls were too thick to allow him to hear more than angry, unintelligible words. By the time he opened the door into the back room, the dispute was already over, the voices low again.

He slipped through the doorway and—

There was Rene. Preacher had been so caught up in the voices that he'd forgotten why he was really here. One glance in Rene's direction and he knew Addie was right. The man was dead. Still, despite what his eyes told him, he had to check.

He pulled off his boots and crossed the floor silently. When he reached the old man, he put his fingers to his neck and then checked for breathing, and the whole time, a voice in his head was saying, *The man's eyes are open. He has bruises around his neck. His skin is cold. Do you have to question everything?* Yes, apparently, he did. So he checked, and he confirmed that Rene was indeed deceased.

As Sophia had said, why bring the old man here on foot, a difficult journey, only to kill him? There was something missing.

Preacher stood there, puzzling it out, until he remembered that the men were still talking in the next room. He ought to have been listening in. When he got to the door, though, he could hear the mayor and Dobbs leaving. Preacher left quickly and ducked through the kitchen doorway as Eleazar walked into the back room.

"Now, what am I going to do with this?" Eleazar mused aloud. "I ought to have had the blacksmith carry it out back to the woods." He sighed and crossed the room, and Preacher could hear him lifting the old man, testing the weight.

"Let's get this over with," Eleazar muttered.

Preacher hurried out the back door.

When Preacher got to the road, there was no sign of Dobbs and Browning. He asked those gathered which way they went. They pointed, but the two men were already out of sight. Had they gone into a house? Headed home? No one seemed to know. They were all waiting for Eleazar.

Preacher caught sight of Doc Adams at the far end of the road. He started that way but didn't get far before someone hurried out to stop him. Maybelle Greene, a widow whose two children had both survived the outbreak. He'd have liked to see that as the grace of God, but it probably had more to do with the family having been ten miles away visiting her sister at the time.

"Preacher," Maybelle said as she hurried up to him. "I heard what they're saying. Is it true? That man brought Charlie Browning back?"

"Seems so."

She stopped, her face clouding as she looked both ways. No one was nearby, but she still leaned in as she said, "I ought to be happy. Thanking God for his mercy. But . . ." She looked up at him. "They say it's God's work, but I can't quite reckon that. Why would God take our children, then send this man to bring some back? Why not just take fewer? Or none at all?"

That was the question, wasn't it? Along with "Why would God take them at all?" but few dared ask that one. In his heart, Preacher believed that God simply didn't concern Himself in the daily affairs of man. He'd given them the tools they needed to survive—the intelligence to discover things like the causes and cures of disease. It was up to them to use those tools against forces of nature that sought to keep the population in check. It was not a popular answer. So instead, he'd babble about God's plan and God's wisdom and the book of Job and such.

To Maybelle, he only said, "This man—Eleazar—claims to do God's work."

"Does he truly do it?" Maybelle asked, her dark eyes searching his.

"I hope so," he murmured. "But that's what I'm trying to find out."

She nodded, seeming satisfied. As he took his leave, he saw Doc Adams coming out of the house down the road.

Preacher broke into a run, garnering a few askance looks from passersby. He reached the doctor as he still stood on the porch, talking to the Osbournes, who'd lost a child three days past. When the Osbournes saw Preacher, he expected them to want to talk, seek spiritual guidance. Surely Doc Adams had been there about their child. But they caught one glimpse of him and immediately withdrew, cutting the conversation short and closing the door.

The doctor saw Preacher then and went still.

"I'd like to talk to you," Preacher said.

"I'm very busy." Doc Adams started to scurry off. "I can speak to you later—"

Preacher swung into his path. "I'll only take a few moments of your time. Were you telling the Osbournes that their daughter can't be returned?"

"No, I was telling them that she can."

"For three hundred dollars."

Doc Adams tried to pass. "You ought to speak to the mayor—"

"He's gone."

The doctor paused. "Gone?"

"He left with Mr. Dobbs. On some task, it seems. So . . . three hundred dollars is the price of a child's life?"

"Yes, and the Osbournes will pay. We will make sure everyone can pay. Now, if you'll excuse me—"

"Three hundred and what else?"

Preacher hadn't honestly expected any "else"—it was an arrow fired wild—but when he saw the other man's expression, he knew that arrow had struck home.

"I heard there was something more," Preacher said. "Something you aren't telling the families."

Doc Adams's face went bright red. He blustered, asking who'd told Preacher and insisting it was merely rumor, people talking, that there was no other price. Finally, when he seemed to see that Preacher wasn't going to back down, he started down the street.

"I have work to do," he said. "Other families to inform of the wondrous news."

"And families to tell that they will not have their children returned. You yourself admitted they cannot all be returned. Has Mayor Browning set you on that task as well? Deliver the good news and the bad?"

"It was not the mayor—"

Doc Adams clipped his words short and kept moving, shoulders hunched, as if against the cold, but there was no more than a light breeze.

Preacher strode up beside him. "So it was Eleazar who sent you on this mission. Then he sent the mayor and Dobbs on another, one that ill suited you."

Doc Adams glanced over, eyes narrowing, then quickly looked away. "I don't know what—"

"I was there. Outside. You left. They kept talking. Arguing, even. Then Browning and Dobbs left. Eleazar wanted to discuss something with them out of your earshot. I'm sure you know it. He sent you away, just as the mayor sent me away when I balked. What did you balk at, Doctor?"

The doctor's expression told Preacher he had *not* balked. Not openly.

"He knew you would," Preacher said. "That's why he sent you off before the subject was raised. Because, like me, you are a fellow of conscience and—"

Doc Adams spun on him. "Good God, man. Do you never stop? You're like a hound with a bone. Leave it be."

"I will not. I'll ask until I have answers. What's the other cost? What else must we pay for our children's return?"

The doctor turned and resumed walking.

"The old man's dead, you know," Preacher said.

Doc Adams glanced back.

"Rene. Eleazar's assistant. He's dead."

Again, it was the expression that gave the doctor away. Preacher had expected shock. He didn't see it.

He's not surprised. He's not horrified. He knew, and however it happened, this man—this good man—has no compunctions about it. How is that possible?

The cost.

When the idea hit, Preacher brushed it aside. It was as wildly fantastical as Addie's claims of demons and possession. And yet it clung there, like a burr, prickling his mind as he caught up and walked alongside the silent doctor.

"That's the price, isn't it? To return life, you must give life."

The older man's shoulders slumped and when he looked over, it was with an expression Preacher saw each week . . . in the face of a parishioner at confession.

"Yes," Doc Adams said. "That is the price. But the old man gave his life willingly. He volunteered."

"And now you need to find a volunteer for each child? Is that what you said to the Osbournes?"

"No, I was told not to tell them."

"Then how does Eleazar expect to get volunteers, if no one knows they're needed? He requires . . ." Preacher trailed off. "That's what they were discussing without you. How to fulfill that part of the bargain. And whatever Eleazar suggested, he knew you would not countenance it. That's why he sent you off."

Doc Adams shifted. "I don't know anything about that."

"I know, which is why I need to find the mayor and Dobbs."

Preacher took off before the doctor could say another word.

ADDIE

Addie had been anxious when Preacher set off in search of answers. Now, almost two hours later, she paced the house, glancing out the windows, stepping onto the porch, and peering down the street. At first, Sophia would tell her to rest, find something to occupy her, not to worry about Preacher. The last few times she'd gone outside, though, she'd come back in to find Sophia standing inside the doorway, waiting for a report. Addie would say she could not see him and Sophia would deflate, only to rouse herself with assurances that Preacher was fine, he could look after himself.

Finally, as the second hour drew to a close, Addie said, "I want to go look for him."

Sophia said nothing, which Addie knew meant she wished to say yes but knew she oughtn't.

"I'll be quick," Addie said. "He's probably down at the hall, talking to the mayor and Eleazar. I'll find him, and then I'll come straight back."

Sophia nodded. Addie gathered her things and went.

Preacher was not in town. Neither was Mayor Browning nor Mr. Dobbs. As Addie learned, Preacher had been asking after them, and someone had last seen Dobbs and Browning heading into the woods, and Preacher had gone off in pursuit.

Addie followed. They'd taken the main trail out of town, which made tracking difficult. She looked for small signs—a broken twig, a boot print in damp ground—and kept her ears attuned. She was no more than a quarter mile from town when she heard Browning and Dobbs returning. She snuck into the forest to watch as they passed. Soon she saw them, trudging along, faces grim, not speaking. There was a purpling bruise on the mayor's jaw. She stared at that, then began drawing back farther to let them pass, when she spotted something on Dobbs's boots. They were light brown, tanned leather . . . and one was speckled red.

Addie crept hunched over through the undergrowth, until she was close enough to see the glistening specks. More on his trouser leg. Blood. There was no doubt of it.

Addie tried to inhale but couldn't force the air into her chest. Her heart pounded too hard.

Mr. Dobbs is speckled with blood. Preacher is missing. Preacher, who dared argue against their plan. Dared suggest it was not the work of God.

She held herself still until they were gone. Then she dashed onto the path and broke into a run.

Addie tore along the path, convinced she would at any moment stumble over Preacher's dead body. She did not, which only made her more panicked, certain it was out there in the forest, where she would not find it, where scavengers would feast—

She took deep, shuddering breaths to calm herself, then began retracing her steps along the path, slower now, searching for any sign that someone had left the path. When she reached the first fork, she heard something. She stopped, her eyes squeezed shut as she listened. Then she tore down the secondary path, branches whipping her face, until—

"Addie?"

Preacher's voice. Preacher's footfalls, pounding along the path. Then he was there, standing in front of her. No blood to be seen.

"Addie? Are you all right? Is it Sophia? Is she—?"

"Sophia is well." She bent, catching her breath. "All is well."

She hiccuped a laugh. *All is well? Charlie is possessed by a demon monster. All is not well. But right now, it is. Preacher is fine. Unharmed.*

Preacher came over, face drawn in concern, hand resting on her arm as she found her breath.

"It's all right," she said. "We were only worried about you. Me and Sophia."

"Sophia and I," Preacher said.

Addie burst out with a real laugh then. No matter how dire the situation, he could not fail to correct her grammar, as gently as if they were at the supper table, saying grace.

When she laughed, Preacher gave a crooked smile and shook his head, murmuring an apology before saying, "Well, you've found me. And I did not find what I was looking for."

"The mayor and Mr. Dobbs? I saw them a ways back. Returning to town."

"They've finished their mission then," he whispered beneath his breath.

"What mission?"

He looked startled, as if he had not meant to speak aloud. "They were out here for something. I know not what. Come. Let's go back to town."

As they began to walk, Addie thought about the blood on Dobbs's boot. He had not hurt Preacher, but he had hurt something. Some animal? She recalled stories of dark magic, with animals sacrificed to the Devil.

"Perhaps we ought to find where they've been," she said.

"That's what I was trying to do."

"No, you were trying to find where they *are*. I can track where they've *been*."

He hesitated. "All right then. I don't want to leave Sophia for long, but if we can discover what they were doing, we ought to."

PREACHER

Addie was indeed able to track where the mayor and blacksmith had gone. And when she found out, Preacher wished to God she hadn't. He wished he hadn't asked. Wished he'd found this on his own, before she'd arrived. A merciful God would have made sure of that.

She'd tracked Dobbs's and Browning's footsteps back to where they'd left the main trail. It had taken time, but she'd eventually determined that they'd taken a secondary one, little more than a half-cleared path through the trees. Preacher had not known where the trail led. Addie had. He was certain of it. But it was not until they saw the cabin ahead and he said, "What's that?" that she said, "Timothy James's place."

Timothy James. An odd creature, like most who made their living in the forest. Preacher had heard whispers about Timothy James, that he'd come here fleeing the Mounties, that he'd been caught with a little girl. Preacher had been furious—if there was a man like that in their midst, they ought to warn the children. But Dobbs said it wasn't true. Timothy James was merely odd. Preacher had always wondered if Mr. Dobbs's reluctance to drive the man out had anything to do with the fact that he brought in good furs and he accepted less than market rates for them.

Now, seeing that cabin ahead, Preacher knew where Browning and Dobbs had been going. What they'd done there. He'd told Addie to wait while he ran ahead.

He found Timothy James behind his cabin. Lying on the ground. Rope burns around his neck. His shirt covered in blood.

"He must have fought."

It was Addie's voice. Preacher wheeled to see her standing there, looking down at the body.

"They tried to hang him," she said. "Or strangle him. Like Rene. But he fought and they had to stab him."

She stated it as a matter of fact, and for a moment, he was frozen there, unable to react. Her thin face was hard and empty, her eyes empty, too. He'd seen that look on her once before. That horrible day two years ago, when Addie had shown up on Preacher's doorstep in her nightgown, her feet bare and bloodied and filthy from the two-mile walk.

Something's wrong with my parents, she'd said.

They'd gone back, Preacher and Dobbs and Doc Adams. Rode on the horses, Preacher with Addie, who they'd dressed in Sophia's clean clothes, her thin arms wrapped around him. They'd gone back to her parents' cabin, expecting they'd taken ill, and instead found . . .

Preacher swallowed, remembering what they'd found. Remembering Addie beside him, her face as empty as this, hollow and dead, looking at the horrific bodies of her parents.

Preacher strode over, took her by the shoulders, and did what he'd done two years ago—turned her away from the sight and bustled her off. She let him take her around the cabin, then dug in her heels and stopped.

"Why did they kill him?" she asked.

"I don't know."

"Yes, you do. That's why you made me stay on the path. You knew he was dead."

Preacher hesitated. She was right, of course. She wasn't a child. That was the problem. He wanted to tell her not to worry, not to think on it. She didn't require an explanation. He was the adult, and he could make that decision, as parents did for their children. Yet he knew that to do so was to loosen his already tenuous grip on his foster daughter. Treat her as a child, and he'd earn her disdain. He would have taken that chance if he thought it would truly stop her from learning the truth. It would not. She'd proven already that she was as curious—and as dogged—as he.

"They killed Rene, too," she said as he tried to decide what to tell her. "Is it the same thing?"

"Yes, it appears so. Eleazar claims that to give life . . ." He struggled for the kindest words.

"They must take it," she said, again as if this were a simple matter, one that anyone ought to be able to see. "They killed the old man to bring back Charlie. And now they've killed Timothy James . . ."

He didn't hear the rest of what she said. He knew the rest. They'd killed Timothy James to bring back another. Then, once that child was raised from the dead, there were five more . . .

"We must go," he said. "Back to town. Immediately."

Preacher heard the weeping before he saw the town ahead. Wailing and sobbing and crying out to God. That's what he heard, and he ran as he hadn't since he was a boy. Ran so fast he could no longer hear anything but the crash of sound, like the ocean's surf, rising and falling.

From the end of the main road he could see the crowd. The entire village it seemed, gathered down at the hall, the mass of them blocking the road. People sobbing. People on their knees. People standing in stunned silence.

He looked back for Addie, but she was right there.

"Go to Sophia!" he said.

She hesitated, but she seemed to see the fear in his eyes, nodded, and veered off in the direction of the house. Preacher kept running. When he reached the crowd, he prepared himself for what he might see. The horrors that could cause such wailing.

On a normal day, if the villagers saw him coming, they'd make way. He was the preacher. But now, even when he nudged through, they resisted, pushing him back until he had to shove past, as if he were at a cockfight, jostling for a better view.

Finally, the villagers seemed to see him, to recognize him. Or they simply realized he would not be held back. The crowd parted. There, at the front, he saw . . .

Children. All six of them. Sitting up in their coffins, looking about, as if confused, their parents grabbing them up, hugging them, wailing.

Now that the thunder in his ears had died down, he realized what he was hearing. Sobs and wails of joy. Praising God. Thanking God.

He looked at those six children and those six families, and there was a moment when he wanted to fall to his knees with the others. To say, *This is a miracle.* To accept it as a miracle.

Then he remembered the body in the woods. Timothy James, lying in the dirt, covered in blood, staring at the sky.

Six children alive. Six people dead.

Dear God, who else did they take? Who else did they murder?

He reeled, stomach clenching, gaze swinging to Dobbs, embracing his child, his big body shaking with joy. Preacher glanced down, about to back away. Then he saw the blood on Dobbs's boot. Timothy James's blood on his boot. Timothy James's murder on his hands.

"What's going on?" a voice cried.

Everyone went still. The voice asked again, and it was a high voice, a reedy voice. A child. Preacher turned to see one of the resurrected—six-year-old Jonas Meek—pushing his mother away as his gaze swung over the crowd.

"Who the bloody hell are all of you?" the boy asked.

Eleazar leaped forward as the crowd gasped and the boy's mother fell back, crossing herself. Jonas began to push up from his coffin, his face fixed in a snarl as he said something Preacher didn't catch.

"Restrain him!" Eleazar said. "Quickly!"

Two men leaped in to do it as Eleazar strode forward, cloth in hand. He pressed it to the boy's face, ignoring his struggles. Preacher caught a whiff of something familiar from his college science classes. Chloroform.

As Jonas went limp, Eleazar's voice rang out over the stunned crowd. "I warned you that this might happen. I will sedate them all now, to prevent further injury. They are confused and will act most unlike themselves for a day or two. But all is well. Your children are returned to you and all is well."

Preacher stepped forward, but before his boot even touched down, Dobbs was there, moving unbelievably fast for a man of his size. He planted himself in front of Preacher.

"You don't belong here, Benjamin," he said.

"I know—"

Dobbs stepped forward. "I said you don't belong here." He lowered his voice. "I would suggest you run on home, preacher boy. Back to your wild brat and your pretty wife. You ought not to leave your family alone."

Preacher looked up into the man's eyes and his gut chilled. There was nothing there. No compassion. No compunction. Perhaps there had been, when he'd undertaken his task, but now that it was done, Dobbs had severed any part of himself that might have felt guilt. He'd done right, and if Preacher dared suggest otherwise . . .

"He's right," another voice said. It was Mayor Browning, moving up beside Dobbs. "Go home, Benjamin. You aren't wanted here."

"But, Preacher," someone said. It was Maybelle, pushing through the crowd. "What do you think of this? Can you speak to us about it?"

"No," Browning said. "He cannot. This isn't your preacher. It's a false man of God, one who would deny this miracle, who would tell you it's wrong, sinful."

Behind Browning, Eleazar stood watching, lips moving, and that chill suffused Preacher's entire body.

It is as if he is putting words in their mouths. As if they are puppets to his will.

"This preacher would take back our children," Browning said. "Steal them from us again."

Preacher started to argue, to say that was not it at all, but there seemed to come a growl from the crowd, and when he looked about, he felt as if he were surrounded by wolves, scenting a threat in the air—a threat to their young and to themselves. He saw that and knew what he must do. The only choice he had.

He closed his mouth, backed away from the crowd, and raced home.

ADDIE

Addie was arguing with Sophia when they heard Preacher coming up the steps. Sophia wanted to go out, to see what was happening. Addie had to block the door to keep her in.

"You ought not to see," Addie was saying. "Preacher doesn't want it."

"I'm not a child, Adeline—"

"But you are *with* child. You cannot be upset. You might lose the babe."

That had stopped her, as Addie knew it would. Then Preacher's footsteps clattered up the steps, and he threw open the door and said, "Pack your things. You're leaving. Now."

Sophia argued, of course. She often did. Addie had never seen a woman who felt herself so free to dispute her husband's word. Or a husband who allowed it. Certainly, in her own home, her mother had only to issue the smallest word of complaint, and she'd be abed for days, recovering. To actually argue? Addie had only seen that once. And when it was over, her mother would never argue again.

But Sophia did. And yet, even as she disputed her husband's word, she did not stand there and holler at him. She could see how agitated he was, and she immediately set about packing as he asked, while arguing about leaving.

Preacher wanted them to go. Her and Sophia. Immediately. He told Sophia what had happened, in the gentlest terms possible, but they still shocked her into a near trance, gaping at him as if he'd gone mad. Addie confirmed it was true, all of it. Rene and Timothy James had been murdered to bring back the children, and there was something very wrong with the children, and they had to flee.

"But . . . but the villagers," Sophia said. "They are almost all innocent in this. We cannot abandon them—"

"I'm not. I'm sending you and Addie on ahead. I need to find out precisely what has happened here and warn those who will let themselves be warned. Then I will join you."

Sophia pulled herself up to her full height—which barely reached Preacher's chin. "I am not going anywhere without you, Benjamin."

"Yes, you are. You and Addie and the baby. Dobbs has already made his threat against my family. You will leave, and I will do what I can here, which I cannot do if I'm worrying about you."

"Preacher's right," Addie said.

She walked up beside Sophia and took her hand. It felt odd, reaching for another person, voluntarily touching another person. But she took her hand and squeezed it.

"You need to go," Addie said. "For your child."

Sophia looked down at their hands, then at Addie.

"All right," she said. "I'll go. For my *children*."

PREACHER

What had Eleazar done? Dark deeds, Preacher was sure of that. Murder. Inciting others to murder. And more. But *what* more? What exactly was wrong with Charlie and the others? That was what he had to discover.

Of the children who'd been raised, only Charlie was awake. The others had all been sedated. Deeply sedated. He confirmed that by paying a visit to the Meeks. They were a God-fearing couple who'd always been kind to him, and he'd seen the look on Ella Meek's face when her son started spewing such venom after the resurrection. She was frightened. So Preacher spoke to her.

Jonas had not stirred since he'd been chloroformed. Eleazar had told them that if he did, and he said anything untoward or concerning, they were to give him another dose, from a small bottle he'd left. The boy was fine, simply not himself. Not yet.

"But he's only six years old," Ella Meek said to Preacher. "He doesn't even know those words he was saying. He's a good boy. A quiet boy."

And so he was, one of the quietest in the town. All his family was, prompting the joke that they truly earned their surname. Meek and mild.

"And the others have been told the same?" he asked.

She nodded. "All of them."

All except Charlie. Who was, by all accounts, resting comfortably at his home. It was time for Preacher to pay the boy a visit.

ADDIE

Addie had lied to Preacher. She would, perhaps, eventually feel guilt about that. But not today. Today did not count by any proper reckoning. Sophia knew of the promise and had participated in breaking it, which proved the world had, indeed, turned upside down.

Addie had promised to stay with Sophia. To ride through the forest, where they'd not be seen, then over to the road and hightail it to Greenville. That was not what she had done. She'd gathered the horses—they had two—and met Sophia on the wide main path. It was quite impossible to hide the taking of the horses, but no one seemed to pay her much mind. In truth, no one had even noticed. They rode until they had to dismount and steer the horses along the secondary path to Timothy James's cabin. Then Addie ensconced Sophia there, shotgun in hand, and went back to town. For Preacher. To keep him safe.

PREACHER

"I've come to apologize," Preacher said, standing on Mayor Browning's front porch, hat in hand. "I was wrong, and I see that now. My lack of faith blinded me. Mr. Dobbs is right. I am not fit to be a man of God. I will be withdrawing from my position immediately."

"What?" The reply came from deep within the house. Dorothy Browning pushed past her husband. "Quit? No. Our town needs you, Preacher, perhaps now more than ever—"

Browning nudged her back. "We'll talk on this later, Benjamin. It's a poor time."

"I know. I didn't come here to resign so much as I came to apologize. I was wrong. I misspoke. A miracle has occurred in Chestnut Hill. Seven miracles."

The whole time he spoke, Browning nodded absently, as if urging him along. *Finish up and begone, man.*

"Charlie is well, then?" Preacher asked.

"Well enough."

Dorothy made a noise, but a glare from her husband cut her short.

"May I see him?" Preacher asked. "Addie is most anxious to speak to her friend again. I've told her this is, as you've said, a poor time. However, she asked me to give him this."

He pulled a stone from his pocket. It was a pretty one, veined with fool's gold. He'd found it two doors down, by the roadside.

Preacher continued. "She says it will lighten his spirits. It's hers, and he always admired it."

"He's not—" Dorothy began.

"I'll take it and give it to him," Browning said.

"May I?" said Preacher. "It would mean so much to Addie if I could tell her his response."

"He's gone," Dorothy said. "With that—" Browning glowered at her, but she squared her thin shoulders and said, "He's gone with that man. They went a-walking a while back. He says Charlie's weak, and then he takes him a-walking. The boy has—"

"That's enough, woman," Browning cut in.

She continued. "The boy—my boy—has scarcely said two words to me. Too weak to converse, that man says. But Charlie can walk and converse with *him*, easily enough."

"Well, I'll leave the stone, then," Preacher said. "And I'll leave young Charlie with Eleazar. The man does not wish to see me, I'm certain, so I will stay clear."

Preacher found Eleazar and Charlie. They had not gone far, just deep enough into the woods that they wouldn't be overheard, and far enough off the path that they wouldn't be seen. Preacher snuck up as best he could. It would not have satisfied Addie, but the two were in such deep conversation that they did not notice him.

"Are you certain that is enough food, boy?"

"I am, sir."

"I don't think it is. My instructions were clear. We will be walking in this forsaken wilderness for at least two days. We need more food."

"I have enough, sir. Much of it is dried."

Preacher paused, shaking his head as if he was mishearing. It was not the *content* of their conversation. While he was startled to hear they were leaving together, that paled against surprise of the voices themselves. Of who was delivering which lines. He was hearing wrong. He must have been.

He crept forward until he could see the two figures. Charlie was bent on one knee, examining the contents of a pack, while Eleazar stood behind him.

"This money and these goods are not the full accounting," Charlie said. "There's eleven hundred dollars and perhaps two hundred more in goods. That's five hundred short."

"Yes, sir," Eleazar said. "I imagine it is. But this is not a wealthy village. They are gathering more, but I presumed you wanted to be gone before the children fully woke."

"Don't be smart with me, boy," Charlie snapped.

Eleazar cleared his throat. "Given the situation, sir, I might suggest you'll want to stop calling me that."

"In private, I'll call you what I want. How long would it take to get more from them?"

"Too long. And that was not the primary purpose of this trip. We got you something far more valuable than money, did we not?"

Charlie snorted. "A child's body is not particularly valuable. Now, a strong young man's . . ."

"It will be such in a few years. We ought to count ourselves lucky that there was a boy of goodly age in the last week who died. You'd not have wanted to be brought back as a toddling child. Or a girl."

More grumbling. When Preacher had first heard them speaking, his mind had reeled. Then something in his gut steadied it, saying, *Yes, this makes sense.* Of course, in the larger scheme of things, the fact that an old man's soul had been put into the body of a dead boy did *not* make sense, but given all that Preacher had seen, it was more sensible than any explanation he'd considered.

The soul was the essence of life. Charlie's was long gone. In heaven, he trusted. And if one believed that, and one believed the scriptures, then a merciful God would not allow a child to be stolen back from paradise. The body would need to be returned to life with a soul still wandering this world. The soul of someone recently departed.

It had seemed odd that Rene had been Eleazar's assistant, but the man had been so doddering that it would have seemed more shocking to realize the situation was reversed. Now it seemed it was indeed the case. The old man—the leader, the teacher—had been in need of a new body, and they had taken it here, in Chestnut Hill.

As for the other six children . . .

Dear God. The other six.

Timothy James's soul. The souls of five others. Murdered, only to awaken in the bodies of children . . . children whose parents they would hold responsible for their deaths.

Preacher turned away from Eleazar and Rene. What they had done was a horrible thing, deserving a terrible punishment, but right now, there were others about to be punished even more terribly, others who'd known nothing of the murders, who'd only wanted their children—

"You do realize we are not alone, I hope," Rene said, his voice as easy as if he were discussing the possibility of rainfall.

"What?" Eleazar said.

"Someone watches from the woods. I trust you plan to take care of that."

Eleazar let out a curse. Preacher began to run, not caring how much noise he made, only that he got back to the village in time to warn them before—

Something grabbed his legs. He did not trip. He was certain of that. He felt the pressure, something wrapping about them as he ran, and there was no time to stop. He fell face-first to the ground.

"Preacher Benjamin," Eleazar said, crashing through the forest behind him. "You are a persistent man. I will grant you—"

"No, you fool," Rene exclaimed. "Not him. I meant—"

"Preacher! Run!"

It was Addie. Eleazar spun toward her voice, back toward the clearing where Rene stood. Preacher clambered to his feet. He could see no sign of Addie, but he had heard her. He had very clearly—

The *twang* of a bow. He saw the arrow. Saw it heading straight for Rene. Saw it hit him square in the throat.

Eleazar let out a howl of rage and ran for the girl, now standing ten paces away, stringing her bow again.

ADDIE

Addie couldn't ready her bow fast enough. She ought to have been able to—she'd made sure she would have time to fire two arrows. One for the monster that had stolen Charlie's body and one for the monster that had helped him. Yet as she strung the second arrow, the ground seemed to fly up under her feet, as if by magic.

She toppled backward, and Eleazar was on her, wrenching the bow away with one hand while grabbing her coat with the other. She went for her knife, but before her fingers could touch the handle, he'd grabbed it himself. Then he whipped her around, knife at her throat, shouting at Preacher to stop.

Preacher halted in midstep, and stood there, his eyes wild with fear, breath coming so hard she could hear it.

I'm sorry, she thought. *I ought to have shot Eleazar first. Let you escape. But all I could think about was Charlie. That monster in his body.*

The monster that was dying now. Lying on the ground, wheezing its death rattle, arrow lodged in its throat.

"Let her go," Preacher said.

"I cannot," Eleazar said. "I need—"

"I know what you need. And I know that what you have isn't satisfactory. What you had wasn't either. So I'm offering you a trade."

"Are you? Interesting . . ."

"Take it," Preacher said. "It's what he'd want. You know it is."

Addie struggled to figure out what they were talking about. Preacher was making sure she didn't. She could tell that, and a knot of dread in her gut grew bigger with each passing moment.

"Take it," Preacher said. "Quickly."

Eleazar seemed to be considering the matter, but then, without warning, he grabbed Addie by the hair and whipped her against a tree. Her head hit the trunk hard, blackness threatening as she fell. She lay there, fighting to remain awake, as she heard them continue.

"You did not need to do that," Preacher said.

"Oh, I believe I did. She's a feisty little one, and I don't think she'll like what I'm about to do."

"Just get it done. Quickly please."

Addie managed to raise her head and saw Eleazar walk to Preacher. She saw his hands go to Preacher's neck, wrapping around it, and she understood what he'd meant. That with Charlie's body dying, the monster—Rene—needed a new vessel. Eleazar had been going to take hers. Preacher had offered his instead.

"No," she whispered. "Please no."

She could see her bow there, only a few paces away. She dug her fingers into the dirt and pulled herself toward it and—

And she passed out.

PREACHER

As Preacher watched Addie lose consciousness, he had a sudden vision of her death, of Eleazar killing him for his master and then walking over, kneeling and wrapping his fingers around the girl's neck. Preacher's hands flew up, catching Eleazar's, stopping them as they squeezed.

"Wait!" he said.

He held the man's hands still as he looked at him.

"You'll not hurt her," he said. "After it's done."

"I have no cause. You'll have given me what I want."

"It was not a question," Preacher said, locking eyes with the man. "You are accustomed to bodies where the soul is long departed. If Rene's soul still lingers now, then so will mine, for a time. If you hurt the girl . . . I cannot lie and say what I will do, because I do not know what I *may* do. But I am certain I can do something, and so I will, if she's harmed."

"As I said, I'll have no cause once Rene has his new body. A girl child is no threat to me. As for telling anyone, I'm quite certain that by now, your village has already realized something has gone very, very wrong."

The village. The other children.

"No," he said. "You—"

Eleazar's grip tightened. Preacher tried to stop him, to say more, but the man squeezed with inhuman strength and then—

Darkness.

Preacher jolted upright. He was lying on the forest floor, Charlie's body beside him. He scrambled to his feet and looked around, but there was no sign of Eleazar.

Something had gone wrong. He'd been tricked.

Addie.

Preacher whirled, searching for his foster daughter, seeing no sign—

No, there she was, across the clearing, still on the ground. He raced over and dropped beside her. He put his hands to her thin chest and—

His fingers passed through her. He stumbled back, falling on his rear. Then he looked down at his hand, the grass poking through it, undisturbed.

Nothing has gone wrong.

I'm dead.

He gasped, the sudden realization as agonizing as a bullet to the heart.

I'm dead. I'm gone.

Sophia. Dear lord, Sophia. I'll never see her again. Never see our child. Never see Addie grow up.

Addie.

He hurried to the girl again. She was breathing. He could see that. As he rose from her side, a scream split the night.

The village. The villagers. The resurrected children.

Preacher ran toward Chestnut Hill. At first, he weaved around trees and bushes, then realized there was no need and tore through them. He could hear more now, shouts and screams and cries for God.

Soon he could see the houses in the distant darkness. Lights flickered. Doors slammed. Shots rang out. And the screams. The terrible screams—of shock, of pain, of horror.

He came out of the woods behind a house, following some of the worst cries. A woman lay on the grass, not screaming now, but making horrible gurgling noises. Atop her was a boy covered in blood, his face contorted and wild as he raised a stone, hitting her again and again, smashing her face until she couldn't scream, until Preacher could only tell she was a woman by her dress.

He ran toward them, shouting for the boy to stop, please stop.

As he drew near, he could see the child under that mask of blood. Jonas Meek. Little Jonas Meek. And the woman below him, gurgling her last? His mother.

"No," Preacher whispered. "No."

The boy flickered, as if *he* were the ghost, beginning to fade. So too did his mother and the blood-soaked grass below them. Something tugged at Preacher. He tried to fight it. Tried to stay, to help, to do whatever he could, but the pull was too great, and as he scrambled for a hold, feeling himself lifting, he caught sight of something moving at the end of the woods.

He saw himself. Standing there, with Eleazar, watching Jonas Meek beat his mother to death and laughing. He was laughing.

ADDIE

When Addie woke, Eleazar and Preacher were gone. It was growing dark, and she knew she wouldn't find them, but she still raced down the path they would have taken, only to get a quarter mile along it and realize she wasn't even sure this was the way they'd gone. She made her way back to the clearing and tried to search again, to no avail.

And what good would it do if I found them? It's too late. He's gone. Preacher's—

She couldn't finish the thought. Her knees buckled, and she fell to the ground, weeping as she hadn't wept when Charlie died, hadn't when her parents died.

Preacher was gone. Dead. Possessed by that thing, and if she found him, all she could do was what she'd done for Charlie—set his body free. Did that even matter? Their souls were gone. In heaven, she hoped. In heaven, she prayed.

Preacher had given his life for her, and she wasn't even his child. Now he'd never see his real child, because of what he'd done for her, a stranger who'd come into his life and slept in his house and eaten his food. He'd let her in and he'd given her everything. Absolutely everything.

There had been, she realized now, always a part of her that didn't quite trust Preacher and Sophia's motivations in adopting her. They were good people. The best she knew. But surely no one could be that good, no one could voluntarily take her, not when her own parents had begrudged every morsel she took from their larder.

She'd always suspected that there was more to it, that the town paid Preacher and Sophia to care for her. That still made them good people—of all those in the village, she'd known them for the shortest length of time, and yet they were the ones who'd taken her in. But surely they were receiving some compensation. They ought to have been.

Except they weren't. She knew that now. They'd taken her because they'd been worried for her. They'd kept her because they cared for her. And now Preacher had given his life for her because . . . well, perhaps because he loved her.

Addie picked herself up then. She dried her eyes, and she walked to Charlie, and she said her good-byes. He wasn't there. He hadn't been there for three days. But she said them anyway, hoping he'd hear, wherever he was.

Then she gathered her bow and her knife, and she set out. She had a job to do. A job for Preacher.

There was death in the village that night. Addie could hear it as she walked back toward Chestnut Hill. Screams. Horrible screams, as the "children" awakened and everyone learned the truth. They'd murdered people outside the village and put them into the bodies of children, and now the children had awakened, possessed by those vengeful spirits.

This was what Preacher had been running to stop when Eleazar caught him. He'd known what was coming, and he'd wanted to warn them. If he were here now, he'd race to that village and save whom he could.

Addie decided he'd done enough for the village. They'd brought this on themselves, and even if Sophia would say there were many who were innocent, Addie disagreed. They'd let Eleazar into their town. They'd ignored Preacher's warnings. Now they should face whatever wrath their actions had unleashed.

They would not all perish. Likely only a few. She supposed that was terrible enough, if they were innocent of murdering Timothy James and the others. But she did not think as Preacher and Sophia did. It wasn't how she'd been raised, and there were parts of her that all Preacher and Sophia's goodness could not heal.

Addie had spent the last two years haunted by the grave sin she had committed the night her parents died. What she'd done. Or, perhaps, what she'd failed to do.

She'd heard the fight. A dreadful one. The worst ever. She'd listened to her father beating her mother. That was nothing new, but this was not like any other time. Her mother's screams were not like any Addie had ever heard.

Addie had lain in her tattered blanket by the fire, feigning sleep as her father beat her mother to death, and she had done nothing to stop it. Her mother never stopped the beatings he gave to Addie, so why ought Addie to interfere and risk turning that rage on herself?

When it was over, the house had gone silent. She'd risen then, and seen her father sitting in his chair, shotgun in hand. Her mother's body lay crumpled and bloody on the floor.

"You'll hang for this," Addie had said, and what she'd felt, saying it, was not horror or fear but satisfaction.

"No, I won't," he'd replied, and put the gun between his legs, pointed it at his head, and pulled the trigger.

For two years, Addie had lived with that. With listening to her mother die and not intervening. With telling her father what she thought and making him splatter his brains across the room. It was her fault. Her sin. For two years, she'd regretted it, and now she did not. Now she realized they had brought it upon themselves, and had she interfered, she'd only have been lying there with them. They had not raised her to interfere, so she had not. As she would not now.

So she circled wide around the village, ignoring the screams, and continued on.

Addie found Sophia in Timothy James's cabin. She told her that Preacher was gone. Sophia wept as if she'd break in two, so much that Addie feared for the child.

She told Sophia what had happened. Or part of it. That Eleazar had returned the old man to Charlie's body. That he'd returned the souls of the murdered to the children's bodies. But there Addie's story for Sophia changed.

In Addie's version, Preacher had made his escape. He'd run to the village to warn them. He'd arrived too late, the children reawakening, but he'd fought for the villagers. He'd warned who he could and then he'd helped fight off the threat. He'd fought for his village, and he'd lost his life doing it. He was a hero.

That part was true. He *had* sacrificed his life—for Addie. And she would never forget it. He'd given her a family, and now she'd protect that family with everything she had, in every way she could.

So she told Sophia the lies that would set her heart at rest, and then she gathered her up, got her on the horse, and took her away from that place of death, off to find a place where she could bear and raise Preacher's babe, and where she could be happy.

Where they all could be happy.

The Collector

THE WOODEN PUZZLE BOX floated on my computer screen, a 3D model perfectly rendered, the liquid display bubbling under my fingertips as I traced the series of twists and turns that would unlock its mysteries. There, and there and . . . yes, *there*. I smiled.

I couldn't resist mousing over to it and clicking, just in case it proved interactive. It wasn't, of course. Simply an amazing piece of art, the splash screen gateway to the website of a small publisher of puzzle books.

I clicked the "enter here" entreaty, feeling a frisson of grief as that perfect puzzle evaporated, replaced by a perfectly boring website. Now I imagined the solution to another challenge—how, as a Web designer, I could make this site so much better. From the looks of it, though, my services would be more than they could afford, so I directed my gaze to the upper right corner where, as I'd been told, there was a second entreaty—this one to try an online puzzle and win a prize.

So I clicked and read, checking it out so carefully you'd think they were asking me to donate a kidney. But you can't be too careful on the Web. Ninety-nine percent of freebies are bullshit. Fortunately, most of those are obvious—badly worded and misspelled missives that never quite explain how a Nigerian prince got the e-mail address of Mrs. Joe Smith in Nowhere, Idaho.

There is, however, that other one percent—legitimate giveaways for promotional exposure—and this seemed to be one of them. Solve a puzzle; win a prize; progress to the next level for a bigger prize. The entry-level contest would win you a downloadable, sixteen-page puzzle book. A reasonable reward for a reasonably simple puzzle, one I solved absently as most of my brain was still occupied reading the page's fine print.

I entered the solution for the anagram and was redirected to a page with my prize available for immediate download. I scanned the file for viruses, of course, but it was clean. And that was it. They didn't even request an e-mail address so I could be signed up for "exciting promotional offers." The page simply gave me a code that would allow me to progress to the next level . . . after a twenty-four-hour waiting period.

I jotted down the code, bookmarked the site and flipped back to my work.

Over the next week, I proceeded through four more levels, solving a Sudoku, a Tangram, a Tower of Hanoi, a Takegaki, and winning a sample e-book, a three-volume e-collection, a limited edition omnibus and a brass-plated n-puzzle with the company logo on the tile's squares. I needed to provide a mailing address for the last, which was fine. I gave my post office box. I wouldn't be rushing to collect it, though. My reward came in knowing I'd already gotten farther than anyone in the puzzle enthusiast e-mail loop that had first announced the contest.

By day eight, I was sitting at my computer, one eye on the clock, waiting for my next twenty-four-hour hiatus to be up.

My cell phone chirped. When I saw the number, I smiled and picked up.

"Hey, there. Did your conference end early?"

Daniel sighed. "I wish. I just called to say hi, see whether you'd be free for dinner Friday when I get in."

"You aren't tired of eating out yet?"

"As long as they don't serve conference luncheon rubber chicken, I'm good."

A message box popped up on my screen, telling me it was time, and I missed what he said next. I um-hmm'd appropriately, but my mind was already on the next puzzle. It was a variation on the classic Zebra puzzle, otherwise known as Einstein's Riddle. Now this was something worth solving.

"And then I rode a camel through Pittsburgh . . ."

"What?"

"Ah, you *are* listening. Working?"

"Caught me."

"On a puzzle?"

I swore, and apologized. He only laughed, then let me go after we set a date for Friday. Even as I hung up, I was pulling over a sheet of paper and drawing my grid for the puzzle.

I solved it, of course. I shouldn't say that so nonchalantly. It was hard. Damn hard. Logic puzzles aren't my forte. By the time I figured it out, I'd passed my twenty-four-hour waiting limit. Even when I submitted the answer, I wasn't certain I had it right, and the site didn't tell me, just said the answer needed to be manually processed and asked for my e-mail address, with a promise to provide a response within twelve hours. I gave them my throwaway one.

Dramatically, at the top of the eleventh hour, the e-mail arrived. My prize? An invitation to try for the grand prize: five thousand dollars. The catch? I had to go to the publisher's office and solve the same wooden puzzle that was rotating on their splash page.

Now, as a small business owner, I could see the point in this. If you're going to give away real money, you want to get your promotional mileage out of it. Have the prospective winner come down, solve the puzzle and film the big event for your website. Travel could be a problem, but according to the address given, it was just over an hour away. Asking me to drive there was perfectly reasonable for a five-grand payoff.

And yet . . .

I didn't buy my house until I could afford a fifty-percent down payment. I'd been dating Daniel for four years, yet had dodged the marriage question, waiting to be sure we'd make it to five. I vetted every client before accepting a new job. I checked the weather forecast before going out. I had never jaywalked in my life.

I don't take chances. Not even when it comes to my beloved puzzles.

So I researched the puzzle publisher. I verified that the address given was correct, as was the phone number. Then I called using a blocked number.

A woman answered the phone. Elderly, by the creaks and warbles in her voice. Her son owned the business and she was his office assistant. She explained the deal exactly as outlined in the e-mail—come to the office, solve the wooden puzzle, win the prize. Of course, if I won I had to agree to allow my name and photo to be displayed on their site, etcetera, etcetera.

I was given an appointment time. There was street parking, but the municipality towed after an hour and was usually waiting to jump, so she advised me to use a strip mall lot a block away.

After the call, I reloaded the company's splash page and started mentally working through the puzzle again.

The office was what I expected—a few rooms in a small building. As I'd been told, there was a tiny lot for the building's other tenants—a nightclub and an after-hours clinic—but it had been split in half, one side for each business, with signs warning that anyone else would be towed, which seemed highly unfair to the publishing company, given that it was open when the others weren't.

With everything else closed, the building was quiet, my footsteps echoing through the hall, the silence ominous in that horror movie "walking down a dark alley" kind of way that made me check over my shoulder every few steps.

When I reached the publisher's office, though, I relaxed. The cheery yellow walls and comfy furniture helped, but it was the rest of the décor that put me at ease. Puzzles. The room was filled with them, from wooden ones on the coffee table to visual ones on the wall to special pieces on pedestals.

As the owner's mother put my coat away, I walked over to a very old Moku-Zougan Japanese puzzle box and brushed my fingertips over the worn finish, shivering.

"You're a collector, Mrs. Collins?" I asked as she returned.

"My son is. Call me Nell."

Nell wasn't as old as I would have guessed over the phone. Maybe sixty, but careworn, her face lined, hair white, a slight stoop in her shoulders.

She looked around absently, as if for a moment forgetting what she was there for, then said, "Let me get the puzzle."

She bustled off. I heard her speaking in the inner office, her voice too low to make out the words. She returned with the puzzle box, held at arm's length like an offering.

"My son's getting the video camera for us. He's so much better at that sort of thing."

I balled my hands to keep myself from snatching the puzzle box from her. It was even more exquisite than it had looked on the screen, each piece worn smooth from countless hands trying to unlock its mysteries.

"It's not easy, I'm afraid," she said as she handed it to me

I smiled. "If it was, you wouldn't be giving away such a prize. Have there been others?"

"A few. But they haven't . . ." She trailed off.

"Haven't solved it."

"Yes. I'm sorry. I shouldn't be discouraging you."

I flashed her a bigger smile. "Oh, I'm not discouraged. The worthiest puzzle is the one no one else can solve." I turned a piece, pulse leaping as it snapped into place. I started to turn another, then stopped. "Should I wait?"

"No, no, that's fine. He'll come when you're closer to the end. It may take a while."

I looked at her. She was leaning forward, eyes fixed on the puzzle, glittering as I turned the second piece. Then the third.

"Do you do puzzles yourself?" I asked.

She shook her head, gaze never wavering from the box as I continued to click the pieces into place.

"You're very good," she said.

I said nothing, only kept turning, kept hearing that satisfying click.

"No one's ever gotten that far," she breathed in an awestruck whisper.

"It's almost done. You might want to get your son."

"He's busy. If you solve it, we can always restage the last few moves."

I set the puzzle box down. It clacked against the glass tabletop and she jumped at the sound.

"But—" she began. "You were almost—"

"I trust you have a standard release form drawn up?" I said.

"Release form?"

"Giving you permission to use my name and image for promotional purposes. As well as guaranteeing me my prize, should I solve the puzzle."

Her eyes narrowed, eying me as if I were an unreasonable child.

"I suppose I could get one," she said, turning away.

"Good. And I'd like to meet your son."

She froze, shoulders stiffening.

"Do you even have a son, Mrs. Collins?" I asked.

She pivoted slowly, not answering. I hefted my purse and headed for the door.

"Stop," she said.

I turned to see a gun trained on me.

"Ah," I said. "That's how it is then."

"I would like you to complete the puzzle, Ms. Lane. In fact, I insist on it."

I walked over and picked up the puzzle box. I turned it over in my hands, the wood so velvety smooth, so inviting that it took all my willpower not to start turning the final pieces.

"A Lamarchand's Configuration, I presume?"

She blinked. "You know it?"

I lifted it to eye level, peering into its dark cracks. "It's a legendary collection of pieces. Every enthusiast has heard the story."

"Well, I'm not an *enthusiast*," she twisted the word like an insult. "My son is. The puzzle is his."

I glanced toward the inner office and heard sounds within—an oddly wet, squelching noise, as if someone was pacing in sodden slippers.

"My son," she said. "He solved it two years ago, and *they* came."

"The Cenobites."

"Yes. The things they did to him . . ." She shuddered. "But he escaped. He came back and I found him. He was in pain, so much pain, and the only way to ease it was to feed him."

"Not with steak and eggs, I presume."

She looked at me sharply and lifted the gun, as if to remind me this was a serious situation and perhaps I should be a little less blasé about the whole thing.

I went on. "So you lure people here with your contests and feed them to your darling boy. And no one wonders where they've gone? I find that hard to believe."

"Do you? Puzzle enthusiasts are a solitary lot, as you might know, Sarah Lane, age thirty-four, self-employed, never married, no children, no siblings, mother deceased, father in Brazil."

"You've done your research. Let me guess: after you kill me, you'll take my keys and move my car from that distant lot, so when someone does look for me . . ."

"You were never here."

It was a far from foolproof plan, but from the burning glow in her eyes, she was beyond caring. However, mad though she might be, outside of bad movies, I suspect villains don't stand around explaining the situation to their victims. Which begged the question . . .

I turned the puzzle over in my hands. "You *do* want me to solve this. That's why you run the contests, looking for someone who can do it. But why would you want the box opened if you've seen what happens?"

"I want to summon them. Those Cenobites. To take him back." She met my gaze. "There is a limit to maternal obligation."

"If I succeed, you'll be free of your son, and if I fail, he'll be fed."

"Precisely. So," she waved the gun at the puzzle, "if you please."

I completed another twist and again heard the satisfying click of success. As I started the next, she leaned in, gun lowering, gaze fixed once more on the wooden box. The piece clicked into place. I pulled my hand back, reaching to the other side to complete the final turn, and grabbed her wrist, shoving the gun up.

She didn't relinquish the weapon. Put up a good fight for her age, actually.

But I was younger, faster, stronger, and when the gun fired, it wasn't *my* head it was pointing at.

As I knelt beside her body, an unearthly wail battered my eardrums. I looked up to see a figure in the doorway of the inner office. He looked as if he'd been ripped apart and haphazardly sewn back together, every joint from his jaw to his fingers gaping, held together with thick black thread, shredded flesh hanging, bones poking through.

When I didn't run away screaming, he hesitated, confused. Then he charged. I lifted the gun and put a bullet through his gut. He fell back with a howl.

"Hurts, I know. I can't kill you, but sometimes, that's worse, isn't it? Not being able to die."

With a roar, he charged again. I fired again. He screamed again.

"I have a few questions to ask—"

"I'm not telling you anything," he said, his garbled voice wheezing through the gap in his severed neck.

"Is that a challenge?" I smiled. "Excellent. Let's begin then."

He eventually answered all my questions. Then I let him feed off his mother and left, locking the door behind me. I took the puzzle box, of course. At home, I put it on a shelf with the others.

As collections went, this one was pitiably small, and had taken me more time and effort to accumulate than I cared to calculate. But it would, one day, be worth it. What I collected was not simply the puzzles, but their stories—the stories of those who opened them, and the mistakes they had made.

Normally, I was there to witness the story unfolding. As Nell Collins said, the boxes were not easy to open, and there were far more collectors who knew the story than those who could unlock the configurations. So they went looking for someone who could. They found me, and I opened all but the last twist. That final one I left for them. They conquered the puzzle . . . then it conquered them, while I hid and watched, and collected their story.

Someday, when I had enough stories, I would solve the greatest puzzle of all—how to use the box properly and win the glories foretold. And then, I would make that final turn myself.

The doorbell rang.

I took one last look at the new puzzle box, running my fingers over the wood. An exquisite piece, and an equally rare story to go with it. An excellent addition to my collection. Then I closed the secret closet. Locked it. Double-locked it. Put the mirror back in place over the door. I am a careful woman.

Daniel was at the door to take me to dinner. As we were leaving, my phone pinged, telling me I had a message. He gave me a look.

"Yes, I'll turn it off," I said.

As I did, I checked the message. It was from a collector who'd heard of my reputation and hoped I could help with a puzzle box he'd just acquired. I would, of course. And it would probably turn out to be a mere imitation. Most were. But I never turned down any possibility, however slight, to add another story to my collection.

Author's Note: this story was first published in *Hellbound Hearts*, an anthology celebrating the twentieth anniversary of Clive Barker's *The Hellbound Heart* and is set in his universe.

GABRIEL'S GARGOYLES

A Cainsville Universe Story

GABRIEL WALSH SHIELDED HIS EYES against the late-afternoon sun and squinted up at the gargoyle, peering back at him from under the eaves of the towering bank. One of Chicago's oldest buildings, his teacher had said. No longer a bank, though. There was no need for such an elaborate financial establishment in this neighborhood. It *was* elaborate, with intricate stone-work and swooping eaves. And, apparently, a gargoyle.

Gabriel hadn't seen the gargoyle before, which meant it hadn't been there. If it had, he'd have spotted it. He was something of an expert. In Cainsville, where his great-aunt Rose lived, there was an annual May Day contest to see which child had found the most town gargoyles. Gabriel had won for the last four years. This year, he was determined to take the grand prize: the honor of having found every gargoyle in Cainsville. The town elders had assured him he had only one left to go.

He sidestepped to get a better look at this gargoyle. The fact it did not seem to have existed a day ago came as no great shock. Cainsville would hardly make such a big deal out of the competition if the gargoyles were always there, waiting to be counted. Some kids claimed they were living things, that when no one was looking they spread their wings and flew about the town and guarded it against all comers. Which was ridiculous, of course. The real explanation? Simple illusion. A visual sleight of hand. A concept Gabriel was far more familiar with than flying stonework.

"Gabe!"

He tried not to stiffen at the voice. Jay Hoover, toughest kid in the fifth grade. Also the stupidest, which had made Gabriel's school days slightly more bearable. And much more profitable.

"Yo, Gabe!"

He didn't turn. That wasn't his name. Which Jay knew very well, and which was why he insisted on calling Gabriel by it.

Jay swung in front of him. He was a big kid, a prerequisite for bullies at this age. The second-biggest kid in class, and that, Gabriel had decided, was the root cause of the issue.

Jay stepped up toe-to-toe with Gabriel, as he did with all his victims. Not too bright and, apparently, lacking proper memory skills, because he always moved right in front of Gabriel and then looked *up* at him before remembering who was the *biggest* kid in fifth grade and quickly stepping back before anyone else noticed the height difference.

"So, Gabe, you didn't tell the class what you're getting your mommy for Christmas."

Gabriel said nothing, just eyed the trio of Jay's hangers-on, bouncing on the sidelines, waiting for the first blow, rather bored by the verbal preamble.

"I've got something you can give her." Jay pulled a crack pipe from his pocket. The others laughed obligingly. It was a poor joke. Anyone who knew his mother would realize a needle was the proper tool and, therefore, would have been much funnier.

"You don't like that?" Jay pulled a ten from his pocket and waggled it. "What do you think I could get from her for this?" He made an obscene gesture. Two of his friends giggled. The third said, "Nah, you don't need that. Everyone knows Gabe's mother isn't a whore. She does it for free."

More laughter now. Gabriel waited it out. Again, neither allegation was entirely accurate. His mother did not take cash from her "boyfriends." That would be asking for a prostitution charge. She did, however, accept and expect "gifts"—either drugs or something she could hock for drugs. Yet there seemed no point in clarifying. So he waited.

"You listening to me, Gabe?" Jay said as the laughter died down.

"Only to see if you're going to say something interesting."

Jay hit him. His first blow went for the stomach, as always. Gabriel deflected it and landed one of his own on Jay's jaw, which was the signal, as always, for the others to join in. Gabriel avoided the worst of the blows but made only a half-hearted attempt to return them. After a few minutes, they tired of the game and strolled off, high-fiving each other on their victory.

Gabriel lay on the cold pavement and stared up at the old bank. No sign of the gargoyle. Something landed on his bruised face. He sat up, put out his hand and caught a fat flake of first snow. He watched it melt on his palm. By then, the other boys were long gone. He rose and pulled Jay's ten from his jacket, along with two fives and three singles he'd picked from the pockets of the others.

A faint smile, one last look toward the perch of the now-vanished gargoyle, and Gabriel headed home.

With the extra twenty-three dollars in his pocket, Gabriel allowed himself to detour out of his neighborhood and into one his mother called "Where the rich folks live." Which was laughable, really, and a perfect example of his mother's low aspirations. It was a middle-class enclave, barely teetering above the line from working-class. Gabriel set his goals higher. At least two zip codes higher. Preferably downtown, close to the Loop. Suburban living would never be for him. A downtown address, then, was his goal. Not a dream or a wish. Those were for the weak. Gabriel had goals.

One goal he intended to achieve very soon lay in that neighborhood, nestled in the glass display case of an antique shop. Before opening the shop door, he checked his reflection in a nearby window. He wiped dirt from the fight off his face. Removed his winter jacket and folded it under one arm, hiding the frayed hems. He ran a hand through his hair, smoothing his cowlick. Another quick check in the glass assured him he didn't look like a street urchin out of a Dickens novel, which was the most he could usually hope for.

The bell over the door rang as he walked in. The elderly shopkeeper poked his head out from the back.

"Andrew," he said, which was the name Gabriel had given him. "Looking for work?"

Gabriel nodded.

"I don't have anything today, but I'll need a pair of strong hands tomorrow to help me move a few pieces from the basement. Think you can do that?"

The old man smiled. Gabriel often felt a twinge of remorse at that— genuinely kind grown-ups who tried unsuccessfully to coax a smile from him. He dipped his head in a nod, murmuring his thanks and hoping civility would be enough. The shopkeeper smiled again and said he'd see Gabriel the next day.

Before leaving, Gabriel detoured past the glass box. Inside was a Victorian tarot card deck. His Christmas gift for Rose. Or, it would be, once he'd saved up enough to dicker over the hundred-dollar price tag.

He didn't *need* to pay for it, of course. Despite the fancy glass box, the deck could easily be stolen. Incredibly easily, given that the shopkeeper had already retreated into the back and would never suspect a ten-year-old boy of stealing old cards. But the man had given him work, and that meant he was off-limits as a mark. There were rules, Rose would say. First, don't cheat family. But a close second: don't cheat anyone who's helped you.

Gabriel took one last look at the cards, mentally ran through the calculations of his funds, what he could earn, and the amount of time remaining before Christmas. As long as the deck remained there for another week, the goal was achievable. With a nod of satisfaction, he left the shop.

Television bored Gabriel. He saw little appeal in the dull, overacted dramas and even less in the screeching laugh-track-plagued sitcoms. His mother felt differently, which meant he could hardly escape the medium, not when she'd turn it up so loud it reverberated through their tiny apartment. In those shows, children would come home after school, bang open the door and yell, "Mom, I'm home!"

Gabriel did not do that. First, he didn't remember ever calling Seanna "Mom." In his head, she was Seanna. In front of others, she was "my mother." To her face, she was nothing at all. It was remarkable how one could simply avoid calling someone by name, if one tried hard enough.

When Gabriel came home, he unlocked the door and eased it open an inch. Then he listened. If he heard a man's voice, he would withdraw and go to the library. Same if he heard Seanna thumping around or grumbling or slamming drawers. That meant she was jonesing for a fix, and he should steer clear. If she was already high, whether he went in depended on his mood. It was only when Seanna was high that the fact of Gabriel's existence didn't annoy her. She could be downright maternal, wanting him to talk to her, asking how his day had been, offering him a Coke or a candy bar from her stash. Some days, Gabriel could tolerate that, if only for the free food. Other times, he saw her smile and heard her wheedling voice, and he wanted to shout and snarl at her. To get angry. Perhaps even to lose his temper. But that would mean she'd won, that she'd made him feel something, that she'd made him care. On those days, he'd rather face the cold and pay for his own snacks.

Today, though, was one of the best days. A day when he opened the door and heard nothing. When he walked through the apartment, he found no one inside. That's when he smiled. A genuine smile as he slung his backpack off his shoulder, grabbed his books and tossed them onto the table with none of his usual care. Then he went into his bedroom, eased the loose floorboard free and took out a warm can of Coke. He turned to go . . . and noticed the corner of his threadbare throw rug flipped back.

With a sigh, Gabriel checked under the rug. This morning, there had been seven dollars and fifty-three cents in an envelope there. Now there was just an envelope. And a penny that Seanna had dropped. Gabriel took two singles from his pocket and put them into the envelope before fixing the carpet. Then he hid the rest of the money—minus a five for dinner—in his proper hiding place, a tiny tear in his mattress. He had seventy-six dollars in there now. Another ten and he'd have enough for the tarot cards if he bargained properly. But he couldn't eat the cards. He'd need twenty more in backup for food before he made his purchase.

As he left his room, he felt a pang of . . . something. Not anger. That was too strong an emotion. Too uncomfortable. What he felt was mostly a weary sense of annoyance. He kept that small stash under the carpet for Seanna to steal because as long as she found money there she'd never think to look elsewhere. After years of addiction she wasn't that smart. The drugs addled not only her mind but also any sense of self-respect, and that's what brought the annoyance close to contempt. She stole from family. There was nothing worse than that.

Yet, as he left his room, his step lightened, and he popped open the Coke can, guzzling half. The missing money meant his mother would be gone for a few days. At school, the teacher had asked what they wanted for Christmas. Gabriel hadn't answered, but if he did, it would be this. An empty apartment. The only thing better was . . .

He glanced at the calendar in his binder. He'd circled this weekend in red. No notation was needed. Red meant Cainsville. At least two days Seanna-free, and then Rose would pick him up for the weekend. Then he'd be back to Cainsville for Winter Solstice. He smiled. Happy holidays, indeed.

Gabriel perched on a stool in Rose's kitchen. It was his stool, an antique his great-aunt had picked up the first time he visited, when he was three and couldn't reach the counter on a normal chair. Now that he was five-and-a-half-feet tall, the stool was admittedly a bit ridiculous. He had to hunch to read the yellowed recipe cards spread across the counter. But the stool was his, and, no matter how many times his mother moved, leaving everything behind as they fled in the night, this stool remained exactly where he'd left it, in Rose's kitchen.

Rose herself was in the parlor with a client. Gabriel could hear her telling an old woman that she saw strife and dissent in her future, and it wouldn't improve until she kicked her freeloading grandson out of the house. Gabriel suspected the cards said no such thing. His aunt might have the Sight, but, when it came to telling fortunes, the only real gift needed was a working pair of ears. Listen to the mark and tell them what they needed to hear. Rose would not approve of his choice of wording there. Clients were not marks. Not all of them, anyway.

Gabriel flipped through the recipe cards. A pointless exercise. He knew which he'd want. Rose knew which he'd want. But it was tradition, and, at this time of year, one did not break with tradition. Not in Cainsville.

Gabriel slid off the stool and poured himself a glass of milk and grabbed an apple from the bowl. Good food, better than he was usually able to afford, though he made the effort. Staying healthy was as important as staying clean if one wanted to avoid the attention of those who might think Seanna should be relieved of her parental duties. That included Rose.

Once he'd shown up at school with a bruise on his jaw and fingermarks on his arm, courtesy of a drunken "boyfriend." The teacher had taken him into a private conference room and asked about the bruises. He'd said nothing of course. But then she'd explained that if his mother was abusing him, he could go live somewhere else, perhaps with a relative.

Live with Rose?

The possibility shone like a star that had always dangled far out of reach, now dropping so close he could almost touch it. A few years before, Rose had tried to keep him, failing to return him to Seanna after the weekend. Seanna came for him, and she'd been furious and Gabriel hadn't gone back for a year. After that, Rose didn't try again. But if she could have him, legally . . .

She couldn't. Gabriel discovered that as soon as his mother learned of his chat with the teacher. Her brain might be muddled by dope, but she had a certain cunning intuitiveness, that part of her that was still a Walsh. She knew what Gabriel had in mind, took him aside and explained exactly why Rose would never get custody of him.

"She has a criminal record," Seanna said.

"So do you."

"Doesn't matter. I'm your mom. She's never been married, and she doesn't have kids, which is a huge strike against her, but the criminal record is worse. Plus, she's a dyke."

"She does date men," he'd said. "I've seen them."

"And what about the women? You think they're just really good friends?"

"No, she dates them, too. I just meant that I'm not sure 'dyke' is the correct term. I think it's 'bisexual.'"

She'd cuffed him for that, her eyes narrowing. "Don't be smart, Gabriel."

One of us has to be, he'd thought.

"You're too smart," she'd grumbled as she walked away. "It's creepy. No wonder you don't have any friends."

Gabriel hadn't taken her word about Rose and custody, no more than he'd believe her if she claimed it was snowing. Every tidbit that came from Seanna's mouth had to be verified. This one, unfortunately, had turned out to be true. Combine "unmarried woman" with "criminal record" and "nonstandard sexuality," and there was no chance Rose could get custody of him. If child services took him away, he'd never see her again. Never see Cainsville again. That wasn't happening. He decided he could manage the situation.

Managing it meant being particularly careful around Rose, because if she had any idea how bad Seanna had gotten, she'd do something, even if it meant losing him forever. When she'd picked him up that morning, he'd been waiting outside. No need for her to discover Seanna wasn't home. He'd showered, trimmed his hair, worn and packed his best clothes—the ones he kept especially for Rose's place. He'd brought his homework bag, complete with two A-graded tests that he'd "accidentally" let fall out when she could see them. He'd even brought a banana to eat on the drive to Cainsville. *See, everything is fine. Not ideal—you know what she is, and there's no hiding that—but she's doing a perfectly adequate job of raising me.*

Rose had noticed the bruise on his face, but when he said he'd made twenty-three dollars off the skirmish, she'd laughed and said as soon as the relationship no longer proved profitable, he needed to show Jay why picking on him was a very bad idea. Which he would, of course.

The mark/client departed, and Rose walked into the kitchen. Gabriel didn't need to look up from the recipe cards to hear her enter. His aunt still towered over him, nearly six feet tall, with the Walshes' usual jet-black hair, light-blue eyes and pale skin. "Black Irish," Rose called it. Or "Gypsy," if she was playing Rosalyn Razvan, as her business card proclaimed her. In build, like him, his aunt was not small. In a novel, she'd be called sturdy, implying she was not thin, but not fat either. Solidly built. Big boned. Whatever adjective worked.

"Picked one?" she asked as she started the kettle for tea.

He handed her a card.

She sighed. "There is nothing festive about chocolate chip cookies, Gabriel."

"You asked what I wanted. There were no restrictions placed on the choice."

"All right, then. I'll decorate them with—"

"No."

"I'll cut them into reindeers and—"

"No."

A quirk of a smile. Year after year, the dialogue never changed. By now, it bordered on absurd. Yet it was tradition, so they stuck to their lines.

"What if I colored the dough green and red and—?"

He handed her a second card. "Sugar cookies. You may make these as well."

Her brows lifted. "May I?"

"If you must."

She laughed and headed for the fridge to take out the eggs and butter. "That bag on the table is for you. A gift for your mother for Christmas. One's from you and the other's from me. I know you never know what to give her."

This too was tradition. He suspected Rose knew perfectly well that, without her contribution, he would buy Seanna nothing. He used to, when he was little. When she still played Santa for him. Then, one year, his gifts mysteriously went missing a week later and turned up at the pawn shop, and he went home and told Seanna he didn't believe in Santa, and there was no need to continue the charade. So she stopped. And so did he. Yet Rose wouldn't let him pass a holiday without a gift for his mother.

There was only a ten-year age difference between Seanna and Rose. His mother had been like a little sister to his great-aunt. An adored little sister. While it was difficult for Gabriel to put himself in the shoes of others, he made the effort with Rose. He had come to understand that, no matter how far Seanna fell, part of her was always that little girl to Rose, who still hoped Seanna could be that again. A vain hope, but Gabriel let her have it.

"How much do I owe you?" he asked.

"An afternoon's work making cookies."

He slid off the stool to fetch the flour.

While the cookies baked and Rose cleaned, Gabriel wandered into the parlor. There wasn't far to wander in the tiny Victorian house. The parlor took up half the main floor space. It was like walking into the antique shop—if the shop specialized in the occult. Rose called it her collection of "old junk," but she was proud of that junk, and for good reason. The pieces were valuable relics from the history of her craft. All the ways people had sought to peer into whatever mysteries lay beyond the everyday, whether it was reading tea leaves or communicating with spirits or catching a glimpse of invisible fae.

Gabriel took down a book on Cornish folktales and laid it on the desk, as if to read, but it was only an excuse for sitting at the desk and poking through the drawer. Getting a look at Rose's cards and making sure she hadn't added to the collection since he'd last been there. She hadn't. There was the Thoth tarot and the Visconti-Sforza tarot and the Tarot of Marseilles. Her favorite—the one she used most—was a replica Victorian deck.

"Yes, a replica," she'd say with a sigh. "Not that the clients know the difference."

The problem was that an authentic Victorian-era tarot was difficult to find. Most from that period originated in France or Italy. A true Victorian tarot was rare, and she'd been hunting for years. Now Gabriel had found one.

He'd filched fifteen dollars from holiday shoppers last week. In Chicago, of course. He didn't pick pockets in Cainsville. The shopkeeper had given him five dollars for helping move things up from the basement and promised another ten for work the following week. Then Rose would finally have her cards.

After dinner, Rose had another appointment with a mark. Gabriel went gargoyle hunting. Night had fallen, but there was no need to be wary. In Cainsville, he could walk around at two in the morning, and the biggest danger he'd face would be locals popping out to see what was wrong.

He read his notebook as he walked. Again, no danger there. He could cross the road, deep in his book, and traffic would stop. Not that he did any such thing. Only a fool tempted fate.

He studied his list of gargoyles and compared it to his hand-drawn maps. While it had seemed likely that the final gargoyle was in one of the regions where he hadn't found any, all of these areas had proven empty, and he'd developed the theory that the last gargoyle was located uncharacteristically close to another. The first would be easily spotted, and children would move on, thinking that area covered. The second would lurk above or below, visible only from a certain angle or during a certain time of day or under certain weather conditions. The solution, then, was a methodical accounting for all possibilities. Today, a light snow fell, which introduced yet another test variable.

He tramped along, snow squeaking under his shoes. A couple of kids passed by with a sled. They didn't ask him to join them. They knew he wouldn't. But they grinned and waved and called a hello, and he knew that if he wanted to go sledding, he could, and there was a comfort in that, a satisfaction.

He continued on down Main Street, nodding at the adults who passed and lifting his head for a more respectful hello when the elders did. Without the notebook in his hand, they'd have stopped to talk, but they saw it and left him to his hunt.

Gabriel had investigated all the gargoyles on Main Street and had turned down Walnut, to take a closer look near the community center. There was one on the rear, there all the time, a sleeping gargoyle on the roof, its misshapen head on its folded arms.

"If you're quiet enough, you'll hear it snore," said a voice behind him.

"Only if there's enough of a wind to make the eaves groan."

The man sighed. "Always need a prosaic explanation, don't you, Gabriel?"

"No, but if there is one, I can't deny it."

"True." The man walked beside Gabriel and peered up. "Yes, I suppose it is the eaves groaning. How dull."

The man had a name. Gabriel didn't know it. Had never heard it. Didn't bother to ask it. If he was being honest, he'd admit that sometimes he forgot about the man altogether. If a few visits to Cainsville passed without seeing him, he'd spot him again and, for a moment, wonder who he was. More sleight of hand, this one in the mind, truth playing peek-a-boo with memory. It was Cainsville. Such things happened.

He looked at the man. He wasn't old. Perhaps college aged or a little more. He had a notebook of his own, sticking from his pocket, and he was often writing in it furiously. Gabriel's own book had been a gift from him, given for "any stories he wanted to tell." Gabriel used it for financial calculations and homework reminders and gargoyle hunting.

"Do you want a hint?" the man said, pushing his hands into his pockets and shivering against the cold.

"No. That's cheating."

"You don't cheat?" A smile played on the man's lips.

Gabriel tilted his head, considering. "It would depend on the definition of the word. In the broadest sense, everyone does. Some more than others. But cheating to reach an achievement implies that you cannot do so otherwise. That you are not good enough. While I appreciate the offer, I am quite capable of finding the last gargoyle on my own."

"You are indeed," the man said. "You're capable of doing anything you want to, Gabriel. Don't you ever forget it."

"I know. Thank you."

The man walked to the community center wall and leaned his back against it as he fixed Gabriel with an appraising look. "Perhaps a small hint? It's allowed for the last gargoyle."

"No, thank you."

"We could bargain for it." The man grinned. "Tit for tat. That's fair."

"No, thank you."

"I hope you aren't bothering the boy, bòcan," a voice said from behind Gabriel. Another voice he recognized. This one a woman's, strong and firm despite her advancing years. Ida walked around the community center, her husband Walter at her side. "You know better."

"Old people," the man whispered to Gabriel. "So annoying."

"I heard that," Ida said.

"I'd hardly bother if you couldn't." The man strolled to Gabriel and said, "I'll leave you with the old folks. You'll be back for Solstice, I hope."

Gabriel nodded.

"Excellent," the man said. "Christmas is well and good, but around here, it's all about the Winter Solstice. The beginning of winter. Longest night of the year." He met Gabriel's gaze. "A very important day . . . and an even more important night."

"Yes, yes," Ida said. "Get along and stop pestering the child. He's cold and in need of cocoa."

The man left, and Ida walked over. "You'll come have cocoa with us, Gabriel? We'd love to hear how your history project went. We know you worked so hard on it." She started back to Main Street as he fell in beside her. When Gabriel glanced down at his notebook, she said, "Ah, out hunting the last gargoyle. We could help with that, you know. It is permitted, with the last."

"No, thank you."

"Not even a hint?"

"I believe I have one already."

She smiled, her wrinkles deepening. "Good. Now, can we drag you away from the hunt?"

"Yes."

The cards were gone. They'd been there Tuesday, when Gabriel came to work for the shopkeeper. On Thursday, the old man had him running errands, so he hadn't been able to check the glass box, but, when work ended and he got his ten dollars, he'd walked to the cards and found an empty display case.

"Andrew?" the shopkeeper said as Gabriel stood there, staring down.

"The cards." Gabriel turned. "Have you moved them?"

"Someone bought them yesterday." The old man made a face as he walked over. "You didn't want those old things, I hope. They aren't real, you know."

"They weren't authentic?" A tickle of something like relief. "The label said they were."

"Well, yes, they were really Victorian. I don't sell fakes, son. I meant, they can't tell the future. Nothing can."

Not entirely true, as Gabriel well knew. He knew better than to say that, though. "I know. They were for my aunt. She's a collector."

"Oh." Genuine dismay crossed the old man's face. "I'm sorry, Andrew. If I'd had any idea you were saving up for them . . . Never mind those. They were too expensive. I'm sure your aunt doesn't want such an extravagant gift from you. Better to save your money for a video game. That's what kids play these days, isn't it? Video games?"

Yes, and Gabriel could not imagine a bigger waste of time or money.

The shopkeeper continued. "How about I find you another set? Genuine antiques, of course. I know where I can get a nineteenth-century Hungarian deck for about thirty dollars. Or an art deco pack for twenty. I'll ask around and make a list. Would you like that?"

Gabriel wanted to say no, but that would be rude, and, despite what others thought, he did understand the basics of civility. He merely applied them sparingly. He nodded, and the old man patted his arm, not noticing Gabriel's reflexive flinch.

"I'll do that then," the shopkeeper said. "And you use that extra money to buy yourself a video game."

Disappointment swirled about Gabriel like a fog. He almost stepped in front of a speeding car on the way back to the apartment. He walked inside without his usual Seanna-check. It'd been almost a week, and he'd grown accustomed to pushing open that door into an empty apartment. When he heard the squeal of her laughter, he stopped short.

"Gabriel, baby." Her voice reached him before she did, and he hovered in the doorway, considering backing out when she appeared.

At one time, Gabriel supposed his mother had looked more like his aunt. She wasn't as tall, maybe five-ten, but her shirt and jeans hung off her like grown-up clothes on children's hangers. Her face was just as thin, with sunken cheeks and eyes that seemed more gray than blue. Today, they were grayer than usual, dull with that heroin glaze. She was only twenty-eight, but she looked twice that.

"This is my baby," she said, and Gabriel realized they weren't alone. A man walked from the kitchen. Maybe thirty, with the bulky build of a construction worker. He had a beer can in one hand and that same film over his eyes. New to the drug. New to the life. His mother knew her marks well.

"Isn't my boy a cutie?" she said.

"He has weird eyes," the man said.

Seanna punched his arm. "Don't be mean. He has beautiful eyes. And he's smart, too. Smartest kid in his class."

"Must take after his daddy."

Seanna spun on the man. "Now *that's* mean. You'd better watch yourself, or you'll be sleeping on the street tonight." She turned to Gabriel. "Can you go get us some burgers, sweetie?"

He nodded and put out his hand. Seanna looked at the man and waited until he passed over a ten.

"That won't feed Gabriel, too," she said. "He's a big boy. Only ten, and look how big he is already. He eats more than I do." She leaned over to whisper. "And the more he eats, the sounder he sleeps."

The man exchanged the ten for a twenty. "Get yourself something good, kid."

Behind the man's back, Seanna raised three fingers. Three dollars. That's what he was allowed to take for his meal. The rest of the change went to her.

Gabriel pocketed the money and headed out.

In Cainsville, Solstice was indeed bigger than Christmas. In first grade, Gabriel's teacher had asked his favorite holiday, and that's what he'd said. She'd looked at him blankly. He'd repeated his answer and explained it— longest night of the year, the basis for Christmas, with feasting, exchange of gifts and all that. The next day, she'd taken him aside for a "chat" about Jesus and how he'd given his life for Gabriel's sins, and that was the proper celebration of Christmas.

Gabriel had corrected her, as politely as possible. Easter was the holiday recognizing the death of Christ, and, while he understood the concept, he thought it rather presumptive to die for strangers. One of the younger teachers had overheard the conversation and reported it, and, ultimately, his teacher had to take him aside and apologize for questioning his religious beliefs. He'd accepted the apology, though he hadn't understood it, not until he was old enough to realize Solstice was considered a Pagan festival. In Cainsville, it had nothing to do with religion. It was a celebration of winter. Nothing more.

The festivities began at sundown. Rose took him down to Main Street, which had been blocked off all day to prepare. Bonfires dotted the road, with a huge one in the middle. Candles covered every surface. Gifts were placed on tables according to age. They were unmarked, suitable for anyone of that age. Children had to bring one for the age group below theirs. Gabriel had brought two books: *The Phantom Tollbooth* and *A Wrinkle in Time*. Both came from the used-book store, but neither looked as if anyone had cracked open its cover, so they could pass as new.

On arrival, every child was given a suet ball and had to find a place to hang it to help the birds through winter. They also got an orange, to represent the sun, and mulled cider, to keep them warm as they hunted for a suitable hanging spot. When they returned, Main Street was filled with tables and tables of food. Afterward, there would be caroling. And, of course, mistletoe, strategically hung for kissing. Gabriel avoided both by helping clear the food away. The night ended with stories and the burning of the Yule log. And that was when Gabriel's night truly began—hunting for the last gargoyle, because he was certain the man had given him a hint. The final gargoyle would appear on the most important night of the year. The longest night of the year.

And it did. In fact, it was rather hard to miss, if you went looking. After the festivities, though, everyone headed home, leaving the streets bare, the bonfires smoldering. That's when Gabriel found the gargoyle, in the most obvious place of all. Right in the middle of Main Street. Town Hall. On the bell tower.

Gabriel stood below the gargoyle as it leaned down from the tower, its twisted face grinning at him as if to say, "Found me!" He looked up through the falling snow and let out a low chuckle that reverberated through the silent street.

"Fitting, isn't it?" said a voice behind him. It was the man, snow crunching under his shoes. Gabriel didn't turn, just kept staring at the gargoyle.

"The bell tower?" the man prompted.

"The Hunchback of Notre-Dame," Gabriel said.

"Very good. You do like stories then, even if you don't write any in that journal I gave you."

"I read the comic book."

The man's laugh rang through the night. "Liar."

Gabriel smiled and shrugged. Then, he made the appropriate notes in his book, giving the exact location and describing the gargoyle, as was needed to claim his victory.

"You did it," the man said as he walked up beside Gabriel.

"Yes, I did."

"You know what the prize is, don't you?"

Gabriel let out a soft sigh.

The man laughed again. "Not as keen on that part, are you?"

"Can I skip it?"

"Nope. You find all the gargoyles, and the town gets a new one, modeled after you."

Gabriel made a face.

"Victory comes with a price," the man said. "You'll survive this one." He looked down at Gabriel. "I'm proud of you. You know that, don't you, Gabriel?"

It seemed an odd thing to say, but Gabriel only murmured, "Thank you."

"Did you get a good present at the festival?"

Gabriel held up a train set.

"Ah," the man said. "Not exactly your style, is it? How about I take that and give you something better."

Gabriel hesitated. The gift, while unwanted, had been given with good intentions, and it seemed insulting to refuse it. Before he could answer, though, the man plucked the box from his hand.

"Happy Solstice, Gabriel," he said as he walked away, the train set tucked under one arm. "And you're welcome."

Gabriel watched him go, frowning in some confusion. Then, as he turned, he saw the gargoyle again, and he nodded. *That* was the gift—the hint about Solstice. Fair enough.

He tried to put his notebook into his pocket, but it wouldn't fit. Something else was in there. Gabriel reached in and felt a box. He pulled it out.

It was the cards. The Victorian tarot for Rose.

Gabriel turned back toward the man to call out his thanks. But the street was empty. He pocketed the cards, smiled and headed back to give Rose her present.

HARBINGER

As hard as Jenna tried to concentrate on the professor's words, all she could hear was water dripping off the drowned girl behind her. She'd even tried threading her ear-buds up through her sweater, popping them in, and cranking the music as loud as she dared. But she could still hear it. That relentless *plip-plop, plip-plop.*

Jenna fought the urge to look over her shoulder again. She'd done it so often now that the students behind her had started to squirm and glower.

There was no use looking because she knew what she'd see. The dead girl, naked, her white and wrinkled skin hanging from her arms and legs like an oversized suit about to slide off. Long, dark hair hung to her shoulders. Her lips were blue. Part of her nose was missing, and one ear. But it wasn't any of that that made Jenna shiver. It was the girl's eyes. Empty and dead, staring straight into hers.

More than once in the last six hours, Jenna had considered the possibility that she'd lost her mind. Yet it seemed to her that if you were truly crazy, you wouldn't consider that possibility. You'd see a drowned girl sitting behind you in Philosophy and ask if she had notes from the lecture you missed last week.

When class ended, she called her roommate, Bree. No reason. She just wanted to talk, make a connection, preferably with someone alive.

It took four rings for Bree to answer, and even then she sounded groggy, her voice thick with sleep. Jenna turned her back on the drowned girl and concentrated on hearing only Bree's voice through the cell phone.

"Don't tell me I woke you up again." Jenna forced a laugh. "I swear, you're worse than my little sister."

"Mmm, no. Just resting my eyes." Bree yawned. "What's up?"

"Not much." Jenna struggled to think up an excuse for calling. "Have you changed your mind about the party tonight?"

"Nah. I need to study."

Jenna couldn't argue with that. Bree was barely passing most of her courses. They'd both struggled at first—university was so different from high school—but it seemed that as Jenna started catching on and catching up, Bree only fell farther behind. One could argue, though, that Bree was still coping better than she was. At least Bree wasn't being followed by a dead girl.

"Jenna!" a voice called.

She turned as the teaching assistant from her Classics course cut through a gaggle of students. Jenna struggled for his name, distracted by the water pooling around her feet.

"Just the girl I was hoping to see," he said with a smile. Trey. He looked like a Trey, anyway—gleaming blond hair, crisp preppy clothes, blindingly white teeth. He certainly didn't look like he needed a TA's salary. Maybe Daddy had cut him off after he totaled the Beamer. The snark was totally uncalled for, but she couldn't help it. One look at Trey, and all Jenna could think was, "I bet he never needs to worry about being followed by dead girls." Live girls, sure. Dead? Never.

"I just read your essay this morning," Trey said. "I wanted to talk to you about it. Do you have time for a coffee?"

"Is something wrong?"

"No, no. It's great." His smile oozed reassurance. "That's what I wanted to talk to you about."

A soft, sighing hiss sounded behind Jenna. She glanced over her shoulder. The drowned girl just stood there, staring, empty-eyed, dripping, water puddling at Jenna's feet, murky now, a thick brown rivulet trickling in from a stream off to the left. Another hiss, and Jenna followed the sound to the source of the brown water and saw a second drowned girl. This one was bloated, like a grotesque doll inflated to twice its normal size, gray skin straining the seams of her sundress, decomposing flesh pillowing over the neckline. A faint pop, skin breaking, gas hissing out.

"Jenna?"

She turned back to Trey.

"You okay?" he asked, full lips pursed in concern.

"S-sorry. I thought I heard someone call me. Coffee, you said? Sure, coffee would be great. Lead the way."

The dead girls fell in behind them, floating above the floor, water trailing in their wake.

According to Trey, Jenna's essay was amazing. Which was bullshit. It was a B-plus effort, and that was stretching it.

If the guy didn't look like he belonged on a prep-school brochure, she'd have thought he was hitting on her. As it was, she figured he was just trying to do his job. Overdoing it, but she couldn't fault him for that. He poured on the praise, encouraging her, then asked about her day, her week, being friendly, taking an interest.

Not the most stimulating conversation ever, but it took her thoughts off the dead girls, who stood against the next table, dripping into the coffee cups of a laughing couple. Eventually, though, Jenna mind wandered back to them and she began to wonder if the girls were actually ghosts. The possibility didn't shock her as much as she supposed it should. She'd grown up in a world where such things were always possibilities, where family and friends would tell stories of seeing Uncle Mike minutes before getting the call that he was dead or seeing Grandma by their bedside, telling them not to grieve for her. They didn't necessarily believe the dead walked among the living, but they were willing to concede that they could return, briefly, to console the living or to pass on a message.

After coffee, Trey left for his last class of the day. Jenna walked through two buildings, then into a courtyard. In fall, it had been jammed with students, studying under the ancient maples, tossing Frisbees, grabbing a few minutes of fresh air before another stiflingly hot class in the old buildings. Passing through it earlier today, she'd noticed a few kids braving the March chill. Now, though, past five, sun dropping, it was empty. Just Jenna and the dead girls.

She found a spot under the biggest maple, tucked out of the way of anyone stepping from the building. Then she turned to the girls.

"What do you want?"

They stared at her, eyes as empty as ever, no indication they'd heard her, no indication they'd even seen her lips move.

"Do you think I know you? Do you think I had something to do with your deaths? Is that what you're trying to do? Haunt me?"

The only answer was a hiss of gas, a fissure splitting on the bloated girl's arm.

"The only person I've ever known who drowned was a guy who rented the cabin beside ours. He got drunk and dove into shallow water. I was five and sound asleep."

They continued to stare.

"Do you have a message? Something you need me to pass on?"

No reaction.

"Is it a message for me? Is there something you're trying to tell me?"

A *plink-plink* as a puddle formed around the first girl's bare feet.

"I can't do anything if you won't tell me what you want. You can stare at me all you want. I'm not psychic. I don't understand."

Jenna waved her hand in front of each girl's face. They didn't give any sign they noticed. When she stepped to the side, though, their gazes followed her.

She leapt forward, trying to startle them. Nothing.

She turned on her heel and headed back inside.

Jenna called Bree and told her she was heading to the library and wasn't hungry, wouldn't bother with dinner.

"Are you still going to Jackson's party?" Bree asked.

"Probably not."

"Why?"

I think I'm going crazy. I'm being followed by dead girls and I have no idea what to do about it, but I really don't think a party is the answer. She sputtered a small, ragged laugh.

"Jen?"

Jenna turned the laugh into a cough. "I just think I'll skip it."

"Hey, I'm the one who has to study. Go have a few beers for me, meet some hot guys, let me know what I'm missing. You could use it." A pause. "You've been a bit off lately."

"Have I?" She looked at the bloated girl. *That might explain a few things . . .*

"Go. That's an order."

"Maybe. I'll hit the library first."

Jenna considered herself a serious student. But that day's three-hour study stint was definitely a record. She was hiding; she knew that. Hiding not from the dead girls, but from what they portended and what she planned to do about it. She'd breezed through her day, trailed by specters. Surreal. Ridiculous, too, but if she stopped, then she'd have to act. Better to just bury her head in a book stack and hope they went away.

She immersed herself in research, cranked up her iPod and eventually the *plink-plink* and the hiss faded into background noise. She was deep in a microbiology text when a crimson drop hit the edge of the table. She didn't look up to see where it came from. She didn't dare.

Another drop fell, next to the first. Then a third, joining the two into a tiny pool. A pool of blood.

Jenna steeled herself and looked up. The two drowned girls stood to the side of her table, silently, patiently waiting. A third figure had joined them. Another drowned girl, fresher than the others, looking no different than someone who'd been out for a long skinny-dip—naked and pale, with wet hair, skin wrinkling on her fingertips. Jenna couldn't see where the blood came from, only that it streamed down the backs of her arms and dripped from her fingertips.

"I don't suppose you'd care to speak to me either." Jenna tried to sound jaunty, but her voice frayed at the edges. She swallowed and looked away. A deep breath. Then she closed her textbook.

If she really was going crazy, then locking herself away like this wouldn't help. She needed someone else to judge. She needed to be around people. She needed that party.

When she got back to the apartment, Bree was taking a study break, napping on the couch. She hadn't changed her mind about the party, but she was happy that Jenna was going, helping her pick out clothes, making Jenna promise to tell her all about it, then retreating to her books.

As Jenna fixed her hair in the bathroom, Bree came back.

"That's a great shirt," she said. "But it really needs something." She held up her hand. Silver flashed in the light.

From Bree's fingers dangled her Celtic cross necklace, one Jenna had admired many times, teasing that if it ever went missing, Bree knew where to look for it.

When Bree reached to put it on Jenna, she protested, but Bree insisted.

"That shirt screams for a necklace." She grinned as she fastened it around Jenna's neck. "And if it disappears, I know where you live."

Jenna laughed, then glanced at the three drowned girls crowded into the bathroom behind Bree. Was it her imagination or were they eyeing the cross nervously?

"Thanks," she said.

"Anytime. Now go party."

If the cross had any effect on the ghosts, it was minimal. They didn't go away. Didn't even shy away. She'd tried waving the pendant at them. Even struck one in the cheek with it. The girl didn't flinch.

By the time Jenna arrived, the party was in full swing. She leapt in, almost hoping someone would say, "You seem a little off, Jen" or give her a strange look and find an excuse to retreat to the other side of the room. No one did. No one noticed the dead girls, either, and Jenna was forced to admit that was really why she'd come to the party—the hope that with all those people around, the booze and dope loosening them up, someone would notice the girls.

As for the dead girls, if they even noticed they were at a party, they gave no sign of it. Just stood there, dripping, rotting, bleeding, leaving a trail on the carpet that no one else could see.

Trey was there, too. He'd come with friends and, while he did pop over and say hi, later bringing her a drink, he hung out with his buddies, only smiling and nodding if their eyes happened to meet.

The drink stayed untouched by her elbow, abandoned when she moved on to talk with a couple of girls she knew from high school. All things considered, adding booze to the mix didn't seem wise.

She tried hard to relax, but it wasn't happening. As long as she led the dead girl entourage, there was no way she could just kick back and party. Eventually she gave up, said her good-byes and slipped out.

Jenna paused on the sidewalk, taking a deep breath, icy air scorching her lungs, a bitter breeze bringing tears to her eyes. Definitely a night for the shortcut home. Common sense, though, kept tugging her toward the round-about route, along the well-lit roads.

The front door slapped shut.

"Leaving so soon?" a voice called.

She turned to see Trey on the steps. He frowned into the dark night.

"Please tell me you've called for an escort."

She shook her head.

He jogged down the steps.

"You shouldn't walk home alone."

She looked at the dead girls and was tempted to say that, unfortunately, she *wasn't* alone.

"Okay, I'll save the speech," he said when she didn't respond. He took a card from his pocket and flashed it. "Luckily, you have a campus escort already here, ready for duty."

"No, that's—"

"I insist. Party sucks anyway. I was just going back to my place to study for midterms. Are you on campus?"

"Just off it." She waved northwest. "But it's a short walk, so you don't have to—"

"—miss much study time. I appreciate that. Come on. We'll take the shortcut."

They walked along the riverbank, talking about the party. It was a comfortable conversation, almost enough to make her forget the dead girls. She did glance back now and then, though, hoping they'd vanished. Once, as she twisted, her foot caught on a root. She stumbled. Her shoe slid on the mud. Trey grabbed her around the waist and yanked her back just as the edge of the embankment crumpled under her feet.

"Close call," he said as she stared down into the fast-moving, spring-swollen river.

She tore her gaze away and looked at the drowned girls. Was that what they'd been trying to warn her about? A premonition of danger?

Trey tugged her back onto the bank. "That drink hit you pretty hard."

She nodded, not saying she hadn't touched it. Better for him to think she was tipsy. As they resumed walking, though, he kept his arm around her. She tried, subtly, to slide away from it. His grip tightened. Her heart picked up speed, but when she glanced over, he smiled and said, "Steady there."

She nodded. A few more steps and his hand slid into her back pocket, which definitely *wasn't* okay and when she moved away this time, there was no subtlety about it. He didn't let go, though, fingers biting into her rear, tugging her so close she almost tripped again.

She realized, then, just how empty the riverbanks were, how far away the nearest buildings were. She thought of the drink he'd given her. Spiked with more than just vodka? And that escort card. She hadn't taken a good look at it—didn't even know if they *carried* ID cards.

She glanced at the drowned girls. They were no help, of course, just trailing along behind her like faithful hounds.

Keep going, she told herself. *It's not far now.*

After a few more steps, though, Trey swung in front of her, cutting her short, his other hand going around her waist. When he leaned in, face coming to hers, she backed up so fast she stumbled. He only tightened his grip, chuckling as he held her steady.

He leaned in again and she was ready to kick, scream, bite, whatever it took, but at the last second, he averted his face, lips going to her ear instead.

"About that essay, Jenna? I lied. It sucked."

She stiffened.

He continued, "That's what I was going to tell you earlier. Warn you, but then . . ." He chuckled again, his breath warming her ear. "I couldn't do it. You're too pretty to get a failing grade."

She tried to back out of his arms. He ignored her struggles and kept whispering.

"I noticed on your file that you want to minor in Classics. You can't do it with essays like that. But I'm willing to give you a little . . ." His fingers slid under her shirt, skating over the back of her waist. ". . . assistance. That's all it'll take. A few weeks of tutoring. And, in the meantime, I can make sure you don't fail that essay." He lifted his head then, teeth glittering in the dark as he smiled. "Or I can make sure you do."

Jenna trembled as his mouth lowered to hers. She forced herself to look up at him with terror-filled eyes. When their lips touched, she stood frozen. Then, as he relaxed and closed his eyes, she caught his lip between her teeth and chomped down with everything she had. Blood spurted into her mouth. He let out a yelp. She punched him in the stomach and wheeled to race away, but he caught her by the jacket.

"Stupid bitch!" He swiped his hand across his mouth, blood spraying. "Do you have any idea how many girls at that party would be happy to be out here with me?"

She wrenched away, dancing backward. "Lots, I'm sure. But that's not the way you like it, is it?"

She tried to run. He caught her again, and dragged her to the embankment. She kicked and punched, but he hauled her to the edge and when she looked down at the water racing by, she knew what the dead girls had been trying to tell her.

"That water's ice cold," he said. "You'll be dead before you know which way is up."

She lashed out, her foot hitting him square in the kneecap. His leg buckled. They struggled. She managed to get free and, with one hard, backward kick, knocked him over the edge.

As she raced away, she heard him cursing, scrabbling to get back up the embankment, splashing at the edge of the water.

Jenna didn't stop until she reached her apartment. She paused in the lobby to catch her breath. Only then did she notice the drowned girls, still following.

"It took me a while, but I figured it out." She managed a smile. "Would have been nicer if I'd been a little quicker on the draw, huh?"

They didn't answer. Didn't react. By now she didn't expect them to. She wasn't even sure they were ghosts at all, not in the usual sense. Just spectral images of girls who had died, unable to do anything but, by their presence, warn of impending danger.

Harbingers of death.

She shivered.

"I'm safe now," she said. "You can go."

They followed her up the elevator. Outside her apartment, she stopped again.

"There's more, right? You want to make sure I do something about it. Well, I will. I'm calling the police as soon as I get inside."

No answer. No reaction.

She sighed and opened the door. It was quiet inside. The apartment was tiny, only one shared bedroom and a kitchen/living room combo. Both were dark. She tiptoed to the bedroom door and peeked in.

Bree's bed was empty.

Had she gone out after all? Good. She deserved it. Jenna only hoped she *hadn't* decided to go to Jackson's party, expecting to catch up with her.

Jenna took out her cell phone. She was about to dial when, in the silence, she picked up a faint *drip. Drip. Drip.* Her gaze shot to the drowned girls. The first was still shedding water, but with a *plip-plop* so familiar Jenna had started to tune it out. This was a different sound . . . coming from a different room.

She stepped back into the hall. Her foot hit a slick spot on the wood and she had to grab the wall to keep from falling. She flipped on the light. There was water on the floor. A tendril stretched from the bathroom door.

"Bree? Bree!"

Jenna raced the few steps to the door. She grabbed the handle. Locked. Twisting it, she threw her shoulder against the wood. The door burst open.

The first thing she saw was the bathroom floor, a puddle of water around the old claw-foot tub. Pink-tinged water.

Drip. Drip. Drip.

Almost reluctantly, her gaze followed the sound to the tub. Water trickled over the side. Bloody water, the tub filled to the brim.

She ran, sliding across the floor.

Bree lay at the bottom of the tub, face barely visible through the red water.

Jenna dropped to her knees, reached in and hauled Bree up as best she could, but as soon as the cold, bloody water enveloped her arms, she knew it was too late.

Bree's head lolled back. Her eyes stared up. Dead eyes. Empty eyes. Eyes Jenna had been looking at all day.

Jenna turned on the drowned girls.

"Why didn't you tell me? Why didn't you warn me!"

Their eyes met hers. Then, the faint outline of a fourth girl materialized behind them, a girl whose dead eyes passed over Jenna without pausing, with no flicker of recognition. Then as one, the harbingers turned and drifted away, off to warn someone else, someone who might understand in time.

V Plates

An Otherworld Universe Story

"YOU NEED TO HELP NOAH lose his V plates," Reese said.

Nick looked up over his laptop as his young Pack brother strode onto the back deck, two icy beers clutched in one hand. Nick reached out. Reese dropped into a chair, popped the top on one and set the other on the deck.

"That's backup," he said. "Fridge is full for once."

"Because I filled it. With *my* beer."

"No wonder it tastes like horse piss." Reese drained the can, wiped his sweaty forehead with the still-frosty empty, then grabbed the second. "If you and Antonio want me on lawn-cutting duty, you gotta keep the fridge full." He leaned back in his chair. "Though I don't see the point in cutting two goddamn acres every week. Back home, we had a few thousand, and I never cut one of them."

"Because you lived in the desert."

"No, I lived on the Outback. The part with grass, because sheep don't live long eating sand." He waved at the surrounding yard. "That's what you need, you know. Sheep."

"Werewolves and sheep, they go so well together."

"Actually, they do, if you raise them yourselves."

Nick shook his head and typed the final paragraph on his marketing plan while Reese's sneaker tapped the deck, waiting for him to be done so he could talk again. For over four decades, Nick had been the one sitting there, impatiently waiting for his father—Antonio—to finish work. Then their household had doubled with the addition of Noah, the teenage son of a former Pack mate, and Reese, running from some mysterious tragedy in Australia. So now Nick got to play the responsible adult. Several decades past due, some might argue.

He closed his laptop. "You're on yard duty until Noah is done with exams. He took it for yours last month. Speaking of Noah, what's this about plates?"

"V plates. You need to help him lose his." Reese watched for Nick's reaction, then sighed. "They don't say that here?"

"I'm sure they don't say it anywhere except the middle of nowhere. On the Outback. With sheep."

Reese choked on a mouthful of beer. "Sheep should definitely not be involved. Which isn't to say they aren't, sometimes, but for the record, no sheep were involved in mine. Though, I admit, the girl wasn't a whole lot brighter than one."

"Ah. V plate. Virginity." Nick glanced around.

"Don't worry. Noah's studying on the opposite side of the house, which in this place means he's a block away."

"Well, I'm sure he'll come to me when he's ready. I'm not going to rush him."

"He already came to *me*."

"What? Noah knows I'm here—"

"For all his questions about girls and sex. You are the undisputed expert. Which means there's no way he is admitting he's eighteen and a virgin to you—a guy who lost his in primary school."

"It was high school." Nick paused. "Well, the summer between the two."

"And by eighteen, you were probably well into double digits. Which is why he's not coming to you." Reese leaned forward, elbows on his knees. "Did he tell you he broke it off with Lexi? He made a date with Leigh Madison for Friday night."

"I don't think I've met Leigh."

"Sure you have. There's one in every school. Can't get laid? Ask Leigh out."

"Oh."

"Right. So, he's dumped a girl he likes to hook up with one who puts out. Then he'll dump *her* and get back with Lexi. That's no way to treat either girl."

"Agreed. We have to help him find a better way."

"I already have. You need to buy him a hooker."

Nick would have been very happy if the conversation had ended there. He'd say, "Like hell," and that would be it. But Reese had gotten it into his head that Noah needed a hooker, and that Nick was the best person to provide one.

Not that Nick had any experience with hookers. True, one couldn't overlook the convenience factor, but really, did you want someone who was only there because you'd paid her? No. Nick liked women, and he liked women who liked him back. That meant no hookers.

As it turned out, Reese didn't expect him to find one. He had that covered. A brothel in Philadelphia, highly recommended by a couple of mutts Reese used to run with. Reese had never been there himself—he had hang-ups about girls, part of the baggage he'd brought from Australia. He'd kept the address, though, which suggested the no-girls situation might not be as dire as Nick feared. There was, however, no way Reese was taking Noah to the brothel himself. That was sex, and in this household, sex was Nick's department.

"I can't believe you talked me into this," Reese muttered as they walked along the dark Philadelphia street.

"We can't come to Philly without seeing Karl and Hope," Nick said. Karl was a Pack mate, Hope his half-demon wife. "When I mentioned it to Hope, she assumed you were coming, too."

"Just as long as she doesn't plan to introduce me to another cute young intern at *True News*." He checked Nick's expression, then let out a growl. "She does, doesn't she? Bugger it. I don't—"

"Oh, look, there it is." Nick pointed at a house two doors down. There was no sign, of course. It was just a house, a rambling old Victorian with tended gardens and a lush lawn.

"It doesn't . . . look like a brothel," Noah said.

Nick glanced over at the boy. Slightly built, five-foot-eight, light-brown hair hanging in his thin face. Eighteen, but looking very young, which really didn't help him with girls. Even setting his "official" age a year younger and enrolling him two years back—to compensate for what he'd lost when he dropped out—hadn't helped Noah catch up.

Noah hadn't said much since they'd arrived in Philadelphia. Not that he ever said much. He'd had a rough time of it in Alaska. While dealing with his Change to a full werewolf, he'd been in juvenile detention. Then he got out, only to lose both his father and grandfather—the former taking off, the latter murdered by mutts—before Noah was whisked across the country to live with strangers.

Nick had grown up with Noah's dad, but that didn't help much—they'd lost touch before Noah was born. The boy seemed to be doing better, though. More talkative. Less moody. Not as easily frustrated. But he was still easily set off—an alcoholic mother left his wiring frazzled. That meant the virginity issue couldn't be ignored, as it could with most boys. For Noah, it was like a sliver, a minor irritation that would inflame and fester until they dealt with it.

"If this isn't what you want . . ." Nick said gently.

"It is." Noah looked over, his expression resolute. "I'm sick of the guys razzing me. They stopped when I told them you were bringing me here."

"You . . . told them I was taking you to a brothel?"

"Uh-huh." A rare grin. "They were so fucking jealous. None of their dads would ever take them to a whorehouse. Not that you're my dad, but you know what I mean."

Reese thumped Nick on the back. "Better let Antonio handle the next parent-teacher night. Though I think you're about to become a very popular choice for school-trip chaperone."

Nick sighed.

"It's very dark," Noah said as they headed up the front walk.

It was. No lights on the cedar-shrouded porch. All the blinds drawn. Nick supposed they were just being discreet. He knocked.

It took a few minutes before the door opened, long enough for Noah to start fidgeting. He didn't stop when it did open, probably because the woman holding it had to be at least sixty. And not a well-maintained sixty.

"Please tell me that's not a—" Noah started to whisper, before Reese cut him short with a look.

"Hello. Liam and Ramon sent us," Nick said, naming the mutts who'd given Reese the brothel recommendation. "We're looking—"

"*He's* looking," Reese interjected, pointing at Noah.

"—for companionship for our friend here."

"Not tonight." The woman started to close the door.

Reese grabbed it and held it open. "What's wrong with tonight? We came a long way and we were told appointments weren't necessary."

"We are busy tonight."

Reese shoved the door open, so they could see into the dark interior. "Doesn't look busy."

"It is not a good—"

A second woman slipped through a hall doorway and tugged the old lady back. She was in her late thirties. Handsome, in a severe way, dressed in slacks and a blouse.

"I'm sorry," she said. "Darlene is a little overprotective of the girls. It's their day off, actually, but you said only one needs companionship?"

Both Nick and Reese pointed at Noah.

"Ah, I see." The woman smiled and winked at Noah. "I'm sure I'll have more than one girl happy to give up her night off for such a handsome young man."

The woman—Angelica, as she introduced herself—led them inside. It was a perfectly normal-looking house, no red velvet to be seen. She took them to a modern room with leather couches, a pool table, bar and big-screen TV.

As they sat, Nick noticed Reese sniffing the air. Nick himself was trying to inhale as little as possible. There were candles burning everywhere, giving off a slightly musky scent that he supposed was supposed to be a turn-on.

With a werewolf's overdeveloped sense of smell, though, the only thing it turned was his stomach.

They'd just settled on the sofa when Darlene returned with a girl. Not really a girl—mid-twenties, Nick guessed, which was good, because he'd gotten to the age where an eighteen-year-old hooker would have made him want to throw his jacket around her and bustle her out of there. Not that this girl needed to cover up. She was still dressed for her night off, in jeans and a pullover. She'd taken a few minutes to put on makeup, though. Too much, really, but she was cute enough, and when she walked in, Noah let out an audible sigh of relief. He got to his feet.

The girl giggled. "In a hurry?"

"Um, no, of course not. I, uh—"

The girl cut him off with a loud kiss. "I wasn't complaining. I like eager. *Young* and eager is even better." She grinned. "We don't get a lot of hot young guys here." She glanced at Nick and giggled. "Or hot guys of any age. I'm sure I could find friends for you two upstairs."

"Nope, we're good," Reese said. "Tonight is all about him."

"Then let's get right to it." She took Noah's hand and led him out. "I'm Sophie, by the way."

"Rob," he said. "I'm Rob."

Once they were gone, Angelica offered drinks from the bar. Nick eyed the Scotch, but Reese grabbed them both beers. Then they settled in, chatting awkwardly, glancing at the clock, as if waiting for Noah to finish an appointment. A short appointment, Nick figured.

After about ten minutes, another girl slid around the corner. This one was older than the first, and she *looked* like a hooker—bleached-blond teased hair, huge breasts that threatened to pop out of her bustier, long legs ending in stilettos.

She flashed her smile at Nick first, but his expression must have said she really wasn't his type, because she plopped herself onto Reese's lap instead.

Reese jumped so fast he nearly sent her flying. Then he lifted his hands, as if to keep them from going anyplace they shouldn't.

"I, uh, I'm not a client," he said. "No offense. I just wouldn't want you to, uh, waste your efforts."

The woman gave a throaty laugh and reached to run her hands through Reese's hair, which brought those huge breasts right up into his face. Reese tensed and Nick thought he was going to throw her off, and Nick tensed himself, ready to run interference. But then Reese went still.

Nick couldn't see Reese's expression, probably because his face was buried in the hooker's boobs, but it probably said something like, "Hmm, this isn't so bad after all." Reese had his hang-ups, but he was still a young were-wolf. God only knew how long it'd been since he'd had sex. That couldn't be healthy at his age. Hell, that wasn't healthy at any age.

As Reese let the hooker coo and rub her breasts against his face, Nick began to think this brothel scheme wasn't so crazy after all. Noah might not be the only guy who solved a problem tonight.

"You know . . ." Reese began.

"Uh-huh," Nick murmured.

Reese pulled the hooker down onto his lap and plucked at the laces of her bustier. "Is there any way I can persuade you to give up your day off. . . ?"

"Sugar, I don't need any persuading," the woman drawled. "You're so damned sweet I'd give you all my days off."

She got to her feet, her hand entwined with Reese's. He stood, then turned to Nick.

"Come with us," he said.

The hooker laughed. "Oh, now that would be a treat. Come with us indeed, handsome."

Nick was all for helping Reese and Noah. He liked taking on the role of guardian. A few years ago, when Clay and Elena—his Pack mates and best friends—had their twins, he started thinking maybe he wanted kids of his own. It didn't take more than a few diaper changes to convince him otherwise, but he'd still felt the wolf instinct to raise the next generation. Taking in two almost-grown young werewolves seemed the perfect solution.

But this . . . this was taking mentorship too far. Of course he'd had threesomes before, but the male-female ratio had always been reversed, and that's how he liked it.

"I need you up there, Nick," Reese whispered.

Shit.

Nick looked at the hooker and tried not to shudder. Maybe he could just . . . be in the room. For moral support. He stood and waved for them to lead the way.

The hooker led them into the first bedroom at the top of the stairs. Which was a good thing, because Reese was almost as eager as Noah had been. Nick barely got the door closed before Reese had her on the bed. Then he pinned her, arms and legs on hers, hand over her mouth.

"Whoa!" Nick said, running forward. "Don't—"

"Find Noah," Reese growled. "I'll keep this one—"

The hooker bucked and writhed, her eyes blazing, jaw working as if she was trying to bite Reese's hand. He wrapped his other one around her throat and leaned down.

"Feel how strong I am?" he whispered. "There's no use—"

The hooker fought harder, her muffled screams loud enough to alert anyone in an adjoining room. Reese's hand tightened on her throat. The hooker glared at him one last time, then her body went limp, gaze emptying.

Reese yanked his hand back. "Shit! I barely—" His fingers flew to the side of the woman's neck.

"Is she. . . ?" Nick began.

"Dead." Reese paused. "And ice cold." He leaned down and inhaled, then made a face. "Decomp. That's what I smelled downstairs. The candles and her perfume were doing a good job of covering it until she got close."

"You mean she's. . . ?"

"A zombie," Reese said, "We need to get Noah."

Nick swung into the hall to see Noah backing out of another doorway, staring into the room he'd just left, his eyes huge. When Nick started toward him, he wheeled. He saw Nick, tensed, and glanced both ways, as if ready to make a run for it.

Nick loped down the hall before Noah could bolt.

"I-I didn't mean to do it," he said. "I swear. I decided since the guys knew

I was coming here, that was good enough. I didn't have to go through with it. B-but when I said I changed my mind, she got mad. I promised we'd still pay, but—"

"It's okay," Nick said, putting his arm around the boy's shoulders.

Noah pushed him away. "No, you don't understand. I tried to leave and she wouldn't let me, so I shoved her. That's all I did, but now she's dead and—"

"You didn't kill her."

"Y-yes, I did. I checked for a pulse and—"

"She was already dead," Reese said, coming up behind them.

Reese took Noah back into the room, where the girl lay on the bed. "See? She—Shit."

Nick pushed past them. There, on the bed, was the girl. Or what remained of her—a skeleton wearing decomposing flesh, a red silk bra and panties.

"Th—that—" Noah began.

"Isn't what she looked like a few minutes ago?" Reese said. "Yeah, I'm sure she didn't."

Noah turned and retched. Nick rubbed Noah's back as he hurled dinner onto the carpet.

"Great," Reese murmured. "More hours of therapy."

"Did I say a hooker wasn't a good idea?" Nick whispered back.

"I didn't expect zombies."

"No one ever does." Nick stripped a pillow of its case and handed the fabric to Noah to use to wipe his face, then frowned at the dead girl. "The last zombie hooker I met didn't look like that."

"You've met others?" Reese said.

"One. With Elena and Clay. Everything like this usually happens when they're around. That zombie had the rotting thing going on from the start. That's what they do. Rot. And it's why they really don't make good hookers."

"Uh-huh. Well, as interesting as this anomaly may be, I say we leave it to Elena and the council, and get out of here before—"

A thump sounded from out in the hall. Then a muted cry.

Nick started toward the door.

Reese grabbed his arm. "Curiosity doesn't just kill cats. Let's go."

Nick hesitated. A few years ago, he'd have agreed. Hell, a few years ago, he'd have been the one grabbing Clay or Elena and saying, "Let's go." But he wasn't the omega wolf anymore. He had responsibilities. Which meant . . .

He turned to Reese. "Take Noah out of here." He waved at the window.

Reese protested, but Nick got them both out. Then he crept back into the hall and followed the sound of stifled cries to a bedroom. The door lock snapped with a sharp twist of the knob.

He pushed the door open. An empty room. Another thump, the muffled sounds louder. Nick followed them to a locked closet. Another werewolf-enhanced twist and the door opened. Inside, a young man lay bound and gagged on the floor. Seeing Nick, his eyes rolled wildly.

Nick motioned him to silence, then pulled off the gag.

"Thank God," the young man gasped. "I didn't think anyone would ever hear me. You must be a—"

He said a word Nick didn't recognize. Probably the Latinized name for half-demons with hearing powers. Reese did say the brothel catered to supernaturals.

"It's okay," Nick said as he snapped the ropes. "I'm going to get you out—"

"No!" The guy grabbed his wrist. "The girls. The whores. They're vetala."

"If that's some kind of zombie, I already know that."

"It's a demi-demon that possesses bodies of the recently dead."

Which explained the non-rotting, Nick supposed.

The young man continued. "I knew what they were as soon as I got here. I'm a necromancer. I can recognize the dead. I confronted the lady in charge and all of a sudden, they swarmed me and locked me in there."

"Okay, but you're out now. So come—"

"My friend. They took him to the basement for some kind of ritual. That's why they're closed tonight. We need to get him out."

Nick knew he wasn't considered the brightest guy in the Pack. Clay was a freaking genius and Elena was damned smart, too, so he never tried to compete, just sat back and let them come up with the plans. But he wasn't dumb. Or, at least, not dumb enough to try handling this on his own.

He clapped the young man on the back. "Don't worry." He took out his cell to call Karl. "I'll get help—"

The young man's eyes bugged. "There's no time for that. Don't you get it? My friend is about to be slaughtered in some kind of demonic ritual."

"Then we'll stall it until my friends arrive." Nick started dialing.

The young man knocked the phone from his hand. "You aren't making this easy, are you?" His eyes glowed orange and his voice changed. "I want your body."

Considering where they were, there was a brief moment when Nick thought, "Whoa, sorry, that's not my thing." Then he realized, given the whole zombie/vetala/demi-demon issue—and the glowing orange eyes—that probably wasn't what the guy meant.

A floorboard squeaked behind Nick, and the stench of rotting flesh wafted past. He spun as three young women slid into the room. The first looked normal enough, her skin just starting to gray. The second's face was covered in blackened boils that bubbled and burst. The third was barely more than a walking skeleton, flesh sloughing off with every step. All three wore silk negligees, thongs, garters and stockings, presenting an image that ensured Nick was not going to be enjoying the Victoria's Secret catalogue for a very long time.

He backed up to the window, watching their outstretched nails, and remembering the zombie scratch that nearly cost Clay an arm. When he reached the window and looked down, though, he saw two more zombie hookers waiting below in the yard.

Shit! Had Reese and Noah gotten away? He should have told Reese to call Karl and tell him where they were *before* he checked out the noise.

"Look, whatever's going on here, it's your business," Nick said. "I'm just going to leave and pretend I didn't see anything—"

"Did I mention I want your body?" the young man said.

"This body?" Nick said. "It's a lot older than you think. I'm a—"

"Werewolf." One of the girls licked her lips with a blackened tongue. "We know. That means your body is in very good condition. You and your friends picked a perfect night to visit. We were just beginning to gather fresh vessels. They last a long time, but not indefinitely. We'll take yours and the handsome young Australian's. The little one is too young, but we will kill him quickly. Mercifully."

Nick hit the man first. A lightning punch to the throat took him down, and he stayed down, the demi-demon abandoning its host. On to the graying girl, who was already running at him, shrieking. A blow to the stomach doubled her over. He grabbed her hair and snapped her neck. When he looked up, the other two were gone, leaving a trail of rotted flesh in their wake.

Nick exited out the window. Only two zombies down there. As he landed, they rushed him. He took the first out with two quick blows. The second ran off. When the first zombie was dead—or dead again—he dropped her and turned . . .

Zombies stepped through the hedges, surrounding him. Six of them. All in lingerie and varying degrees of decomposition.

A figure raced through an opening in the hedge. Reese. The young man ran to Nick's side and flipped around to cover his back.

"Noah?" Nick said.

"Safe."

The zombies began to circle.

"You need to watch their—"

"Nails, I know." Reese lowered his voice. "Where's the necromancer?"

"Huh?"

"Zombies are controlled by a necro. Where's—?"

Reese stopped as they spotted Angelica hidden in the shadows.

"I got her," Reese said. "Cover me."

Nick raced after him, knocking zombies aside as they charged. But not many charged. Not as many as should have, if Angelica could order them to guard her. Nick realized it just as Reese grabbed Angelica. Reese already had his hands around the woman's neck. Her eyes flashed orange, then emptied as the demi-demon left her.

"Goddamn it!" Reese said, dropping the corpse.

"The old woman," Nick said as he surveyed the zombies, closing in on them again. "Darlene. Where's—?"

A white-haired figure stepped through the gate, lips moving, hands fluttering. The zombies shifted forward, rumbling and hissing.

A shadow appeared behind the old woman. Noah knocked her to the ground. His hands shot up to snap her neck. The zombies turned and rushed him.

"No!" Nick yelled.

He raced over, shoving zombies out of the way. Killing the undead was one thing. Killing a living person—deservedly or not—wasn't something the boy needed on his conscience.

Nick grabbed the old woman away from Noah. A quick wrench broke her neck. The zombies hesitated. They didn't evacuate their shells, though. They just watched him, as if confused.

Because they weren't zombies. Shit. They were vetala, whatever that was. Normal rules didn't apply.

"What do you want with us?" the one in front said. She had trouble speaking—her jaw hung by a few threads of tendon. Of all the zombies, she was the most decayed, barely more than a walking skeleton wearing a sweatshirt and thong.

Nick hesitated. They continued to watch him warily.

"You killed the one who summoned us," the leader said. "We belong to you. What do you want from us?"

"Nothing."

A rumble went through the pack, and they shifted, foot to foot.

The leader tilted her head. "We are free to go?"

"Yes," Reese said, walking up behind them. "You're free to go."

She continued to study Nick.

"Go," he said,

The leader dipped her head. "Thank you."

Her body collapsed. The others did, too, one after another, corpses falling onto the grass and starting to rot.

Once Nick had moved the bodies inside, checked the house and made sure there weren't any more zombies hobbling around, he called Elena. She'd contact the council and decide what to do about a brothel filled with corpses. Maybe he'd be back to clean it up. Maybe he wouldn't. Not his call, thankfully.

They walked back to the car in silence. As they got in, Noah said, "So that should work, right? If I tell my friends I went through with it? They won't . . . know?"

It took a moment for Nick to realize what he meant.

Reese beat him to an answer. "They won't know. We'll give you a few tips to make it sound good."

Noah relaxed in the back seat and Nick realized it was what the poor kid wanted all along. Not to lose his virginity. Just to get his friends off his back. If only he'd figured that out sooner . . .

"I'm going to call Lexi," Noah said. "Do you think I can get her back?"

"Just don't mention the brothel," Reese said. "If she finds out, tell her the truth—that nothing happened. I'll back you up."

"And as for winning her back," Nick said. "I have some tips for that, too."

Reese and Noah looked at each other.

"Um, maybe not," Noah said. "I appreciate your help, Nick, but after tonight . . ."

They both laughed.

"Excuse me?" Nick said. "This was *not* my idea."

But they were talking again, and neither heard him. He sighed and started to drive. Suddenly, changing diapers didn't seem so bad. Teenager's messes were a lot bigger and a lot tougher to clean up.

LIFE SENTENCE

An Otherworld Universe Story

DANIEL BOYD had overcome many obstacles in his life, and mortality was simply the latest challenge. He'd been born into an illustrious family of sorcerers, owners of a multinational corporation. Money and magical powers. The proverbial silver spoon . . . or it would be, if your father hadn't screwed the company over and gotten himself—and his sons—disinherited. But Daniel had surmounted that barrier, and so he would with this one.

"We're heading down to the laboratory," Shana said, her voice coming through his computer speaker. "It's underground, so let's hope we don't lose the connection."

They'd better not, considering how much Daniel had paid for the equipment. He leaned back and watched the screen bob as Shana descended the steps, the camera affixed to her hand.

The doctor had given him the death sentence two weeks ago. Inoperable cancer. Six months to live. Daniel didn't accept it. He had money, he had power, he had connections; he would find a way to commute this sentence. So he'd begun his search, delving in the black market of the supernatural world.

Shana finally reached the underground Peruvian laboratory. As much as Daniel wanted this cure, he wasn't flitting across the world to get it. There was no need to when he had Shana.

She was, as he'd always said, the perfect assistant. Loyal enough to follow orders without question. Astute enough to anticipate his every need. Attractive enough to make everyone presume he was bedding her, and smart enough never to correct that presumption.

She'd been with him for six years, and he didn't know what he'd do without her. Luckily, he didn't need to worry about that.

"Still there, sir?" Shana asked.

"I am. Audio and visual working fine."

A man's face filled the screen, coffee-stained teeth flashing. "*Hola*, Mr. Boyd! I'm delighted that you've taken an interest in my studies. May I be the first to welcome you to—"

"I have a meeting in twenty minutes."

"Of course. You're a busy man. I mustn't keep you—"

"No, you mustn't," Shana said. "Now, this is the lab, I take it?"

The camera panned a gleaming, high-tech laboratory. Dr. Gonzales was funded by a European Cabal that wouldn't appreciate him double-dipping with a Boyd for a client, but he'd been unable to resist Daniel's offer.

Gonzales walked to a table full of beakers and tubes and started explaining how he'd distilled the genetic component.

"Not interested," Daniel said. "I only care about the end result."

"You can fax the results to me," Shana said. "So our scientists can check your procedures."

"Yes, of course. Well, then, on to the subjects."

The screen dimmed as they returned to the hallway. Daniel answered three e-mails while they walked and talked about the cure. It wasn't a cure for cancer; Daniel had realized early that was a band-aid solution to avoid tackling the underlying problem of mortality.

Vampirism seemed the best solution. Semi-immortality plus invulnerability. But as it turned out, the process of becoming one was far more convoluted than he'd expected, and promised only a twenty-percent chance of success . . . and an eighty-percent risk of complete annihilation of life and soul.

Most vampires, though, were hereditary, and therein, he believed, lay the answer. After some digging, he finally found a lead on Gonzales, a shaman who claimed to have isolated and distilled the genetic component that would make anyone a vampire, for the right price.

"Sir?" Shana murmured.

He glanced at the screen to see what looked like a hospital ward. He counted eight subjects, varying ages, all on their backs, unconscious, hooked up to banks of monitors.

"We began clinical trials five years ago, starting with rhesus monkeys—"

"Could you tell us about these subjects, please," Shana cut in. "Have they completed the trial? How much attrition did you experience? Have you managed to induce invulnerability as well as semi-immortality?"

"They've all completed the procedure. We had two subjects whose bodies rejected the infusion. One survived. One did not. As for invulnerability, naturally, that is part of the package—"

Gonzales stopped as Shana stepped up to a sleeping subject and slid a knife from her pocket.

"—though it hasn't been perfected yet," he hurried on. "It will be, though."

Shana wrote something on her tablet notebook. Sweat trickled down Gonzales's cheek.

"Why are they unconscious?" she asked, still writing.

"We had some difficulty finding willing subjects, and while I'm sure they'll be pleased with the results, we thought it best to . . ."

"Ease them into the reality of their new life."

His head bobbed. "Yes. Exactly. Thank you."

"Wake one up."

Gonzales stared at her. Then he looked into the camera.

"When Ms. Bergin speaks, she is speaking for me," Daniel said.

Gonzales blathered on about the danger of reversing an induced coma. Shana set the camera down, so he could speak directly to Daniel, then walked away, as if giving them privacy. She walked behind Gonzales, quietly opening a medical cabinet, taking out a syringe and scanning the bottles before choosing one. Daniel smiled. The perfect assistant. Always resourceful. Always anticipating his needs.

As Gonzales continued, Shana filled the syringe, stepped up to the nearest subject and plunged it in.

The man bolted upright, gasping and wild-eyed. Not unexpected, under the circumstances. The screams were. Unearthly shrieks filled the lab as the man grabbed at his skin, fingers and nails digging in, ripping, blood splattering the white bed, the white walls, Gonzales radioing for help as he ran to the medicine cabinet.

Shana walked over to the camera, then glanced back at the subject, still screaming and rending his flesh as if acid flowed through his veins.

"Well, now we know why they were sedated," she said, and turned off the camera.

You didn't reach Daniel's position in life by giving up easily. Yet neither did you get there by clinging to hope past all reasonable bounds. He spent another month researching promises of vampire life, before giving up on that particular cure.

"They've been making huge strides in zombification lately," Wendell said, between bites of his burger. Wendell was Daniel's second cousin, a VP in the family Cabal. Relations with his family had greatly improved a decade ago, coinciding with his own company's appearance on the NYSE. An independently successful Boyd could be useful to the Cabal, and Daniel felt the same about them.

Wendell swiped the linen napkin across his mouth. "Did you hear what I said?"

"I heard. I'm ignoring it, having no overwhelming desire to spend my eternity in a state of decomposition."

"Oh, you don't rot forever. Eventually the flesh is gone and you're a walking skeleton." He leaned over to thump Daniel's shoulder. "I'm kidding. Well, not about the rotting part, but scientists have been working to overcome that little drawback. We had our own R&D department on it for a while before we decided it was simpler to monitor the independent guys, wait until they're done and then buy the research."

"For zombies?" Daniel's lip curled with distaste. The server—thinking he didn't like his meal—rushed over, but he waved her away.

"Sure. Think of the applications. We've got a lawyer on his deathbed right now. Guy's been with us almost fifty years. A wealth of information is about to disappear. We could change that."

"Huh." Daniel tore off a chunk of bread and chewed it slowly. "You have any names?"

"Not on hand. I can get them, though. If this works, though?" Wendell smiled. "Biggest favor ever."

Biggest favor ever was right. Savvy businessman that he was, Wendell had known exactly how much his information was worth. If it worked, he wanted a new job—with Daniel's corporation. That was fine. Wendell would make a good addition to the firm. Besides, if he had a stake in Daniel's continued survival, he'd make damned sure he gave him every contact the Boyd Cabal had. Plus, if it worked, he'd be able to swoop in and snatch up the research from under the Cabal's nose, in which case Wendell wouldn't have a job anyway . . . and might be in need of the immortality solution himself.

Wendell got Daniel the names, and Shana started making the appointments. The first was with a whiz-kid half-demon who'd recently parted ways with a renowned researcher and had accidentally walked out with the man's work, which he'd refined and was now prepared to sell.

Daniel sat in the boardroom as the kid gave his spiel, Shana hurrying him along with reminders that Mr. Boyd was a very busy man.

"Your time is valuable," the kid said. "Especially now, huh?"

He grinned. Daniel and Shana remained stone-faced.

"I believe you brought a test subject?" Shana said. "One you have successfully transformed into a zombie."

"Right. Yes. He's in the . . . Just hold on."

The kid hurried from the room and returned with another college-age kid. He walked a little slow and his face was paler than Daniel liked, but at this point, he wasn't being fussy.

"How long has it been since you turned him?" Shana asked.

"Three months."

"Any side effects?"

"His reflexes are a little slow, but we're working on that."

Shana motioned for the subject to turn. He did a one-eighty.

"He's breathing," she said.

The whiz kid smiled. "Yep. Breathing, got a pulse, eats, drinks, just like a living person."

"Impressive."

"Does he talk?" Daniel asked.

"Sure," the zombie said. "What do you want me to say?"

"Recite the multiplication tables, starting at six."

As the zombie performed, Shana eased behind them and removed a gun from her purse. She hesitated, just a second, but at a look from Daniel she nodded and shot the zombie in the back. He fell, gasping and clutching his chest. The whiz kid stared, then dropped to his knees beside his subject, who was bleeding out on the floor, eyes glazing over.

"Not a zombie," Daniel said. "Next time, Shana?"

"I'll ask for a demonstration of resurrection."

"Thank you."

"Is the lighting adequate, sir?" Shana asked.

She swept the camera around the dark cemetery. The image jittered as she shivered. November really wasn't the best time for such things, but she hadn't complained, of course.

"Dr. Albright is—" she began.

The shower turned on in his hotel suite's adjoining bathroom, drowning her out. Daniel glowered, then scooped up the portable screen and moved into the sitting room. The girl in the bathroom called out, asking if he wanted to join her. He closed the door and settled onto the sofa, then asked Shana to repeat herself.

"Dr. Albright is setting up at the gravesite. I'm heading there now."

A yelp, as she tripped over a half-buried gravestone.

"Careful, Shana. That equipment is very expensive."

"Y-yes, sir," she said through chattering teeth.

"Get yourself a stiff drink when you finish," he said. "That'll warm you up. Bill the company."

"Thank you, sir."

He smiled. Little things, but crucial in employee relations. Even watching the screen made him chilly. He reached over and jacked up the heat on the gas fireplace, then poured himself a brandy.

He turned up the sound as the girl in the bathroom yelled for the shampoo. He supposed she had a name, but he couldn't remember it. Just another young woman in a bar who'd assessed the cut of his suit and spread her legs, a Pavlovian response to the smell of money.

Shana finally found Albright. Along with two assistants, he'd begun digging up a recent grave. It was long, cold work, and partway through, Daniel had to turn off the screen and bid farewell to the girl. Apparently, she'd expected to stay the night and complained bitterly about being sent out with wet hair, so he'd handed her the suite's blow-dryer and hurried her out the door with couple hundred bucks "for the taxi."

By then they'd dug down to the casket and were waiting for him, all shivering now, breath steaming in the air.

"I've resurrected the corpse inside," Albright announced, talking loudly to be heard over the muffled bangs and cries.

"Mr. Boyd can hear that," Shana said. "Now, the ritual you used is supposed to return the body to its original form, free of any after effects of death, correct?"

"Absolutely, as you will see in a moment."

The assistants opened the casket. The man inside jerked, all limbs flailing, then sat up, gulping breaths of air before frowning, as if only just realizing he didn't need those breaths. He squinted up at the people surrounding his casket.

"Wh-what's going on?" he asked.

"You've been resurrected, Mr. Lang. Congratulations."

The man's frown deepened as he seemed to consider this. Then he nodded and tried to stand. Shana motioned to Albright, who stopped him. Shana ran her tests, confirming he did, indeed, appear to be dead. Or undead, as it were.

She took out a folder and consulted a list.

"And you are James Lang, who died in an automobile accident on February 20?"

He nodded.

"You're sure?"

"Course I'm sure."

She plucked out a sheet of paper and showed it to him. "Because you don't look like Mr. Lang. And I noticed, Dr. Albright, that you began digging before I arrived, contrary to our agreement."

"I knew it would take a while and it's a cold night—"

"I appreciate your consideration. I do not appreciate your duplicity. You started because you wanted to disguise any indication of recent digging; perhaps to lay a fresh zombie in Mr. Lang's grave."

"I didn't—"

"Then you won't mind me returning Mr. Lang to our offices, where he can be monitored for signs of decomposition." She turned to the zombie. "Don't worry. Having skipped the embalming phase, it shouldn't take long."

As expected, the zombie rotted and, in the meantime, Daniel knocked three more names off the list Wendell had provided, grumbling each time he did so, well aware that his cousin seemed to be getting the best of this deal. If Daniel succeeded, Wendell got a cushy new job. If he failed, Wendell could go to the Cabal board of directors and tell them he'd used Daniel to cull their list of zombification experts.

Of the five rejected so far, only the whiz kid seemed to be a career conman. The rest were serious researchers, seriously researching the subject, but years from selling a perfected cure. Typical underfunded scientists—desperate for that big windfall that would let them continue their work—they tried to trick him into funding their work. He understood, though that didn't mean they hadn't paid dearly for the mistake.

Two more researchers came and went, and Daniel was nearing the end of the list when one at the bottom, perhaps hearing rumors, took it upon himself to make the initial contact. He came; he requested an audience; he was refused; he stayed. When Daniel left work, the man was still there. When he returned the next morning, he was still there. Daniel decided he could find a few minutes to hear the man out. And a few minutes was all it took because the man followed Shana into Daniel's office and announced, "I don't have the cure you're looking for."

Shana sighed and started ushering him out, murmuring apologies to Daniel, but the man stood his ground and said, "I don't have it, but I can get it. I'm just missing one crucial ingredient."

"Money," Daniel said, leaning back. "Lots and lots of money."

The man gave a strange little smile, almost patronizing. "No, Mr. Boyd. I have many investors. What I lack are test subjects. Seems there aren't a lot of people willing to die at the risk of being reborn in a rotting corpse."

When Daniel didn't respond, the man took that as encouragement and stepped forward, opening his briefcase on Daniel's desk. He took out a folder the size of *War and Peace*.

"I'm asking you to take this and have your scientists go through it. My work, I believe, will speak for itself. All I need is someone to provide me with an unlimited supply of test subjects."

"Unlimited?" Shana said.

"My projections suggest I need between ten and fifty, depending on the number of stages required to perfect the serum. That is, however, an estimate at this point. More may be needed."

"More than *fifty*?" Shana caught Daniel's look and dropped her gaze, an apology on her lips. She stepped back.

Daniel took the file. He leafed through it. For show, of course—in high school, he'd blackmailed a fellow student to get him passing grades in science.

"Leave your card with Ms. Bergin. I'll get back to you."

Two days later, Daniel had Shana call and tell the man—Dr. Boros—that he'd get his test subjects, with a cap of fifty. Not that Daniel really intended to cut him off at fifty, but one had to set limits. And it placated Shana, which was, admittedly, important. He couldn't afford to lose her now.

Within a week, Boros had the first subjects ready for Daniel's inspection.

"They aren't nearly at the stage you need," Boros said into the camera.

"But I want complete transparency, Mr. Boyd. You can see how far I've progressed and how far I need to go. No charlatans' tricks. I believe you've had enough of those?"

"I have."

Boros clearly wasn't putting his money into his laboratory—a shabby set of basement rooms. It was clean and the equipment was top-notch, but hardly the high-tech, gleaming lab such experiments should have.

Boros also lacked assistants. Again, not for want of funds, but in this case, apparently, understandable paranoia. He trusted only one young man, a fellow scientist and fellow necromancer. Daniel understood the sentiment—he felt the same about Shana. But more staff would mean faster results, and at this stage, with only three months to go, Daniel desperately needed fast.

Boros's assistant brought in the first subject . . . strapped down on a gurney. Shana's sigh whispered across the audio connection.

"At least he's conscious," she murmured to Daniel.

"This subject has been zombified for a week, and if Ms. Bergin would care to examine him, she'll see no signs of decomposition. However, we have another problem."

Shana waved at the restraints. "He's unstable?"

"In a manner of speaking."

The assistant undid the restraints. The man lay there, blinking at the ceiling.

"Rise," Boros said.

The man didn't move. He should have—zombies had to obey the necromancer who resurrected them.

"Well, you've cured the control aspect," Daniel said. "Thankfully."

"Actually, I haven't. On examining his brain activity, it seems he would respond, if he could. In attempting to remove the necromancer's control, it seems he has lost all control."

As if in response, a wet spot spread across the subject's pants.

"That's a problem," Daniel said.

A small smile. "I suspected you'd say that." Boros waved, and his assistant brought in the second subject. To Daniel's relief, this one was walking.

He was also leaving a trail of decomposing flesh, falling like dandruff in his wake.

"That, too, is a problem," Daniel said.

"Agreed."

Boros turned to the subject. "Clap three times."

The man only looked at him.

"Touch your toes."

"Why?" the man asked.

Boros stepped between the two subjects. "In one, I've stopped decomposition at the expense of bodily control. In the other, I've freed him of the necromancer's control while accelerating decomp. Which problem would you like me to solve first? I know you'd like me to work on both, but my resources here—"

"You're not working there anymore. Your study is coming here. I'm clearing my laboratory and putting my specialists under your control."

"I'd really rather not—"

"You will. Or you don't have a client. Now, if you'll excuse me—"

"Sir?" Shana cut in. "The . . ." She paused and motioned for the assistant to remove the test subjects. When they were gone, she turned to Boros. "Can they be saved?"

Boros shook his head. "One will remain in a permanent state of paralysis. The other will continue to rapidly decompose."

"So they'll be terminated? Humanely?"

"Not so fast," Daniel said. "If there's still something to be learned from them, keep them."

"But—" Shana began.

"Bring them to the lab. There's a storage room we can use. We'll keep them there."

He flicked off the screen.

Within two months, Boros was getting so close to a cure that Daniel started postponing his visits to the doctor. His symptoms all but disappeared, as if driven away by the knowledge that cancer wasn't going to be a death sentence, not for him. Even if it ravaged his body tomorrow, Boros was far enough along that Daniel could take the temporary cure, then wait out the final one.

He didn't know how many subjects they'd gone through. Shana kept him updated every week, when Boros put in his requisition, but he paid no attention. It was during one of those weekly updates that she said, "We can't keep this up, sir. He's demanding ten more in the next week. There's a limit to how many transients can disappear from a city before someone starts investigating—"

"Then send the team to another city."

"We're doing that. But it's a slow process. He needs healthy, clean subjects. Do you have any idea how hard it is to find them among that population? We test them, but he still rejects a third of the ones—"

"Then we need to come up with an alternative."

A soft sigh of relief. "Thank you, sir. Now, I've done the calculations, and if you were to take his cure in its present form, we could slow the testing, meaning we could cut back the number of subjects significantly and—"

"I'm not taking a substandard cure unless it's an absolute last resort."

"I understand, sir, but we *are* reaching that stage—"

"No, we aren't. I want you to comb through the employee files. Find anyone with a terminal illness. Offer two years' salary to their families in return for their participation. Emphasize the benefits of the procedure and minimize the side effects."

When she didn't answer, he looked up from his computer golf game. She was staring at him.

"Employees, sir?"

"That's what I said. If we don't have enough with a terminal illness, make it a general offer and increase it to triple salary."

She continued to stare.

"How's Lindsey, Shana?"

She blanched. When Shana came into his employ, her eleven-year-old daughter had been suffering from a rare liver disease, on a transplant list and failing fast. As her signing bonus, Shana got that liver for her daughter, and all the care she'd needed to make a full recovery. And Daniel got the perfect assistant—one indebted to him for life.

"I-I think we can fill this latest requisition with transients," she said. "I'll split the team and send them farther afield."

He smiled. "Thank you, Shana."

She started to leave. He called her back and handed her a check for ten thousand dollars.

"A bonus. Buy something special for yourself and Lindsey."

She stared at it and, for just a second, he thought she was going to hand it back. After only that brief hesitation, though, she murmured, "Thank you, sir," pocketed it and left.

Finally, the day came. And not a moment too soon, as Daniel struggled to get into work every day, ignoring his wife's nervous clucking, ignoring the little voice inside himself that said, "Take the cure as it is, before it's too late." Boros was close, though, and Daniel willed himself to hang on. The pain and exhaustion were simply more obstacles to overcome.

And then, it was ready.

Daniel made Boros go through the final stage twice—two batches with four subjects each time. When he was assured of the results, he ordered six of those subjects killed, the other two left alive and stored for long-term monitoring and potential future tests. He wasn't sure what Shana objected to more—killing successful subjects or holding the other two captive. He had assured her, though, that once he'd been treated, all the failures could be terminated and sent on to their afterlives. That satisfied her.

Killing the successful subjects and keeping two for testing was but one of the precautions he took. He knew he was heading into the most dangerous phase of the testing. He was about to die and put his rebirth in the hands of others. It would be the final test of loyalty for his assistant, and while he trusted her more than anyone in his life, he took precautions with that, too, guaranteeing she wouldn't decide at the last moment that he could stay dead.

Then he let Boros kill him by lethal injection. Not pleasant but, according to his research, the quickest and most reliable method. The next thing he saw was Shana's face, floating above his, her pretty features drawn with concern, worrying that the cure might have failed. While he'd like to think she was worried for his sake, he knew better.

"Sir?" she said when he opened his eyes.

He blinked hard. "Yes?" He had to say it twice. When he spoke, the relief on her face . . . there was a moment there when he wished it was for him.

He tried to sit up. She helped him. She gave him a glass of water. She wiped his face, made him feel more himself, and he was grateful.

Daniel had undergone surgery a couple of times in his youth, and this reminded him of that, coming out of the anesthetic, slow and groggy. Boros bustled around, administering tests, checking his reflexes and responses to visual and audio stimuli. Shana kept him comfortable.

At last, Boros declared the conversion a success. He had Daniel get up and move around, doing a few tasks on his laptop, making sure his physical and mental capacities were normal.

"All right, then," Boros said. "Go back to bed."

Daniel didn't want to go back to bed—he felt fine and he needed to relocate to the safe room in the basement, where he'd remain for a few days, presumably "on vacation" until he was fully recovered.

When he tried opening his mouth to refuse, though, he couldn't. Instead, he found himself walking back to the bed. And, as he lay down, he realized with no small amount of horror that he'd been tricked.

Boros walked over. "Did you really think I'd give up the chance to have a man like yourself as my personal puppet?"

Daniel started to sit up.

"Lie down."

He did.

Boros smiled. "Yes, I know, you checked and rechecked, making sure I gave you the right formulation. And I did. You can ask Ms. Bergin. Unfortunately, it appears there is no way to remove the control a necromancer has over his zombies."

"But—"

"I know, I demonstrated it to you. With subjects raised by my assistant, meaning they would have no reason to obey *me*."

Daniel tried to look at Shana, but she'd disappeared behind Boros.

"Don't bother appealing to her. She's been paid well for her cooperation. Yes, you're holding a chit on her, but considering that you're under my control, that's a problem easily remedied. So let's start there. Please release—"

The muffled hiss of a silenced gunshot cut him short. Boros slumped forward, a small-caliber bullet through the back of his head, Shana behind him with a gun. As Boros lay on the floor, blood oozing down his balding scalp, Daniel sat up, slowly, eyes on the barrel. She lowered it to her side.

"I trust you'll make that call now, sir?" she said.

He did, having her daughter released, then giving the phone to Shana. Out of Daniel's earshot she spoke to her daughter.

"You'll be well compensated—" he began when she returned, and for the first time since they'd met, she interrupted him.

"I know. I'll be very well compensated. And, as soon as I've set you up in the safe room, my employment is at an end."

He understood and said as much. She called a pair of guards to come for Boros's body and detain his assistant, then called in two shamans who'd been part of the research team and, as such, knew Daniel's secret and would be tending to him during his recovery. The four of them set off for the room that would be his temporary home.

"There's one last thing I'll ask," Shana said as they took the elevator to the basement. "You promised to release the other subjects—"

"Excluding the two successes. I may still need them."

She nodded. "The others, though . . ."

"Can have their souls released immediately. And there won't be any more. I presume that's why you killed Boros."

She nodded and he felt a small prickle of disappointment. Had he really thought she'd done it to protect him?

She handed him a form authorizing the subjects' release. He arched his brows, surprised at the formality, but she met his gaze with a level stare. She didn't trust him, and he'd earned that mistrust, so there was nothing to do now but make a clean break of it. When they reached the basement lab, she faxed the signed forms to the records department.

Outside the safe room, Shana slid her card through the reader, coupled with a retinal scan. The electronic door whooshed open. Daniel walked in and looked around. He hadn't seen the work they'd done to prepare it. He hadn't even told Shana what he'd wanted. But it was exactly as he'd expected—a storage room converted into a luxury hotel suite.

The shamans hurried in to help him sit, then retreated behind Shana. She hadn't said a word since the elevator. He supposed he couldn't expect more, under the circumstances, so he made a call, wiring a million dollars into her account, and she waited in silence until she received confirmation on her cell phone. Then, with the shamans flanking her, she closed the door.

Daniel was just settling onto the bed when the speaker overhead clicked on. It was Shana.

"The records department has received the fax on releasing the zombies. I'm going to do it now, before I go."

Daniel smiled. There was no need to tell him that, but it was obvious she couldn't bring herself to walk away. As angry as she was, she had a good job, and she'd hoped—expected—he'd try to convince her to stay.

"How much, Shana?" he asked.

"Sir?"

"To stay. What do you want? More money? A bigger office?" He chuckled. "An assistant of your own?"

"No, sir. I was simply calling to confirm that it's all right for me to release the zombies."

He sighed. She was going to be difficult. "Yes, yes. Release them. Now about—"

A *whoosh* cut him short. He glanced at the door. It was still shut.

"You!" snarled a voice behind him.

He wheeled to see a section of the wall had opened. One of the zombie subjects stood in the opening, squinting at him with its good eye, the other shriveled.

"You did this to me," the zombie said, struggling to speak through rotting lips.

"No," Daniel said slowly, carefully. "A scientist—"

"You don't even remember me, do you? But I remember you. Sitting there, barely paying attention, busy talking on your cell phone as you sentenced me to this." He waved at his rotting body.

Daniel looked up at the speaker. "If this is your idea of a lesson, Shana—"

"No sir," her voice crackled. "*This* is my idea of a lesson."

Another zombie appeared behind the first. Then a third, crawling on stubs of arms. A fourth slithered past him. They crowded into the doorway, grumbling and grunting, all glowering at Daniel. Then the first stepped aside and they rushed forward, zombie after zombie, running, lurching, dragging themselves toward him.

Daniel ran to the door. Pounded on it. Screamed.

"Don't worry, sir," Shana said. "Your procedure was a success. No matter what they do, you can't die."

A click, and the speaker went silent as the zombies swarmed over him.

PLAN B

Deanna lifted the charm bracelet and shifted closer to the bedside lamp for a better look.

"Oh, god," she said. "Reminds me of the bracelet my dad gave me when I turned thirteen. I asked for the new Guns N' Roses tape, and he gave me one of these. Bastard."

Gregory double-checked his tie in the mirror. "Think Abby will like it?"

"Shit, yeah. If any grown woman was made for charm bracelets, it's Abby." Deanna rolled onto her back and draped the bracelet around her breast. "Looks better on me, though, don't you think?"

Gregory chuckled, but continued adjusting his tie. Deanna slid the bracelet down her stomach, spread her legs and dangled it there.

"Wanna play hide and seek?" she asked.

She wrapped the bracelet around her index finger and waggled it closer to her crotch. Gregory stopped fussing with his tie and watched. Before the bracelet disappeared, he grabbed her hand.

"Uh-uh," he said. "Tempting, but no. I've heard of giving your wife a gift smelling of another woman's perfume, but that would go a bit far."

"Like she'd notice." Deanna flipped onto her stomach. "Probably doesn't even know what it smells like. The only time Abby lets her hand drift south of her belly button is when she's wiping her twat, and she'd avoid that if she could."

"That, my dear, sounds remarkably like jealousy."

"No, *my dear*, it sounds remarkably like impatience."

He shrugged on his jacket. "These things take time. Every detail must be planned to perfection."

"Don't pull that shit on me, babe. You aren't dragging your heels plotting how to get away with it. You've got that figured out. Now you're just trying to decide how you want to do it. You're in no rush to get to the reality, 'cause you're too busy enjoying the fantasy."

He grinned. "This is true. Shooting versus stabbing versus strangulation. It's a big decision and, sadly, I only get to do it once."

"At this rate, you'll never get around to doing it at all."

"How about Friday?"

Deanna popped up on her elbows, then narrowed her eyes. "Ha-ha."

"I'm quite serious." Gregory patted his pockets and pulled out his car keys. "Does Friday work for you?"

She nodded, eyes still wary.

"It's a date, then," he said. "I'll see you tomorrow and we'll talk. I'm thinking stabbing. Messier, but more painful. Abby deserves the best."

He smiled, blew her a kiss and disappeared out the door.

Deanna sat up and looked out the window. The cottage Gregory had rented for her was perched on a cliff overlooking the ocean. Below, the water looked mirror-smooth, with brightly colored yachts and sailboats bobbing about like children's toys. Cotton-candy clouds drifted across the aquamarine sky. Farther down the shore, a freshly painted red-and-white lighthouse gleamed like a peppermint stick. It was a picture so perfect that if you painted it, no one would believe it was taken from life. Yet if she looked down, straight down, she found herself staring into a maelstrom of mud and garbage. All the trash those distant boats tossed overboard wound up here, at the bottom of the cliff, where beer cans and empty sunscreen bottles swirled in whirlpools crested with dirty foam.

Be not deceived; for as ye sow, so shall ye reap. The Bible quote came so fast it brought a chill, and she shivered, yanking down the window shade.

For as ye sow, so shall ye reap. How deeply the lessons of youth burrow into the brain. She could still hear her father in the pulpit. The lessons of youth, driven in with the help of a liberally wielded belt.

At fifteen, Deanna had run from those lessons. She'd fled all the way to Toronto and found the hell her father prophesied for her. At seventeen, she mistook Satan for savior, becoming a wealthy businessman's toy in return for promises of gold rings and happily ever after. After two years, he discarded her like a used condom.

Before he could pass her apartment to his next toy, she'd broken in, intent on taking everything she could carry. Then she'd found the photos he'd taken of them together. And they'd given her an idea. For as ye sow, so shall ye reap. There had to be consequences. A price to be paid . . . but not by her.

It had been laughably easy. Of course, she hadn't asked for much. She'd been naive, having no idea how much those photos were worth to someone who valued his family-man reputation. But, with practice, she'd learned. For ten years now, she'd made her living having affairs with wealthy married men, then demanding money to keep her mouth shut.

Now, finally, that had all come to an end. One last mortal sin, and she'd be free.

Deanna opened the drawer of her bedside table and reached inside. Beneath the pile of lingerie was a postcard of the French Riviera. She didn't pull it out, just ran her fingers over its glossy surface. She closed her eyes and remembered when they'd bought it. She'd seen it in the display rack and pulled it out, waving it like a flag.

"Here! This is where I want to go."

An indulgent smile. "Then that's where we'll go."

He'd said Friday. Did he mean it? Could she book the tickets now? She stroked the postcard. No, not yet. Give it another couple of days. Make sure he meant it this time.

"How retro," Abby said, waving her wrist above the plate of mussels.

She snaked her hand over her head and wriggled in her seat like a belly dancer, her laughter tinkling chime for chime with the bracelet. The tiny dock-turned-patio held only a half-dozen tables, but every male eye at every one of those tables slid an appreciative look Abby's way, and an envious one at Gregory. He snorted under his breath. Fools.

He stabbed through his chowder, looking for something edible.

"It's so cute," Abby said. "Did you pick it up in London?"

"You could say that. So, you like it?"

"Love it." She fingered the charms. "Which one's for me?"

"All of them."

"No, silly. I mean: which charm did you buy for me? That's the tradition, you know. If you give someone a charm bracelet, you have to buy them the first charm, something meaningful."

Like hell. He wasn't about to waste money on another trinket. Not when it'd be lying on the ocean floor by the weekend. He peered at the charms. A key, a train, a saxophone . . .

"The lighthouse," he said. "I bought you the lighthouse."

"Oh?" she said, nose wrinkling as she examined the charm. "That's . . . interesting. Why'd you pick that?"

He waved his hand at the ocean. "Because it made me think of here. Your favorite restaurant."

"But the lighthouse isn't—" She leaned as far back in her chair as she could. "I guess maybe you could see it from here. On a clear day. If you squint hard enough. Well, it's the thought that counts, and I *do* love it here. The lights over the water. The smell of the ocean. Heaven."

Heaven. Right. They lived in a town with two four-star restaurants, and Abby's idea of heaven was a wharf-side dive where the specialties were beer, beer, and mussels soaked in beer. At least in town he might hope to make a contact that would lead to a sale. But none of the summer people came here, only locals, and no local bought a thousand-dollar painting of the Atlantic Ocean when they could see it through their kitchen window.

The screen door leading to the patio creaked open. Out of habit, he looked, half hoping it might be one of the American celebrities who summered in town. He caught a flash of sun-streaked blond hair and a male face hidden by the shadows of the overhang.

The man scanned the patio, then stepped back fast. The door squeaked shut. Gregory's eyes shot to Abby as her gaze swiveled back to the harbor.

"Was that Zack?" he asked.

"Hmmm?" Her bright blue eyes turned to meet his, as studiously vacant as ever.

Gregory's jaw tightened. "Zack. Your summer intern. Was that him?"

"Where, hon?"

Gregory bit off a reply. This wasn't the time to start sounding like a jealous husband, not now, when all it would take was one such comment passed from Abby to a friend to give him motive for murder. If Abby wanted to cheat on him, she'd had plenty of opportunity to do so before now. As lousy as their marriage was, Abby was satisfied with it. She was satisfied with him. And why not? She had a wealthy, handsome husband who owned a successful art gallery, where every pathetic seascape she daubed onto canvas found a prominent place on the walls. The perfect catch for a pretty, young art student of mediocre talent.

The moment he'd laid eyes on Abigail Landry at a Montreal art show, he thought *he* had found his perfect catch. A beautiful, lauded, young painter, the ideal showpiece artist for his new Nova Scotia seaside gallery, and the ideal showpiece wife for him. The trouble had started three months after the wedding, when she'd refused to paint a custom-ordered portrait of a Schnauzer wearing sunglasses. He'd lost his temper and smacked her. She'd said nothing, just gone into her studio and started the dog's portrait. Then the next day she'd waltzed in on a private meeting with two of his best clients, her black eye on full display, leaving him stammering to explain, all the while smiling sweetly and asking if anyone wanted iced tea.

Before long, divorce was out of the question. Her silly seascapes accounted for seventy percent of the gallery's income. Then, two years ago, when the stock market plunge had wiped out his finances, she'd glided to his rescue with her own well-invested nest egg, offered as sweetly and as easily as the iced tea. So he was trapped.

"But not for long," he murmured.

Another vacant-eyed "Hmmm?"

He smiled and patted her hand. "Nothing, my dear. I'm glad you like the bracelet."

———

Abby lifted the crimson-coated brush, in her mind seeing the paint move from the brush to the canvas. No, not quite right. She lowered the brush and studied the picture. The red would be too harsh. Too *expected*. She needed something more surprising there. She laid the brush aside. Tomorrow she'd be better able to concentrate on finding the right shade. Tonight . . . She smiled. Well, tonight she had other things on her mind.

She moved the painting to the locked room in the back, then picked up the canvas propped against the wall and placed it on the now-vacant easel. She looked at the half-finished seascape. No room for surprises there. Blue sea, blue sky, white and gray rocks. Assembly line art. This was what her talent was reduced to, putting her name on schlock while her true work was shipped out of the country and sold under a false name so Gregory didn't find out. Seascapes made money. Money made Gregory happy. So Abby painted seascapes, seascapes, and more seascapes, with the occasional crumbling barn thrown in for variety.

She glanced at the clock. For once, they'd have all night. Gregory had taken off after dinner and told her not to wait up. No excuses given. He was long past bothering, and she was long past caring.

She lifted the crimson-soaked brush to clean it, then stopped, and stared at the painting. As if of its own accord, her hand moved to the canvas and the brush streaked red across the surf. Too much red. She daubed the tip in the white and brushed it lightly through the red, thinning and spreading it until it became a pink clot on the wave. The surf tinted with blood. A small smile played on Abby's lips. Then she took a fresh brush and blotted out the red with indigo.

As she painted, a blob of blue fell on her arm. She swiped at it absently, then stopped, seeing the blue swirl on her pale arm. It looked like a Maori tattoo. She dabbed her finger in the paint and accentuated the resemblance. There. Cheaper than henna, less permanent than ink. As she laughed, she caught a glimpse of herself in the mirror across the room and grinned.

Any minute now she'd hear the key turn in the back lock. And then . . . A rush of heat started in her belly and plunged down. She looked at her reflection again, gaze dropping to the twin dots pressing hard against the front of her sundress. She rolled her shoulders and sighed as the fabric brushed her nipples. Still looking in the mirror, she unzipped her dress and let it fall. She grinned at her reflection. Not bad. Not bad at all.

Her eyes went to the blue tattoo on her forearm. An unexpected burst of color. She turned to the easel, lifted the paintbrush and grazed it lightly over one hardened nipple. She sighed, then tickled the brush hairs around the aureole of her other nipple.

Another dip of paint, ochre this time. She stroked lines down her torso, shivering at the cool touch of the paint against her skin. Next, the red, on her stomach, drawn in lazy circles and zigzags. She parted her legs, lowered the brush and swirled it across her inner thigh. As she painted lower, she let the end of the brush dart between her legs, prodding like an uncertain lover's finger, hesitant yet eager. Each time it made contact, she moaned and glanced at her own expression in the mirror. She forced herself to finish her work, painting the other thigh to match the first, letting the brush tip probe her only when it came in contact naturally. Then, when she finished, took the brush and turned it around, so her hand wielded the plastic tip instead of the paint-soaked bristle. She spread her legs and used the tip to tickle the hard nub within.

The back door clicked open. Abby grinned and lifted the brush, painting one last stroke of red from her crotch to her breasts. A bustle of motion in the doorway, silence, then a sharp intake of breath.

Abby looked up, and flourished a hand at her painted body.

"What do you think?" she said. "A work of art?"

"A masterpiece."

Gregory switched the cellphone to his other ear and took his keys from the ignition.

"Yes, that's right, a room on the west side. Not the east side. There was construction on the east side last time and it kept me up all night." He paused. "Good. Hold on, there's more. I want extra towels. Your housecleaning staff never leaves enough towels."

The hotel clerk assured him everything would meet his satisfaction. It wouldn't, though. Gregory would be sure of that. He'd find something to pester them about at the front desk, raise a little fuss, just enough so that when the police asked the clerk whether she remembered Gregory, she'd roll her eyes and say, "Oh, yes. I remember him."

Once he finished here, he'd stop by Deanna's cottage and make sure everything was ready. He chuckled. Deanna was ready, that was certain. Ready, willing and chomping at the bit. She wanted to be free of Abby almost as much as he did. Last night when he'd gone by to finalize the plans, he'd barely made it through the door before she'd pounced and given him a taste of what life would be like post-Abby. He felt himself harden at the memory. A remarkable woman, Deanna was. He only hoped everything went well tonight. It would be a shame to lose her.

Last night she'd suggested—not for the first time—that she join him at the hotel, so she could corroborate his alibi. He'd gently reminded her that wasn't a wise idea. When the police dug into his personal life, he knew they'd find he had a history of infidelity, but there was no sense doing their homework for them. Or so he'd told Deanna. The truth was Gregory didn't want anyone seeing them together tonight. Better to leave her behind . . . in close proximity to his about-to-be-murdered wife.

Not that he had any intention of offering up Deanna as a scapegoat. But, if things went bad, it always helped to have a plan B. Deanna had bought the weapons and the tools, so it would be easy enough to steer the police in her direction. If the need arose, he had a speech all prepared, the heart-rending confession of an unfaithful husband who had realized he still loved his wife and told his mistress it was over, then made the tragic mistake of leaving on a business trip to Halifax that same day, never dreaming his scorned lover might wreak her revenge while he was gone. He'd practiced his lines in front of the mirror until he could choke up on cue.

But that won't be necessary, he told himself as he headed for the gallery. Everything would run smoothly, and when the furor died down, he and Deanna would start their new life together.

He pushed open the door to the gallery. A muted laugh tinkled out, followed by a deep chuckle that grated down Gregory's spine. He paused, holding the door partly shut so the greeting bell wouldn't alert Abby and Zack. The murmur of their voices floated out from the back room. Zack laughed again. Gregory eased the door open, trying to slide in before it opened wide enough to set off the bell. He was almost through when it chimed.

The voices in the back room stopped suddenly. Zack peeked around the corner, saw who it was, then said something to Abby, too low for Gregory to hear. The intern backed out of the studio.

"Ab? I'll grab coffee on my way back, okay?"

Abby appeared from the back room, carrying a wrapped canvas, and beamed a smile at Zack. "Perfect. Thanks."

As Zack strode out the front door, he slid a smirk Gregory's way, as if being allowed to play errand boy for Abby was some great honor Gregory could only dream of. Art student, my ass. The kid looked as though he should be riding the waves, not painting them. Not that Gregory cared. If Abby wanted to play teacher with California Picasso, she was welcome to him. He only hoped the kid wouldn't cause trouble later.

"I sold the new Martin's Point oil," Abby said, laying the canvas on the counter. "Got the asking price, too."

"Good, good. I just stopped by to make sure everything was okay before I left for my meeting."

"You'll be staying for the weekend, I assume."

Being little more than an hour from Halifax, there was no need for him to stay the weekend, and they both knew it, just as they knew he usually stayed anyway, and why he usually stayed. Yet Abby asked as casually as she'd ask whether he'd take Highway 3 or 103, a matter of no interest to her either way. The thread of anger that rippled through him surprised him, as it always did, and, in surprising him, only angered him more.

"Yes, I'll be staying the weekend. With a friend."

He hated himself for tacking that on the end, hated himself for studying her reaction, and hated her even more for not giving one.

"Don't forget we're having dinner at the Greenways' on Sunday," she said. "Eight o'clock."

"I'll be there."

She nodded, then disappeared into the back room. He stifled the urge to call out a good-bye, turned on his heel and left.

"You've reached the voice-mail of Gregory Keith—"

Abby sighed and hung up.

"Still no answer?" Zack asked as he flipped the gallery's "open" sign to "closed."

"He must have turned off his cell. Maybe he's still in a meeting."

Zack cast a pointed look through the window into the darkening night. "Uh-huh."

"Sometimes his meetings run late," she offered lamely. "I'll try once more from home, then call Mr. Strom back and tell him we're still considering his offer."

She turned off the main lights as Zack locked the front door. He followed her into the studio, and trailed out the back door after her, walking Abby to her car.

"Go," Gregory hissed.

Deanna lurched from behind the bushes as Abby parked at the top of the long drive. Gregory had to squint to see her. For a kilometer in either direction, the only lights were the security floods beaming onto the renovated farmhouse.

Abby climbed from her car. She started to lock it, then stopped as she spotted Deanna stumbling up the driveway, her clothes torn and bloodstained. From this distance, Gregory couldn't see his wife's expression, but he could imagine it. Eyes wide, mouth dropping open, a whispered "oh."

Abby jogged down the driveway toward Deanna. Smatterings of their conversation drifted to him.

"—accident—help—"

Abby gestured at the house. "—911—?" She didn't have a cellphone, hated them.

Deanna grabbed Abby's arm, her voice shrill with panic. "—son—trapped—please—"

Then Abby did what Gregory knew she'd do. She followed Deanna. When Deanna stumbled, Abby grabbed her arm and draped it around her shoulders, supporting the injured woman. Very heroic. Also very stupid, because when she reached the shadows of the cedar hedge, all Deanna had to do was trip Abby, throw her weight on top of her and Abby went down. Deanna shoved a chloroform-soaked cloth over Abby's mouth and nose, and she stayed down.

Deanna turned toward Gregory's hiding spot, but he didn't step out. Not yet. First, he was making damned sure Abby was out cold. If anything went wrong, Deanna's would be the only face she remembered seeing. He motioned for Deanna to slap Abby's face. She did. When Abby didn't move, Deanna slapped her again, the sound cracking through the silence.

"I think that's enough, my dear," Gregory said, stepping from the bushes. He didn't want any bruises to be found on Abby's body later.

He tossed Deanna the rope and watched her tie Abby up. Then he took over.

Deanna slapped Abby again, the sound echoing the rhythmic smack of the waves against the boat's hull. Gregory shifted, fighting the growing worm of pique in his gut. Abby wasn't waking up. What if she didn't? He'd have to go through with it, of course, killing her, but he'd really hoped she'd be awake when he did it. He wanted her to see who wielded the knife, to regain the power she'd sucked from him over the years.

Gregory grabbed the knife. "I'll wake her—"

Deanna snatched it from his hand. "No, let me."

Deanna lowered the knife tip to Abby's cheek and pressed it against her pale skin. A single drop of blood welled up. Abby's eyes flew open. Gregory reached for the knife, but Abby bucked suddenly, startling them both, and the knife clattered to the deck. Abby jerked against her bonds, wriggling wildly. Deanna dove to hold her down. In the struggle, Deanna's foot knocked the knife across the deck.

"She's tied up," Gregory said. "She's not going anywhere."

Deanna nodded and pulled back from Abby. His wife looked around, gaze going to the knife by the cabin door.

"I'll get that," Deanna said.

As she pushed to her feet, Gregory took her place, looming over his terrified wife.

"Ah, now she's afraid," he said, smiling down at her. "Smart girl. Don't worry. This won't hurt a bit." He grinned. "It'll hurt a lot."

"Gregory?" Deanna said behind him.

His lips tightened at the interruption. He faced her. "What?"

"Yesterday you asked if I was looking forward to this. I said I wasn't." She bit her lip, looking sheepish. "Well, I just wanted to let you know, I lied. We are looking forward to this."

"Good. Now—" He stopped. "We—?"

Deanna smiled. Her gaze moved to something beyond his shoulder.

"Yes," she said. "We."

He turned, following her gaze. Behind him, Abby sat up, tugging the rope from her wrists.

"Wha—?" he began.

Something cracked against the side of his head. He stumbled and managed to turn just enough to see Deanna raise the fire extinguisher again. She swung it.

Abby and Deanna stood at the side of the boat, watching Gregory's body sink into the inky water. A late-night fog was rolling in, a dense gray blanket barely pierced by the distant lighthouse beam.

"You're sure he won't wash up on shore?" Deanna asked, nibbling her thumbnail.

"Which way is the tide going, hon?" Abby asked gently.

"Out. Right. You said that. I forgot. Sorry."

"That's okay. You did a good job."

Good, but not perfect, Abby thought as she bent to wipe a smear of blood from the deck. She'd have to bleach that later. If the first blow had succeeded, there wouldn't be any blood. It took a second hit to the head to induce bleeding. But Deanna hadn't known that and Abby hadn't thought to mention it and, really, it wasn't as if Abby would have changed her mind when the first blow failed.

She stood to see Deanna frowning as she squinted overboard, trying to see Gregory's body through the fog.

"It's okay, hon," Abby said. "He's definitely heading out to sea and will be for a few hours yet. Even if he does eventually wash up on shore, it won't be near here."

"But they'll identify him, won't they?"

"Yes. But then what? He wasn't shot. He wasn't stabbed. He hit his head and drowned. Happens all the time. Even if they suspect something, it can't be linked to us. We were careful."

"You're right," Deanna said, forcing a small smile. "You're always right."

Abby walked over to Deanna, smiling. "Not always. I married that bastard, didn't I?"

She put her arms around Deanna's neck and leaned in. Their lips met. Deanna's parted, hesitant at first, as always, as if unsure, maybe still a little shocked at herself. A minister's daughter in spite of everything, Abby thought. She kept the kiss gentle and tentative, their lips barely touching. After a moment, Deanna tried to pull Abby closer, but she held back, teasing Deanna with modest kisses.

Abby reached down to the bottom of Deanna's blouse and began to unbutton it, her hands moving as slow as her lips. Deanna gave a soft growl of impatience, but Abby only chuckled. Only when the blouse was fully unbuttoned did Abby let her hands touch Deanna's skin. She pressed her fingertips against Deanna's stomach, then traced twin lines up her ribcage. She cupped Deanna's bare breasts, and slid her thumbs over her hard nipples. Deanna groaned, grabbed the back of Abby's head and kissed her, all shyness gone. As Abby returned the kiss, heat throbbed through her. Perhaps just once more . . . But no. She couldn't.

She wrapped her hands in Deanna's hair and eased her back a step. Deanna's balance faltered. She tore her lips from Abby's to shout a warning that she was too close to the edge of the boat. But Abby already knew that.

She put her hands around Deanna's torso and thrust her away. Deanna started to fall. She grabbed blindly and caught Abby's charm bracelet, but the clasp broke. Deanna's arms windmilled as she fell over the side.

Abby walked to the back of the boat and pulled up the anchor. In the water below, Deanna thrashed and screamed. As Abby headed to the pilothouse, she looked down to see Deanna frantically trying to find a hold on the smooth side of the boat.

"I can't swim!" Deanna shouted.

"Yes," Abby said. "I know."

She walked into the pilothouse and started the engine. She moved the boat out of Deanna's reach, then waited and watched as Deanna's blond head bobbed like a beacon through the fog. When Deanna finally sank and didn't resurface, Abby pushed the throttle forward and headed for shore.

Abby parked at the top of the driveway and rubbed her hands over her face. God, she was so sick of playing the distraught wife. How much longer did she have to do this? The last week had seemed endless. Pretending to look up expectantly each time the bells chimed over the gallery door. Murmuring, "I'm sure he will," whenever someone reassured her that her missing husband would come home soon. Enduring Zack's constant, mooning, "I'm here for you" glances.

It hadn't taken long for the police to discover that her missing husband had been renting a cottage outside of town for his mistress who was, conveniently, also missing. A quick check of their shared bank accounts showed that Gregory had slowly drained out nearly ten thousand dollars over the last month. That had been Abby's idea, passed through Deanna to Gregory. As Deanna had warned Gregory, he couldn't be seen dipping into the accounts right after his wife's murder. Better to siphon some out early so they'd have celebration cash during the mourning period. Now, with a missing husband, a missing mistress and missing money, it didn't take a genius to realize Gregory had cut his losses and left. Too bad all their assets were jointly held, meaning his abandoned wife could now use them as she wished. She even had the ten grand in cash Deanna had squirreled away for them.

Abby grabbed the pile of mail from the passenger seat and climbed out. As she circled around the front of the car, she leafed through the bills, flyers and notes of sympathy. An unfamiliar postage stamp caught her attention. France? Who did she know in France? When she looked at the handwriting on the front, she froze. It wasn't possible. It *wasn't*.

Hands trembling, Abby tore open the envelope. In her haste, she ripped it too fast and the contents flew out. A postcard sailed to the ground.

"No," Abby said. "No!"

Deanna stood by the water's edge, arms wrapped around herself, shivering despite the warm night breeze that blew off the Mediterranean. Behind her the lights of the French Riviera flickered in the darkness, a scene that nearly matched the one on her postcard . . . the postcard Abby now had.

Deanna felt the sharp edges of the charms biting into her palm. She looked down at the bracelet in her hand. When she'd dove into the ocean, leaving Abby to think she'd drowned, Deanna had still clutched the bracelet. She'd kept it, thinking maybe she'd send it back to Abby as proof that she was alive. But then she decided the postcard would be enough . . . the postcard they'd picked out together, when they'd first hatched their plan, when Deanna still thought—hoped—that Abby and her promises had been real.

Deanna fingered the charms on the bracelet, stopping at the lighthouse. She remembered her last evening with Abby, sitting behind the cover of the lighthouse, dipping their feet in the surf, their clothing strewn over the rocks and bushes. Abby had asked, oh so casually, how well Deanna could swim. And, as accustomed as she was to lies and deceit from her lovers, Deanna still almost fell for it. The truth had been on her lips, ready to tell Abby she'd been captain of the swim team before she'd dropped out of school. Instead, when she opened her mouth, she heard herself say, "Me? Can't swim a stroke. Never learned how."

Deanna had tried to look past it, told herself she was too suspicious. And yet . . . Well, it never hurts to have a plan B.

She let the lighthouse charm fall from her fingers. A lighthouse had been *her* lucky charm that night, when the unexpected fog rolled in. She'd followed its beam back to shore. Then, before she'd left town, she'd returned to the lighthouse one last time, to leave something for Abby. On the postcard, she'd written only one line, instructing Abby to look for further "correspondence" at the "charmed" place. There, in the very spot where she'd deceived her lover, Abby would find detailed instructions on how to make her penance, on the exact penalty she must pay. The demand was fair. Not enough to send Abby into bankruptcy, just enough to hurt. For every action, there is a price to be paid. Deanna knew that, and now, so would Abby.

Deanna drew back her arm and pitched the bracelet into the ocean. Then she turned and headed back to the hotel.

THE HUNT

A Cainsville Universe Story

WILLIAM ENVIED HUNTERS whose wives allowed them to decorate the family home with their trophies. He sometimes even envied hunters who didn't have wives to complain, like Teddy, who'd just sent him a photograph of his latest trophy, hanging in his living room.

"Did you get the pictures?" Teddy asked when William called.

"They're right here on my screen."

"Nice, huh?"

"Not bad. A little sloppy with the cutting."

Teddy only laughed. "Yes, I'm not at your level yet. But I'm working on it. So, have you given any more thought to that hunting trip?"

"Some."

"I've done my research. It's kosher. Zero risk. Zero responsibility. We pay our money, show up and hunt. A real English hunt. Horses, hounds, the whole works. Like nothing we've ever done before."

That was the kicker, the reason William was even considering it. Novelty. There'd been a time when he'd counted the days between his hunting trips. Not anymore. He was bored.

"Okay," he said.

Teddy paused so long William prodded, "You there?"

"Sure, I just . . . You said okay?"

"Yeah. Go ahead. Set it up."

Teddy babbled away after that, making plans. William half listened as he admired Teddy's trophy—a necklace hanging from a picture frame—before flipping back to the ones he liked best, those of the woman herself, lying dead on her apartment floor.

William stood in the middle of the forest clearing and stamped his feet.

"Little chilly, huh?" Teddy said, blowing into his hands.

William shrugged.

Teddy glanced over. "You aren't worried, are you? It's risk-free, like I said. We're just along for the ride."

That wasn't the problem. The forest . . . it just wasn't what he'd expected.

When Teddy first suggested this excursion, William's pulse had quickened. Like most of his kind, he was an urban hunter. Born and raised in the city. Stalked his prey through back alleys. Took them down in abandoned buildings. There was, however, an allure to the forest. The domain of hunters like Dayton Rogers and Ivan Milat and the Larsens. Raw and feral, primitive and wild.

Except . . . this was a little more wild than William liked. Around them, gnarled trees shot up and slammed together overhead, blocking the moon and stars. The wind didn't bluster and blow like city wind. Here it whispered and moaned and shrieked. And it smelled like death. Not good death— bright coppery blood and fear. This was dank, dark death. Rot and decay.

He glanced at Teddy. "Are you sure—?"

The bay of a hound cut him off. Hooves pounded along the hard path.

The hounds appeared first. Six beagles, noses to the ground, long ears dragging. Four horses followed. Ordinary looking horses with ordinary looking riders—guys between thirty and fifty, wearing hunting jackets and jeans and boots.

Just regular guys. Except they weren't regular at all. William could tell by the way their eyes took in everything and gave away nothing. Hunters, like them.

"Sorry we're late," said the bearded man in front. "Had some trouble with the fox."

A fifth horse stepped into the clearing. The rider led a sixth. A bound woman lay draped over the saddle. When he yanked the rope, she tumbled to the ground. A leather mask obscured her face, but William could see her eyes, rolling in terror.

"Looks good," Teddy said. "Young. Strong. Healthy. Scared."

The men chuckled, and the leader motioned for William to mount.

"Where's mine?" Teddy asked.

"Coming."

William swung onto his horse, remembering how from summers at his grandmother's farm. As his boots found the stirrups, he caught a flicker, like fire, to the left, and he looked over, startled, but it was only a lantern held by a rider.

"Release the fox," the leader said.

The man holding her rope yanked again and, with a snap, her bound hands and feet came free. She pushed to all fours and started to run, still hunched over, so blinded by the mask that she headed for Teddy, who laughed and backed up.

As she ran, her skin seemed to blacken, as if swallowed by the shadows. William gave his head a shake and blinked. When he opened his eyes, the girl was gone. In her place was a massive black dog, running straight for Teddy.

As the beast sprang, Teddy wheeled and ran. The hounds ran too—not beagles now, but huge black dogs with blazing red eyes, tearing after Teddy so fast their paws never seemed to touch the ground.

The leader shouted, "Ride!" and William turned to see five figures in dark green cloaks, hoods pulled up. Beneath them, their steeds had become great ebony horses with manes and hooves of flame.

The Wild Hunt.

William heard his grandmother's voice from all those years ago, when she'd seen what he'd done to the barn cats. "The riders will come for you, boy. Mark my words. The Wild Hunt will come."

William's horse plunged after its brethren. He tried to stop it. Tried to scramble off. But he was trapped, watching his friend run headlong through the forest as the hounds pursued, the riders pursued, *he* pursued.

As they rode, more hunters joined, coming from all sides, silent wraiths atop fiery steeds. Ahead the hounds bellowed and roared, jaws snapping so loud William could hear them.

Teddy ran, but he did not run far. The beasts took him down. William tried to look away, but he couldn't move his head, couldn't shut his eyes. He was forced to watch as the hounds tore his friend to pieces.

When he couldn't turn his horse around, he tried to dismount, but the stirrups snapped like traps, iron teeth chomping into his feet. As he screamed, the reins leaped up, like snakes, wrapping around his hands, tightening until the leather was embedded in his flesh.

The leader's empty cowl turned toward him. "Ride!"

As the group shot forward, William's steed joined them, with a blaze of fire that seared him to the bone and bound him to his mount, and he understood what his grandmother meant. The riders had come for him and now he would hunt forever.

DEAD TO ME

I SAT ON THE SOFA and watched my dead ex-husband take the last pizza slice from the box. I suppose I should say, "My dead ex-husband's ghost," but he didn't look like a ghost. Or act like one. I'd think he wasn't dead at all if it wasn't for the way his head lolled to the side, neck broken.

I suppose, too, that I shouldn't call him my ex when the divorce hadn't been finalized. And, no, that impending divorce had nothing to do with his accident. I'd been there, but I hadn't killed him.

"You know what would go great with this?" he said, lifting the dripping pizza slice. "A cold beer. Any chance, babe?"

"You don't need a beer. You're dead."

He shrugged and leaned back into the couch, feet propped on the coffee table. "That's a matter of opinion."

"Well, you're dead to me."

He met my gaze. "Am I?"

I got up and went to bed.

As I tried to sleep, I could hear him downstairs. Not giving me a moment's rest. Selfish bastard.

My mother had warned me not to marry him. With my mother, though, there were few things in life she hadn't warned me against, from riding a bike to buying my own business. She had her reasons—I was her only child, and she'd been an invalid since the accident that killed my father, so it was in her best interests to keep me safe and close. Whenever I suggested getting my own place, she'd peer over her glasses, cold eyes glittering, and say, "Go on, but remember this: If you walk out that door, you're dead to me."

Those were the last words she'd said when I finally did leave to get married. Six months later, she was dead, and the house was mine. I'd rented it out until, sadly, her predictions on my marriage proved all too accurate.

Despite her dire prophesies, it hadn't ended badly. We separated by mutual agreement. I returned to my mother's house. He kept the condo, which he'd had before we married. As a lawyer, he made more money, but I pulled in enough not to bother with alimony. No kids, no pets, no fuss, no muss. He'd even given me a convertible as a parting gift . . . and to make sure my bedroom door stayed open.

I walked into the bathroom the next morning and found him in the shower. I tried to pass by, but he threw open the door and leaned out.

"Wanna join me?" he asked, waggling his brows.

"No, thanks."

He only grinned. "Then I guess I'll have to take care of it myself."

He wrapped his fingers around his cock and met my gaze, his grin inviting me to watch. There'd been a time when I would have—a lot of times when I *had*. But there was nothing sexy about a dead guy whacking off in my shower.

I turned away and started brushing my teeth. A couple of minutes later, the door squeaked open again.

"Grab me a towel, babe?"

"You're dead," I said, not looking up from the sink.

"Matter of opinion."

I turned then. "You want an apology, don't you? That's what this is all about. Yes, I'm sorry you're dead. But I have no reason to apologize."

"No?"

"No. Now go away."

"Til death do us part, babe," he said, grinning. "And you're not—"

I strode out and slammed the door behind me.

I spent the morning in my home office trying to balance the bar's books and ignore the noise from downstairs. It was him, demanding my attention, as usual. That's the misleading thing about strong-willed people. You figure if they're so capable, they won't need you. Bullshit. First my mother, then my husband, always demanding, always expecting, always needing. Death didn't change that.

At first, he'd liked what I'd done with my life. He'd been tired of dating lawyers and doctors and PhDs. A bar owner with a high school education better suited his bad boy self-image.

After we married, though, he started expecting more. More of my time, more of my attention. Why couldn't I host dinner for his colleagues? Why wouldn't I join the other wives at their charity luncheons? Why didn't I try harder to fit in? Why didn't I make more of an effort to better inform myself, better educate myself, just *better* myself?

He began to notice my deficiencies. Not that he'd ever say so outright, but he got in his little digs, always joking that he might not have the smartest wife in the room, but he always had the hottest one. Eventually I decided I was more mistress material than wife. He didn't disagree. So we split, he got the stuck-up, straight-laced lawyer girlfriend, and I was the woman he came to when he wanted to hang out and kick back, to talk and screw until morning.

That was fine by me. I got as much out of it as he did . . . until two days ago, when I told him it was over. He didn't like that, and he died because of it. But I didn't kill him.

When I went downstairs to head out to work, he was there, crouched at the bottom of the stairs, fingering a dent in the baluster.

"Seems I left a mark," he said.

"Yes. A year ago, when you ripped out my mother's chair-lift for me. Remember?"

"Are you sure?"

"Of course I'm sure. You fell—" I pointed "—over there."

He looked at me. His eyes had started sinking into his skull. I glanced away and tried to walk past him, but he stepped into my path. Tried again. Blocked again.

"What?" I said.

No answer.

"I didn't push you down those stairs and you know it."

He didn't argue, only slid his gaze to the side, conceding my point.

"So why are you—? Oh, I know. You wanted a proper burial—big funeral, fancy headstone, scenic plot." I crossed my arms and looked up at him. "You know I couldn't do that. How would it look? You break your neck on my stairs three days before our divorce is finalized? The cops would have ripped me apart, and your bitch girlfriend would lead the charge."

He didn't argue, which was as good as agreement. He didn't get out of my way, either.

"What if one of your clients called with the same story?" I said. "Her soon-to-be-ex died from a fall down her stairs after an argument. You would have told her—off the record, of course—to do exactly what I did."

Again he said nothing. This time, when I tried to get past he let me.

After work, I lay in bed, listening to him downstairs. He seemed to be getting quieter, but I could still hear him. Damn him. Tenacity was a fine trait, but there comes a time when one needs to accept the inevitable. He never could, and that's what had gotten him killed.

He'd come over Thursday night, as he always did, telling his girlfriend he liked to work late and wrap everything up before the weekend. We had our routine down pat. He'd bring takeout. We'd watch TV, maybe a movie. Then we'd adjourn to the bedroom, euphemistically speaking. There were rarely beds involved.

That day, over Chinese takeout, I'd told him there would be no more

Thursday nights after the divorce. I'd had enough of his jealous girlfriend, always sending her friends to my bar to check up on me, driving past my house when he didn't come home on time, cornering me in the grocery store to warn me that once the divorce was final, I'd have no reason for contact with him. At first, I'd been amused. After a year, I was sick of it. Besides, I'd met someone, a firefighter who came into the bar now and then, and we'd hit it off and, well, you know . . . Point was, it was time for us both to move on.

He hadn't liked that.

We'd argued. When it was obvious he wasn't listening to me, I'd retreated up the stairs. He followed. At the top, he'd grabbed my arm. I'd wrenched away. He'd fallen. The end. Not my fault.

It was over, and he couldn't accept that now any more than he had on Thursday. It was time for another chat. So I went downstairs.

He wasn't grinning and teasing now. Again, nothing new. His grins had always been quick to turn to scowls when charm didn't get him what he wanted.

"Get over it," I said.

He glowered at me, sunken eyes narrowing.

"Don't give me that look. Remember Tim from your softball team? Paralyzed in that ski accident? What did you say?"

He only glared, his shriveled lips tightening.

"You said you wouldn't want to live like that. So now you've changed your mind?" I snorted. "Great. And who did you think would have looked after you? That girlfriend of yours? Give up her hotshot lawyer job to play nursemaid to her drooling boyfriend? Not a chance. You know exactly who'd have been stuck with it. Your not-yet-ex wife. Well, no way. No fucking way."

His lips parted in something I didn't catch, but I knew it wasn't complimentary.

"You would have been miserable. Just like her." I waved at my mother. "On her death bed and she calls me home, begs me to take care of her. I look after her for a month, and what were her last words? Told me I was still cut out of her will. Vindictive bitch. So I did what I had to do. But I'm not a murderer. I didn't kill her, and I didn't kill you."

"I'm not dead," he rasped.

I ripped off a piece of duct tape, then leaned into the basement crawl-space, where he lay beside the skeletal body of my mother. He thrashed his head from side to side, feebly protesting in the only way he still could. I slapped on the tape.

"You're dead to me," I said.

I rose, relocked the hatch and went upstairs.

Peace and quiet, at last.

DEVIL MAY CARE
A Cainsville Universe Story

A S A WINE GLASS whipped past Patrick's head, he reflected that he might
enjoy breakups more than he should. It wasn't that he took pleasure in
inflicting pain on a woman he'd come to know. No, what he appreciated
was the efficiency of it. No protracted dance of relationship disintegration.
Just a sharp, clean break. One minute he was enjoying a post-coital glass of
wine with Tracey, and the next he was being forcibly ejected, amidst curses
and broken glass, and there was no chance she'd grieve the loss of him. No
chance she'd try to win him back and suffer the ego blow of his refusal.
That was the beauty of his breakup ploy, one that had served him well for
over a hundred years. Tell a woman that your wife is pregnant—when she
never even knew you were married—and you guarantee a swift parting.

Of course, he wasn't married. That would be wrong. And very inconvenient, he thought, as he jogged down the apartment stairwell. His was
not a life conducive to long-term relationships. He had too many secrets,
too many facets of himself he couldn't share with a lover. Also, it would
bore him to tears. *Boinne-fala* had their place. Rather like those plastic
puzzle boxes that seemed all the rage, the ones with the colored squares.
Fascinating for a time, until you figured them out and then . . . well, then
the challenge was gone, the shine worn off.

"You look pleased with yourself today, *bogan*," a voice said as he swung
through the building's back door. "Causing trouble, I presume?"

He glanced up sharply to see the face of a stranger—an old woman with long graying hair drawn back in a braid. Just because he didn't recognize her didn't necessarily mean they weren't acquainted. Fae affected glamours to pass for human, and while their disguises were based on their true selves, immutable in features and form, they could age it anywhere from eighteen to a hundred-and-two. He peered into the old woman's eyes.

"No, *bogan*," she said. "You do not know me."

Bogan. One of many names for his kind: *Bogan, bòcan*, hobgoblin, puck . . . She was another kind of fae—he could see the glimmering fae light behind her glamour. He tried to focus on that light enough to see her properly and determine her type.

"The polite way to do this is simply to ask," she said.

He snorted. "You've been among the *boinne-fala* too long."

"*Boinne-fala?*" She arched her brows. "Ah, that's right. You're Tylwyth Teg. Welsh. *Boinne-fala* meaning a drop of blood. An insult for humans who are no more than a drop of fae. You Tylwyth Teg still think yourselves above mere mortals. You refuse to admit exactly how far we have fallen."

"One only falls if one allows oneself to stumble. Now, if you'll excuse me, I have—"

"—things to do. Many, many things to do, which ultimately amount to nothing except pleasing yourself."

"Which is all that matters." He gave a mock bow. "Now, my lady, I take my leave."

"Aren't you even going to ask what I am?"

"Why bother? A true fae wouldn't tell me. It quite spoils the game."

"I don't play games."

"Then you aren't a true fae." He headed for the sidewalk. She seemed to stay where she was, but a moment later, her voice sounded at his ear.

"There is one type that does not dabble in petty bargains and mischiefs. One that deals in truth."

"Mmm, sorry. Not ringing a bell."

"Liar," she said. "You know all the types, Patrick of Cainsville, the legendary scholar with the legendary library."

"Scholar?" He snorted. "I'm a writer. A dime-store novelist. Your sources flatter me, but they're wildly mistaken."

"My sources are never mistaken. As you well know because you've figured out that I must be a korrigan."

"Never heard of it."

Her laughter rippled along the silent street, the laughter of a much younger woman.

"A korrigan has the power to see the future. But you know that."

"Fortune telling? Excellent. Perhaps you can use your scrying ball and tell me when I'll rid myself of your company."

"In about two minutes. First, though, make a mental note of this address. You'll need it." She rattled off an apartment in the city and then said, "Now, I have one minute left. One minute to warn that your future is about to take a most unwelcome turn. A fate that is, for a *bogan*, worse than death."

"Boredom?"

She gave him a pat-on-the-head sort of smile. "No, my dear Patrick. Worse still. You're about to find yourself in a position of responsibility."

He laughed. "I've managed to avoid that particular fate for many, many years. I believe I'm something of an expert."

"You were," she said. "Until now." She touched his forehead, so briefly that he didn't have time to pull away. Then, with one final unsettling smile, she walked away. He hesitated, and then walked to the corner, but she was gone.

Patrick didn't get home until late that night. His phone was ringing when he unlocked the door to his apartment. He considered ignoring it but, while he was indeed an expert at shirking responsibility, there was a difference between ducking it and merely postponing the inevitable.

He barely had time to say hello before Tracey said, "It's not going to work, you son of a bitch."

"I know," he said. "But I will always remember you fondly."

"I mean the money. I just got a call notifying me that my post-divorce credit card debt has been paid off. If you think you can buy me back—"

"I have no idea what you're talking about. Maybe your ex finally stepped up. I'm happy to hear that, Trace, but it wasn't me."

"Bullshit. You paid it in case you want to screw around with me again on your poor pregnant wife. The answer is no. If you want your money back, just tell me and I'll take out a loan, because there is no way in hell you're getting in my bed again. You wouldn't have gotten there in the first place if I had any clue you were married."

"You have my word that I won't bother you again. I'm glad someone paid that debt, and I wish you all the best—"

Click. He looked down at the receiver and smiled. *Good girl. You deserve better.*

She also deserved to get out from under that divorce debt. Which was not why he'd done it. Not at all. It was simply a matter of balancing the books. All fae understood the concept of give and take, but none more than the *bòcan*. Treat them well, and they'd return the favor. Treat them poorly, and expect trouble, which was only fair, after all. As for Tracey, he owed her for the pain of their parting, and a *bòcan* always paid his debts.

After the phone call, Patrick went to bed. Like most modern fae, he'd adapted to human life centuries ago. While fae wouldn't die without regular food and drink or go mad without sleep, sustenance did give them energy and rest kept them mentally sharp. They did not require as much as the *boinne-fala*, but they conformed to the social norms of meal and sleep schedules all the same.

What Patrick did not share with humans was the phenomenon of dreams. His sleeping mind would occasionally tug out a forgotten memory in answer to some nagging question. But it did not mangle memory and anxiety and fantasy, as human dreams did. Which was why, when he found himself standing on the balcony of a fairy castle, it was, to say the least, disconcerting.

There was no doubt this wasn't a memory. Patrick hadn't lived in the time of fairy kingdoms. Having spent centuries enduring his elders' reminiscences on those past glory days, he was glad to have missed them. It was as bad as when humans over-imbibed and waxed nostalgic about high school. From what he knew of high school, if those were the best days of their lives, he didn't begrudge them one drop of that alcohol. Likewise, when he heard the ancient fae prattle on about castles of gold and fairy kings, he could only roll his eyes and opine that while he liked a good feast as much as anyone, he rather preferred ones that came with cutlery, well-seasoned food, and easy access to indoor plumbing.

In human folktales, fae lived in another dimension. As usual, the *boinnefala* had no idea what they were talking about. Fae had always inhabited the same plane as humans. In the early days, the world had been big enough for both races, and the fae made their homes in the wild places where humans rarely ventured, and if they did, charms and compulsions could make them forget what they'd seen.

Humans, though, bred like rabbits. At least compared to the long-lived fae. They were also an adventuresome and curious race. This was, perhaps, the aspect that made Patrick feel quite at home living among them. Between the questing and the breeding, human culture spread. Soon they'd encroached on the borders of the fae kingdoms, and the seers warned this was no temporary crisis. They'd foretold a day when humans would map every inch of the earth, when there would be no place to hide. So the fae, ironically, embraced the method that human populations often used when threatened by a dominant culture—they adapted and they interbred and they kept their own culture in hidden enclaves.

That night, in the vision—because he'd not call it a dream—he stood on the balcony of a golden castle. A young fae man leaned over the railing, his hands gripping the edge as if to keep himself from vaulting over it.

"Of course she chose him," the man whispered in Welsh. "Did I truly expect anything else?"

Patrick looked down from the balcony to see a woman running across the moor, toward the forest, where riders waited, men on black steeds that breathed fire.

Cŵn Annwn. The Hounds of the Otherworld. The Wild Hunt.

One of the huntsmen broke from the pack and rode toward the woman. And with that, Patrick knew exactly what he was seeing, *who* he was seeing.

The story of Mallt-y-Nos. Matilda of the Night. It was one of the most important stories in Tylwyth Teg history, so pervasive that a warped version of it could even be found in human folklore.

On the night of her wedding to the fae prince Gwynn ap Nudd, Matilda had wanted one last ride with their childhood friend, Arawn, prince of the Otherworld. One last hunt. What she didn't realize was that the two young men had made a pact that if Matilda went to Arawn before her wedding day, she was his and the world of the fae would close to her forever. A preposterous agreement, exactly the sort of jealous romantic nonsense one would expect from two arrogant princes.

"You're an idiot, you know that?" Patrick said to Gwynn. "If you and Arawn were characters in one of my books, you'd both come to horribly tragic ends, in just punishment for your stupidity. And Matilda would live very happily ever after without you two clods."

Even as he said it, he couldn't quite muster the proper level of disdain. He saw the anguish on Gwynn's face, and remembered what it was like to be young and foolish and madly in love and thoroughly convinced you were not good enough to hold onto your beloved.

Patrick knew what came next, and he didn't care to witness it. Didn't care to stand at Gwynn's side and see him endure it, because as moronic as these boys had been, they did not deserve this next part. So Patrick turned to walk into the castle—and hit an invisible barrier.

"No!" Gwynn whispered. Then louder, "No!" Then the young man did indeed vault over the railing, grabbing it with both hands and dropping to the ground below and somehow, in a blink, Patrick was right there with him as he ran across the palace grounds.

"No!" Gwynn shouted. "I made a mistake. Forget the pact. She can go to him. If that's what she wants, he can have her. Just don't—"

Patrick heard a distant scream, and he could make out Matilda, on the back of Arawn's horse, scrambling off as she saw the kingdom of the fae disappearing behind her. Disappearing in fire.

As Gwynn ran for Matilda, he shouted that he was coming, just stay there, please stay there. But she couldn't hear him and Patrick doubted she would have stopped running even if she could. This was the worst, because this was the moment when Gwynn realized his mistake, that she hadn't left him for Arawn, that he'd been too blinded by jealousy to see the obvious: that she'd gone to her old friend for one last hunt and nothing more.

Patrick could hear Arawn shouting too, as he rode for Matilda, upon realizing his own mistake, that he'd never stood a chance, that she loved Gwynn and he'd been willing to condemn her to misery because he couldn't face that.

Patrick supposed Arawn's situation was as much a tragedy as Gwynn's, but he barely paid it more than a flicker of notice. His attention was fixed on Gwynn, and everything he felt was Gwynn's, and when the fire between the kingdoms consumed Matilda, the pain he felt was Gwynn's, an agony unlike anything he'd experienced, unlike anything he ever cared to experience, and he bolted up in bed, gulping air, his body trembling, sweat pouring off him.

He hung there, between sleeping and waking, and then he ran his hands through his hair and took a slow look around the room. With a sharp shake, he pushed from bed, yanked on his clothes and headed out to find whatever might banish the vision.

Patrick was unsettled. And it was really starting to piss him off.

It'd been a week since the vision. A week of trying to get the damned thing out of his head. Day and night it was there, cropping up at the most inconvenient times. It was not the images that bothered him; it was the emotions.

Patrick made his living exploiting human emotions. A teller of stories, a merchant of fantasies, but mostly, a dealer in the drug of secondhand emotions. Finding just the right twists of tragedy and heartache to keep readers turning the pages, sinking ever deeper into the characters' despair until . . . victory. Redemption, love, joy. Happily ever after. Sigh. Close the book and smile, and when life sends you swirling into tragedy of your own, pick up the book again and relive that ride, knowing it will all work out in the end, as real life rarely does.

The best stories—the ones he strove to tell—were the ones that lingered after that last page was turned. The ones that kept readers thinking and, more importantly, feeling.

Which was all very fine for the humans on the other end of the process, the ones who filled his bank account and let him lead his devil-may-care life, unsaddled with such petty inconveniences as having to drink cheap wine in order to afford the rent. He'd been there; he never intended to return.

What he did *not* appreciate was being on the receiving end of a story he could not banish from his brain. For him emotions were as inconvenient and annoying as forgoing good wine. Emotions were messy. He did not do messy. Not anymore.

The situation had become dire. He was at a nightclub, charming two lovely young women, his biggest concern how he'd choose which one to take home . . . and then getting those subtle hints that suggested he wouldn't need to choose at all. He'd been on the brink of closing the deal when he'd forgotten what he was saying. Not a momentary lapse, but a dead stop mid-sentence, all because he'd caught a glimpse of a man passing by and thought, "He looks like Gwynn." Except the man didn't, not beyond the most superficial way. It was proof of his distraction that his brain snagged on such a vague resemblance and then stayed there, spinning off into thoughts of the vision.

"Patrick?" one of the girls said. He wasn't even sure which, the blonde or the brunette, which wasn't like him at all. Whatever else one might accuse him of, he was attentive in his seductions.

"I . . ." he began.

Focus, Patrick. You've got this. They're hooked. Now reel them in and enjoy.

He looked from one very attractive young woman to the other, practically smelling the pheromones pouring off them, and all he could think was . . .

"There's something I need to do," he said, sliding from the barstool. "I'm sorry. I hope you have a lovely evening, ladies."

He couldn't even come up with a more charming way to break off the seduction. His mind was racing down another track, and he could barely remember to give an apologetic nod before he was out the door.

Enough of this. He needed answers. Even if the best place to get them was the last place he wanted to go.

Cainsville.

The thing Patrick loved most about Cainsville was the warm greeting he got after being away for months.

"What are you doing here?" Ida asked when he came face to face with her and Walter on the Main Street sidewalk.

"I live here," Patrick said.

She grumbled, as if she sorely wished she could change that. Which meant she must have been in a good mood, because normally she'd *tell* him how much she wished she could change that.

Ida, her consort Walter, and the other elders had founded Cainsville about two hundred years before. Patrick hadn't been there—founding a town, particularly when Chicago itself had been little more than an offal-filled shit hole, was not his idea of a pleasant way to enjoy the New World. He'd been in San Francisco, reveling in the chaos of the gold rush. But when he wandered east—for a reason he'd rather forget—he stumbled onto Cainsville at a time when they were in dire need of a fae with a few tricks up his sleeve. So he'd cut a deal with them. He would solve their problem and earn himself permanent residency. An iron-clad deal . . . the only kind he made.

Patrick continued past Ida and Walter, which was easy enough, given that the other elders all followed the practice of using glamours to make them appear well beyond the age to start collecting Social Security. Which didn't mean they were actually saddled with the physical disadvantages of senior citizenry. But the problem with looking old? You had to act your age, at least on Main Street in full view of the *boinne-fala*.

Patrick zipped past them into the grocery store and made straight for the wine aisle. No trip to Cainsville could be endured without a stop here first. He took his selections to the register, where a solemn young woman rang through the customer ahead of him. When she turned his way, he got one look at her bright blue eyes, smiled, and said, "Rose."

She fixed him with a cool, assessing gaze. She didn't remember him, of course. The last few times he'd been in town, she'd been off seeing the world and then, if rumors were correct, spending some time as a guest of the state penal system. The latter was to be expected for a Walsh. The family had been in Cainsville for generations, and there was more than a sprinkle of fairy dust in their veins. A family with the sort of special fae talents that did not encourage a life on the proper side of the law.

Rose had one of the rarest gifts: the second sight. Which explained that careful stare as she looked him over. His face tweaked a buried memory that overcame the compulsion that made most humans forget Patrick when he left Cainsville.

"It's good to see you," he said, still smiling.

"It's been a while," she said, in a way that hunted for a hint to help her place him.

"You were just out of high school the last time I was in town."

She nodded, as if that was good enough. As she rang through his wine, she said, "Glad to be back?"

He chuckled. "I wouldn't exactly say that. You?"

She paused, as if this was a question she hadn't considered. Then she nodded. "Yes, I am."

"Good." Which it was. If Rose Walsh was happy here, this was the best place for her, where no one would judge her for her talents or her past.

Outside, he found Ida and Walter waiting.

"How long are you staying?" Walter asked, in a tone that prayed for a short visit.

"Don't worry, old chap," Patrick said, clapping him on the shoulder. "I'm only popping in for a day or two."

Ida sniffed. "Just come and go as you please. Leave all the work of running this town to us."

"You do it so much better," he said, and then bid them a fair day and left.

And here was the root of their issue with him. Oh, they certainly didn't like the fact that he refused to hide under the glamour of age. Or that he made his living in such a public way. Yet their real issue was this paradox. They did not want a *bòcan* around, particularly him, but if he did not stay, he could claim all the benefits of Cainsville's sanctuary while taking on none of the responsibilities.

The greater problem was that Ida had no interest in resolving the paradox. Patrick did alter his appearance, sometimes leaving as a forty-year-old and returning at twenty or reversing the process. If anyone thought he looked familiar, he'd say his father used to live here. Or his cousin or nephew. As for the writing career, he used pseudonyms and cultivated the personae of the reclusive author.

He also made it clear that he would carry the weight of his responsibilities as an elder. Just not the boring ones, like sitting on the housing committee, deciding whether newcomers should be allowed in. The tedium would kill him. But there were many ways a *bòcan* could be an asset to a community. He was, despite what he'd told the korrigan, something of a scholar. He could play a trick or broker a bargain or answer a question, and would do so quite happily. But Ida and the others preferred to grumble. And that, he'd realized long ago, was a problem best handled with a few glasses of fine Bordeaux.

As he approached his house, he felt what might be called a tremor of pleasure. His house. His home. The one place that was truly his own, where he could retreat and close the door, and the world could not follow. That feeling didn't last much past the porch. One step into that house—dark and silent and heavy with the stink of dust and disuse—and he confronted a problem of his own making. The house was his, but he refused to make it his own.

His home was—for want of a more descriptive term—ugly. Not outside. He'd had it built exactly as he wanted it. But inside? There had been a time when he'd done that right too, selecting every furnishing with care, building a nest. A true refuge from the world. But then when he left Cainsville, he ached for home, and every other place he stayed made him feel like Goldilocks, endlessly seeking exactly the right bed, unable to sleep until he found it. Except in his case, he knew exactly where the right bed was: at home in Cainsville. He didn't want to be in Cainsville. Hence the conundrum, which led to this new version of his home, where as furniture aged and rotted, he replaced it with whatever was cheap and available.

He moved quickly through the front rooms, heading for the one that was still his, still exactly as he wanted it. Or exactly as he'd wanted it a hundred years ago. It might not quite match his tastes now, but it retained a familiar comfort.

He stepped into his library and flicked on the light. However much it showed his age, he still felt a mild wonder each time he did that. To come home, after months away, hit a switch and have light? For one who'd lived most of his life with candles and lanterns it was a small miracle.

The room looked like a library straight out of a Victorian novel. Or it would, if one ignored the word processor in the corner. The hulking beige box might ruin the ambiance, but to be able to type out a story and edit it as often as he liked? That was yet another miracle, at least for a writer.

The room was small. He'd often thought of taking out a wall to expand the library, but that moved too far into making this his ideal writing place, which would only make leaving more difficult.

Patrick walked to a bookshelf and ran his fingers over the spines of the old and worn tomes. He selected two. As he pulled them out, the books repaired themselves, the gilt fonts shining, the leather bindings gleaming, rips and tears disappearing.

He sat in his overstuffed chair, the one piece in the house left from the original decor, reupholstered and repaired throughout the decades, because when one found the perfect reading chair, one really could not relinquish it to the trash heap. He settled in, opened the first book and flipped through pages of Welsh until . . .

Mallt-y-Nos. Gwynn ap Nudd. Arawn.

He ran his fingers over the words and whispered to the book as if she were a reluctant lover. "Come now. Open for me. Show me your secrets, you beautiful—"

The words swirled, and he tumbled through the page, into the story, landing on a golden balcony, with a fair-haired young man gripping the railing, watching his betrothed run into the night.

"No!" Patrick snarled, and forcibly wrenched himself back into the present, throwing the book across the room.

He rubbed his palms against his eyelids. Not that. He'd seen quite enough of that already.

He opened the other book, this one handwritten, and proceeded more carefully until he found what seemed to be what he wanted. Once again, he fell through into a castle, but a human one. Perhaps only a few hundred years old. English. He looked around to see an Edwardian Christmas ball in progress.

"Who is she?" asked a voice beside him, and he turned to see a dark-haired man, perhaps forty. He'd been coming in, his overcoat half-off, bringing the chill of the night air with him. There was a woman on his arm, young and beautiful. The man's gaze, however, was fixed across the room. Patrick followed it to see a raven-haired woman, no longer young, no longer beautiful, but shining as bright as the North Star while she laughed and danced with a man, handsome as he grinned at her, his own face lighting up.

Patrick turned to the man beside him, staring entranced at the woman. He did not look like the fairy prince on the balcony, but Patrick could see past that. No, he could *feel* past that. While his connection to this man wasn't as strong as it'd been to Gwynn, it was still there. He glanced at the couple on the dance floor.

"Matilda and Arawn," he murmured.

Not them exactly. Not reborn. Not even reincarnated. Not exactly.

The legend of Matilda, Gwynn and Arawn. A cycle endlessly repeating. Humans with fae blood taking the place of the originals, spending their lives seeking one another, seeking answers to questions they could not even fathom.

"Who is she?" the man asked again.

"Lady Fairfax," said the footman taking his overcoat. The servant added, "With her husband, Lord Fairfax."

"They look very happy," said the young woman with them.

"They are," a matron said as she came up behind them. "I've known them for many years, and I've never seen a couple more deeply in love."

"Then you ought not to be staring at them, my dear," his companion said softly. "Particularly not in front of your wife."

The man mumbled an apology and tore his gaze away.

The scene faded and returned on a dark summer night, to a woman sobbing as if her heart would break. When the fog of the vision cleared, Patrick saw Lady Fairfax bent over the body of her husband, lying dead on the grass, a sword still clutched in his hand. The dark-haired man stood a few feet away, his own sword hanging at his side, bloodied. He stared at the man on the ground as if he didn't know how he'd come to be there.

"Why?" Lady Fairfax shouted, staggering up as she wheeled on him.

"For you," the man whispered.

"Me?" Her voice rose. "Me? I barely know you. Why would you do such a thing?"

"I . . . I do not know."

Lady Fairfax flew at him, hands out, fingers curved into claws as the men's seconds rushed in to hold her back.

The scene went dark, and Patrick drifted back to his chair, still clutching the book. He flipped more pages, only reading now, sifting through accounts of the trio through the ages.

The legend of Matilda, Gwynn and Arawn. Or, as it should be called, the tragedy of Matilda, Gwynn and Arawn. That's how it usually ended— in death or madness. Or abject loneliness, never finding one another, and endlessly feeling like they'd missed something crucial in their lives.

For the fae, the story was more than a sad legend, and the humans more than tragic actors. In the original version, Matilda, Arawn and Gwynn had been the best of friends. The Tylwyth Teg and the Cŵn Annwn, living in harmony, two sides of the same coin, light and dark, meadow and forest, day and night, the fae and the Wild Hunt. But on Matilda's death, lost in their grief, Gwynn and Arawn blamed each other. The princes became kings, and the two sides became enemies. In their old age, they tried to repair the damage, but it was too late. Today, the Tylwyth Teg and the Cŵn Annwn still lived somewhere between allies and enemies, forced to stand together to survive in an increasingly human world with share ever-dwindling resources.

That was where the legend came into play, for it said that when Matilda returned, if one side could win her over, their survival would be ensured. It was not a matter of which man she chose—that was romantic melodrama. Yet if she did prefer one, either as a lover or a friend, it would naturally sway her toward whichever side he represented.

That, then, was the legend. An interesting piece of fae lore. But what the hell did it have to do with Patrick? That was the question, and the books weren't answering it.

Patrick read a few more books, drank a full bottle of wine, and then ventured onto the nighttime streets. It was quiet enough that he'd hear the other elders coming before they spoiled his stroll. When one walked up behind him, though, he made no move to escape. He even slowed his pace until an arm hooked through his.

"Hello, Patrick."

He looked down at the elderly form beside him. "Hello, Veronica. Let me guess. You heard I was in town and remembered you needed something from me."

"But of course. Why else would I seek your company, *bòcan*?"

She smiled at him, and he returned it with genuine affection.

"Your timing is perfect," he said. "Because I need something from you."

"Excellent. We'll walk to the park, and you can tell me what trouble you've been up to, and I can properly chastise you for it."

It wasn't far to the park, giving him time only for a single story, one of his more outlandish adventures. Veronica did not, of course, chastise him. She laughed and teased, and before he knew it, they were opening the gate.

A wrought-iron fence bordered Cainsville's tiny park, because even the best parents might turn their heads for a moment. Every child here was treasured as a symbol of the elders' success, that the town they'd built lived forever in these children, who'd grow and leave and then return to have little ones of their own.

The park was a monument to that love—from the play equipment to that fence, the posts topped with chimera, shiny from generations of children kissing them and rubbing them for luck. There was a bench inside, but Veronica settled onto one of the swings. Patrick joined her.

Her question involved research, as usual. Veronica was the unofficial town historian. She also managed the festivals—open to all—and the rituals—open to none but the fae, and sometimes not even them. He answered her as best he could and promised to seek out more on the subject.

"And you need. . . ?" she said.

"Just a settling of curiosity."

"Is that possible?" she asked. "For your curiosity to ever be settled?"

He smiled. "Hopefully on this one matter. I . . . heard something about

Mallt-y-Dos." Her folklore name was Mallt-y-Nos—Matilda of the Night—because that had been her initial choice, however unwittingly. To the Tylwyth Teg, she was Matilda of the Day, signifying the choice they hoped her human descendant would make.

As soon as he said the name, Veronica's head shot up and her glamour rippled, revealing her true form, a black-haired fae with bright green eyes. A much more attractive form, and one Patrick had seen in its entirety on a few occasions. Romping with humans had a definite allure, but every so often it was nice to return to your own kind.

"Mallt-y-Dos?" Veronica said, and it took a moment for his wandering mind to recall what had prompted that glamour-affecting surprise. "You've heard something of her? Here?"

"Actually, that's what I was going to ask you. Whether there's any scuttlebutt rippling around these parts. A boggart in the city mentioned her name, and I wondered if it portended anything."

"I've heard nothing. Is there any way you can pursue it?"

The hope in her eyes made him genuinely regret having mentioned it. Being so close to the third-most-populous city in America, Cainsville was in dire need of a Matilda. The elders pretended all was well, but Patrick no longer felt the same surge of natural energy when he returned from his wanderings.

"It really was just a chance eavesdropping," Patrick said. "I couldn't even pursue the fellow to ask what he meant."

"But if there is any way, any at all, to get more details . . ."

Veronica watched him, her glamour all but gone now, her fae form pulsing. The one elder who welcomed him here, who treated him as if he wasn't a pariah, was asking him for a favor.

Cach.

"I'll see what I can do," he said.

The korrigan was at home and far too pleased to find him on her doorstep.

"I don't appreciate games," Patrick said as he walked into her house.

"You love games. Just not when they're foisted on you. We could have

avoided that if you'd spoken to me sooner. I presume you got my message."
The vision, she meant, her lips curving in a satisfied smile.

"Matilda is returning," he said. "Here."

"Yes."

"Has she been born?"

"Not yet."

"When?"

"Eventually. That is all I know of her, *bogan*, so do not press me for more."

"On *her*. But you know more about Gwynn, don't you. That's who I saw." *Who I felt.* "What's my connection to him?"

"Oh, I'm sure you've figured it out."

"I have no idea."

"You lie so well, *bogan*. All right. Let me spell it out for you. Gwynn is returning, and you will be his sire."

"Me?" Patrick snorted. "I know your kind see truth mixed with false-hood and you cannot tell one from the other. So I'll help. I cannot sire the new Gwynn, because I am fae. He has fae blood, at least some from the line of the original, but his parents are human."

"No, *he* is human. Even a drop of mortal blood makes a child mortal."

He knew that, of course. He'd just thought—hoped—that the legend implied both parents were human.

"You will sire the new Gwynn," the korrigan said. "The mother will have fae blood, including the line of the original. She is a daughter of your town."

"Cainsville?"

"Yes, and again, that's all I know."

"Then this new Matilda will be forever lacking a Gwynn," Patrick said, getting to his feet. "You just told me the mother is from Cainsville, which is going to make it very easy for me to stop this prediction from coming true."

Part one of avoiding the korrigan's prophesy? Get his ass back to Cainsville. That might seem counterintuitive, but avoiding the town was just asking for trouble. The solution to this problem was education and preparation. Return to Cainsville and make a list of every woman who might someday serve as baby-mama.

Compiling that list was not easy. It'd been years since he'd done more than pop into Cainsville to use his library or annoy the elders with his presence. He could speak to Veronica—he'd need to at some point—but he hadn't yet decided what he'd say about Mallt-y-Dos, and asking her to list eligible young women so he could avoid them would be . . . problematic under the circumstances. Even if there didn't need to be a Gwynn to win the new Matilda, it would certainly help Cainsville's cause if there was. If Patrick refused to play daddy, even Veronica might turn her back on him.

He sat in the coffee shop with his notebook, pretending to work while he watched the Saturday foot traffic. In two hours, four women fit the criteria. Three he recognized from old Cainsville families and made a mental note of their features. He asked the kid behind the counter about the fourth, and learned she'd recently moved to town, no familial connection, which meant no fae blood. Rose also strode past on her way to work. While she definitely fit the list, Rose Walsh was not a fun weekend romp. He respected her family enough to steer clear.

When the coffee shop door opened, he glanced up to see a possible addition to his list . . . in about ten years. A gangly teenage girl, maybe fourteen, but already showing signs of beauty, with long dark hair and rich brown eyes. She had fae blood, too, because he recognized the older woman who followed her in. Daere Carew, from another very old Cainsville family.

"How about a hot chocolate, Pams?" Daere said to the girl.

Pamela. Yes, Pamela Bowen. Daere had left Cainsville after her marriage to a Bowen, but she returned to visit family. Her grandmother had been one of their success stories, having unique powers with none of the negative side effects that often accompanied fae blood.

Daere asked her daughter about the hot chocolate again.

"What I'd really like is to get out of this town," Pamela muttered.

Her mother sighed, and the girl said, "Sorry, Mom. It's just . . . creepy. All the gargoyles and the old people." Her mother gave a deeper sigh.

Patrick chuckled. *Pamela Bowen, I do believe I like you. I'm almost sorry I'll have to add you to my do-not-touch list. I bet you'll be something else in another ten years.*

He looked at the girl again, to commit her face to memory, but when he did, the vision flashed. He saw the girl, Matilda, leaping onto the back of Arawn's horse. Then Lady Fairfax, laughing as she danced.

Could Pamela Bowen *be* Matilda? No, the korrigan said the new Mallt-y-Nos had not been born.

Not Matilda herself. Mallt-y-Dos's mother.

Patrick shook the thought from his head. Save the romantic fancies for his books. Young Ms. Bowen would not appreciate that one.

After Daere ordered the hot chocolates, she leaned over and whispered to Pamela, "Well, there aren't any gargoyles in here. Or senior citizens."

Pamela glanced around. Her gaze fell on him, and she went still. If she'd been a dog, her hackles would have risen. Even the hairs on his own neck rose under her stare.

You see me. You know what I am.

A rare power, to see a fae's true form and know they were not human. Most times, those with the gift gaped in wonder, as if gazing upon angels. This girl's stare, though . . . He'd never seen such hate in a child's eyes.

She saw him, and she hated him. Had she had some negative experience with fae? Whether she had or not, no one with fae blood was going to woo this girl. So how could she be Matilda's mother?

Wait. The original Matilda had been half Tylwyth Teg and half Cŵn Annwn. That meant her human representative needed the blood of both, like the original. Pamela, then, would find a boy with Cŵn Annwn heritage . . .

Another sharp shake of his head. *Really, Patrick? Stick to novels.*

He looked at Pamela, still staring with the look that dared him to comment, to react, to reveal himself. When he did nothing, she sniffed and turned away.

"Can we drink in the park instead?" she asked her mother.

"It's rather cool out . . ."

"But we have hot chocolate."

Daere smiled. "So we do. To the park then."

Pamela took her drink and walked past him without a backward glance.

Patrick made his list, checked it twice, and then got the hell out of Cainsville before he was either naughty or nice. Christmas came shortly after that, and he carried on with his life. He wrote. He caused a little trouble. He balanced the scale by doing some decent things in return—slide a hundred-dollar bill into a homeless man's pocket, break into a run-down apartment and leave gifts for the kids. Easy enough to do good at holiday time. Also easy to find women to share his bed, those feeling a little lonely this time of year . . . or just sick of hanging out with their families. The only difference was that he now insisted on using his own condoms, rather than relying on the ones they'd kept in their purse for who-knows-how-long.

Did he feel a little guilty that he'd ducked Veronica during his Cainsville visit, to avoid having to tell her anything? Yes, he was capable of guilt, at least when friends were involved. He'd figure out what to tell her before he returned, which would not be soon if he could help it.

Before he knew it, spring had arrived. He was heading home in the early hours, having spent the night with a young woman who dreamed of being a porn star and studiously practiced her craft. If she'd made extra effort for him because of a few cagey comments that may have led her to believe he was involved in the adult entertainment industry, well, he'd never said that outright and practice makes perfect. He'd just been helping her reach her goal.

He was currently providing yet another community service. Housesitting, in a beautiful Victorian manor, the owners of which were in the south of France for the month. Their house was on the border of one of the sketchier Chicago neighborhoods, and they'd forgotten to hire someone to watch it. Patrick had come to their rescue and taken up residence. He'd already protected the home from two raccoons, a marauding tomcat and an infestation of mice.

The future porn star lived only a few miles from his temporary residence, and it was a lovely morning for a walk, the sun just beginning to rise, the air clean and sharp. Yes, it was another sign of his age that he'd never grown accustomed to motor vehicles. He owned one, of course, but he kept it in storage unless traveling to Cainsville. Otherwise, if he needed a car, he could always liberate one from the curbside. When he could, he preferred to walk.

Heading through that unsavory neighborhood never bothered him. He was a three-hundred-year-old *bòcan*. Petty criminals were hardly a match for him, and he emanated an aura that said as much—they'd glance his way, only to look off again with a snort, as if telling themselves he wasn't worth their time.

Patrick was heading down a side road when he heard a cry from one of the alleys. A young woman who hadn't been quite as successful in scaring off the local predators. He slowed to listen. Had it seemed like a sexual assault, he'd have gotten involved, but what he overheard sounded like a simple mugging. He supposed the victim would not appreciate him calling it "simple," but if you walk through these streets alone, you'd best leave your valuables behind, lest you be forcibly parted from them.

Still, he had not yet decided against helping. He weighed the current balance. While he could—and did—argue that sex with an aspiring porn star and squatting in an empty manor were acts of community service, he would allow that they did not quite equal sneaking holiday gifts to needy children. One might even consider them zero-sum acts, neither contributing to his debt nor relieving it. And a few recent indiscretions may have tipped the balance more to the debt side of his personal ledger. He'd take a closer look at the situation and see if the trouble warranted the reward.

He crept to the mouth of the alley and peered down it to see a teenage boy with an equally young girl pinned to the wall. The girl's face was battered and bruised, and she wheezed, as if she'd been struck in the ribs, too.

"Where's the dope, Seanna?"

"I don't do that no more."

"Bullshit. You must have lightened some dude's stash at that party. I know how you operate. Been your victim myself a few times. Flash those big blue eyes while you slide your fingers into my pocket."

"I was at the party for a friend. Not to score. I need to stay clean or my aunt will kick me out."

"Boo-hoo. And bullshit."

"I'm serious. You already got all my money and my necklace. Go ahead and pat me down. There's nothing else."

"Oh, I'll do more than pat you down, Seanna. We're going to have some fun. And then you'll show me where you hid the stash."

"Uh-uh." Patrick walked over. "You don't want to do that."

The boy turned, his broad face scrunching up. "Who the hell are you? Her father?"

Well, that was a little insulting. Not biologically impossible, of course, but still . . .

"Just a concerned citizen strolling past," Patrick said.

"Keep strolling, pops. This is none of your business."

"The safety of the streets is everyone's business. I've already called the police from a pay phone. If you want to entertain yourself while we wait, I'd suggest taking a swing at me."

The boy sneered. "Not much entertainment when I could knock you over with one hand behind my back."

"Let's not overdo it. You can use both. And while we're at it, how about a wager on the outcome?" Patrick removed a crisp hundred from his wallet. "Will this do?"

The boy dropped Seanna and bore down on Patrick. "Oh, I think your entire wallet will do."

"We'll start with this." Patrick let the breeze catch the bill, and he released it, sending the boy scrambling. He was about to tackle the distracted teen when distant sirens sounded. The boy caught the bill and looked up, following the sound.

"I'd say they're about thirty seconds out," Patrick said. "Perhaps you just want to take that hundred—"

The boy was already running. Seanna turned to bolt, too, but Patrick caught her by the shoulder, saying, "I don't think you want to go with him."

"The police—"

"First thing you need to learn if you like picking pockets? The difference between a police siren and an ambulance. Second? Don't carry drugs while you're lightening wallets, because the sentence for that will be much harsher."

"I don't have—" she began.

"Then you wouldn't be in such a hurry to get out of here."

"I'm holding it for a friend."

"Yes, yes. Now, as there are no actual police coming, Seanna—"

"How do you know my name?"

"Because your friend there used it."

Which was true. Yet he also knew her surname: Walsh. Seanna Walsh, niece of Rose, the aunt she'd undoubtedly referred to.

As bruised and bloodied as the girl's face was, he had only to see those bright blue eyes, put them together with her black hair and fair skin and unusual name, and he knew this was Rose's niece. He'd last seen her in Cainsville before she ran away from home, which made her about eighteen now.

Eighteen years old. Growing into a young woman. An attractive one, with plenty of fae blood and a penchant for trouble. Yes, Seanna was definitely on his do-not-touch list. And now he'd just *happened* to rescue her from a mugging? He'd written enough romances to know that's what fate was scripting in this scene. They'd meet now, under these circumstances, and then when she was a more palatable age to him, they'd meet again in Cainsville and he'd look at her very differently.

Forewarned was forearmed. And now he was forewarned.

"You should get yourself to a doctor," he said as he started to walk away. "You sound as if you cracked a rib."

"I don't have any money."

He should shrug, keep going, and leave her bleeding in an alley. Prove he wasn't her knight in shining armor, so when they did meet again, her memories of him would be less than rose-tinged.

And yet . . . Well, the sort of romances he wrote were not the sweet kind. He was particularly partial to gothics, and in those, the hero could indeed be an ass. The allure of the bad boy. One look at Seanna—and the former friend who'd just fled—and he suspected she understood that allure all too well.

"You mentioned an aunt," he said. "I'm sure she'll take you to a doctor."

"Then I have to explain how I got beaten up, when she thinks I was working at an all-night coffee shop."

"Tell her you got mugged leaving work."

Seanna shook her head. "She won't buy it, and then she'll start asking questions about where I work, and she'll know I lied about the job."

True. Rose was a sharp one. Having the second sight didn't help.

He took three twenties from his wallet. "This will cover a visit and anti-biotics. Now scram, kiddo."

She took the money without a word of thanks, no more than she'd thanked him for rescuing her. A girl who thought the world owed her. Which was unfortunate, because it was going to prove her wrong, time and again.

Patrick let Seanna walk on ahead to the mouth of the alley. Whichever way she turned, he'd go the other. She was about to step from the alley when she staggered and grabbed a trashcan, pulling it over with a clatter as she collapsed. She lay on the sidewalk, taking deep and pained breaths. She tried to rise, only to whimper and double over.

Another moment passed, and she glanced at Patrick. "Aren't you even going to help me?"

Not if he could help it. At least he hadn't been rude enough to walk straight past her.

"I think I broke that rib," she said.

"Possibly," he said.

Another minute of silence. Then, "Could you help me up? Please?"

It was the please that did it. A tough little girl who was, in all likelihood, not nearly as tough as she thought. Or as she'd like.

He walked over and helped her stand.

"Can you just hail me a cab?" she asked. "I can take it from there."

"I thought you didn't have any money."

"I have enough to get me to a doctor."

At least she didn't try to squeeze cab fare out of him. He supported her over to a wall and then looked around for a taxi before realizing the impossibility of hailing one at this hour, in this neighborhood. He told her he'd need to call from the pay phone and got about five paces before she let out a yelp, and he turned to see her on the ground again.

He sighed, went back and helped her to her feet.

"On second thought," she said. "A doctor can't do much for a broken rib.

All I really need is a place to rest and clean up." She looked up at him, biting her lip and widening her eyes. "You wouldn't happen to live around here, would you?"

He had to bite his own lip to keep from laughing. Her attempts to look seductive would work so much better without that calculating gleam in her eye. This was her new plan then—to get *him* to tend her wounds so she could pocket his sixty dollars.

"I do live nearby," he said. "But I'll warn you that my wife isn't at home this week."

She gave a sly smile. "Good. Then we won't disturb her."

"That wasn't a hint, Seanna. I was letting you know that I'm married. Which means I'm doing this out of the kindness of my heart, and I don't want anything in return. *Anything.*"

It may have just been his ego, but he swore disappointment flickered across her face.

"Under those circumstances," he continued, "do you still want to recuperate at my house?"

"Yes, please."

Seanna Walsh was a mess. And not just because of the beating. That hadn't been particularly severe. The blood came from her lip, where she'd bitten it, and once she washed up, the facial bruising appeared to be from a single blow. She did seem to have cracked a rib but was breathing fine now. The damage she'd done to herself over the past few years was worse. Far worse.

When Seanna had argued with the boy about drugs, Patrick thought it was probably marijuana. Or perhaps that new drug circulating at parties, the one amusingly called ecstasy. Yet he'd only needed one look at her in a post-bath oversized T-shirt, and he knew the problem ran much deeper. He didn't dare try recreational pharmaceuticals himself—the effects on fae were unpredictable—but he partied enough to understand the culture and realize that the needle marks on Seanna didn't come from a medical condition.

Fae blood made humans more susceptible to addiction. Perhaps they sensed something missing in their lives, a mystery about themselves they couldn't solve, and they took comfort in alcohol and drugs. Or maybe the booze and dope stilled an inner voice that said they were different, that they didn't quite belong with the *boinne-fala*. Or perhaps it was simply a facet of being fae, like that part of his own self that he overindulged in his fondness for wine, women and song.

Whatever the reason, it did not mean that every human with fae blood was a roaring drunk or stuck needles in her arm. Some, like the Carews, seemed to have avoided that lifestyle altogether. Those like Rose had a wild side, but it didn't run to addiction. Or perhaps with the Walshes that predilection was always there, and they fought it by indulging their wild side in pickpocketing and con artistry. The Walshes were a tough bunch. Seanna, though . . . Seanna was different. Not yet out of her teens, she'd already tumbled down the rabbit hole of addiction and lost herself there.

As he tended to her and let her rest in the guest bedroom, he discovered that he felt something for her plight. Not sympathy, because that presumed he understood how she could have fallen so far so fast. No, it was closer to pity, an emotion that always seemed to carry a thin thread of contempt, as if recognizing that the recipient was in a very bad place, but not entirely free of the blame for it. Whatever their faults, the Walshes had strong family ties, and no one could say Seanna had a difficult childhood, particularly not in Cainsville, where no child was as special as those with the old blood. So her situation smacked of—while he hated to be so cruel—weakness.

The more time he spent with her, the more he wondered if he was being too harsh. Perhaps the addiction-prone properties of her fae blood were simply stronger. She did not resume her awkward attempts at seduction, which made him suspect she'd simply presumed he'd expect sex, and rather than wait until he demanded it, she'd taken control and offered. That *did* speak to strength. An almost animal cunning and strong survival instinct, which he admired.

As he wrote in the back room, listening to Seanna sighing and whimpering in her sleep, he found himself putting fewer and fewer words on the page and instead staring out the window, immersed in his thoughts. Immersed in thoughts of Gwynn.

Seanna was the one. He was certain of it. She fit the profile—or she would in a few years—and the way they'd met suggested the meddling hand of a cosmic matchmaker.

He'd avoided Veronica because he didn't dare admit he was supposed to father the new Gwynn and had no intention of doing so. Because that made him feel . . .

Guilty, damn it. It made him feel guilty.

He knew Cainsville was in trouble. While extinction didn't lurk right around the corner, they saw it coming. Fae were not like humans, hearing scientists talk of the dangers of ozone depletion and thinking, "I'll be dead by then, so who cares?" The fae would not be dead when trouble hit.

If a new Matilda was coming, having a Gwynn would help. Without one, it would be like with Lady Fairfax—Arawn would swoop in and snatch her up. Patrick knew the local Cŵn Annwn well enough to predict that.

The elders wouldn't understand why Patrick was so resistant to the idea of siring Gwynn. It wasn't as if he'd be expected to raise the boy. There could be a financial obligation, if the mother knew who'd fathered the boy, but Patrick certainly had the funds to support a child.

The korrigan was right—he didn't want the responsibility. That was all there was to it. Responsibilities came with attachments, and attachments, as Patrick well knew, only led to pain.

But did he have the right to say he wouldn't even lend his seed to the cause of saving his people? Yes, he had the right to refuse. But *should* he? Putting Cainsville and the Tylwyth Teg aside, weren't his own survival instincts better honed than that? True, if Cainsville fell, he could move on—he had before. But even if he wasn't particularly fond of living in the town, he appreciated having it there, for sanctuary and an energy recharge when he needed it.

By the time Seanna awoke, it was the dinner hour. He picked up takeout, and they ate, and she talked, opening up a little about her hopes and dreams. They were silly hopes and dreams, not unlike the ones he'd heard from so many young women. Rather underwhelming, and there was a part of him that wanted to shake her and say, "You can do more." You can *be* more. She wanted an apartment. She wanted a puppy. She wanted a job. Someday, she might even finish high school, because it would make her aunt happy. They were the dreams of a child, covering the basic needs of a human—shelter, food and love, if only from a pet. Sad and pathetic fantasies, and as she talked he realized . . .

Did he even dare put it into words? Hardly. It was too far outside the realm of his experience. No, that was a lie. It was too far outside the realm of his current personae, of the life he'd crafted for himself.

What if he accepted that she would be the mother of Gwynn, of his child, at some future—hopefully *distant* future—point in time? While she was in no way a suitable parent, she *could* be, and he could help with that. Tackle the addiction. Get her a job and an apartment. Buy her a damned puppy if that helped. He was sure Rose had done her best, but she wasn't much older herself. Perhaps what Seanna needed was a fairy godfather.

He sputtered a laugh at the thought, making Seanna ask what was so funny, a guarded look in her eyes that said she suspected mockery. He talked her hackles down and then brought wine up from the cellar. Fae wine, very hard to come by in the modern world, which was why he usually made do with decent *boinne-fala* vintages. Yet he always kept a couple of bottles with him. He poured her barely a shot, teasing that was enough, given she was underage. It *would* be enough. Not to intoxicate her but, well, there were different sorts of intoxication, and fae wine heightened the senses, better connected one with the surrounding world. It might satisfy a need in Seanna and ease her addiction. Which meant, he supposed, that he'd already made up his mind on the matter.

Seanna would be his new project. The Eliza to his Henry Higgins. She ought to be at least seven years older before she attempted motherhood, which left plenty of time for gradual changes. He'd do this right, from start to finish, no rushing through it, no half measures, no wandering off when he tired of the hobby.

They drank the fairy wine, and they talked, and he lit the fireplace, which seemed to please her in a childlike way. Then he wrote for a while as she listened to music on her Walkman. He'd already agreed to let her spend the night—in the guest room—and he'd drive her back to her aunt's in the morning.

Near midnight, he relented on the alcohol and allowed her to select wine from the basement, hiding his amusement when she brought up the bottle with the fanciest label . . . the cheapest in the collection. She opened it in the kitchen and poured them each half a glass, as per his instructions. Then they talked some more, as he sought to get a sense of his first step: concentrate solely on the addiction or get her back into school while she battled those demons.

This would not be a small project, but it was the right one. And he was the right person to tackle it.

That night, Patrick slept even more poorly than he had with the Gwynn-vision. At least then he'd managed to yank himself out of the nightmare. That night, the visions from both the korrigan and his book looped endlessly in scattered and frenzied fragments.

When he finally did wake, sunlight streamed through the window and he stared at it, wondering why he hadn't drawn the blinds the night before. He was very careful about that—a basic security measure, particularly when the bed was not your own. But all the blinds were open and . . .

And his head hurt. That gave him pause, wondering if he'd struck it and forgotten. Every movement sent stabbing pain through his skull, and the sunlight was so bright, so damnably bright.

I'm hung over.

That wasn't possible. The closest he'd ever come to it was after drinking nearly four bottles of fae wine back in the days before that cost a small fortune.

Last night, he'd had half a glass of fae wine and half a glass of human. Nothing more.

He looked down at himself, saw he still wore his clothing from the day before, and realized he didn't remember coming to bed. He'd been talking to Seanna, regaling her with some wild tale from his life, telling her it was a plot from one of his books. She'd been laughing, and then she'd . . .

Brought him more wine? Yes.

"Only for you," she said. "I know I've had enough."

Cach. She'd dosed the wine. Mixed in some human drug. Combine that with the fairy wine, and it had sent him . . .

He had no idea where it'd sent him. He didn't dare guess . . .

Oh, no.

He spun to look at the other side of the bed, but it was empty. He was lying atop the bedspread.

Also, you're fully dressed.

He exhaled in shuddering relief. All right. So if not seduction . . . He blinked harder and looked around the room. Then he let out a deep sigh. He may have collapsed in bed fully dressed, but he'd apparently had the forethought to remove his watch and wallet. Or, more likely, it had been done for him. His Swiss watch was gone and his wallet flopped open on the nightstand, emptied of all cash and credit cards. She'd even taken his new ATM card, which would be useless without the code. Unless she'd managed to get that from him while he was under the influence.

"*Cach*," he muttered and rolled out of bed, cursing again as pain stabbed through his skull. He had to call the bank and put a stop on everything before she did too much damage. Unfortunately, given this wasn't his house, making a call meant getting to a pay phone. He really needed to invest in one of those new mobile ones.

He lurched into the living room and stopped to spew a volley of far more eloquent curses. Every item of furniture had been pulled from the wall, books strewn across the floor, pictures yanked down as Seanna had searched for wall safes. A quick survey of the house revealed similar disarray in every room, along with the theft of every portable item of value. She must have left with pillowcases of loot over her shoulders.

There was no way he could hide this damage. Time to collect his things and flee the scene.

And thus Patrick's plan to rescue Seanna Walsh died within hours of its birth. Oh, he did attempt to find her, though part of that search was so he could teach her that stealing from a *bòcan* was a very bad idea. That didn't bother him nearly as much as the fact she'd stolen from someone who'd done nothing except help her.

If such a scenario had been put to him before this, he'd have laughed at the suggestion that he might be offended—and even a little hurt—by such a thing. He understood tricks better than anyone, and he would have bowed to Seanna and said, "Well played, miss." Yet that was not how he felt. Not at all.

It was one thing to stuff a bill in the pocket of a homeless man or leave gifts for underprivileged children. Those involved no actual contact with the recipient. Do his good deed and leave, and the scale returned to balance. With Seanna, he'd gone well beyond anything he'd done in many, many decades. He'd let her into his life for a few hours and shown her every kindness. How did she repay him? Robbed him blind.

Anyone with basic self-awareness realized it was wrong to hurt someone who'd helped you. But it also violated her family's code. For the Walshes, the world was full of marks, to be conned and robbed and cheated. But you didn't do that to family, and you didn't do it to friends, and you didn't do it to people who'd been good to you.

He'd heard rumors that Seanna had stolen from her family before she ran away. Yesterday, he'd dismissed them as just rumors. The Walshes had never complained, so the stories must be false. But they wouldn't complain, would they? Seanna's betrayal would be a private matter, a private shame, their failure to indoctrinate her in the code.

Patrick did hunt for Seanna. He even swung through Cainsville a month later, tracking down Rose and subtly asking after her niece. The girl had not been seen. And so, it seemed, his plan was, at the very least, on hold.

Five months after Seanna's betrayal, Veronica sent a note to his post office box. Had it come a half-year before, he'd have ignored it, presuming she was annoyed that he'd left Cainsville without speaking to her about his Matilda findings. To be honest, he'd have been surprised if she did. Complaining wasn't Veronica's way. She would be disappointed in not getting more answers but would not chase him for them. She respected his privacy, which was why she was the only elder with his postal box number.

The note was simple and to the point, which was also very unlike Veronica. Enough so that he didn't even take the time to hot-wire a car. He hailed a cab for the hour-long trip and told the driver not to spare any rubber getting him to his destination.

Once settled in the taxi, he looked at the message again. Five words. *Get to Cainsville, Patrick. Now.*

He did have the driver make a stop along the way. At a pay phone so he could call Veronica and see if she was at home, rather than arriving and being forced to run pell-mell through town searching for her, which would hardly befit his image. She was there, and she wouldn't tell him over the phone what the summons was about, just said to meet her at his house.

When he got there, he hurried through the front door and caught a glimpse through the entryway of Veronica in the living room. He slowed and added a little jaunt to his stride as he walked in, saying, "All right, where's the fire?"

Veronica pointed to a young woman seated across from her. Seanna Walsh. A very pregnant Seanna Walsh.

"She was looking for you rather desperately," Veronica said. "I can't imagine why." She cast a pointed look at the girl's protruding stomach.

"No, that's—It can't . . ." He trailed off as he flashed back to the night he'd been drugged. The night he couldn't remember. While the fact he'd woken fully dressed had suggested he hadn't done anything to Seanna, it did not mean she hadn't done anything to him.

"It's not like that," he said weakly, and Veronica tilted her head, her expression severe, but her cool gaze thawing slightly, as if willing to grant him the benefit of the doubt.

"I'll leave you two to chat," she said, rising. "You'll come talk to me afterward?"

He nodded, and she left. Patrick stayed standing just inside the doorway.

"What's this about?" he said to Seanna.

She put her hands on her belly. "I think that's obvious. Even the old bat knew."

He shot her a glare. "She has a name. I'm sure you know it."

A shrug, as if she did but didn't care. She leaned back, her arms stretching across the top of the sofa, possessive in a way that set his teeth on edge. He forced himself to relax and walked to the chair Veronica had vacated.

"How did you find me?" he asked.

"Magic."

That gave him pause, but one look at her smug expression said she was only being sarcastic.

"I've seen you around," she said. "I know what you are."

Again he had to struggle not to outwardly tense. "And what am I?"

"A writer. A rich one. Someone pointed you out at the coffee shop once and said you were a famous novelist. I didn't remember seeing you before, but he said you'd been living here for years. The most famous person in Cainsville. And the richest. Even if you don't look it." A pointed stare at his clothing. Then she glanced around. "You don't spend your money here either, do you? This place is a dump."

"No, it's just old."

"Same thing." She shifted to put her feet—complete with dirty sneakers— on his sofa. "But you have the fancy house in Chicago. Or you did—I went there and someone else lives in the place now. I guess you didn't want me coming back and cleaning out the rest, huh?" Before he could comment, she continued, "A fancy house in Chicago and this dump in Cainsville, so no one knows you're rich."

"I'm not rich, Seanna."

"Of course you are. You're a novelist."

He had to laugh at that. "Which is definitely not a path to fame and fortune."

"Don't bullshit me. I pawned your watch for almost five hundred, to a guy who usually gives me twenty bucks. And I got the balance on your bank card before you shut me out. Nearly a quarter-million. In your *checking* account."

"So you knew me from Cainsville. And then you bumped into me in Chicago—"

She snorted and rolled her eyes.

"You didn't bump into me," he said, slowly, as he worked it out. "You set me up. You even staged the attack. You spotted me in Chicago and planned out how to take down a rich mark."

"Oh, I'm just getting started with that." She smiled and rubbed her belly. "And you just started paying the price for being a Good Samaritan."

Her smile grew, so very pleased with herself and not the least bit ashamed.

"That's not my baby," he said.

The smugness faded from her eyes, just a little. "What?"

"Perhaps you missed that class on the birds and the bees. Probably shooting up behind the school, if you were still bothering to attend. But conception requires sex. I am quite certain I didn't have sex with you." He curled his lip. "Quite certain I *wouldn't* have sex with you, little girl."

She blinked, straightening. Then her eyes narrowed. "Well, you did, and I can prove it."

"How? Did you take photos? I'm sure you didn't. They'd hardly be flattering. Given that I woke up fully dressed, I know anything between us wasn't consensual. As a lover, I'm much more involved. I can't imagine how much work you needed to do to get me where you needed me."

"Oh, not much at all. You were willing. You just didn't know it."

Fury burned through him. Fury and outrage, and he wanted to walk over there, grab her and tell her what she'd done—exactly what he'd thought he saved her from in that alley. But she wouldn't see it that way at all. Never would; never could. That would require intelligence and the ability to put oneself in another's shoes, and Seanna Walsh had not a drop of either.

"You are the father," she said. "There are ways to prove that now."

He reined in his anger and only said, "Are you sure?"

Her expression said she wasn't, not entirely. She'd probably heard about DNA tests but not enough to know if it was even feasible to get one.

"Well," he said, getting to his feet. "You do have a point. You're pregnant and in need of help." He took a twenty from his wallet and tossed it at her. "Buy yourself a few cartons of milk. I hear that's good for pregnant women. Now, if you'll excuse me, I have someone I need to set straight on this misunderstanding." He stepped toward Seanna. "I'll escort you out. And don't think of coming back. I think you'll find I protect this place a little more carefully than my one in Chicago. They say booby-traps are illegal but no one tramples on my right to protect my property."

Patrick did not actually turn Seanna out on the streets to fend for herself, pregnant with his child. He needed to deny paternity to her—he wouldn't put it past Seanna to have brought a hidden tape recorder to catch an admission. But he knew the child was his, and his son would not suffer for the sins of his mother.

He spoke to Veronica first. He told the truth, that the girl had decided a "rich author" was the perfect baby-daddy, the perfect sucker to be fleeced. Veronica clearly knew the girl, because she only said, "I wondered if it was something like that. She's a troubled child."

"That's an understatement."

She nodded, but her look held only sympathy for Seanna, perhaps touched with guilt. If a child of Cainsville had gone so wrong, then they were all to blame. Which wasn't true. Patrick suspected nothing had broken in Seanna Walsh. It simply hadn't formed. The worst possible consequence of fae blood: sociopathy, taking a fae's underdeveloped conscience and annihilating it entirely. However, to be perfectly honest about it, that too was their fault, was it not?

"What does this have to do with Matilda?" Veronica asked.

"Matilda? Nothing."

"Let me rephrase that. Obviously since the Walshes have no Cŵn Annwn blood, the child cannot *be* Matilda. But there is a connection. Is she . . ." She trailed off as if struggling to keep the hope from her voice. "Is Matilda coming?"

"Yes, but can we not discuss this further? Please?"

A few moments of silence. Then, "All right. But if the birth is significant, that girl is in no shape to be a mother. Or even to carry a baby to term. If she hasn't already done irreparable damage with drugs or alcohol, that is."

He was trying not to think of that. Trying very hard.

"I'll look after it," he said.

Which he did. As best he could. He'd hoped Seanna would stay in Cainsville. From what he heard later, Rose had tried—desperately—to take the girl in when she realized she was pregnant, but she'd been unable to convince her to stay.

Seanna fled to Chicago. Patrick followed. He found ways to get money to her, secretly. He even called in a sizable favor from another fae to impersonate an outreach worker offering free medical care and healthy food and prenatal vitamins and whatever Seanna needed. He'd half-expected the girl to demand cash instead, but to his surprise, she'd accepted the help. *Happily* accepted it even. She went to the appointments and she ate the food and she took the vitamins.

From what Patrick could tell, she'd been clean since the pregnancy began. Well, as clean as she could get—still sneaking the occasional cigarette and beer. But she was taking care of herself and, more importantly, the baby in her belly, and that gave him hope. Seanna might be little more than a wild animal but, like an animal, she seemed to extend that self-interest and well-tuned sense of survival to her child, and the pregnancy proceeded without a hitch.

Patrick was even there the day his son was born. He knew Seanna's time was close, and he'd had her apartment bugged since the "outreach worker" helped her get it. He heard Seanna call for the ambulance, and he'd followed it to the hospital, affecting an older glamour, putting him in his seventies. Then he'd charmed the nurses into thinking he was someone's grandfather, and they left him alone, there in the hall to hear his son's first squall.

A big, strapping, healthy boy—that's what the doctor said. The next day, Patrick returned to the maternity ward in his old man guise, and "wandered" into Seanna's room. She was reading a magazine, the baby sleeping in a basinet. She didn't recognize Patrick—one glance at his gray hair and wrinkles and she stopped looking. He apologized for being in the wrong room and asked what the child's name was. Seanna took at least five seconds to look up from her magazine, pointedly letting him know he was interrupting her rest time.

"Gabriel," she said.

A nurse walked in, bathing supplies in hand, and overheard. "Oh, that's lovely, dear. Is it a family name? Or is it after the archangel?"

Seanna turned a level gaze on the woman. "No, it's from my favorite childhood story. About the Wild Hunt, riders from hell that stalk the living. They're also known as Gabriel's Hounds."

Patrick coughed to hide his snort of laughter at the nurse's expression. And he had to laugh, too, at the irony of naming the Tylwyth Teg's future champion after the opposing team.

"Actually," he said. "The Wild Hunt sends souls of the damned into the afterlife, not the Christian hell. It's an old Celtic legend."

The nurse's expression said that wasn't much better. "It's time for the baby's bath. No visitors allowed."

"I understand. But may I . . ." He looked at the sleeping child. "May I hold him for a moment before I go?"

He expected Seanna to protest, but she only shrugged. It was the nurse who gave his aged body a dubious look.

"He's big for a newborn," she said. "You'll want to sit down."

He took a seat in the visitor's chair, and the nurse brought the baby from the bassinet.

"He's been sleeping, so he might fuss," the nurse said.

The child—Gabriel—did not fuss. He opened his blue eyes, and Patrick would not say the child looked pleased to find himself in the arms of a stranger, but he did seem resigned to it.

There was little of Patrick in the child, at least in outward appearance. That was common with fae *epil*—offspring. Gabriel was a Walsh through and through, from the thatch of black hair to the pale skin to the blue eyes, already brighter than most. His solemn expression reminded Patrick of Rose, as did the keen gaze that traveled about the room and then rested on Patrick's face, as if assessing him.

"He's a bright one," the nurse said. "Inquisitive."

"Babies can't see much past their noses at birth," Seanna said. "I did my homework."

"I'm glad to hear that," Patrick said. "You'll make a good mother."

She turned to the nurse as if he hadn't spoken. "Show me how to bathe him."

The nurse took Gabriel, and if Patrick felt a twinge of reluctance to let him go, it was balanced by the reassurance that all would be well. Whatever kind of person Seanna was, she would be a good mother. Their child was safe with her.

———

A few days later, Patrick was again summoned to Cainsville. The note came from Veronica, but clearly at the behest of the other elders, and included the line, "I've said nothing to them," which told him he would not enjoy this visit. He'd go, though. He might avoid Cainsville, but he didn't hide from it.

They met at Ida and Walter's house. Veronica was there, along with a few of the other elders. The silent majority, as he called them. Non-entities who could be counted on only for one thing: to follow Ida's lead.

"I hear Seanna Walsh had a son," Ida said before he could even settle in. "Congratulations, Patrick."

He glanced at Veronica, who reiterated her earlier message, mouthing it.

"We heard she stopped by while she was pregnant and was rather desperately looking for you, Patrick. We'd hoped we were mistaken about the obvious conclusion. But when a source brought us the news that she'd given birth, I went to see the child myself. He's half fae. Half *bòcan*."

"I—"

"You impregnated a drug-addicted *child*?"

He could tell the truth. Tell them how he'd been tricked. Which would lay him open to their mockery yet not exonerate him from the accusation, because they wouldn't believe him. Oh, they'd accept that he'd been tricked—that was too rich an irony to ignore. But they'd think he'd gone along with it in the end, that Seanna drugged him and that lowered his inhibitions, but he'd still been an active participant in the process of conception.

"She wasn't on drugs at the time," he said. "That would hardly be a worthy conquest. And the age of consent in Illinois is seventeen. So . . ." A careless shrug, coupled with a faint smile. "I didn't mean to knock the kid up, but condoms don't always hold under rigorous conditions." His smile grew as he leaned back against the couch. "With me, it's always rigorous."

He got the full contempt-dripping glare from Ida for that. Veronica shook her head, but the look she gave him said she understood his choice. Embrace misbehavior rather than suffer humiliation. He was a *bòcan*. Misbehavior was expected.

"If that's all . . ." he said, starting to rise.

"We're going to switch the child," Ida said.

Patrick stopped. "Switch . . ."

"You know what we mean."

He did. Human legends told of changelings, fae stealing a human child and replacing it with one of their own. Like most lore, it had arisen to explain the inexplicable in ancient times. How could two perfectly healthy humans give birth to a child who grew up disabled or mentally deficient? There was only one answer: that the child wasn't human, that a fae child had been swapped for their own. But within that nonsense there was a shred of truth, perhaps from parents who'd instinctively realized that while their child might resemble them, the resemblance was only superficial, and he or she was not truly theirs. That their child was, indeed, a changeling.

Fae did not leave full-blood offspring with humans. Fae had enough difficulty conceiving that they'd never part with a child. Beyond that, they had no magics that would disguise a fae child permanently. No, true changelings were a very different thing.

Fae were well aware of the problems that could come with their blood, and sometimes, the cycle needed to be broken. If a child was born to a fae-blood family deemed too damaged to care for it, they'd find a human child with the same basic appearance—and far superior parents—and swap the infants, using compulsions and charms to hide the switch until the parents grew attached to the new child.

That's what the elders wanted to do with Gabriel. Find him a new family. Which meant Patrick would lose him. *They* would lose him. Their new Gwynn, gone before they even realized he existed. Patrick might be able to keep tabs on the child, but there was no reason for the swap here.

"Seanna will be a fine mother," he said.

Ida laughed at that. "You *have* met the girl, haven't you? Presumably had a few minutes of conversation before taking advantage of her? She's a high school dropout with a juvenile record. Addicted to drugs since she was fifteen—"

"She's clean," he said. "If you saw the child, you know he's fine. She gave up drinking, drugs and even cigarettes for the pregnancy. She ate well. She found an apartment. She's making plans to get her high school diploma." He straightened, finding a smug smile for her. "One could even say I did her a favor. Helped her turn her life around."

Ida fixed him with a cool look. "You did nothing of the sort, *bòcan*. If Seanna seems to be a good mother, then she's plotting something. That's the kind of girl she is. She won't change."

"Now that's a little harsh, Ida," Veronica said. "If Patrick is right—and we can easily check that—then while he certainly didn't do her a *favor*, the child may have given her a purpose. Perhaps that's all she needed."

Ida opened her mouth to protest, but Veronica silenced her with, "Let's just go see. We'll 'bump' into Seanna in the city, check the baby, talk to her. If she's properly caring for the child, then taking him away would be unnecessary, even cruel."

"Veronica is right," Walter said. "We lose nothing by checking. We all know Patrick is almost certainly stretching the truth. If so, then we proceed with the switch."

Ida and Veronica did "bump" into Seanna and the baby in Chicago. They took mother and child to lunch, and even Ida had to agree that the baby had made an immense difference in Seanna. She'd cleaned up—both figuratively and literally, her hair sleeked back in a ponytail, face scrubbed clean, dressed in a peasant blouse and long skirt. Gabriel was just as clean and well dressed, pushed in a fancy new stroller, courtesy of a mysterious benefactor.

When the baby spit up at lunch, Seanna whipped out a fresh jumper from her diaper bag. When he fussed, she had rattles to amuse him. Ida grumbled that she wasn't thrilled that Seanna had chosen formula over mother's milk, but as Veronica said, she had to find some fault and if that was the best she could do, then the answer was clear: mother and child were fine and would stay together.

Over the next week, Patrick periodically checked in on Seanna and Gabriel. He had to be completely certain this change wasn't a whim, abandoned after a few too many sleepless nights. But Seanna kept it up, and their son made it easy—he rarely cried or fussed.

One day, when Patrick swung by their neighborhood, he saw Seanna come out of the apartment building looking even better than usual. She was dressed almost like a schoolgirl, in a modest skirt, white blouse, flats and a sweater. Her hair left free and brushed until it gleamed. Going to meet someone, it seemed. Normally, he'd have contented himself with that few minutes of watching, but this made him nervous. It wouldn't be a job interview so soon after the birth. A young man? That's what he was afraid of, that a new lover would distract Seanna from their child. So he followed.

She took Gabriel to a nearly empty park. Patrick wore his old-man glamour, knowing she hadn't paid enough attention at the hospital to recognize him again. But approaching them would seem odd when there was no one else within fifty feet. He stayed back while she sat on a bench and took Gabriel from his stroller and dandled him on her knee and cooed at him. The perfect picture of an adoring young mother.

A few minutes later, a couple approached, seemingly to *ooh* and *ahh* at the baby. They were in their thirties, dressed in business wear, as if taking a stroll through the park on their coffee break. Except there were no office buildings within a mile radius. And when the woman sat on the bench, she perched on the edge, as if not quite committed to staying. The man stayed standing, casting anxious glances around. Seanna held the baby out for the woman to hold. The woman pulled back, shaking her head, but the look in her eyes, the longing in her eyes . . .

No. No, no, no.

Patrick darted from one tree cluster to another, getting as close as he dared.

"The doctor says he's the healthiest baby he's seen," Seanna was saying.

"I . . . I can see that," the woman said haltingly. "He's . . . he's beautiful."

"Smart, too. Everyone says so. He has to look at *everything*. His dad is super-smart. He's a writer."

The woman nodded, unable to tear her gaze from Gabriel.

"And he's a really good baby," Seanna continued. "Sometimes, if I didn't get him up for feedings, he'd sleep right through the night. If he cries at all, it means he's hungry or he's wet. Oh, and about feedings, while I would have *loved* to breastfeed, I knew that wouldn't be right, under the circumstances. He's on formula. The best kind. I don't have a lot of money, but I made sure he got the best of everything. He deserves it. I . . ." Seanna's voice broke. "I wish I could keep him. I really do. But this is for the best. I'm only sixteen. I'm not ready for parenthood. I need to finish school and then go to college. That's what the money is for: college. Otherwise, I'd give him to you for free. I . . . I never thought I'd be able to go to college. My parents . . ." She swallowed. "They were really young when they had me, and I saw how hard it was, as much as they tried. I want to do better. For him. Because it's all about him."

"We can see that," the woman said. "You've taken such good care of him. It's just . . ."

"It's not an easy thing," her husband said. "We've talked to people, and they've warned us of all the things that can go wrong. Falsifying adoption records is expensive, and someone could blackmail us later. Or you might change your mind and want him back."

"Never," Seanna spat out, before she seemed to remember her role and softened her voice. "As much as I love him, I know this is best, and I'd never interfere with his new life."

"We'll think about it, but we really aren't convinced it's as easy as—"

"No," Patrick called out, strolling from his hiding place, his usual glamour back in place. "Buying babies isn't easy, shockingly. It's also very, very illegal." He flashed the inside of his wallet. "Detective Jones, CPD. You aren't the first couple this girl has tried selling her baby to."

"Sell?" the man said, backing up. "You think we were trying to buy. . . ?"

His wife was on her feet. "Never. We just stopped to tell her how beautiful her son is."

"All right then. On your way. I need to have a chat with this young lady." They fled at a near-run.

"You bastard," Seanna hissed.

He met her gaze. "You stone-cold bitch."

She all but threw Gabriel back into the stroller. Patrick snatched him out, and she grabbed for him, but Patrick backed up, holding his son tight as the boy peered at him.

"This is what you planned all along, isn't it?" he said.

"No, it's what I planned after you refused to help me out."

"I did help you out, you little—" Patrick stopped himself. This was the mother of his child, and while he might not feel one iota of regard for her, after what she'd done to him and nearly done to Gabriel, she had the power here. Legally, the child was hers. *All* hers, since he could not come forward and claim paternity.

"I did help," he said. "Or did you really think social services would subsidize your apartment and buy you designer baby equipment?"

Her sullen expression didn't change. He didn't expect it to. He understood her now, as only Ida—damn her—had really understood her. Seanna Walsh was incapable of caring for anyone but herself. She'd played the role of perfect mother for the sake of the prospective parents. Gone clean during the pregnancy and cared for the child to ensure the viability of the product. That's all Gabriel was to her. A product. A means to an end. That had been the reason for his conception, and it was the reason for his continued existence. To handle that, Patrick had to handle Seanna on her own terms, the only ones she understood. The ones he understood, too.

"I have a deal for you," he said.

"Unless it involves marrying me—"

"It won't. It can't. That isn't legally possible, and besides, we both know it wouldn't last. I'm no more a father than you are a mother, Seanna. What I have is money. What you want is money. So here's the deal. You will take Gabriel to Cainsville and move in with Rose. You will stay clean. You will care for our child with her help. In return, I will provide whatever you need."

"How much?"

"When I said money, I meant it figuratively. I will pay your bills. I will buy what you need."

"I need money. Now."

He leaned back, cradling Gabriel as the child fussed at his mother's sharp tone.

"I'm sure you do, Seanna, but—"

"No, I *need* it. I was counting on that deal you just fucked up."

"Those people weren't going to buy him. You've watched too much TV if you really think it's that easy."

"I owe money."

He sighed. "How much?"

"They were paying me twenty grand."

"Then I'll give you ten, because I'm sure you aren't that deeply in debt. I'll take Gabriel to Rose while you settle—"

"He's a newborn *baby*. You don't have any idea how to care for him."

"Then you'll have to tell me. I'm taking him to Cainsville."

"Fine. But not to Rose. She's *my* aunt and he's *my* son. I'll take him to her. You'll keep him overnight at your place. I'll settle my debts and come get him tomorrow." She handed him the bag. "Bottles, formula and diapers in there. Figure it out, same as I had to. Now let's go get my money."

Patrick had indeed "figured it out"—with a stop at the nearest library and a book on basic baby care tucked under his jacket when he left. If he did anything wrong, Gabriel didn't complain. He snuck the baby into Cainsville, and they spent the rest of the day and the night together, with no more than a few whimpers, easily fixed with food and diaper changes.

Seanna came for Gabriel the next morning. Was it hard to let her carry him out that door? Yes. Harder than he would have imagined. But it was how it had to be.

That afternoon, Patrick was in the grocery store, picking up supplies. He'd stay in town for a week or so, be sure Gabriel settled in.

Rose was at the till.

"So," he said. "I hear you have a new addition to the family. Congratulations."

She frowned at him. Then her eyes clouded as she dipped her chin in a nod and murmured, "My niece had a baby. Yes. I haven't seen him yet."

Patrick went still, and it took a moment for him to say, "Haven't seen. . . ? Wasn't she in town today?"

Rose looked up sharply. "What?"

"I thought I heard Seanna and the baby were here."

"Not as far as I know." Hope flickered in her blue eyes. "Did you see them?"

Patrick extricated himself from that conversation as fast as he could. He went to the coffee shop and the restaurant and asked around. No one had seen Seanna and the baby, though one person recalled seeing "a girl" dropped off by a cab, which had then waited for her as she'd walked up Patrick's street.

By evening he was standing in the entryway of her empty apartment. Completely empty, only trash left on the floor.

"You know her?" asked a voice behind him.

Patrick turned to see a short, overweight man with a permanent scowl, and he decided that the proper answer was no, and then added, "I was given this address to pick up some stuff, but there doesn't seem to be anything here."

The man snorted. "Neighbors said she had a couple guys come by and clean it out in the middle of the night. The guys gave her cash. Some of the stuff wasn't hers. I rented this place partly furnished." He peered up at Patrick. "You sure you don't know her?"

"No, but a friend of mine does." He took out his wallet and handed the man five hundred dollars. "This should cover whatever she took. If you can get a forwarding address, I'll quadruple that."

The man's rheumy eyes gleamed. "For that much, I'll find the kid myself."

Patrick gave his home phone number. "I'll pay for *any* information. Just leave a message on the machine." He peeled off another hundred. "Please."

Seanna was gone. Patrick spent a month looking for her. Paid two separate investigators to look for her. Had Veronica speak to Rose, saying she was worried about the baby and if she heard anything, anything at all . . .

Finally, he returned to the korrigan, and found her at home, in a younger glamour. She motioned toward the living room, but he stayed in the front hall.

"There's a child," he said.

Her brows lifted. "So soon? I thought you'd decided against it. Or was the choice not yours to make, in the end?"

When he glared at her, she said, "It's not going well, I take it. Yes, I did foresee that."

"And you didn't bother to tell me?"

"You were already resistant. I was hardly going to say anything to discourage you. We need this child, Patrick. He may primarily serve the Cainsville Tylwyth Teg, but he will help all of us."

"His mother took him. I don't trust her to care for him, and I need your help to find him."

She shook her head. "I can't demand glimpses of the future. They are presented to me. If I get one of the boy, I'll tell you. Otherwise, I have seen far enough to know he'll be fine." She paused and pursed her lips. "Well, *fine* might be an exaggeration. One cannot grow up like that and be truly fine. But it's not necessarily a bad thing. It will make him stronger. Like tempering steel."

Patrick bristled. "My son is not a weapon."

"Oh, but he is. Whether you want that or not. Whether he wants that or not." She eased closer and draped her hands around his waist. "I know that doesn't please you. You're angry and frustrated. May I offer a temporary respite?" Her fingers slid to his rear. "I believe I can distract you for a few hours."

Patrick pulled her hand away, turned and walked out. And with that, he had to admit he'd run out of options. He'd been thoroughly and repeatedly duped. By a drug-addicted high school dropout. The irony of that . . . The humiliation of that . . . It should have been unbearable, but what he felt wasn't humiliation. That would make this all about him, and for once in a very long time, it wasn't all about him. It was about a child he'd left with a sociopathic addict who couldn't be trusted not to sell him for her next hit.

Except she could, in her way, be trusted not to do that. He'd miscalculated paying Seanna the money, but she had still come back for Gabriel. That didn't mean she gave a damn about him; it meant she didn't want to lose the one thing of value she had in her pathetic life. The one thing of *monetary* value. As long as she had Gabriel—and kept him healthy enough that social services wouldn't come for him—he was worth something. Not to strangers—she'd seen that wouldn't work. No, she had a more reliable nest egg now. One that would last for as long as she had the child. She had Patrick.

When the money dried up, she'd be back. That might be a couple of months. It might be a couple of years, while she ran her petty scams and robbed her marks and made Patrick worry and stew until he was ready to hand her whatever she wanted to guarantee his child's continued safety.

That meant that he had to be ready for her return. He had to be where she could find him. Whether it was a month from now or five years.

Patrick stood on his porch, his hand on the doorknob, fighting every instinct that screamed for him to run, to get the hell out, to forget the child, because it was just a child and hardly his first. But Gabriel wasn't *just* a child. He wasn't even just a special child. He was a child that Patrick had inadvertently condemned to this life. To that mother. Patrick had made mistake after mistake, and this was how he'd pay.

He opened the front door, walked in and put down his suitcases.

Home, sweet home. For as long as it took.

ABOUT THE AUTHOR

KELLEY ARMSTRONG was born in Sudbury, Ontario. In her youth, when asked to write stories in school, she consistently wrote about dark, paranormal, undead, or evil characters. According to her alarmed teachers, she couldn't—or wouldn't—write "normal" stories. Despite this early censure, Armstrong continued to pursue her dream of becoming a professional writer while completing her degree in psychology at the University of Western Ontario and then studying computer programming at Fanshawe College.

Armstrong's first novel, *Bitten*, beginning her blockbuster thirteen-novel Otherworld series, was an instant *New York Times* bestseller. Her many other successful series in multiple genres include the teen paranormal novels Darkest Powers/Darkness Rising (*The Rising, The Summoning, The Awakening*), the Nadia Stafford crime series (*Wild Justice, Made to Be Broken, Exit Strategy*), and the Blackwell Pages middle-reader adventures, upon which she collaborated with M. A. Marr. Armstrong is currently writing the Cainsville supernatural-gothic novels (*Visions*, *Omens*) and the teen fantasy series Age of Legends (*Sea of Shadows*), which debuted in 2014. *Bitten* has recently been adapted into a TV series, now in its second season on the Syfy Channel.

When not spending time in Western Ontario with her husband, three children, and animals everywhere, Armstrong reports that she continues "to spin tales of ghosts and demons and werewolves, while safely locked away in my basement writing dungeon."